THE SWORD AND THE FLAME

THE SWORD AND THE FLAME

PAMELA HILL

St. Martin's Press
New York

Library of Congress Cataloging-in-Publication Data

Hill, Pamela.
    The sword and the flame / Pamela Hill.
        p.   cm.
    ISBN 0-312-07091-8
    1. Mary, Queen, consort of James V. King of Scotland, 1515–1560—
    Fiction.   2. Mary, Queen of Scots,   1542–1587—Fiction.
    3. Scotland—History—16th century—Fiction.   I. Title.
    PR6058.I446S9   1992
    823'.914—dc20   91-34909
                                                                          CIP

First published in Great Britain by Robert Hale Limited.

First U.S. Edition: January 1992
10   9   8   7   6   5   4   3   2   1

Author's Note

The Clan MacGregor was not outlawed until fifty years after the events described in this story.

P.H.

m. (1) Jeanne d'Harcourt
(no issue)

François Comte de Laubecq Killed 1524	Antione Duc de Lorraine m. Renée de Bourbon	Nicolas	François	Anne	CLAUD DUC DE GUI m. ANTOINETT DE BOURBO

François Anne — d. in infancy

Isabella	Jean	François Duc de Lorraine	Nicolas Comte de Vaudémont	Anne	Antoine d. young

Isabella Jean — d. young

MARIE b. 1515 m. (1) Louis Duc de Longueville	François Duc de Guise b. 1519	Charles Cardinal de Lorraine b. 1524	Claud Duc d'Aumale b. 1526	Louis Cardinal de Guise b. 1527	Ant Ab Farr b.

(2) JAMES V of SCOTLAND

François d. 1556	Louis d. in infancy	James, Duke of Rothsay b. 1540 d. 1541	Robert d. in infancy

orraine
c de Lorraine

(2) Philippa of Gueldres

Louis	Claude	Catherine	John		Ferry
mte de			Bishop	Others	
démont	d. young		of Metz		
. 1528			and Cardinal		
			of Lorraine		

François	René	Renée	Pierre	Philip
Grand Prior	Marquis	Abbess of		
of Malta	d'Elboeuf	Rheims	d. young	
b. 1534	b. 1536	b. 1538		

MARY, QUEEN OF SCOTS
b. 1542
m. (1) Francois II
m. (2) Henry Stewart, Lord Darnlly
m. (3) James Hepburn, Earl of Bothwell
Executed Ash Wednesday, 1587

The Royal House of Stuart and
the present Royal House

orraine
ıc de Lorraine

(2) Philippa of Gueldres

Louis Comte de ıdémont . 1528	Claude	Catherine	John Bishop of Metz and Cardinal of Lorraine	Others	Ferry

Claude / Catherine — d. young

François Grand Prior of Malta b. 1534	René Marquis d'Elboeuf b. 1536	Renée Abbess of Rheims b. 1538	Pierre	Philip

Pierre / Philip — d. young

MARY, QUEEN OF SCOTS
b. 1542
m. (1) Francois II
m. (2) Henry Stewart, Lord Darnlly
m. (3) James Hepburn, Earl of Bothwell
Executed Ash Wednesday, 1587

The Royal House of Stuart and
the present Royal House

THE SWORD AND THE FLAME

Part I

'He may be a Lorrainer; he is not dark enough for a Frenchman.
I hope that his features will resemble his father's, but it is hard to
tell at less than two years old.'

I remember that those were the exact words of Madame Marie
de Guise-Lorraine, the widowed Duchesse de Longueville,
because it was the first time she had been able to mention her
dead husband without weeping. Now, she watched their small
son, Duc François, who had been called after the King of France,
stagger and play on the cushions at her feet. We were not cold in
the solar, although there was no fire lit; outside, it was autumn,
and whatever may be said for or against mourning it kept us
warm. The severe pleated barbe outlined Madame's piquant
face, hiding her chin and her long throat. As for the gown, its
looseness did not disguise the fact that her second pregnancy
was not far off term. Duc Louis had chosen an unfortunate
moment to die of fever lately at Rouen.

Madame Marie had loved her husband and he her. I had
often envied them their happiness together, brief though it had
been. They had been allowed to choose one another instead of
being forced into marriage. I felt my own thoughts grow bitter,
accordingly, and caused my mind to alter its direction. I put
down the sewing I was at, rose from my chair and went to the
window to look out at the September day.

'Here is a party of riders,' I said idly. 'They are coming from
Amiens.'

Madame did not turn her head. Her long fingers were playing

with the little Duc, causing him to make small chuckling noises, 'It is no concern of ours,' she said. 'Puiguillon will receive them.'

But I did not think the leader of the party, who bore the royal blazon, would be content even with so high-born a household official as Gilbert de Beaucaire, Seigneur de Puiguillon. This message was almost certainly for Madame herself, and callously invaded her mourning, although she had withdrawn here from Paris in order to be left in peace. The King was not considerate in such matters. I wished, though I did not often wish it, that Madame Marie's mother, Duchesse Antoinette, were here with her now instead of coming later, when she would travel as promised to Châteaudun for the birth. That lady had a way of sending messengers to the rightabout in a way I could not do. Nevertheless I stayed by Madame, ready to help her in any way I might. Presently the tramplings of arrival sounded in the hall, and Puiguillon himself, embarrassment making his face red, appeared at the door, having been told to admit no one and being obliged nevertheless to do so.

'Madame la Duchesse, they say that they must see you. It is a letter from the King.'

'Then admit them,' she said calmly. She had risen to her tall height, and gathered her child to her. The little boy's hand strayed to the unfamiliar barbe, pulling at it to try to reveal his mother's half-hidden face. Madame handed him to me and I took him in my arms, noting that I had not been instructed to go. Madame remained composed, and told them to enter.

They came in, some of them I knew, from Vendôme and Fontainebleau; they were dressed as one expected, with great padded shoulders and round hats with a jewel wrought in goldsmith's work, high soft boots for riding, and shirts so delicately smocked they might have been worn by women. But there was nothing womanly about the messengers of King François, as I knew well. I saw their glance pass me by briefly, as of no account; they knew me only as the quiet companion of Madame. She herself had taken the letter, presented with formal kissing of hands; its coloured seals swung as she opened them expertly. She spread out the letter, and her pale face gave away nothing. Then, as if she could not help herself, she crumpled the parchment in one hand, and faced the messengers, high-born as they were, selected for this special and unwelcome errand.

'You may tell His Majesty that I cannot accept his proposal. I am in mourning for my husband, and desire nothing but to be left in quietness to await the birth of my second child. You have ridden far on this journey; they will see to it here that you are given refreshments before you leave. I will write to the King myself, declining his offer. Pray inform him, in the meantime, that I am grateful for his remembrance; and now, I pray you, leave me.'

As soon as they had gone she was like an unleashed fury. 'Do you know what he said?' she asked me. 'He has arranged – there is no question of my being asked what *I* prefer – for me to marry the King of Scotland. How could I do other than refuse? How can I leave my son and go to a foreign country? And there is the other child to come.' She laid a hand over the place where the unborn child lay. 'They have chosen the wrong time for their plans,' she murmured. 'I grieve for my own beloved husband, newly dead. How can I take another?'

A thought came to me, which for once I did not put into words. The King of Scots was himself grieving for his dead young bride, Madame Madeleine of France. Perhaps the pair could comfort one another. But having no real experience of such matters, I kept silent.

I could remember King James V of Scotland well enough; everybody in France knew him, from the time he had come over two years since to seek a wife, running up and down the Paris market stalls buying ostrich plumes and diamonds, to the time he had jilted Mademoiselle de Vendôme, Madame's own cousin. They said the poor girl had never recovered from it. There had been tourneyings and great expense at her father's castle, and Monsieur and Madame de Longueville and I had been there, and I remember the handsome red-haired Stewart King, with whom all the ladies were in love. In the end he had met Madame Madeleine, the King's daughter, in her invalid carriage, elsewhere, and the pair had fallen in love at sight; nothing would do but that they must marry, and so they were married at Notre Dame, and followed the Court afterwards for some months till it was time to set sail for Scotland. But Madame Madeleine was consumptive, and died a few weeks after landing in that inhospitable country. The King, they said, was quiet for a long time.

What was this love at sight? I knew nothing of it. I set down the little Duc de Longueville, who went straight to his mother and hid his face in her gown, against where his expected brother or sister lay. Madame clasped him to her, as if he could protect her; but we both knew that he could not. Against the King of France's fiat, if he was determined, nothing would prevail.

The weather worsened as it had done for the new Queen of France's recent coronation, but that did not prevent other parties of riders from coming to disturb Madame. News of her refusal of so auspicious an offer had alerted those in high places, not least her parents, who rode over earlier than expected from Joinville. Duchesse Antoinette was as usual in her closed old-fashioned coif, the like of which nobody else had worn since the time of Louis XII; and my father wore his armour, with the great double cross of Jerusalem and Lorraine floating behind him on his banner, and a train of sixteen men. They tramped into the hall and I was permitted to greet them all briefly, and then was sent up to my room. My tall father was as handsome as ever; he was like a man made of gold. It was astonishing that he was by now devoted to his little brown wren of a wife, and that they would produce, in the end, twelve children. No doubt Duchesse Antoinette would ride straight to Châteaudun with Madame for the lying-in; that meant there would be no place there for me.

I watched them go in from the turn of the stairs, hiding myself behind one of the balusters. Wine was brought up from the kitchens; I saw it come. I knew they would try their utmost to persuade Madame to the Scottish marriage, for it would be an honour to have a Queen in the family; our grandfather Duc René had been forever dreaming of crowns and in his way, achieved one in Sicily. I went and got on with my sewing, then heard them disperse to their different rooms. They would stay for a day or two, having come so far, although Duc Claud disliked in these days, now his youth and his ambitions were fading, to be any-where but at Joinville.

Madame Marie sent for me presently and I asked her no questions. It would have been impertinent, and I could tell from her sad face that they had been troubling her deeply over the matter of the Scots marriage. She called her little son to her, as she had done when the first messengers came, and winced from time to time as if the unborn child gave her pain.

*

The Guises did not themselves persuade Madame, but the King of France would take no denials. He sent word to say that as Madame de Longueville was to marry his son-in-law the King of Scots, the widower of Madame Madeleine, he had created her a Daughter of France. This was the highest possible honour, and assumed acceptance. But Madame still said nothing. Last of all came a reason which induced her compliance in the matter, if not her goodwill. That old devil the King of England demanded her hand for himself, and went on demanding it well into the following spring. The prospect of marrying Henry VIII, after the fate of four of his other wives, was alarming; anything else could only be better than that. His proposal was made, certainly, to spite King James, who was his sister Margaret's son. James V was, as I have said, young and handsome; Henry VIII was old and obese. He had the insolence to say that as he himself was big, he needed a big wife. 'But my neck is small!' Madame replied. It was the first sign of returning spirit in her.

She had by now gone into labour at Châteaudun, and had given birth to a second boy. She named him Louis, after her dead husband. The child only lived four months. I myself think that the troubles they made her endure in course of the pregnancy killed him, but perhaps not. Meantime, the little François was all that was left to her; and when she set sail at last for Scotland she would have to leave him behind. Being of the *haute noblesse*, and Hereditary Grand Chamberlain of France, the child could not be permitted to leave its shores with his mother.

I have said nothing of my own story, as the above events are of greater importance. It may have appeared, from my description of myself as in attendance on Madame Marie, that I was a servant; but I was not.

I, Claudine de Vouvray, am the natural daughter of Claud Duc de Guise, by my mother who is dead, and who was in waiting upon Duchess Antoinette in the early days of the latter's marriage. Although they say that that was a love-match, I do not believe that it was so, although later, as I have said, husband and wife grew devoted. The Duc being handsome as a god, his eye often strayed from his bride to his pleasures, in that first year at the least; and my mother, they say, was a hoyden. Also, she was in an unfortunate position, not having been sought in marriage because her family were poor, her father having gambled away what should have been her marriage-portion. As time passed, and she saw younger women finding husbands, my mother forgot her duty to her mistress, and set out to attract Duc Claud, who was not only handsome, as I have said, but had already some reputation as a soldier, though Marignano had yet to be fought. Also, he was a friend of the King.

Duchesse Antoinette was not yet pregnant – that took two years – so it was hard on her when she learned that my mother was with child by her husband. Being herself, she made no scene, merely cast her wise grey eyes down to the ground and no doubt said her prayers. She was a curious little creature, with the big nose of the Bourbons, hooded eyelids, and a full underlip. Perhaps the last after all signified passion; by the time they were done, the Duc and Duchesse made many children between them, beginning with Madame Marie, who was conceived before I was born, so that we were almost of an age, though I was always the smaller. No more children came to the Duc and Duchesse for four years, so Madame Marie and I shared a nursery between us.

It was as well there was somebody to look after me, because my own mother was dead. She had died of a fever within a few days of my birth, and Duchesse Antoinette, out of compassion, visited her in her chamber. I was lying on the bed unwrapped, for nobody had thought to buy me a cradle or swaddling bands; I think I had been born without assistance from anyone. Almost with her last breath my mother begged that I might be called Claudine, and although this cannot have pleased Duc Claud's wife, she permitted it. Later she saw my mother buried with the proper obsequies. After that, as there was nobody else to bring me up, the Duchesse did so herself, and strictly at that. She endeavoured, I am convinced, to make sure that I would not develop the character of my mother, whom I resembled, having brown hair and water-green eyes. During my childhood, therefore, I was often chastised, perhaps less out of unkindness than a sense of duty. I did not appreciate this, naturally, and I can recall often weeping with pain and disgrace, and my dear Madame Marie, who was so good herself she never needed reproof, putting her arms round me.

'Take comfort, Claudine,' she would say. 'It is to make you good. Already you are better than before it happened.'

But she had no devil, as I had, to get the upper hand; when a little sister, Madame Louise, appeared in the cradle, and later a little brother, who would take away her inheritance, Madame Marie was not jealous; she hung over them and played with them like dolls. The years passed, with the arrival of more and more babies. Duc Claud was now a hero in the eyes of France, because at the time of Madame Marie's birth he had been pinned beneath his horse with twenty-two wounds at the Battle of Marignano. They thought he was dead, and his serving-man flung himself across the body, and was himself killed when the enemy galloped past; but Duc Claud was saved and carried back afterwards to his tent. His handsome face was unscarred, but one arm and the other thigh had received fearful slashing; for the rest of his life he wore a spiked iron bracelet on the arm, to remind him of his youthful sins. I will not say he desisted from these altogether: I have a bastard half-brother named Claud, and possibly others, but I have never met them. Plenty of legitimate sons grew up at Bar, and later at Joinville when Duc Claud and his brother Antoine exchanged inheritances. All that had to do with the marriages of old King René, the first of which had been childless if not landless, the second producing eleven children all told, including my father. Their mother, the second wife of René, was a most beautiful woman named Philippa of Gueldres, of high-born blood and knew it. Nevertheless she astonished everyone, as soon as she became a widow and had reared her children, by entering, somewhat to their embarrassment, a Poor Clare convent, as she was said to be dying. She did not die and instead lived to the ripe old age of eighty-five, sleeping on a pallet. I mention her because when Madame Marie and I were eleven years old, Duchesse Antoinette, who was exceedingly devout, thought that the convent would provide us with an education and possibly, if we had vocations, a future.

We were accordingly sent to Pont-à-Mousson, not far from Nancy where Duc Antoine, who had kept the title of Lorraine, had his palace. The Abbess received us and took us straight to Madame Philippa. Poor Clares are not permitted to receive visitors in the ordinary way, but as one of her sons was a Cardinal an exception had to be made for Madame. I was amazed at her cold, unchanging beauty beneath the coif; her face was as smooth as a lily, and she did not like me.

Our education proceeded. Joyful as I was to be with my young

Madame, I remained unimpressed with life as led in convents, at least as strict a one as Duchesse Antoinette had chosen for us. Some nuns are holier than others. The Poor Clares were indeed so, and perhaps the wearing of open sandals does something for the soul besides producing chilblains on the feet in winter. Likewise, some good is no doubt done, in the encouragement of Christian charity, by ringing a bell in a tower to let the world know that everybody inside the building is hungry and to ask for food to be placed in a bowl left outside the gate. All I know is that I myself never felt any better for living on a wretched dole of bread scraps and fatty remnants of meat, sleeping on the floor on a thin straw pallet, and being forever cold. Although she said little and never complained, I do not think Madame Marie liked it greatly either, and once she fell ill with a fever and had pain in her joints for some weeks. It may be that her parents had wanted her to copy her saintly grandmother, and it was certainly possible for clever young women to do well in the position of Abbess, better than they might have done in the world as wives, because husbands are not, as a rule, so considerate as God. But I do not think Madame Marie fancied such a life, and no doubt, like myself, often wished she was back in the comforts of Joinville, especially in the fruit-picking season, when there are ripe lemons and pomegranates in the gardens, and the juice from the latter runs down one's chin.

In any case Madame would have been wasted in a veil; she grew very beautiful, and very tall indeed, with red-gold hair that hung to her knees, and a tender curve to the upper lip that gave her oval face great softness. Her grandmother sent for her often to her cell, and talked gravely to her; occasionally I was sent for also, but was not regarded with the same approval, in especial after certain remarks I once made to Madame Marie when we were lying on our pallets and supposed to be asleep. We had been talking about the foundress, St Clare, who had been the friend of St Francis and had cut off all her beautiful long golden hair to follow him, and had given away her jewels.

I remember saying that I thought she was mistaken. 'If God gives one beautiful long golden hair, why not keep it?' I said. 'She could have married St Francis, then he need not have gone round with a begging bowl. They could have lived on her money and given a great deal to the poor, and done as much good with less discomfort.'

'Claudine, do not let them hear you,' said Madame Marie warningly. 'It would hurt them very much.'

But someone had heard, and next day I was sent for to the Abbess, who talked to me about chastity, humility, and the harm of owning property. Did I not know that the blessed Francis would not permit St Clare to walk along the road with him, lest it lead to unchaste thoughts? I kept my eyes down; I knew the answer to that one; they had said they must not walk together unless the thorns on the hillside blossomed into roses, and the thorns did. But blossoming hillsides were very far from Pont-à-Mousson; I was sent to Madame Philippa in order that she might whip me herself. She made such a good job of it, that old woman, that for two days I could neither lie nor sit. 'You are full of sin, and will come to a bad end,' she said. After that I held my counsel about long golden hair. They made me cut mine off, as a penance.

There was a further sadness; Madame Marie was taken away from me. This was in no way part of my punishment. Her aunt and uncle called, to see old Philippa, and were shown the eldest daughter of Duc Claud, to assess her beauty. They were astonished; she must not, they insisted, remain one single day longer in a dreary convent; she must come with them to Nancy, and meet their children and the great world.

They would have taken me also, at Madame Marie's particular request; but here the Abbess intervened. I was not, she stated, in a proper state of mind to be permitted to go out into the world; it would be of benefit to me to remain with them for at least another year. So, hating everyone, I had to watch Madame Marie ride off with her relations, the sunlight glinting on her hair beneath her hood. She turned and waved to me.

I stood there with my cropped hair, watching the cavalcade out of sight, till one of the nuns beckoned me inside. There were the tasks to perform that we had always had, but I had not formerly minded because they were shared with Madame Marie: weeding the kitchen garden, preparing the vegetables, cutting up such meat as came, cleaning the pots with sand until one's nails broke. It was not an education, except in one sense; I knew that I could not bear it any longer. As soon as I might do so, I would myself escape to Nancy, which was nearer than Joinville and would save me a journey across the mountains; and there I would join Madame Marie. It should not be impossible to find the Duc de Lorraine's palace: after that, I would think what to do. Meantime, to plan it was difficult, certainly; but I was determined upon it.

For weeks it rained and froze. I waited until a dry day, when it was my task to dig the garden ready for planting in the spring. It was very cold, and my hands and feet were red and hacked with frost. I dug for warmth for some time, setting my rough shoe firmly against the spade; then, having looked about me to see that I was not watched, I left the spade sticking in the soil, quickly climbed over the wall at a place I knew, and found myself on the high road to Nancy. It is not so difficult to escape from an enclosed convent as everyone thinks; the people inside it stay there because they have chosen that way of life, not because they are imprisoned. I had not, and I swung my way along the road in the direction of the capital of Lorraine, knowing the hills were behind me and the flat Moselle valley in front. Only now did I begin to feel myself somewhat unprotected; I had never been out alone before, and I knew that I might be set upon, though it was not worth any robber's while, as I had no possessions. I had not even any money with me, and could not have paid for a lift on a cart; in fact, none passed me by. I walked quickly, putting as much distance between myself and the convent as I might before they discovered my absence. In any case – and I laughed to myself – there was nothing they could do about it; they were forbidden to come out beyond the walls of the enclosure. I was free.

I passed through the town, and later through the village of Dieulouard, where pigs rooted in the streets. Nobody heeded me, as I looked like one more young peasant girl in rough clothes and a close coif, with hands accustomed to work and clogs that had seen service. I took time to wonder what they had done about Madame Marie's beautiful hands to fit them again for Court circles; no doubt they had treated them with rosewater. How I looked forward to seeing her again! I knew that she would not repulse me; but meantime the way was growing solitary and strange, with hills rising on either side the powerful river. I trudged on, not admitting to myself that I was growing frightened; it was still a long way to Nancy, and perhaps I should not reach it before night. Also, I was growing hungry; there had been no chance to save any of the miserable scraps the

Poor Clares issued, being of course no worse than they ate themselves. Once I made my way to the swift-flowing river, lay down and drank some water; it was cold as ice, but made me feel better. As I came up, I heard singing.

I stood where I was, and listened. It was the sound of men's voices, two of them, making plainchant. The sound itself was extraordinary in the thin cold air, full of gladness, springing naturally from the singers' throats, a hymn. I saw them presently come round the turn of the road; two Franciscan friars, in brown habits with white girdles, and their heads tonsured; one was tall, the other short and stout. Both appeared full of happiness. As they approached, they smiled at me, and held out their begging-bowls. I, in turn, held out my hands, helplessly.

'I have nothing to give you,' I said, 'but may I walk with you while you sing? I am going to Nancy, and have no protection.'

'Come with us there, by all means, mademoiselle,' the tall one said. 'It is a long way still.'

'I do not mind, as long as I have company.'

'Then say a prayer while we sing, and perhaps a cart will convey us into Nancy.'

They began their joyful chant again, and I said a prayer as the tall friar had bidden me. It must have been heard, because shortly, from the direction of Dieulouard, came lumbering and creaking a cart. It was full of chopped logs from the mountains, and drawing it was a great one-eyed destrier of Brabant, once used in battle to carry a knight in full armour. These horses are bred for such, and withstand the full onslaught of the enemy; they are often wounded themselves, and when that happens are of no further use to their masters and are sold, like this one, for heavy draught work or for breeding. I laid my hand on the destrier's neck, wondering what battles he had seen, and wondering also if it were worse to draw a heavy weight of firewood than bear a panoplied knight. The tall friar meantime was speaking with the driver. He seemed to do most of the talking when it was needed; I had yet to hear the little stout one say a word, but he smiled on.

'He will take us. May God bless you, little brother,' said the tall friar to the driver, who was muffled well against the cold, his hands in mittens. His breath steamed, and the horse's breath. We climbed all three on the back of the cart, sitting uncomfortably on the sharp logs; but it was an act of Providence to have sent the cart. I felt myself jolting agreeably, and soon slept, finding the stout little friar's arm about me to prevent my falling off. I shall be forever grateful to those friars, and I was able to give them nothing, and said so.

'Pray for us,' they said again. The driver set all of us down at the Franciscan church, and I did not like to ask him to direct me to the palace. I said goodbye to the friars, and went in; and beheld a great ornate tomb rearing up by candlelight, with gilded arms resplendent upon it. I knew it must be that of René Duc de Guise, called King of Sicily. There were two figures kneeling in front, and to my joy I recognised Madame Marie herself. The other I did not know. I almost ran, in defiance of respect, to where she knelt, and placed myself behind her till she should have finished her prayers for her grandfather. When she rose at last, she saw me; and to my great joy did not frown. Her tilted blue-grey eyes widened and she smiled. She was grandly dressed already, far more so than in our days at Joinville. She wore a little velvet cap shaped like a closed crown, and trimmed with ermine fur; and the sleeves of her gown were turned back to show an ermine lining also.

'Claudine! My dearest! What are you doing here? How did you come? Did you –' Her glance, which was always shrewd, ranged over my red hands and peasant clothes, and her smile grew. I murmured that I had climbed over the wall, and had walked much of the way. 'Let me stay with you,' I said. 'Do not send me back.'

'My darling, I am to go to Court. I cannot take you with me there; everywhere is full for the Queen's crowning. But wait; meet my cousin. You can perhaps stay here at Nancy.'

She made me known to one of the surviving children of her father's brother Duc Antoine, who had accompanied her. That young lady, Madame Anne, seemed easy-going, and made no difficulty as I was escorted back to the palace. It was a relief to have hot water to wash myself, clean clothes given to me, and a comfortable bed to sleep in. Next day I was taken before the Duchesse, Duc Antoine's wife, a vague lady of Bourbon blood who said she supposed I could stay, if I conducted myself suitably; but Madame Philippa must of course be informed. I was troubled at this, thinking that the old woman would claw me back again; but no doubt she was as greatly relieved to be rid of me as I was to go. At any rate, I heard no more from Pont-à-Mousson.

*

There were only two days of Madame Marie's company to be enjoyed before she was taken by Duc Antoine and his Duchesse Renée to join the Court. When she left, I have never seen anyone look more regal. She had grown even taller by now, with a white column of a neck, and her red-gold hair shone; I forget which costume she wore to depart, but one had the sensation of jewelled radiance, and the softness of fur. The fashions were changing, and close coifs were worn nowadays solely by old women and nuns; only Duchesse Antoinette continued to wear hers, and her big nose was not enhanced by it. Now, there were these little round hats, perched on top of the hair, and the hair itself had to be beautiful, no longer hidden as it had been since the days of St Paul. I had not made any speeches about him at the convent, which was perhaps as well; but I think that he was hard on women, both in causing them to cover their hair and to keep silent, also to obey their husbands. A husband is not always wiser than his wife. However these are only my own thoughts, and after Madame Philippa's whipping I kept them to myself. At any rate, Madame Marie when she rode off with her aunt and uncle looked very beautiful, and as once before turned and waved to me. I was left with the three young people, sons and a daughter, who had remained behind at Nancy, which was a great deal better than being at Pont-à-Mousson; but I wished that I could have gone with Madame Marie, to see the new Queen Eléonore crowned and to meet the Court. Yet who was I to meet the Court? I was nobody.

Having decided that I was nobody, I made sure, in the company of the two young sons and remaining daughter of Duc Antoine, that I was somebody; or rather that they should think I was. The generosity of the Duchesse had made over one or two gowns to me that her daughter had discarded, and they were grander and more comfortable than the coarse robe I had been forced to wear at Pont-à-Mousson. My hair, which had been so ruthlessly cropped, was beginning to grow again, with a slight curl; and over the past year I had become a young woman, with pretty breasts and a neck almost as long as Madame Marie's. I was at an age to tease very young men, which the Duc's sons were beginning to be. With their parents away, they were ready to enjoy freedom from the formal life they led by custom in the palace; after all, they were the descendants of Dunois, the

Bastard of Orléans, who had helped to save France from the English with the Maid's help; and they lived like kings. They were never, as a rule, allowed to forget this, but I led them round and round the corridors in games of hide-and-seek, their sister running after them, the governess, a sour-faced creature named Madame de Joigny, helpless to do anything about it. Often when I was caught in the game, the elder son, M. François, would kiss me; and presently the younger, M. Nicolas, followed suit. It became less a game of hide-and-seek than that of seek out Claudine, and kiss her when found; and though I struggled and pretended to mind, I did not mind very much. It was agreeable to be pretty, well dressed and shod, and permitted to laugh and talk, and be kissed by young men. A letter came from Madame Marie to say how much she was enjoying life at Court, and that she had been presented to the King and Queen. I did not envy her by now; I also was enjoying life.

It had to come to an end, of course. One day the sour-faced *gouvernante* approached me to say that there would be no more games of hide-and-seek. She had written both to Duc Antoine's wife at Court, and to Madame Antoinette at Joinville, to say that I was not behaving myself, was leading the young princes astray, and should be sent for at once. 'An escort has arrived,' she said triumphantly. 'You had best pack your gear; you may take the gowns with you.'

I was not even permitted to say goodbye to Duc Antoine's family. Madame stood over me while I got my things together, then came down to see them strapped in the saddle. I was mounted behind a serving-man, and we set off for Joinville. The journey was uneventful, but I was filled with apprehension about my welcome when I should reach the castle; the sight of its fairylike turrets rising at last in the distance filled me with no pleasure.

I was well thrashed on arrival, as I had foreseen. Afterwards, as I lay howling, little Madame Louise, the one who died early, came and put her arms round me as Madame Marie would have done. 'Do not cry, Claudine,' she said. 'Soon you will have your own household, and nobody can beat you except your husband. I heard Maman say that as you are not prepared to be a nun, you are to be married.'

I struggled up, my scarlet buttocks screaming. 'To whom?' I

demanded, forgetting to address her formally. 'Did you hear?
Do you know?'

Madame Louise looked reflective; in such a mood she
resembled Madame Marie a little, except that her colouring was
darker, like the Bourbons. 'I do not think that my mother has
found anyone yet,' she said uncertainly. 'When she does, you will
be informed.'

That, at any rate, was some comfort; they might have marched
me to the altar without knowing whom I was to meet there. At
least, I told myself, there would be an end of having my skirts
flung over my head and my backside whipped till it stung with
pain. A husband could perhaps be persuaded not to beat me.
I would make him want to kiss me instead, as I had contrived
with the sons of Antoine, Duc de Lorraine, in their palace at
Nancy.

To say that Duchesse Antoinette seized upon the first offer that
was made for my hand after my leaving the convent and Nancy
sounds uncharitable, but that is what she did. The reasons were
at least made clear to me; she always performed her duty. Being
a bastard, as she said, I was in any case few noblemen's choice as
a bride unless I had brought a large dowry. 'While I am
prepared to see you fitted out suitably for your wedding,
Claudine, I cannot be expected to provide more,' she said coldly.
In fact she had to be extremely provident at Joinville, as the
estate had to be made to pay for all of us and also for Duc
Claud's expenses at Court, which were considerable. Riches,
accordingly, could not be my lot; and the Comte de Vouvray,
whose second wife I was to become, was poor.

It was explained to me that his poverty arose from honourable
reasons, not gaming or other extravagance. He had gone to war
with King François against the Emperor, and like him had been
taken prisoner and held in Spain. Later the Comte ransomed
himself to freedom, and this cost a great deal. Having few
resources left after this except his estate, and being old, it was
hard for him to find a wife who would maintain his position.
'You have been suitably reared,' said Duchesse Antoinette. 'If
you mind your manners, there is no reason why you should not
make a châtelaine, and bear your husband sons; his first wife
had no children.'

Her full underlip firmed itself a little, primly, and at the time I did not guess why; how could I? Madame la Duchesse continued with such information as she thought it necessary for me to have.

'The Comte resides in the château of his name beyond Thorigny, where his ancestors have lived for some generations,' she continued. Her habitual distance of manner to me, so different from the warmth she used with her own children, chilled me; I had never heard of Thorigny, did not know where the château might be; and found myself desolate at the thought of parting forever with young Madame, whom otherwise I might have hoped to see again. I did not dare, however, to question Duchesse Antoinette in any detail, even about the appearance of my future spouse. Like many brides, I would not see him until the wedding. Meantime I made such cheer as might be done over the cutting and fitting of my bridal gown, which was of good cloth and would last. However, it was not fashionable or grand, like those I had worn at Nancy. It was made for a provincial châtelaine, after the habit of the Duchesse herself, something left over from the last reign; and down the middle was a lacing arrangement, which I knew would be loosened when I was expecting the sons I was to bear my husband. The Duchesse herself bulged notably here prior to taking her chamber every few years, after which all was decorously quiet until a new baby appeared. This much I knew, but not how the babies got there. It was not discussed at Joinville, even the servants being made to remain discreet. There was likewise a dark cloak of heavy stuff, two pairs of shoes for the country, hose, and chemises, all of linen. I was told again that I must consider myself fortunate; I was to become a Comtesse, bear an ancient name, and in a year or two have full control of my household.

'Not now, madame?' It was the first question I had asked, and the Duchesse frowned a little above the narrow ruff that she favoured. 'You are young,' she said, 'and imprudent, not yet accustomed to order servants. The Comte agrees with me –' I doubted initially if the Comte had had any choice – 'that for the first two years, at the least, you should be subject to a *gouvernante*, a good woman he has himself recommended, a Madame Sanserrato. Her husband, I understand, was the Comte's valet, and was with him in the Italian wars, but is now dead. She herself has been the housekeeper at Vouvray for some time, and will teach you a great deal concerning such things as they are contrived in a smaller household than that of Joinville. Her son is the steward there, and the Comte has a high opinion of his abilities. That is all. Remember, your first duty is to please your husband. Do not disgust him by the outlandish behaviour of which you are, unfortunately, capable despite all my care.'

By now I was in such a state of abject terror and gloom that I hardly dared raise my eyes to the Comte de Vouvray when at last he stood waiting for me at the altar beside the priest. I was relieved, when I did so, to find that he was no monster, though old. He was tall and thin, stooped a little, and his hair was grey and his nose long. In his youth he might have been handsome. When the vows were exchanged he fixed a mournful dark gaze on me. I guessed his age to be about sixty-two. He had taken my hand in his firmly, in a dry grasp, and appeared pleased with me in my old-fashioned lacings. I felt the ring slide on my finger, and found myself married. On leaving the altar I observed that my husband walked with a limp, and learned later that it was from a wound taken in Italy. This made him kin to my father, and I began to warm towards him.

Madame Louise had begged for a little feast for me, and there was a roast of spring lamb with rosemary, a pressed tongue, a dish of eels, and some subtleties. I ate very little, because I was still miserable about going away to Thorigny. When I knew my husband better, I decided, I would ask him if there were places we might visit that I knew. At the same time I wished that he had not agreed to the continued presence of the *gouvernante*. It would be no different from life under Duchesse Antoinette, with no Madame Marie. I longed fiercely for a sight of the red-gold hair and tilted eyes; if only she could have been here! Perhaps she would not have let them take me away: she could persuade her mother, whose favourite she was, to anything. It did not matter that I was now a Comtesse.

At the wedding ceremony, and afterwards at the feast, I had noticed a woman present whom I did not know, and nobody thought to point her out to me. She might have been about fifty, tall and thin. She wore dark clothes, as widows do who have been in that state some time, and a long peaked hood hanging down her back such as peasants still wear, with a laundered coif

beneath. Her face was curiously long and pale, with features like
our Gothic ancestors, and a thin mouth of purple-red beneath a
prosy upper lip. I have observed in the course of my life that
persons with such a colour enjoy a long allotted span and do not,
as is supposed, succumb to heart trouble. Accordingly, this
woman came in with Madame Louise to undress me ready for
my bridegroom, and I realised that she must be the *gouvernante*,
Madame Sanserrato. I did not speak to her, being too greatly
overcome by the situation. I let them unlace me, remove my
shoes and hose, and Madame Louise took a comb and ran it
through my hair, spreading it about my shoulders on the
pillows. Then she kissed me.

'A good night, Claudine, darling,' she said, and went out of
the room. The *gouvernante* followed. I took it that she had the
status of a servant, and also, Madame Louise being still
unmarried, it was proper for some older woman to have been
present at my disrobing. Of Duchesse Antoinette there was no
sign; she had done, as usual, her duty, and having graced the
wedding ceremony had taken herself afterwards to her own
apartments.

The room that had been given us was one of the best in the
castle, signifying the Comte's status. He came in presently,
without attendants; there had been little ceremony used of that
kind. He limped to the bed, drew the curtains and got in. I said,
by way of making talk, 'How did you hurt your leg, husband?'

'At Pavia, and it got no better in a Spanish prison. Do not
trouble your pretty head about it, my dear. I hope to please you
otherwise.'

I was about to say that he did not displease me, for he did not;
but he had already reached out towards me, and had begun to
ease up my chemise, which action troubled me; I had never been
permitted to see my own naked body, for even when I took a
bath Duchesse Antoinette had ruled that I must cover myself
first with a white sheet with a hole in it for my head, the rest to
be draped over the bath's edge, so that I saw nothing. Now I felt
the Comte's hands, which were thin and dry, travel intimately
over my stomach and hips, then between my legs, which
troubled me greatly. I dared say nothing, however, having been
brought up to endure certain things in silence, though never
this. He had edged himself nearer, and presently lay on top of
me, and I felt the part that men keep in their codpieces raise

itself gently, then subside again. He took his hand and tried to
aid it, but to no avail; then he sighed, and began to fondle my
breasts, which aroused a curious sensation in me; by this time I
had grown blushing and confused in the dark. Mercilessly, the
dry hands caressed and stroked my body, missing no part back
or front; and I concluded that this was what was meant by
marriage, and that in some way it would get the Comte his son. I
remembered what Duchesse Antoinette had told me of my duty,
and prevented nothing that my husband might try to do; in the
end he sighed, and to my relief turned over on his back.

'Let us sleep now,' he said. 'It may be better tomorrow, or the
day after.'

I did not sleep at once. I lay awake, a prey to conflicting
feelings. What had happened was not, in its way, unpleasant; but
it had roused sensations in me I did not know I possessed. There
was nobody I could ask concerning these; even Madame Marie,
if I wrote to her, would not know, for she had never been
married. As for the *gouvernante*, I did not fancy asking her. The
notion that she had gone through the same process with the late
M. Sanserrato made me laugh to myself, then begin to shake
uncontrollably with laughter; I bit my lip and made myself stop,
afraid of waking my husband.

Next day, Duchesse Antoinette sent for me; had I pleased the
Comte? Had I become a wife to him? She seemed anxious to
know, and, in my innocence, I smiled and said that I had done
so. 'That is good news,' she said, and kissed my cheek, a thing
which had never happened before. In important marriages they
test the sheets, but there was none of that. The Duchesse then
gave me a little purse of gold coins to use for myself, whether
out of kindness, or because she was glad to be rid of me, I do not
know. I thanked her, and made my way down to the Comte's
waiting coach.

The coach was of black leather, very old, square in shape, so that
the corners had cracked and when it rained the roof leaked, but
it was not raining that day. I was in tears, because my dear young
Madame had written me farewell and had promised to write
again, but it still meant that I would no longer see her. My
husband dozed, which meant that he did not perceive my tears;
as for the *gouvernante*, she took no heed of them. The driver was

a fellow from Thorigny who had been put up in the servants' quarters overnight; we saw nothing but his back. The coach was uncomfortable, and lurched on the road, because the horse was frisky. Suddenly the lurching woke my husband, who smiled at me and reached out to fondle my hands.

'We have had to buy him lately, because the last one dropped in the shafts,' he said. 'Madame Sansarrato uses the equipage on market day, when she goes to Troyes. Perhaps the weight of cheeses and salt marts was too much for poor Lopi.' Madame smiled, and said nothing.

I resolved to ask later if I might ride the frisky horse, to take some of the devilment out of him; I had been taught to ride very well at Joinville. But I would wait, I thought, till Madame Sanserrato was out of the way. I had already guessed that no favours would be granted me in her presence. She sat silently in the opposite seat and did not say a word during the journey, only staring down at the straw-laden floor.

At Troyes, we stopped at an inn. By then it was growing late, and any bustle of activity at the booths was long over. I saw several pairs of lonely knitted hose hanging on their frames, and flatirons for sale. My husband pointed out the cathedral and the abbey of St Lupus, then escorted me to the inn. We all had supper together.

I was weary, and dreaded a repetition of the night before, longing to be left alone in my own bed. This happened; I was shown into a room, with a bed in it, and at the foot a pallet, as is customary. When I had been undressed and had lain down, Madame Sanserrato came in again and folded my clothes, then took off her gown, leaving herself in her petticoat with a linen band round her head, and lay down on the pallet. There was no sign of the Comte that night, so my prayer was answered; but no word was spoken of why he had elected not to visit me. No doubt he was as weary as I, and doubted his powers.

The Château de Vouvray, beyond Thorigny, was built in a hollow, so that I saw the high-pitched roofs before anything else. As we approached I noticed some ducks in a stream, and a large dovecote, big enough to have been lived in, nearby. The cobbled courtyard was grass-grown, and our horse, his high spirits a trifle abated by the journey, dragged us across it to the front door, over which was carved in stone my husband's coat of arms. He got out, lent me his arm, and followed by Madame Sanserrato we made our way inside. A man was standing on the threshold, neither young nor old by my estimation; he might have been thirty. This fact did not interest me, but his features did; he was the image of my husband, and might have been the Comte himself in his youth. I sensed the dark eyes pass swiftly over me, then lower themselves; he bowed, and made us a formal greeting. 'This is your new mistress,' I heard my husband say. He made known the man to me; his name was Andelot, and he was our steward of stated abilities. An instant's resentment had shown on his face at the Comte's words, and I took it that my position here was not popular, at least with him. A few servants in linen caps huddled at the back of the entrance; they did not care about my arrival one way or the other, from the look of them, except for one little girl who laughed behind her hand at the widow. As far as that went, Madame Sanserrato was to have charge of them in the meantime, not myself.

In bed that night, my husband still did not visit me, and I knew the hope that perhaps what was required had been done, and that he would not return. Madame slept in her own place, and I enjoyed a night's quiet sleep between worn sheets scented with herbs, which smelled pleasant. Soon, I hoped, the carrier from Joinville would come, and I would dispose the rest of my clothes, including the grand gowns from Nancy, in their place. There was a long-saddle, a chest which opened, fitted as the step of the bed, and it was carved like a door-lintel with the arms of the De Vouvrays. I knew nothing about that family, and resolved to ask my husband concerning it; to show an interest would be civil.

There was an opportunity next day, for he elected to show me round the estate, which was small, and could be covered on foot. I took the opportunity to ask him if I might ride the carriage-horse, and he looked doubtful for moments, then said he supposed there was no reason why not. I thanked him before he changed his mind; then put in my request to know more about his family. Nobody can say that I lack my share of guile. They were not, in fact, very interesting, though they had been known since the time of St Louis, but so have a great many families. There had been soldiers among them and, emulating these, my husband had followed the King to his defeat by the

Emperor at Pavia, and like him had been taken prisoner to Madrid. 'This marriage to the Emperor's sister is not a success,' the Comte remarked unexpectedly. 'The King is not interested in her, and when he is not interested in a woman, he ignores her. The coronation was grand enough, but since then Madame Eléonore has been a grass widow, and will remain one.'

I remarked that the previous Queen had been a grass widow also. 'Ah, you knew that,' replied my husband. 'Queen Claude passed her time making jam. There are worse things for women to do, no doubt.'

'Will you require me to make jam?' I asked; I was beginning to enjoy his company. Never before in all my life had I been permitted to say whatever was in my head, and now I was able to do so. He smiled at me in a loving manner. I did not find him in the least unpleasant.

'You are to do whatever you wish, my dear, until, perhaps – but we will see –' He tailed off, and I knew that he was thinking of the son I was expected to bear him, according to Duchesse Antoinette. I had no objections, except that I was still unsure whether or not the matter had been set under way; yet there was no one here to ask concerning it.

That evening, after dark fell, the Comte took out an old fiddle and played tunes on it, while the fire leaped, and Madame Sanserrato got on with her sewing. Behind us, the man Andelot came and went, and I resolved to ask Madame who he was, and why he was so like my husband in appearance. There was no opportunity that night, however, because the Comte came again to my bed, and caressed me all over in the way he had done at Joinville. Perhaps our walk round the estate, and the fact that we got on well together, had made him feel young; or perhaps the fiddle-playing had cheered him. Whichever it might be, I was left, as before, feeling confused, excited, and all on fire. But apart from his hands, which as before had been everywhere, the Comte had done nothing in the way of consummating our marriage, as I later found to my cost.

The time passed dully at Vouvray. One day was exactly like another. The chief excitement was the midday meal, at which family and servants came and sat at old-fashioned trestles, which were brought into the hall by the men. The day after my arrival they had drawn a goose's neck, and we proceeded to eat the roast bird after it had been carved by Andelot. On the other days we had, always and unfailingly, pigeon stew or pigeon pie. The birds were taken from inside the great dovecote, selected from those which were not laying or sitting on eggs. It was, again, Andelot who chose these, having an unfailing eye for the right pigeon and a quick way of despatching it. The limp corpses were brought in for plucking, and every feather saved to stuff pillows or quilts. Madame Sanserrato saw to that, and said to me one day, without ceremony, 'You can pluck some of these.' I was unaccustomed to being so addressed, and replied with equal hauteur that I intended to go for a walk, and she could pluck them herself. 'It is part of your duty,' she replied, and I felt myself flushing.

'As you have undertaken my duties, you can carry them out yourself,' I told her, and marched out of the door, but not before seeing a delighted smile on the face of the little maidservant, plucking assiduously at her end of the table. I hoped she would not suffer for the smile.

Another day, wearied with the long evenings spent in sewing, I decided to ride the carriage-horse, whose name was Pierrelot. I met my husband limping across the cobbles, and asked him; he agreed with a friendly smile. 'Tell Andelot to tighten the girths for you,' he said. 'He is in the dovecote.'

I picked my way across the yard, which was foul with ducks' droppings among the grass. The dovecote loomed ahead of me like a great house. I reflected that I had never been in it. I ducked my head to enter – it had been built in days when people were evidently smaller than they are now – and despite myself observed hundreds of walled nests, tier upon tier of them, and a sound of cooing. I also observed Andelot and Madame Sanserrato. She had her hands on his shoulders, and was kissing his cheek.

I gasped, and the woman whirled round, her face patched red against white. I ignored her. 'I am to ask you,' I said to Andelot, 'to tighten the girths for me. I require to ride Pierrelot today.'

'You cannot ride him today; he is to go into market tomorrow,' put in the woman, with an insouciance which amazed me. Andelot spoke up, smoothly, as if he were never at a loss. 'Perhaps Madame la Comtesse will accompany us into Troyes,' he suggested. As it would displease the widow, I agreed; turned on my heel, and marched out.

Next day we set forth, a large basket of ducks' eggs with us. If Madame Sanserrato had expected me to report on her behaviour to my husband, she was disappointed, or perhaps pleased. We rode in silence, while Andelot sat up in front, driving the horse. I resolved in future to make my rides occur at the end of the week, unless a drive elsewhere interfered with them. Next time Madame crossed me, I resolved to ask my husband. After all he had agreed to my riding.

Troyes was busy, as it had not been the last day we came through. I bought two pairs of additional knitted hose for the winter with some of the money Duchesse Antoinette had given me. I was aware that the man Andelot followed me at a little distance, and presently I turned round and asked him what he wanted. He smiled; nothing would disturb his self-satisfaction, evidently. He was handsome as well as able, and knew it; a part of my mind registered the fact, while at the same time reminding me that he was a servant, and must be kept at a distance.

'It is easy to lose oneself here, madame,' he said. 'Allow me to take your packages, and to escort you through the market. There are many things to see.'

He took my purchases, and also took my arm; I was not comfortable with the latter situation, or with the pressure of his fingers against my sleeve. He showed me, however, the gingerbread stall; the stall which sold oranges; the ribbon-seller; the makers of lace, still working at it on bobbins, with separate white lengths for sale; and a fortune-teller. At the latter's tent he took my hand.

'Let us go in, and see what she predicts for us.'

'No, I will not.' I had wrenched my hand away. 'Take me back to the coach, if you please. I do not care for your manners. They are familiar.'

An unpleasant expression passed for instants over his face, making it no longer handsome but ugly. He said nothing more, but preceded me back to where the coach waited, and held open the door for me to enter. Madame Sanserrato, having sold her eggs and bought some cheeses, joined us shortly, and we set off for Vouvray. I kept silent on the journey, as I had done before. Perhaps it would have been better if I had spoken up, then or later, to my husband. But Andelot was young and strong, and the Comte old and frail; also, I did not know what exact relation they bore to one another, although I could begin to guess.

*

Two days later I had my ride, and Andelot was sent to tighten the girths. I would have hoped that he had learned his lesson from my manner at the Troyes market, but when I was in the saddle, with the girths tightened, he suddenly slid his hand up my leg inside my skirts, past my garter, feeling towards the place which is private. I brought down my crop on his arm not once, but twice.

'Take your hand away,' I said, 'or I'll slash your face.'

He sneered, withdrawing his arm. 'Used to it from him, aren't you? Why not put up with it here? Nothing wrong with me, is there?'

'You are insolent. Let me go, please; I doubt if the horse would ride you down, but I will try.'

He backed away, and I left him nursing his arm. I could see the hatred in his eyes as I left him. I do not suppose any young woman had refused him favours before. He would have to make do, I decided, with Madame Sanserrato.

Our life went on in this way, I do not know for how long, winter came and went, and the ducks' stream froze over, making it necessary to break the ice in the mornings before they could swim and drink. I was glad of my knitted stockings that I had bought at Troyes, but had not been back to the market with Madame and Andelot. The latter troubled me no more in the way he had done, but followed me constantly with his eyes as though I were naked. However I could not complain to my husband about that. He himself continued very kind and grudged me nothing, and I had accustomed myself to his fondlings in bed, which by now had made my breasts swell, if nothing else.

With regard to that, one day a joyous letter came from Madame Marie. She was to be married to the young Louis, Duc de Longueville; by the time I got the letter the wedding would be over. I burst into tears; not to have seen Madame Marie married, not to have made one of the glittering throng at Court, where she was now, in waiting about the Queen! My husband came over to discover what ailed me; it was some time, with my sobbing and crying, before he was able to find out.

'And they are going to Fontainebleau,' I wept, 'but will not be able to visit us here, because of Madame Marie's duties. I am forgotten; I am nobody. I will be hidden away here for the rest of my life.'

I heard the last word rise on a wail, and was already ashamed;

but he did not reproach me. 'It is true that we cannot afford the rich clothes needed for Court,' he said gently. 'However, I will take you to see Fontainebleau before they get there; it is not a long drive from here.'

I dried my tears, and reflected that what he had suggested was better than nothing; next day was fine, and we got into the coach, and to my relief it was the driver who had brought us here the first day, not Andelot. Madame did not come either. I began to be more cheerful in the company of my husband, and we talked and laughed in the way we often did, bowling along a smooth road on either side of which young trees were bursting into leaf.

'There are many miles of forest on the other side,' said the Comte. 'The Kings of France have hunted there for centuries; there are trees so old nobody knows their age, and rocks where a quarry can hide.' This kind of information was often forthcoming from him, and made him interesting to talk with. I looked out of the window for the palace, and saw it at last, with a great sheet of water in front, and swans gliding gracefully.

'It is in process of alteration,' said my husband. 'The King brought Italian notions back from his wars, and will have everything built after their manner.' He helped me out of the coach, and gallantly limped about with me to show me the Pavillon du Roi, the Pavillon de la Reine, the Pavillon des Enfants de France, the Pavillon de la Porte Dorée, the Chapelle de St Saturnin, the great staircase, the Pond of Frogs. I was transformed by the sight of so many round dormer windows, so many round arches, so many winding outside stairs in graceful formation. I wandered from one to the other, forgetting the poor Comte whom it pained somewhat to walk, and who had brought me here out of kindness. At last I heard his shortened breaths and turned to him. 'Forgive me,' I said. 'I have kept you too long.'

He pinched my cheek. 'We will make it up tonight, eh?'

I smiled, and let him think the prospect pleased me. In fact, the thought of his dry lascivious hands was growing less pleasant; why not leave me alone when he could go no further with me as I was beginning to desire? But I must be grateful for today, and picture Madame Marie, happy with her new husband, riding presently into the courtyards on splendid horses, in magnificent clothes, behind the King.

The Comte exacted payment from me not only that night, but

also the next; on both occasions the bed-curtains were still drawn late into the morning. I was ashamed that the servants should know, particularly Madame Sanserrato who helped me from my nakedness into my clothes. Where she met her lover I did not know or care, but envied her in that he did at least more than finger her lean body. I myself, by now, with much caressing, was no longer thin but almost plump; I had little breasts like two ripe fruit, and my mouth had swollen with my husband's kissing. Anybody who met me would have taken me for a young woman of experience, but nobody ever came to Vouvray, except the curé twice a year. He would drink wine with my husband, take some silver, and then go. I do not recall that he ever troubled to speak to me. If he had, I might have asked his aid in what happened next.

On the second night, my husband laboured in his breathing, and as he lay above me made grunting sounds, as he often did, then his hands faltered between my thighs. Presently they grew still and cold, and his gruntings stopped. I did not think what had happened for some time, being far away in a dream of Madame Marie; it was a pleasanter way of passing the interlude than in thinking what was happening. When I came to myself it was to be aware that the Comte had not moved for a very long time. I spoke to him and he did not answer. I suddenly had the certainty that he was dead, and tried to draw myself out from under him; but my hair, which had grown long again, pinned me there, and I could not move. I began to cry out for help, and Madame Sanserrato came running, in her nightgown and linen headband, unseen. 'Help me, help me,' I called, and she drew back the curtain and saw us as we were; the Comte dead and cold, and myself spreadeagled beneath him.

She lifted him aside; she was strong. 'Get up,' she told me. 'Go to my bed.' I crept shivering out of my own, and pulled my chemise over me; lately, the Comte had preferred to caress me naked. The thought that he was dead was not yet real. I made my way to Madame's bed, not too willingly; I did not want my head to lie where hers had lain. But I did not know what to do with a dead body, and I knew she would call the servants and lay out my husband, and light candles at his head.

I heard footsteps coming and going, and finally knew they were carrying the Comte's body downstairs. I had begun to wonder what would become of me, and lay awake in the starlight, having pulled Madame's covers over me to try to warm myself, as I was shivering. Then I heard footsteps in the room; I thought it was Madame, and took no heed. They came to the bed, and suddenly the covers were taken up and plunged in a fistful against my mouth; and when I could no longer cry out, pulled up also from the side, so that I lay naked, with my chemise above my stomach. Then there was a man's weight upon me; then while I struggled, the man did those things which men commonly do with women and which had not before happened to me; and once he was in full possession, let the bundle of clothes at my mouth go, and thrust his tongue in. I would have sobbed aloud, but could not; the hurt of my robbed virginity was great, and his stiff member thrust on and up me. Presently he removed his tongue, and said, 'Be silent, you little bitch. I've waited long enough for this, and I intend to enjoy it. If you cry out, my mother will come and whip you. You should be glad of a lover by now.'

I thought of the poor Comte lying dead belowstairs, and of how I would have to go and mourn for him tomorrow; then realised a certain thing. Madame Sanserrato was Adelot's mother, not his mistress. That meant that he was the Comte's son by her. I felt the jerking of the bed and of my own body. I was being used, and would be so again if I let it happen. It must not be permitted to happen. It must not. I would prevent it in some way, when I had leisure to think clearly. Now, despite everything, I felt ecstasy rise, and heard myself give the great cry women emit when they are fulfilled; it must have sounded through the house. He crushed his mouth down on mine, saying amiably, 'Quiet, now, quiet, my girl. We want them to think it was the old man.'

What did he mean? I endured his kisses, loathing them despite the pleasure that had risen in me. He continued to enjoy me till near morning, for I could not escape, then when it grew light rose up and went away. As soon as he had gone, Madame Sanserrato stood there. She must have been waiting and listening.

'You are fortunate that my son was here,' she said. 'If you are proved with child, we can say it was the Comte's. In that way Andelot will inherit what has been his right since he was born. In those days it was the barren first Comtesse who prevented it, and lately it has been yourself. Now, you will atone. Tomorrow night my son will come to you again; after that it is not prudent. Two nights, perhaps, should be enough. You will stay in this room, and I will have food sent up to you. We must have mourning made in Troyes. The woman will come to measure you, but otherwise you must see nobody.'

I had lain still, my face swollen and wet with tears, my eyes closed, as though I had not heard her. My body was bruised, much handled, ravished; my mouth tingling with unwelcome kisses. I wanted it now to happen again and yet I knew it must not. Somehow, I must escape from Vouvray; after she had gone I began to make my plans, lying alone in the grey light of morning.

Next day was teeming with rain, and far from cowing me it cheered me; Madame would be the less likely to look out of the door, or to follow across the sodden yard. I lay naked, and waited for my breakfast to be brought, hoping it would be sent by one of the maids; and it was, by the little girl who had giggled the first day I came, mocking Madame Sanserrato; I felt that she would support me, for Madame beat her often. Her name was Germaine. She was discreet today; it was impossible, with myself in a strange room, and the bed bloodied, that she should not know something had been proceeding the night before that should not. She set down my breakfast, a crust of new-baked bread and a large stoup of foaming house-ale warmed by stirring it with a red-hot poker. I reached down and drank some of the ale; it gave me heart. Then I let Germaine begin to dress me. She must have seen the bruises on my body, yet said nothing. I winced as she laced me up.

'Germaine,' I said, 'lend me your cap and shawl for a little while.' But she looked round fearfully.

'Oh, madame, I dare not. If *she* should find out –'

'We must risk that, and I have nothing to give you. But I will leave the things in the stable; you would find them there almost at once.' I had determined to saddle Pierrelot, and get away on him; the rain would help.

'Madame, I will aid you,' she said shyly, and when I was dressed put the cap and shawl on me. I stole quickly downstairs, having neither money nor a change of clothes; and saw Madame Sanserrato seated at the head of my husband's open coffin, between the burning candles. Her peaked hood was pulled forward over her face, her black sleeves over her hands. She might have been his widow; in a way, she was so. There must have been a time when she and the Comte were young enough to beget a son together. I did not want to think of it, and vanished out of the door, into the teeming rain. It soaked me by the time I had reached the stables, but I cared nothing; my hands were slippery with wet and trembling with haste, and I fetched the harness and put it on Pierrelot. The good beast was used to me by now, and in any case was not of a temper to be difficult; I only hoped he would get me out of Vouvray before my absence was discovered. I remembered to leave Germaine's cap and shawl in a little limp bundle, knowing she would come to find them soon; and cantered off, my sore inner parts solaced by the saddle. I could hardly see the way for rain.

We rode on, for I knew which road I was taking; the road to Fontainebleau. Somehow, I would find Madame Marie, and she would help me. My hair streamed down into my eyes, and my clothes were like a cold bath round me; every now and again I raised a hand from the reins to wipe the water from my eyes. At one point I had seen a laden donkey come past; it was the maker of mourning-gowns, come to fit me with her pins. She did not know me, and I gave her no greeting. She had come from the opposite direction in which I was travelling, but I knew I was on the right path, because the other day when I was driving with my husband, we had remarked on a strange twisted tree that grew in the way.

Pierrelot did well. I do not know how old he was, but he liked a swift ride when he could get it. As we began to near our destination the rain stopped, and I flung back my hair and began to see clearly. There was now less danger of pursuit; in fact, and I laughed to think of it, they had nothing on which to pursue me. Nor were they likely to know which way I had gone; it was possible that they thought I had returned to Joinville, in which case fear of Madame Antoinette would prevent their trying to retrieve me from there.

I became aware that the horse was having his head by the time we reached Fontainebleau. He galloped past the entrance to the great château and I tried in vain to make him turn. I had a brief glimpse of the lake, the round dormers, we had seen the other day; no more, and he led me into a forest of thick trees. There were rides cut through, and down one of them he plunged, as

though drawn irresistibly by some scent or other; I had to keep
my head down to avoid low branches, which would have caught
me by the hair or whipped my face. 'Pierrelot,' I murmured, but
he took no heed, and galloped on. I was beginning to be
frightened; when would he stop? There were sounds among the
thick old trees, half heard through my fear; hunting horns, the
baying of dogs, the movement of men and horses. The King was
at the chase. I heard my husband's voice, wearily for I had
begun to grow very tired and frightened; he was telling me again
that the Kings of France had hunted in these forests for
centuries. Philip the Fair had died here, mysteriously, at the
hunt. Perhaps I too would die: or gallop on and on, for a
hundred years. I almost regretted Vouvray, desite my pain.

Suddenly a terrified stag charged out of the trees across our
path, his nostrils distended, his eyes staring and bloodshot. I
could smell his acrid scent, see his branched antlers, like
candlesticks; his tongue lolled out of his mouth; he was almost
spent. The baying hounds sounded in the near distance.
Pierrelot reared, and the stag veered in direction and plunged
into a thicket of trees to our right. I was thrown from the saddle,
but before reaching the ground was caught in the strong arms of
a man in a round jewelled hat. His oblique lecher's eyes surveyed
me, not favourably; his great strong neck was like a bull's. He
had the most incredibly long nose I had ever seen. Pierrelot had
vanished; I do not know what became of him. The man thrust
his hand at once into my breasts, feeling them in an impersonal
way; they were still sore from Andelot's handling. All about us
huntsmen with angry faces were clustering by now. The dogs
leaped about, aimlessly. Their collars were jewelled also. I
noticed all such details, in the way one does, they tell me, before
death.

'You have lost us our quarry, young madame,' said the
long-nosed man. He was immense, a giant. Vitality exuded from
him. He held me across his saddle like a caught fish, and the
familiarity of the greeting brought home to me what I must look
like; soaked with rain, my loose hair plastered against my face,
my skirts sullied with mud from the ride. I might have been a
nobody or a whore, and as such he had already treated me.
Andelot's hands had acted in the same way at the beginning as
this man's were doing now; and I had no crop to bring down,
having dropped it in the confusion. In any case I would hardly

have dared use it; this man was the leader of the party, and I had lost them their stag. I could picture the great, panting beast, saved for the time from a bloody death; and was glad, for I love all animals. It was gone by now among the rocks, back to its own kind.

The jewelled giant jerked his head to a nobleman – they were all noble, judging by their gear – who rode by him. 'Take her back, and see that she is given food and made dry,' he ordered. His eyes swept briefly over me, then he lost interest for the time. 'We must find another quarry,' he said, and turned away, leaving me to the nobleman, who was not best pleased. 'We will meet again, madame,' said the giant smoothly, and his deputy, enraged at missing whatever new victim they might find, said nothing at all to me as I was borne back to the palace on his saddle-bow. I asked uselessly for Madame de Longueville. 'I have my orders,' he replied curtly. Afterwards I found that he was Anne de Montmorency, Constable of France. At the time, he might have been anyone. I was so weary, wet, and cold that I felt almost dead, and even the thought that the giant personage had it in his mind to behave with me later as Andelot had lately done aroused no interest in me. I was too tired even to think of it.

The Constable made me dismount at a courtyard, and flung the reins to a waiting groom. There seemed to be servants running everywhere; one escorted me up a stone staircase, wherein an alcove was set with, carved in stone, a head and shoulders like a satyr's; that of the man who had held me in the forest, but without his hat. I knew that I need ask no questions; that had been the King of France, and I was in his power. My escort had gone, making his way, without doubt, back to the hunt, having disposed of me for the time. I turned to the servant, who wore the royal livery, and said that I desired to be taken to Madame de Longueville.

His face was blank. 'As madame pleases.' I knew that he would never take me to Madame Marie; he also had his orders, which were to convey me to just such a room as we reached now; a small room, with a carved marble mantel, chairs, and a bed. I glanced at the bed, knowing that the King of France would come and tumble and use me on it, when he had done with his day's hunt and had his supper.

I reminded myself that I had eaten nothing since breakfast; I was swaying with exhaustion, the long ride, and the forgotten usage of Andelot. I asked the servant if I might have some food. His answer was the same. 'As madame pleases.'

However, food was brought. I picked at it, finding that I could not, after all, eat. My wet clothes chilled me and I had begun to shiver, but there was nothing into which to change them. I sat down in one of the chairs, hardly aware that I marked its tapestry seat with damp. There was a case of jewels in the room. Everything was very elegant. No doubt this was a place to which the King often brought young women.

I tried to think what to do. At one point I got up and tried the door; it was locked, as I expected. Even if I won out, I had not the beginning of a notion how to find Madame Marie in the whole of Fontainebleau. I saw now that I had been mad to come; but had I the choice, I would not return to Vouvray. By now, they must be aware that I had gone, and would have made their plans accordingly; first, there would be the funeral of the Comte, lacking his widow. I thought of my husband coldly; was it pride of blood that had made him marry me? He could have married Madame when her Italian husband died, and had his son made legitimate, satisfying everyone. But I myself, now? What was to happen to me after the King had tired, as he would do, of me in an hour? To find Madame Marie would be useless then; even she could not take pity on a young woman whom His Majesty had used as a whore, after coming upon her alone in the forest.

Time passed. I could find no way of escape. I had even looked up the chimney from the mantel, but the tall stacks I had seen outside would defeat me, and in any case, shivering and weak as I was, I had no heart for such an attempt. I do not know what would have happened except what was intended for me, but after what seemed an eternity there was a sound of the lock turning, the door opened, and a tall noblewoman stood there in a blue gown and cloak, her fair hair smooth beneath a round fashionable hood banded with gold. She regarded me with calm interest, and asked if I was comfortable. I flung myself at her feet.

'Madame, madame, I beg of you, help me to free myself! I have no money and I cannot pay, and have nowhere to go, but to be out of here is all I ask. I am the Comtesse de Vouvray, madame, and I seek my friend the Duchesse de Longueville. If you know her, and know where to find her, tell her Claudine is here, in great distress. I beseech you to do this; otherwise what will happen is that I shall be used, then abandoned; I know it too well.'

I was clasping her knees, and could feel the rich stuffs which made up her gown and underdress. At first she had seemed disinclined to listen to me, and I learned afterwards that she made a practice of looking in to ensure that the King's casual young women, often in distress like myself, were clean, fed and prepared to await his attentions. His habits seemed to amuse her, like the antics of a favourite brother. Later I learned that she was François' mistress, had made a marriage of convenience to an old husband, and had twenty brothers and sisters of her own. No doubt that was where she had acquired her detached amusement at the vagaries of life. Her name was Anne de Heilly, Duchesse d'Etampes, and she was a Huguenot by conviction. All this I did not of course learn till later; at that time I was only conscious of the beautiful hands, loaded with precious rings, running over me, and the voice exclaiming, in the unmistakable accents of Picardy, that I was soaked.

'Whatever else becomes of you, you must be put into dry clothes at once,' she said, and with a quick generous gesture swung off her blue velvet cloak and put it about me. It made me feel a little warmer, but my sodden clothes were still clinging to me underneath. 'Come,' said the Duchesse. She led me out of the room – I bade it farewell with a shudder of thankfulness – and down a great corridor; and thence by devious little staircases and through rooms each one of which contained a box of gleaming jewels like the first, to a door, at which she knocked. A servant opened, and against the light from the window I saw a couple sitting, their hands in one another's like two children; my dear Madame Marie, and a tall young man I did not know, who must be the Duc de Longueville, her husband. He had not gone with the rest to the hunt.

'Here is a young lady to see you,' explained the Duchesse. 'She is wet and cold, and needs a change of clothes. I do not know any more than that; I have not asked.'

She smiled, whipped her cloak from off my shoulders, and was gone before I could thank her. I wondered afterwards how she dealt with the King when he came back to the palace to find his prey gone; no doubt she had her own methods. Meantime, I did not consider that; Madame Marie had sprung to her feet.

'Claudine! My dearest! You are soaked! How is it that you are here? Louis –' she addressed her young husband, who appeared anxious to do everything she asked, and made ready to disappear, in order that she might undress me and put me into dry clothes – 'Louis, I think she should be put to bed; look, she is shivering. I will tell the maids to fetch a hot brick, and you, Claudine, get your clothes off, and then they will dry you; once you are in bed, you may tell me about it.' And she went off to instruct the maids to do their duty, while the Duc removed himself, I know not where. I was so greatly filled with relief and thankfulness that I was almost fainting. I undressed and felt them dry me, and put me into a clean chemise of Madame's, and see me into her bed; the luxury of the silken pillows and sheets claimed me, and I fell asleep at once, like a child. When I awoke, Madame Marie was sitting by me, alone

'And now tell me everything, if you can,' she said gently. 'What has happened to your husband? How did he permit you to come here, in this state?'

I suddenly broke down and told her everything that had happened, not omitting my treatment at the hands of Andelot the steward and his mother. She listened very gravely. She said, 'My husband will see that a proper man of business is sent to Vouvray, to put your affairs to rights and see that you receive your jointure. These people must not be permitted to continue as they have done. As for yourself, we must wait to see whether you are with child, which may have happened, or not. If you are, it will be cared for. I imagine that the next legitimate heir will want his rights, in either case.' She spoke wisely, and I tried to imitate her calm.

'That is a cousin, I believe,' I said. 'I have never met him. He never came to Vouvray.' I was beginning to feel better, with the possibility of a child mentioned openly between us. I had been fearful of it ever since Madame Sanserrato's speech. Now, it could leave my body in time, and be no longer a part of me; as Madame said, it would be cared for. In the event, there was to be no child; but I did not find that out till after my illness, which lasted a long time.

Next day I began to be ill, flushed and feverish, tossing in the bed Duc Louis had kindly vacated to allow me to grow better undisturbed. Madame Marie slept with me herself, and showed me every kindness; I did not know till later that she was indeed with child, and most happy about it. The contentment of the couple with one another was something I had never before seen; the Guise husband and wife had achieved something like it over the years, no doubt, but it was not to be witnessed except in private; the Comte and I had certainly not achieved it, by reason of our disparity in age and his impotence, though he had been kind enough. Otherwise, all I knew of bodily passion was force and ugliness, both with Andelot and, by expectation, with the King. As regarded the latter, when after some weeks I was recovered, and appeared behind Madame Marie in one of her made-down darker dresses, he might never have set eyes on me. The soaked waif of the forest was a different person from the protégée of the Duchesse de Longueville. He respected Madame Marie greatly, admired her beauty, and treated her as one of his daughters.

After my recovery I was early taken to make my curtsy to the Queen, Madame Eléonore. King François had neglected both his wives, the first of whom had been Claude de France, daughter of Anne of Brittany and Louis XII. She had borne him five children, including beautiful Madame Madeleine: this second marriage to the Emperor's sister was to bring him none. Madame Eléonore had been a pretty woman in her youth, and no doubt her first marriage to the King of Portugal had been happy enough; but disappointment and homesickness, and the fact that she knew very little French and spoke that with a Flemish accent, had made inroads on her appearance. She should have been attractive still; her father had been known as Philip the Handsome, and his Spanish wife, though mad, had been very beautiful, and Madame herself had also evaded the Hapsburg lip, unlike her brother. However she sat, listless and obedient, and did not enchant the King. She would make no mark on history. It was left to the Duchesse d'Etampes to do so. The latter spoke kindly to me now and again, having no reason not to remember me. I once said that I hoped I had not ruined her velvet cloak. 'There are plenty of others where that came from,' remarked quiet Duc Louis, Madame Marie's husband, when he heard: he spoke seldom, but within himself had wit. He was not much known by anyone, except his wife; their happiness burned with a steady, pure flame. I envied them. As for Madame d'Etampes, she was loyal to the King, but also a good friend to the Huguenots, like King François' sister Marguerite. The persecution against them was not yet known in France.

I did not meet all the King's children at Fontainebleau, or indeed before we left it for Châteaudun, for Madame Marie to prepare for her own child. The two I remember most clearly were the princes, because they were so different they were hardly like brothers at all. The Dauphin, named François, was very charming, manly and brave, with a word for all, beloved by everyone; his brother Henri was taciturn and shy. Both young men had been returned from captivity in Madrid on payment of a large ransom, for they had been sent as hostages to the Emperor when their father was allowed by him to return to France. I do not understand all of it, but I believe King François broke certain promises to the Emperor afterwards by permission of the Pope, which did not make Queen Eléonore any happier as his wife under the terms of the treaty. The King was a personage who would please himself, whatever befell. We left him hunting and dancing at Fontainebleau, and ourselves returned to Châteaudun.

This was always Madame Marie's favourite residence, through her marriage and her widowhood. It had belonged to the great Dunois, the Bastard of Orléans, her husband's ancestor, who with the Maid of Orléans herself had saved France from the English. We lived in a tremendously high tower, from which a road wound down to the banks of the river which later became the Loire. The tower was so old that its stones struck a chill through one; those who lived in earlier times must have had strong constitutions.

For a season, Madame Marie knew great happiness. Her husband asked nothing more than to be near her, and they awaited the birth of their child in delighted anticipation. I watched Madame's body thicken without any feeling of envy; I was too greatly relieved to have escaped the consequences of Andelot's ravishing of me to want to imitate her state.

With regard to that, there was the interview with the Duchesse Antoinette to be endured. I knew that she would come, both to see Madame Marie before the birth and to visit her own relations, the Bourbon Vendôme family, who lived not many miles off. Having seen her daughter she sent for me privately. I went in fear and trembling, and I was not mistaken. The grey eyes beneath the closed coif were like steel.

'You have returned to trouble my daughter, I see.'

'Madame, I could not help myself.'

'Do not answer me. A suitable marriage had been arranged for you, better than many young women in your position had any right to expect. Yet you ride away, in a fashion lacking in dignity, and compromise yourself with the King, having done so already with your house-steward. Nobody but my daughter would have had the good nature to take you in.'

'Madame, I did not compromise myself. It was misfortune.'

'Do you tell me that you did not make great eyes at this servant, in your husband's lifetime? Do you tell me that he had not been in your bed before?'

'It is useless for me to tell you anything, madame, for you will not listen.' I had flung my head up, and looked her in the eye; perhaps that impressed her. She resumed her discourse, however, not any more pleasantly than hitherto.

'I have tried to persuade my daughter to part with you, and send you back to me at Joinville, where your behaviour would be supervised; but she will not. All I can say is this; if you are to stay with her, it must be in the guise of a nun. You will not raise your eyes to any man. You will behave like a servant. If there is any further scandal concerning you, I myself will see to it that you are put out on the streets.'

My knees were trembling, but I dared not answer her. I made my curtsy, turned, and went out.

Thereafter I was, as the Duchess de Guise had instructed me, a nun. I wore Court dress, but did not dance; nor did I raise my eyes. I think now that Madame Antoinette had been afraid, not knowing the degree of devotion Duc Louis had for his wife, that I might sow dissension between the couple, in the same way as my mother had done between the Duc and Duchesse de Guise to the extent of my own conception and birth. Otherwise I do not know why Madame Antoinette should have been so cruel to me. I was not, in any case, in a state to enjoy frivolity, or to want to trespass against her instructions. The Court, whether at Fontainebleau, Blois, Paris or Vendôme, where we all went later, grew accustomed to the sight of me creeping, like a dark-clad shadow, behind radiant Madame Marie at Court functions; radiant because, at the Duc's palace of Amiens, she had given birth to a healthy son, François, at the end of October. That he was called after the King signified her acknowledgment of the royal favour; everyone knew His Majesty looked on her as a daughter. She was so beautiful that it was difficult to deny her anything, and it seemed as if good fortune would follow her always.

Ill fortune, however, eclipsed the Court. The Dauphin François died, after a few days' illness. Even his father was plunged into mourning. There were no more hunts, for the time, in Fontainebleau forest. The King spent many hours alone; and it was difficult to envisage the shy Henri as Dauphin. It was as though a limb had been cut off; even I felt it. The Court was no longer lighthearted.

Part II

We first saw the King of Scots at the château of Vendôme, where
he had gone from Paris with the supposed intention of
betrothing himself to the daughter of the house. Like all
Bourbons, Mademoiselle Marie de Vendôme had a big nose, but
was otherwise handsome. I saw a good deal from my imposed
position as nun and servant. In fact I did not have to be entirely
as abject as I had once been. Duc Louis' man of affairs had
settled matters at Vouvray for me and had arranged that my
jointure should be regularly paid, so I had a little money of my
own, enough to buy myself clothes and cosmetics. I had,
moreover, asked that Madame Sanserrato and her son Andelot
should remain where they were instead of being cast on the
world. This was less out of charity – I felt none for either of
them – than from a fancy I had that, were they deprived of a
home and a livelihood, they would in some way seek me out for
revenge; and I wanted more than anything at that time to be
free of them for life, and left in peace. I followed, therefore, the
Duc and Duchesse de Longueville in their happiness and beauty,
and as their destination was Vendôme I went as well. We were all
of us grandly dressed, as the Vendôme family kept great state,
almost as though they were kings. No doubt Duchesse
Antoinette, having been brought up among them, had imbibed
a sense of her own worth accordingly.

This was manifest also in Mademoiselle Marie, who was a
young lady of great force of character. She would stride about
with sweeping assurance, and state without hesitation whatever

it was she wanted to convey. She had been indulged by her parents, and her every wish was law. This was evident in the matter of her rumoured engagement to the King of Scotland, whose portrait she had procured in some way, and kept in a chest. I may state now, though I did not see it then, that the appearance of James V was quite unlike that of anyone else. For one thing his hair was red, and the face above his neatly trimmed beard was pale and oval. His eyes had a narrow look, giving him the aspect of an elfin, enchanted creature; they say he used to go about in disguise among his subjects, but he must have been known by them wherever he went. When we heard he was in France, it was like expecting to see the King of Elfland among us, especially as, Duc Louis told us, the Scots fleet had scattered the Emperor's ships which had been sent against King François; seeing what they took to be a hostile English navy appear, they turned about and went home. King François was so grateful to the King of Scots for this that there was nothing he would not do for him subsequently, though the matter of the ships had been unintended.

The hall at Vendôme was full, and Madame Marie and her husband, who were seldom apart, were talking together with some acquaintances at one side of the hall. I observed a man and his servant, the servant having narrow eyes and red hair, come in, and stand among the common folk, where I was myself. It was the King of Scots, intent on taking a look at his intended bride before he put pen to paper on the matter. Instead of having the discretion to keep silent and let events take their course, Mademoiselle Marie came marching up, smiling broadly, the portrait with her, filched from the chest. She took King James by the hand, which was forward of her.

'Sir, you stand over far aside,' she said. 'Therefore, if it please Your Grace to talk with my father or me, as you think for the present, a while for your pleasure, you may if you will.'

The King flushed a little, but went with her to the Duc de Vendôme and all politeness was exchanged with him and his Duchesse: but personally I believe that it was from that first moment that James Stewart decided not to marry a managing young woman with a large nose. The decision bewildered everyone in the event, as nobody could see anything wrong with Mademoiselle de Vendôme.

King James was hardly honest about the business. He allowed

the Vendômes to feast him, bring musicians, fill the hall with dancing, a masque, a play, a farce; and outside there was jousting, with the King of Scots himself running at the tilt in a horse with great nodding feathers on its head that he had bought for the purpose in Paris. Besides all this, Vendôme erected a pavilion for him, hung with silk and cloth of gold, and a gold canopy set with gems to put over his head. Incense and sweet waters were poured out abundantly, to make everything pleasant; and poor Mademoiselle Marie and the King exchanged rings and chains, tablets with diamonds and rubies, and almost as many different jewels as there had been in the boxes in the guests' rooms at Fontainebleau, from which one could help oneself. My own Madame Marie, naturally, met the King of Scots in process of these entertainments, and I heard afterwards that his facile heart was meantime hers until he learned that she was happily married already. What she thought of him I did not know, or ask, then or later.

That was the situation, and there it remained. James V announced with diplomacy to the Vendômes that he must go directly to the King of France to confer about the marriage, and departed, leaving them with an immense bill for the entertainments. They never saw him more. The silk and cloth of gold were finally folded and put away, and there was a feeling of flatness at Vendôme, with Mademoiselle herself betrayed and disappointed.

I first set eyes on Madame Madeleine de France, the King's daughter, when she was married to James V at Nôtre Dame on New Year's Day, 1537. It had been a love-match and everything had happened quickly. I was among the spectators outside, as only the *haute noblesse* had been bidden to the ceremony, which was crowded. Seven cardinals were present to officiate. My own Madame Marie and her husband Longueville, in ducal coronets of gold and cloaks lined with fur against the weather, had gone in; also the royal party, King François in his plumed hat, conducting the bride in white and gold, with a small jewelled cap on her head, and her bridesmaids behind in gowns with green sleeves. Her head, with its profusion of bright brown hair, was bowed as she went in, and I did not see her face; but as she came out, with her new husband by her, she was radiant with happiness, like a tall languid lily which has acquired the flush of

a rose. She was very beautiful. Behind her was Madame
Marguerite, the King's sister who had brought her up after the
death of her mother Queen Claude. The low-growing peak of
dark hair on Madame's forehead always intrigued me; she was
supposed to have one of the finest minds in France.

King James himself, with his bride on his arm, wore a short
cloak of blue velvet, lined with sable fur, and a suit of white satin
beneath. It was one of the few times I have seen that
unpredictable creature looking happy. He and Madeleine had
fallen in love at sight while she was lying in her invalid chair at
Blois, as she had consumption. Her doctors had forbidden her
ever to marry and have children. James V had been told of this,
but it made no difference; he must have Madeleine, or nobody.
Both he and Madeleine herself, her health having improved
greatly with being in love, begged the King to let them marry
without delay. King François had a kind heart in such ways;
besides, he was anxious to show gratitude over the matter of the
Emperor's ships. He gave his consent; he was also grateful for
the lifting of the gloom that had covered the court since
Dauphin François' death. The shy new Dauphin Henri, coming
upon King James in a church in the Lyonnais, had run to him
and embraced him, later taking him straight to his father at the
palace and waking François from his customary afternoon nap.
'Who is it that knocks so loudly at my door?' the royal voice
demanded, and when told it was King James, hurried out in his
shirt-sleeves to embrace him also. Now, the latter was his
son-in-law. The crowds roared their welcome. I thought, when I
saw the new Queen of Scots pass by, that I had never in my life
seen anyone with such long eyelashes. I wished them happy, and
for long. As for the forsaken Mademoiselle de Vendôme, she
had announced her intention of going into a convent, although
King James had, somewhat callously, offered to give her away at
the altar to whatever bridegroom the King of France might
select for her.

Six earls, six lords, six bishops, and twenty great barons had
meantime come out of Scotland dressed in their best, at the
King's command; and at the wedding feast, gold cups were set
before the guests containing not the expected wine, but, when
they were uncovered, gold dust and small lumps of gold. 'These
are the fruits of my country,' the King had said. My Madame
Marie related this to me particularly, and in after years herself

followed the practice, already begun then, of mining gold on Crawford Moor. There were bonnet-pieces in gold too, in a dish, showing the King's handsome profile wearing his round hat. Altogether the poorer country had shown itself up well in face of the rich profuse gifts of France. These last were astonishing: during the days that followed, King François told his daughter to help herself to anything she chose, and Madeleine and her ladies did not hesitate; tapestries, rich beds, cupboards of plate, bolts of cloth, velvet, silk, cloth of gold, cloth of silver, rich tablecloths, twenty Persian carpets, dresses, jewels; everything except money, for that was in short supply. In the end King François had to give King James certain properties in France in lieu of the balance of Madeleine's dowry. It did not matter; all was happiness, jousting and dancing, as in the days of Vendôme.

They spent the months of winter in France, travelling from one château to another till the milder weather should have come to Scotland, for Madeleine's sake. When it did, as far as that goes, King François fitted out two great ships to convey his daughter and her gear; and the night before the pair left there was an immense carouse, everybody being drunk till all hours of the morning. The King and Queen of Scots went off down the Seine, and I believe had a great welcome at Rouen; I remember being astonished, as we all were, that delicate Madame Madeleine should stand up to the constant feasting and public demonstrations of joy; it was rumoured that she was with child; consumptives breed easily. She weathered the welcome and, worse, the voyage: it was stormy, and the King of England, ever disobliging, had refused a safe-conduct to them to land in his realms; they were nearly taken hostage off Scarborough, and the poor people from the Pilgrimage of Grace, rowed out in small boats, begged King James to come into England and rescue them from their heartless tyrant. 'Ye English would have hindered my return, or I had been home forty days ere this,' he said to one man. 'But now I am here, and will be shortly at home, whoever sayeth nay.'

They landed at Leith, and the new Queen kissed the ground, thereby pleasing the Scots folk immensely; her beauty, the evident fact that she loved their handsome King, the rumour, quickly spreading, that she was already with child, made her at once beloved. Queen Magdalen, as they called her, could do no wrong; her wisdom and kindness were much spoken of there, extraordinarily so for a girl not yet seventeen.

*

We ourselves left them in our minds, nor did we hear more for some time. Madame Marie had her own glad news presently; she was expecting a second child in early August. She continued meantime at Court; and though he seldom left her, Duc Louis was obliged to do so briefly to transact certain business in Rouen.

I cannot recall any feeling at the news that Queen Magdalen was dead, forty days after she had landed in Scotland, where the cold had killed her. There was too much grief of our own by then. Duc Louis had contracted a fever in Rouen, and had died of it. I do not know which news reached us first. I can remember going to Madame Marie and putting my arms about her, as she had so often done for me. It did not seem to me that any trouble I had endured equalled hers. They had loved one another so much, and had had so short a time together; scarcely three years.

She was staring ahead at nothing with her blue-grey eyes, and suddenly said, 'At least I have known happiness. You, Claudine, have known none. I have my children; we must pray that this second birth takes place safely. Stay by me; do not leave me. You remind me of the time when he was here,' and then she broke down into weeping. It was the only time, till years later, that I ever saw her tears. Then she said, 'I do not doubt my mother will come, but I want to see no one else. We will go to Amiens, and later to Châteaudun. I may be quiet in both those places. I am finished with the Court. From now on my life will be that of a widow, bringing up my children.'

Then the mourning clothes were brought and put on her, and she had her little boy sent for for a time: and thereafter sat alone.

As I have said at the beginning, the proposal for the Scots marriage, or rather the King of France's command for it, was most unwelcome to Madame Marie, in mourning as she was, and pregnant by her dead husband. Three things made her fight her way out of despair; the first was the necessity of safeguarding little François' inheritance, which they had tried to eat into to provide her second dowry. She would by no means hear of this, and in the end King François, short of money as he was, had to find the sum himself. The second thing was a visit from her mother. Duchesse Antoinette had been paying a visit to her relatives at Vendôme before her own coming child was born.

She rode over, heavily pregnant, sitting astride in the old fashion, with the familiar closed coif on her head, hiding her forehead, and her narrow ruff round her neck, so that only her big nose, full underlip and chin showed. I watched the indomitable little figure come, and almost felt an affection for her; if only she had been fond of me, I would have rendered fondness in return. As it was, I hid myself while she was shown to her chamber, for she would stay with us a day or two before returning to Joinville for the birth.

She and Madame Marie sat together as mother and daughter will, and I unwittingly heard what they were saying. There is a place against the upper stone embrasure at Châteaudun, where one can curl up with a cushion and enjoy the sun, and not be seen by anybody. I had thought myself well hidden, and in fact had dozed off with the warmth; when I awoke, it was to hear voices, and I realised that Madame Marie and the Duchesse were placed near the solar window, saying intimate things to one another. I did not know how long they had been there, and if I revealed my presence now they would blame me for eavesdropping; on the other hand, if I did not reveal it, and was later discovered, the results would be even worse. I decided, on reflection, to stay where I was. Nothing of what they said would be repeated by me, and perhaps after her mother had gone I would approach Madame Marie and confess everything. In the event, I did not.

They were discussing the marriage, and Duchesse Antoinette was explaining why it was best for her daughter to become Queen of Scots rather than remain in her château, a widow, caring only for her child.

'You loved your husband, it is true,' I heard her say. 'Nothing, however, can bring him back, and you have a great deal of your life left to you.'

'That is small consolation, Maman.' All of the Duchesse's children addressed her in this informal way; there was great love between them.

'Hear me out,' said the Duchesse Antoinette. 'You are not as other women, my daughter. You have more in your head than is needed for surveying a household, looking after children, hiring and dismissing nurses and servants, picking the fruit when it is ripe to make jam. You have power, which could be used in ruling a country. Now is your opportunity; if anything befalls

King James, yours would be the task of dealing with ambassadors, writing to other crowned heads, imposing your wishes on the people, perhaps saving the church. I hear that there is much unrest in Scotland from these so-called reformers; you have the intelligence and the faith to deal with them, to see that they do not overcome the established rule with their teachings. All that you could do, and more; and you talk of sitting here, at Châteaudun, in mourning! It is not enough for you; as the years pass, you would regret having denied yourself the opportunity of a crown, and it will not come again – unless with the old monster of England, when you would not last long.'

She ended on a wry note, which was like her; and I heard Madame Marie give a little laugh, almost her first since the Duc de Longueville's death. 'I do not want that, certainly,' she admitted; and to my relief they rose and went away from the window, and I was able to escape with my cushion and my cramped limbs.

The third thing which helped Madame Marie change her mind was a letter from the King of Scots himself; he had mourned alone a long time over the death of Madame Madeleine, but now knew that he must father an heir.

He had had a strange boyhood. His mother, Queen Margaret, was a sister of Henry VIII, endued with many of that monarch's less endearing qualities. After bearing many dead children to her husband James IV, she was left with one son only, a year old, after his father had been killed fighting the English at Flodden with most of the Scots nobles fallen round him. Queen Margaret then made a foolish second marriage with a Douglas, the young Earl of Angus, with whom she soon started to quarrel. The Earl took the boy King prisoner and held him for some years, debauching him in the process, and threatening to cut him in pieces at an attempted rescue at Linlithgow. In the end James V managed to escape by himself, and rode to Stirling, where the castle was instantly barred by his orders against the Douglases. He never forgave them, exiled them for life from the country and from his presence, and even burned one of their women at the stake. Angus and his brother, of course, went straight to Henry VIII, who maintained them for many years as spies for his own benefit. This royal uncle was hardly a friend to his sister's son; his attempt to marry Madame Marie himself was only one aspect of his spiteful enmity.

James V touched on some of this in his letter to Madame, which was shown to me. '*I am only twenty-seven years old and life already weighs as heavily upon me as my crown does ... there is not a noble in my kingdom who has not been seduced by the King of England's promises or suborned with his money. There is no safety for my person, nothing to guarantee the execution of my orders or the enforcement of equitable laws.*

'*All this alarms me, Madam, and I await your support and counsel ... I wish to overcome all obstacles so that I can open up for this nation the way of justice and of peace ... All along, my power and that of my forebears has rested on the commons and the clergy, and I am obliged to ask myself if this power can last much longer ...*'

'He has not tried to deceive me, at any rate,' said Madame Marie. 'Perhaps I can help him.'

She sat for a long time with the letter between her hands, its royal seals dangling. Thereafter she seemed a trifle more content with the marriage. Later, I was convinced, though I never told her so, that it was not the King who wrote that letter at all, but Cardinal Beaton on his behalf: that man was a statesman.

'It would please me greatly, Claudine, if you would go to be with little François at Joinville. I know that my mother will be kind to him and that he will have playmates – some of his uncles and aunts will be like brothers and sisters! – but I do not want him to forget his mother. When I am far away I shall think of him constantly, and you will be able to keep me in his mind; otherwise, children forget.'

I was horrified. To go back to Joinville, under the supervision of Duchesse Antoinette, who had just given birth to another child of her own! There was a full nursery, which would make a different life for the little boy who had hitherto, since the death of his baby brother, been quite alone. I was not, however, concerned with him, but with myself. I had expected to accompany Madame Marie to Scotland, never to be parted from her. I decided that the only thing to do was to tell her the truth. I flung myself on my knees.

'Madame, madame, let me come with you, I beg! The little Duc will have all the love he needs, except yours; and your mother will see to it that he does not forget you. But as for me, she does not like me; I think the circumstances of my birth are responsible. I would never be permitted to be alone with the little Duc, to speak to him freely: I would be watched always. When I came back to you at Fontainebleau, your mother spoke to me afterwards; she said that if I ever so much as raised my eyes I would be put out on the streets. That would be my position, madame, and I beseech you not to send me to Joinville. I will be your servant; I will be your maid. You may trust me. Let me come with you. I will not betray you.' I was weeping; I felt the hot tears run out of my eyes and scald my cheeks. Madame Marie, who had frowned at first, was listening calmly.

'As that is the case, my Claudine, you must come. I would not make you unhappy. I shall be glad, also, to have your company in Scotland; it is a foreign land, and I must feel my way. Come, then; prepare your gear to set sail, and let us pray for a good crossing.'

I seized her long-fingered hands, and kissed them. There was no more talk of my going to Joinville. Duc Claud, and Madame Louise, were to come on the voyage, but first there must be the proxy wedding in Notre Dame, after the articles of marriage had been signed at Châteaudun. That first day there had been music; later on there would be much pomp, with the King of France present in the great church that had witnessed so much history. He, after all, had set the matter on foot. I wondered if he would recall that former wedding, only a year ago, of King James to Madame Madeleine, who had gone in on his arm clad in white and silver, with a wreath of jewels on her head; and now lay in dust.

The party of Scots did not impress me. Lord Maxwell, an elderly peer who stood proxy for the King, was grey-bearded; when he was younger, he had not distinguished himself by the way he handled certain of the Scots ships at the time of Flodden, arriving with them two days after the battle was over, when they could no longer be of use. The other commander, Arran, lost the fleet altogether, driving it in storm at last against the coasts of France, where it was dispersed. All that was sad old history; but the King of England did not seem less of an enemy now. Piqued at having been refused the hand of Madame Marie, even up to the last, he refused to allow her safe-conduct through England, or a safe harbour if she met rough weather. King James, hearing of this, had sent a vessel to survey the English ships and others to strengthen the fleet that was bearing his bride north. 'We must pray for a calm crossing,' murmured Madame Marie. Neither she nor I had ever been to sea.

We rode to Dieppe, and there a quarrel broke out between Lord Maxwell and another of the party, a churchman whom I had last seen, on King James's visit, in the purple robes of an archbishop; now he was in the scarlet ones of a cardinal. He seemed to expect to be preferred before anyone else, and to go on the same galley as the Queen; when Lord Maxwell would not permit this, the two men almost came to blows. The cardinal's name was Beaton, naturally. He was a handsome man, with dark greying hair beneath his scarlet cap, a thin face and shrewd eyes; their glance passed over me as of no importance.

Mary of Lorraine, Queen of Scotland, passed to her ship, accompanied by our father Duc Claud, her sister Louise, and others. When all was set fair a squall arose, and it was evident we would not have the calm weather Madame had prayed for. The sea worsened, but the wind was to the north, and to our advantage; so the great prows furrowed on, the grey sea breaking round them; I thought of delicate Madame Madeleine a year ago, braving just such seas.

Many were sick, but not Madame or myself. She sat pensive, and at one point said quietly, 'Louis has been dead a year.' I knew also she was thinking of the little Duc François her son, to whom she had said farewell at Dieppe. I did not intrude on her, lest she remember how I had refused to go with him; but indeed it was not the child whose company I had objected to, but that of his grandmother. I rose from my place, and went and walked about the ship, coming presently about a sight which would have made many laugh, though I did not; that famous warrior Duc Claud de Guise, leaning over the side, sick as a dog. He looked in actual danger of falling out, and I went and held his arms for him; he winced, and I knew I had touched the spiked iron bracelet of penance, and took my hand away. I had felt the wounded arm, twisted and misshapen, beneath his padded sleeve. He had served his King well. At the end, he looked round and thanked me, scarcely knowing who I was for sickness. It was one of my few encounters with my father.

The coast of England was passed; we did not venture too near. The Scottish coast came in sight on the Sunday, the twelfth of June. It seemed grey and uninviting. A castle reared above us on a cliff. This could not be St Andrews; there was no town.

'It is Balcomie,' voices murmured. 'They have put in over soon. The Laird of Learmonth will make her welcome.' In the Scottish way, they were chary of titles.

Madame Marie had travelled well, and appeared to have recovered from her sadness. She murmured to me that she was glad to find herself a good sea voyager; it would not be so hard to go again to France. We descended the ship's side together, and were rowed in a small boat on shore, to Learmonth's castle.

The thing that struck me about Scotland was the pervasive cold, even in mid-June. It was worse in the east, for a wind blows constantly beyond the headlands off the sea. It is a treeless country, only the stout old buildings standing up to the constant blast; the cathedral, built in the time of Bruce to house St Andrew's bones; the places they call the pends; the New Inns, where the Queen was lodged, after King James had galloped to Balcomie with a fine array of horsemen and escorted her to the waiting town. He was dressed very fine, with a jewel in his hat; we ourselves were in the latest fashion and this may have been part of the trouble. Formerly, in France, gowns had been high-necked, with a little ruff to finish them, hardly successful or comfortable unless, like Madame Marie, one had a throat like a swan. Now, they were low-cut, square to the shoulder, leaving a great expanse of bare flesh exposed to the blast, with a little fitted cap on the head to balance but not protect. The Queen, on one of her first public appearances with the King, wore such a gown, with her tall column of a neck thrusting up from her uncovered shoulders, rich sleeves, furred with ermine, turned back to show the lining, and her slender arms covered to the wrists with purfled stuff. There was no warmth where there ought to have been, and too much where there need not; such is fashion. The King looked gallant and handsome, with fur on his coat.

I do not think that it was a happy marriage; that could hardly have been expected, though at first, at any rate, he showed her courtesy and she, first and last, showed him tolerance. The King of France had brought them together, and they both left sorrow behind them; in another instance they might have comforted one another. But there were factors which prevented this. There was a dark-browed boy, the King's bastard son James, eight years old, made the Prior of St Andrews; his mother was Margaret Erskine, a flame of the King's, who had been forced by her father to marry Douglas of Lochleven, that last being a castle in a loch. James had taken her from her husband, and kept her with him as his mistress till she bore his child; afterwards she went back to Lochleven and produced a large family. Madame was always good to the boy, who hardly repaid her. There was also a bastard daughter, Lady Jane, by another mother; Madame Marie took charge of the little girl also as though she were her own. Altogether the King had nine bastards, all by different women. But none of that, except for the presence of the young Prior, was made evident the first day, when there was the wedding in St Andrews Cathedral, grand and glittering like that in Nôtre Dame, with the King in a hat embellished with gold thread, and the folk crowding beyond the doors as they had done in Paris. Prominent at the ceremony was Cardinal Beaton, whose castle, with his mistress in it, jutted up nearby, and their children.

Later, I helped to undress the Queen, and comb out her magnificent red-gold hair. Lying on the pillows, I saw no happiness in her eyes. She reached out a hand and drew me to her, and whispered, 'Claudine, pray for me.' I did so, all that night.

'Is he not handsome? Does he not fight better than younger knights, even after all these years? They say he is a ladies' man and at the same time faithful to his wife.'

That was Joanna Grisenoir, one of the Queen's ladies whose acquaintance I had already made on board the galley. She spoke to the other, Marie Pierres, and together they occupied a place which made it permissible for them to wear her Grace's chosen colours of purple and white. As I wore the same, and they were uncertain of my position and rank, they avoided me. I did not care, for by the Queen's favour I occupied an excellent place to view the tourney, and the sight of my handsome father, Claud de Guise, thundering past, his ruined arm disguised by a padded sleeve, his ruined leg in protective armour engraved in delicate patterns on the metal. He threw his spear well, farther than the King; and the thunder of applause proved how popular the House of Guise had become since Duc Claud's advent. The Queen and Madame Louise, his daughters, sat together, clapping proudly. All about me was the sound of Scots spoken, and I knew that Madame Marie and I would have to learn the language if we did not want to sit silent on every occasion. I did not mind doing so, but Madame liked to show her wit. The King spoke French a little, but not enough. He was happy now, his great horse preening and curvetting in the tourney as he rode. Soon it would be all over and we would progress to the different palaces; Linlithgow, Falkland, Stirling, Holyrood, then St Andrews again. Madame had been taken to walk about the town on the day after her wedding, with the people again crowding to see her and exclaiming at her tall height. She had not kissed the ground of Scotland as Madame Madeleine had done a year ago; but there was greater hope that she would bear the Scots king a living heir, in time.

Linlithgow is a beautiful palace, Falkland a jewel; but I like Stirling the best, mounted on its rock, with the clouds often forming a crown above it, and the Abbey Craig, where they find their hawks, rising green in the near distance. It was from Stirling that the Queen decided to pay a visit to her mother-in-law, Queen Margaret, who lived with her third husband and their children at Methven, not far from Perth. The marriage was in straits, for Margaret Tudor had quarrelled with Lord Methven in the way she had quarrelled earlier with Angus, and what is more wanted to divorce the former to remarry the latter. Needless to say the King did not take all this seriously – he would never in any case have permitted Angus to return to Scots soil – and so the bickering went on, making everyone unhappy. I think in fact that the old Queen had been an unhappy woman since the time of Flodden, because James IV had been good to her and had put up with her ways, and had even desisted from his mistresses during the time of his marriage. At any rate we all of us, Joanna and Marie and two Scots ladies whom the Queen had appointed, Lady Craigie and Lady Drummond, rode eastward through the hills, and finally came upon the plain stone castle, with servitors hurrying about the yard and slops poured steaming on the midden, and grooms springing to attention when it was seen there were horses to take. Her Grace had sent no word of her coming to Methven, as she thought it best to meet her mother-in-law without formality. The situation could be difficult; King James approved of young Methven, and relied on him to keep his turbulent mother in order; he had conferred the title on him that Henry VIII, as Margaret's brother, who approved the Angus marriage, referred to as 'Muffin' and lost no chance of ridiculing the young man, who it was rumoured in any case had a wife and children elsewhere. He was not present on the day we visited the old Queen, as she and he were barely on speaking terms. However that might be, the Queen herself went up; and we ourselves were bidden to wait below in the hall, having dismounted and refreshed ourselves. Whatever was said beween the old Queen and the young, we met Margaret Tudor later, and she had enough to say.

She was a stout pock-marked woman, with a cyst on one eyelid. It was hard to think of her as the English Rose who, a generation since, had filled the land with joy when she rode as a bride through Edinburgh on James IV's saddle-bow, with her golden hair hanging loose, fourteen years old, and the town's streets running with wine. Now, it was different.

'The King my son owes me a debt, and Scotland also,' the petulant voice made clear. 'When there were riots in Edinburgh when he was a child – why should I not marry again if I chose, and I the King of England's daughter? – I took him in my right hand, able to walk he was by then, and on my left arm my sweet babe Ross, born after the King died; that child pleased me well, and he died at scarce two years old – and I walked to the gates of Edinburgh Castle, and the folk were pressed against them. I called out, "Ring down the portcullis" and it was done, and the crowd went home. I never lacked courage, and now no one heeds me.'

She went on in this way for a time, and Madame Marie echoed her agreeably, being anxious to make a friend and not an enemy of her; but it was known, even by the King, that Margaret sent information into England, for which in his lifetime she had been paid something not very large by Cardinal Wolsey; by now, I do not know what she did. I did not take to her whining ways, and was glad when the visit was finished; before we left, a small boy and girl were brought in, the children of Queen Margaret and the absent Muffin. There was also a daughter by Angus, the Lady Margaret Douglas, who was kept close at Henry VIII's court in London. I understand that her mother had not seen her since she was an infant.

My own pleasure in the journey was less that of seeing the old

Queen than of my talk with Lady Drummond. She was a jolly
soul, not young, with a swelled stomach which showed beneath
her kirtle, but did not appear to trouble her. She also had
memories of Queen Margaret as the English Rose, and agreed
that it was a pity she had become as she was.

'You will know,' she said as she rode home next to me, 'that
King James IV would have married my husband's kinswoman,
whom he loved. They say Margaret Drummond was poisoned,
with her sisters. It may have been the English, but it may have
been the Scots lords in council, who did not want a third
Drummond Queen. The first, who married King Davie, took
herself before the Pope with a pillow stuffed down herself, to
pretend she was pregnant when she was not.' My lady shook
with laughter. 'Then the second, Queen Annabella, was very
beautiful; and a third would have been too much for them,
doubtless. At any rate, King James IV married a Tudor; and so
we have our King James V.' The last phrase was made out of
belated prudence, for Joanna and Marie were nearby. I
reflected that my Scots was progressing; I had understood
almost all that Lady Drummond said, and would remember it.

I had the chance to see history in the making at Edinburgh that
February, a time of year when the capital is very cold. That day,
in a window-embrasure, the King stood with the King of
England's envoy, Sir Ralph Sadler, much coming and going with
written papers shuffled between them. Nearby stood Cardinal
Beaton, the centre of a group; and whether he or the
Englishman had the sharper glance I do not know, but each was
keeping an eye on the other. Further off, old Queen Margaret
Tudor was talking with some noblewomen; and I kept close to
my own Queen, who had already spoken with the English envoy
and assured him of all our close feelings for Henry VIII. I
watched; and suddenly saw Sir Ralph Sadler whip a spare paper
out of his doublet, and show it to the King. It concerned the
supposed vices of churchmen. James looked at it, laughed,
shook his head, and the audience was over. Later I learned that
King Henry was trying to persuade the King of Scots to follow
his own example, abandon the Pope, rifle the monasteries, and
grow rich. King James would have none of it, nor did he heed
his uncle's advice to stop the peasant-like habit of breeding
sheep on his moors. There has been more money made in

Scoland over wool than there ever was from gold. Wool we certainly needed in that cold February, when such high matters were set under way: and at other times as well.

The King leaped down from his French saddle, wearing his black velvet coat made likewise in the fashion of France. Such fashions were to be seen in Scotland everywhere, in the ladies' hats, in the long trains attached to dresses, copying the Queen; citizens' wives were made mock of for wearing them, for they trailed in the mire of the streets. King James liked the splendour in what he wore, and his lords copied him; today his familiar, Oliver Sinclair, wore a black coat also. I had never liked Sinclair, without knowing why; he was an official of the household, older than the King, with a bluff manner many people would think of as reliable and honest. I did not, and what the Queen thought I did not know, for she kept her own counsel. She, at any rate, was not riding the streets, nor wearing black velvet; she had ordered a loose gold-and-purple gown for late pregnancy, and kept her chamber. Only I knew – she had said little of it to anyone – how great a relief this coming birth was; over a year had passed since the marriage, with still no sign of a child. Madame Marie had occupied herself with building and gardening, sending for fruit-tree cuttings to graft on native stock, hopefully in this cold climate; and talked of mining again on Crawford Moor to extract more of the gold King James had brought to his wedding with Madame Madeleine. But none of that would satisfy the Scottish people, or the King, unless there was an heir; and the heir was long in coming. I myself believe that unwillingness caused the delay; there had been no love in the marriage. With Longueville, Madame Marie had conceived at once, and again shortly after the first birth. However, a pilgrimage to the Isle of May had set matters on foot here, and it only remained to pray for a prince.

I was seated with my sewing – I have few accomplishments, but I can smock neatly, and this was to be a little coat for the baby, made of linen as he would be born in the spring – near the window, for light, and did not look up when a shadow fell on me. 'Why, little nun, raise your eyes,' said a voice. I not only raised them, I sprang to my feet, and made my curtsey. It was the King. His narrow hazel glance regarded me, then my sewing; he evinced some interest in that, and handled it. His fingers were

not as long as Madame Marie's, but shapely enough. He handed
the little garment back to me.

'It is a pity you have not a child of your own for whom to make
kickshaws,' he said. 'Why do you sit forever solitary, never
dancing, never laughing with the rest?'

'Sir, it is not my nature.' This was not the entire truth; once I
had been eager enough to dance and laugh, but Duchesse
Antoinette's dire threat as to what would happen to me if I
raised my eyes had long since bitten into me, and although she
could not now see me or punish me herself, I could not but
believe that if I transgressed in any particular, vengeance would
somehow follow. I heard the King laugh. His fingers pinched
my cheek.

'Permit me to change your nature,' he said. 'A pretty creature
like you should not be a nun, as I said, with eyes on the ground.
Do you know that your eyes are the colour of green water, when
you raise them? Do so, and look at me.'

His hand had left my cheek and travelled down my arm, and
squeezed the upper part of it. I drew back, angering him. 'Do
you deny your King?' he said, and I remembered that his blood
was part Tudor; in many ways, he resembled his royal uncle of
England, whom to deny was death. I flung back my head and
answered proudly.

'No, but I deny my Queen's husband,' I told him, and he
turned away. I knew that he did not forgive anyone who crossed
him, and that I had lost his favour. As long as I kept that of the
Queen, this did not greatly trouble me. In any case, His Grace
was shortly to set out for the Isles; and perhaps when he came
back there would be good news of a prince to take his mind from
lesser matters such as myself. The Queen's coronation had
already taken place when she was six months pregnant, and
everyone came from near and far to Holyrood, the commons
sitting outside on wood scaffolding specially erected, the rest of
us within, having a clear sight of Their Graces in purple and
white, their gleaming crowns fashioned of gold from Crawford
Moor, the Queen's sceptre of silver, and on her belt a great gem.
The King had twenty-four jewels in his crown, garnets and an
emerald, and a turquoise on his finger. Everything gleamed; the
chapel furnishings which had been brought from Stirling, the
reliquaries, the great ring Cardinal Beaton wore which had been
blessed and sent from Rome. My friend Lady Drummond,

gossiping beside me, hardly troubled to lower her voice at sight of the lean impressive figure in its flowing scarlet robes.

'The Pope told him not to trouble himself to come to get his honours, like other folk, so they were sent to him,' she murmured. 'The best of all worlds, Master Davy Beaton has; an Ogilvy for his fancy woman, and eight children they've made between them, all living together at St Andrews and Arbroath.'

Someone looked round and hushed her, and the Cardinal began to sing Mass; he had a voice which was not notable, but true enough. I thought that he must be a clever man to have got himself where he had, in the counsels of France and Scotland, though they said the old ogre in London did not trust him, which weighed nothing against the Cardinal.

The King and Queen came down the aisle at last; the voices of the choristers soared. Madame Marie looked at me, and gave me a little smile, as much as to say, 'Behold me, after all; I was not wrong to come.'

That had all happened three months before, and now Lady Drummond was dead.

We had been walking together to the Pends, for the birth was to take place at St Andrews. My lady's breath laboured a little as she walked, but I took no heed, as she was talking on as usual. Stout, ageing Queen Margaret Tudor was to be the baby's godmother, and was in town, and Lady Drummond pursued her favourite topic without fear of being quietened in the open air.

'She is here bold enough, but were it I, I'd think shame of myself to show my face. Three husbands, and the last one young enough to be her son, and her saying – this was a while back, grant you – that the second marriage was not valid, for King James IV was not dead at Flodden at all, but gone on a pilgrimage for his sins. Well, I know a tale worth two or three of that. The King fell fighting a lance's length from Surrey, the English commander, and they took his body to England, and there it still lies unburied. King Henry fancied himself then as a good son of the Church, whatever has happened since; and King James was excommunicate for aiding the King of France. The body lies in an attic at Sheen, and there it will lie till somebody has mercy on his soul; *she* cares nothing, except for her own lusts, good as he was to her. I think I will sit down.'

She lifted a corner of her skirt to wipe a tear from her eye, and sat on a stone wall, the sill of a church; and I admitted then that I did not like her colour; it was as grey as the wall. 'My lady, are you well?' I asked anxiously, but she gave no answer, only a kind of whistling groan, and then a quantity of fluid gushed out of her, below her skirts, flooding the ground. A few people came and stared, and I said to them, 'Go to the palace and say that Lady Drummond is ill, and get a litter,' and a child went, and I took the poor soul in my arms and said, 'Be of cheer, now; you will soon be in your bed.'

'I will soon be in a narrow box, my dear.' Her eyes were closed, and she was smiling a little: I saw that the great swelling had subsided.

They fetched a litter soon, and a priest came from the church: but before we reached the palace she was dead. It was as though she had confided her last secret to me before she went. Her husband came to the funeral from his estates, but shortly married a young bride.

I missed Lady Drummond greatly. The two French ladies-in-waiting, whom I had never greatly liked in any case, had both by now been wedded to Scots lords. I myself, still keeping my eyes down, was not considered as a bride by anybody. My chief companion thereafter was another old lady, this time of a great age; the Dowager Lady Maxwell, herself a Stewart of Garlies, born in Galloway and a distant relation to the King. She had borne six children and had seen much history pass. She was not so prodigal in relaying it as Lady Drummond had been, but she would describe the odd terse thing like, for instance, the eelskin leather straps and girths the Galloway men used when they rode into battle. Her Maxwell marriage gave her an acquaintance all across the Border, but she chose to stay a good deal at Court. She helped the Queen meantime at the latter's embroidery of white and gold; Madame was always fond of working with threads, and used to make up her own designs of flowers and leaves. The old lady's eyes were too dim now, and her fingers too stiff, to contrive the stitches, but she would hold and wind the gleaming hanks with me, while the Queen sewed and we all listened to the sallies of Senat the woman fool, who had come from France. There was a dwarf named Jane also. Their clowning passed the time.

The old lady was present, as I was myself, with a great number of

others, at the lying-in, which being towards the end of May
made the chamber very warm with the close press of bodies.
Two great beds had been made ready for Her Grace to labour,
one of yellow damask and the other of white, with cool taffeta
sheets; nevertheless it was often needed as time passed, to wipe
her face with cloths wrung out in rosewater. She lay biting her
lips, not anxious for so large an assembly, half of whom she did
not know, to hear her cry out. How different it was from
Châteaudun, where she had twice given birth in privacy! The
first time, Duc Louis had however stayed near; now, the King
was gone to the Isles. His nature was such that to have him about
her at such a time would have agitated her, as well as him; it was
a good notion to take ship, with as many lords as he preferred,
and to sail to those remote places. Old Lady Maxwell had told
me certain things about the former Lords of the Isles, and how
the last of them was still kept in prison, having been there all his
life except for one occasion, when he had broken out and raised
fire and sword through the Highlands to obtain his birthright.
That was long ago, before this King's lifetime; and his father,
James IV, had gone to the Isles shortly thereafter, and made the
wild folk love him. This King would not do that, I thought; but
maybe they would take heed to the sight of him, handsome as he
was, with his red hair. At any rate, he had gone; or at least we
thought so. The Queen was troubled by news of storms, and
once feared he was lost.

Suddenly she gave a cry, and called for me. 'Claudine, hold
my hands; it is coming.' I hastened forward and grasped her
beautiful long-fingered hands, and she pulled hard against me
till at last the child was born. It was a handsome little prince, an
heir for Scotland. I took no heed of etiquette, but leaned over
and kissed the Queen's cheek, whispering the news in her ear, to
the accompaniment of sour looks from those of high degree,
who no doubt thought the task should have fallen to them.

They lifted the Prince of Scotland away and wiped him clean,
and laid him in his carved cradle, while the Queen's women saw
to her. I wondered how soon the news would reach the late
Madame Madeleine's ladies, who had left the Scots court at the
time of the second marriage, but lingered still in England. Poor
Madeleine would have borne the King a child of her own, had
she lived.

King James himself was accosted as they weighed anchor at

Dumbarton, and told that he had a handsome son. The Isles were forgotten, and he came hastening home; he hung over the baby, and made much of his wife. It was so seldom that one saw him happy that it was like looking at a different being; his hazel eyes glowed, his mouth smiled above the pointed beard, his pale long-featured face was flushed with pleasure. The baby slept, and thrived with his wet-nurse; when she could, the Queen would often go to look at him, for as soon as might be he would be taken away from her, to live in his own establishment here at St Andrews, while she followed the King on the prescribed rounds of Court residence. Meantime, the child almost took the place of little François for her, except that his name would of course be James.

The torches flared orange against the summer night, illuminating the faces of the crowded watchers, some gentle, some humble, for all could not get into the Cathedral. Everyone had seen, by torchlight, nonetheless, the Prince of Scotland borne in to his christening in the arms of the stout old Tudor Queen, the King's mother, his godmother; and, behind her, the heir he had displaced by his coming, the Earl of Arran, his godfather, with a twitch to his face and an air of uncertainty about him. Then there was the King himself, in his jewel-coloured clothes, and the Cardinal, in scarlet and lace. It was at that point that I became aware of two women talking nearby, who seemed to know everything. They were fieldworkers, who wore the barrel-shaped coif such folk do, and their skirts turned back to show the petticoat and save the stuff; but they knew all of Scotland's history from the Bruce down, and were relating it while the choir sang inside the building. They had remembered, when the old Queen passed by, how once a pavilion of leafy branches had been made in the woods for her and her son, to their honour, and all manner of rich foods brought into it. 'She'll be pleased to be bairnswoman,' said one. 'It'll be the Queen's Grace that will ha'e made muckle o' her in such a way.'

'She wasna heeded otherwise,' reflected the second woman. The first began to recite the woes of the Stewart Kings, now happily ended.

'Twa dee'd o' broken hearts, and the heir o' the last starved to deith in a tower. He was one for the women, they say, that Duke o' Rothesay, and young and handsome with it.'

'This bairn will be Duke forbye.'

'Ay, 'tis the heir's title. Then there was,' the gossip went on, 'the first King Jamie, his brither, stabbit in a drain after long enough in English prisons; and the second, the only son that lived, was blawn to pieces at war wi' a cannon; and the third fell in battle agin his ain son.'

'I mind King James IV,' said the listener. 'He didna die in his bed.'

'Na, Flodden was nae man's bed. And this yin lost his queen, and her wean wi' her, and that was muckle dule. But now all's merry. The sixth James, this'll be. They say he's a fine strong bairn.'

'The Queen's a good strong woman. She'll ha'e ithers.'

I moved away as best I could in the crowd, as I had no wish to listen to comments about Madame Marie: but I was in time to hear the first speaker say, placidly,

'Yon's Lady Marion, the Cardinal's liking, with her bairns.'

The light flared on a woman's handsome resolute face, in a hood of no particular fashion; she was surrounded by a clutch of children of different ages. I perceived a likeness, in their dark hair and eyes, to the Cardinal, having had the matter pointed out to me: otherwise I might not have done so.

The singing soared in the Cathedral, the christening was over; and presently the torches melted into the night. When it was dark, bonfires blazed out on every hill, from the wild northern glens to the distant Borders, telling the English nation, and their King, that our own had got an heir.

I had often had cause to remark the King's strange nature, although its vengeful quality had not yet touched me. At this time, when he should have continued happy after the birth of his son, he did a thing within three months which outwardly resembled his vengeance against the Douglases, exiling them and burning their sister Lady Glamis to death, not for witchcraft, as many mistakenly thought, but for attempted poisoning. She was guilty of neither. I understand she died very bravely. I had all this from my old Lady Maxwell, the same who had told me about the Galloway eelskins. Now, nobody could understand the sudden arrest of Sir James Hamilton of Finnart, who had appeared to be the King's close friend. Lady Maxwell knew, however, and told me; the reason went back many years.

Hamilton of Finnart was a bastard son of Arran, and had done well for himself in acquiring land. He was always richly dressed, and his wife, who had been a Livingstone, likewise. I did not know them at all well, for they were far above me, strutting about Court, he in his capacity as Master of Works of Linlithgow and other palaces, as well as Principal Steward to the King. He had an abrupt manner, something like that of Oliver Sinclair, and appeared to be as close a favourite. Then we heard that he had been made prisoner, tried, and executed the same day, in the same manner as Lady Glamis had been.

There was a buzz of talk at Court, and I heard some of it. Some said that when the King first set out for France to seek a bride, he fell asleep on the boat, and Hamilton of Finnart turned the rudder and brought him back to Scotland against his will. Others said the Church authorities had laid hold of Hamilton and made him agree to confiscate reformers' property. Still others said he was hand in glove with the Douglases, plotting to murder the King and the Prince, and that the King had discovered it.

'It is none of these,' said old Lady Maxwell. 'When the king was a boy in the hands of the Douglases, the Earl of Lennox, whom he loved well, tried to rescue him from them, not far from Linlithgow that would be. The Earl of Angus and his brother held the King's rein, and said they would cut him in pieces rather than let him go free. He had to watch while Lennox was slain by Hamilton of Finnart. They say Hamilton's own father, Arran, came and wept over the Earl's body, for Lennox was much loved. His young sons escaped to France, and are there yet.'

'So the King has harboured his vengeance all these years,' I said, 'and made a friend of Finnart, or pretended to do so. Now the man is dead.'

'Do not speak so loudly,' she said to me, as others had said to Lady Drummond.

That was not all. The King took Finnart's possessions, including his chapel furnishings, his crucifix, his holy water stoup, his candlesticks, his silver bell, his pyx, had the baby Prince's arms engraved on them, and made them over to the child in gift. Dead men's shoes bring no fortune, and I thought the King was risking a great deal when he acted in such a way; but of course I said nothing to the Queen.

She herself continued very kind to me, and even took me with her in her great new litter of black, with the thistles of Scotland and the lilies of France worked on the frames in gold. Soon, however, she was riding again, and told me that she and the King would shortly visit Glamis together; it was the first time he had taken her there.

'They say it is very beautiful,' she told me. 'All I know is that the King loves to visit it there often, and once brought back twelve great silver flagons to melt down for the mint.' She turned her head against the cushions, and smiled at me. 'You will come, Claudine?'

I flushed with pleasure; there were so many others, of more importance, whom she could have asked to accompany her and her husband rather than myself. I packed my gear – I had no maid, and did not need one – and was ready to ride behind the King and Queen with all their train, on the appointed day in autumn.

Scotland is a country of so many contrasts that it bewilders one a little; I have still not seen it all. After the jagged steeps of Stirling and the Abbey Craig, and Edinburgh Castle, the flat plain of Forfar reminded me of France. The trees were already changing colour, and ahead of us I saw a great new forest rise: and against it, as a background in a tapestry, the figures of the King and Queen, riding superbly in their rich bright clothes. Mary of Lorraine is so often thought of as still and unmoving that one does not often remember her as a splendid horsewoman, Duc Claud's daughter, descendant of the mighty Dunois, the warrior of France. Her red riding-cloak flung behind her in the autumn wind, with the speed of her going; we all raced to keep up with her and the King, who had a tugging feather in his hat pinned by a jewel. It was a moment of happiness; and suddenly we came upon Glamis Castle.

Her Grace had spoken of its beauty. It was so beautiful it took my breath away. Its clustered turrets reminded me of Joinville, and its great retaining wall. I saw the Queen rein in and look, and say something to her husband. 'Yes,' he replied, 'it is a fair castle.'

His profile was towards me, and the expression on his face was one I can only describe as smug; it reminded me that this was the man who had taken dead Hamilton of Finnart's chapel furnishings and given them to his baby son. Twelve great silver flagons, too, had come from here. What else was there to know about Glamis? The name fretted at me; I had heard it already.

Now was not the moment to ask, but I would find out, in my own way, when I could do so.

I did so soon. We had been allotted our chambers, and I was to share mine with Lady Grant of Freuchie, an elderly widow who attended on the Queen; the latter tried nowadays, especially since the marriage of Joanna and Marie, to replace French attendants with Scots. I hoped that she would not replace myself. I did not make talk with Lady Grant meantime, but wandered off in my own company upstairs, into the turret rooms and along the half-staircases. It was only just beginning to grow dusk; late sun pierced through the further windows. By its light, I saw a figure, that of a young girl. Her hair was brown and her dress plain; she might have been a servant, or else might not. At the risk of being officious, I went up to her and said, 'Are you looking for anyone?' It was, after all, my duty, with the Queen in the house, to see that everyone was accounted for.

Her eyes looked up at me, and I have never seen such an expression in any that belonged to someone young. They were like an old woman's, full of resigned despair. They were hazel in colour. 'No,' she said in a flat voice. 'Are you?'

'I have come with the Queen's Grace. My name is Claudine de Vouvray.' I had decided that she was not a servant, though how I knew was not certain. She had the air of a ghost.

'My name is Margaret Lyon. My brother is Lord Glamis. He is held prisoner in Edinburgh Castle, with my second brother. My sister's husband they executed. My mother they burned alive.'

'Child –' The horror of it and the flat way she recited it, made my flesh creep. 'Who did this thing? When did it happen?'

'The King. It happened three years ago. That is why I will not go down and meet him. He said my mother was a poisoner. She was not. She was good and beautiful and never harmed anyone. It was because she was a Douglas born that the King took his revenge. The jury said she was innocent, but he said she must burn. He likes to come here, by himself, to gloat over the castle, which he has taken for his own. He does not know I am here; he has forgotten me. My mother bade me hide at the time, and so I was not arrested.'

'I will speak to the Queen about your brother,' I said. 'They must not be left in prison. Her Grace is kind, not vengeful. Will you not meet her?'

'I will meet none of them. I will stay here alone till I am an old, old woman. No one dare marry me, because of the King's anger. He does not forget.'

She turned away, and I went downstairs thoughtfully. I was certain the Queen would do something to release the Glamis brothers – they could only be boys – and that evening, when I went to her, I was ready to tell her all I had found out, and about Margaret Lyon. But Her Grace turned a glowing face to me.

'You are to be the first to know, my Claudine, except my husband,' she said. 'I am with child again: so soon! Yet it is true; I must be growing like my mother.'

I kissed her hands, nor did I say what was the truth, that she would never resemble Duchesse Antoinette. But it was not possible, in face of her news, to trouble her with the Glamis matter at present. I would do so when I could; like the King, I would not forget.

I did not. Our stay at Glamis was short, but I felt that something should be said concerning the matter before we rode on to Dundee. I thought it over, then, after all, as she seemed a discreet person, discussed it with Margaret Grant one night when we were in our shared bed, the curtains safely drawn against servants and eavesdroppers. She had of course heard of the Glamis burning: there had been much sympathy at the time. 'Lady Glamis died bravely,' she said. 'Her young second husband – they were not long married – was put in ward in the Castle likewise, and the day after the burning tried to escape, and was killed falling from the Rock, as the rope was too short. It was a sad business. I think that, as you cannot speak to Her Grace at present, you should speak to the King. It may be that his first anger has abated, and he has no doubt forgotten the existence of the two boys, and will free them readily enough.'

I pondered it, saying little, as she did not know the King's attitude to me or the fact that I myself had already angered him. Perhaps, however, he would have forgotten that also. What I did not know was that, at this time, King James was greatly troubled with nightmares, taking the form of Hamilton of Finnart, with a sword in his hand, ready to cut off both the King's arms, and saying he would return on a third night, and cut off his head. It was, in short, the worst possible time I could have chosen to trouble him; but I was not to know.

Next day I came upon him deliberately, for I had caught sight of him going into the forest beyond the wall. I did not follow him at once, thinking that after all he might have wanted to relieve himself. I walked about, and presently heard his voice hail me, without anger in it, though we had not spoken since the earlier episode when I had refused him his pleasure. Now, with his son thriving and another on the way, he would surely be quit of that.

'Why, it is the nun: good-day, madam.'

I made my curtsey, and deliberately fastened my eyes on his face. He looked, it is true, like a man who has had no sleep; he was paler than usual, and there were shadows under his eyes. He had brought none of his gentlemen with him, and I hoped that I had not made him angry by interrupting his solitude. But he took my arm, and I did not draw away.

'And what may I do for you?' he said courteously; he could be very charming. I smiled, and reminded him in few words of the young boys held in prison in Edinburgh. 'Sir, would this happy time not be a pretext for setting them free?' I said, and saw his thin eyebrows fly up under the red hair.

'You are a little busybody,' he said. 'Where heard you this?'

I was prepared for that, and merely said that I had heard it among the women's gossip when we were riding to Glamis; it was near enough the truth. I would on no account mention Margaret Lyon.

The King suddenly turned and, taking my chin in his free hand, planted a kiss on my lips. 'You please me,' he said. 'Come; let us go among the trees, where none will see us. Give me what I ask, and I'll release the Glamis brood.' The narrow hazel eyes regarded me. I wrenched away.

'Give them their freedom,' I said clearly. 'I'll not be your whore. Your Queen is to bear you another child; does not that suffice you? It is not a time for unfaithfulness.'

'By God, you deserve that a man should lift up your skirts and take you whether you will or no. Get your nun's face out of my sight; if you speak so again I'll have you whipped.'

'But not burned on the Castle Hill of Edinburgh; was that why Lady Glamis suffered death?'

I do not know what made me dare say it, and hearing the hiss of his breath behind me I picked up my skirts and ran; out of the forest, away from the King, back to my own kind, having accomplished nothing; not having saved the imprisoned boys, and as for myself, no doubt having built up a grudge that would fester in the heart of James V of Scotland, in the same way as that implanted there by Hamilton of Finnart long ago.

Later that day, we rode to Dundee.

I was at first anxious on my own account, more I must say than on that of the Lyon family whom, after all, I did not know; the fate of the girl left alone into old age in the upper part of Glamis Castle seemed as pitiful to me as her brothers', who lay in prison. However nothing occurred to alter my days in any such particular; I stayed near the Queen, kept my silence, and moved with her thankfully to Falkland at last, where she had decided to await the coming child while the King moved elsewhere. There was no ill-will about it; the pair at this time dealt excellently together; but I could not help thinking to myself that were it Longueville whose child were expected, she would not have been absent from his side for a moment, or he from hers. But that had been in another life.

Falkland is a pretty little hunting-place built in the woods, a short ride from St Andrews. I knew the Queen had chosen it deliberately for that reason; King James preferred his son to have his own separate household, not coddled by his mother. The Prince had chaplains and nurses; that would do. The King himself loved to visit him, and used to take him gifts specially made; a bear's tooth in gold for when the child was teething; a gold whistle which he was too young to blow; a silver spoon while he was yet sucking at his wet-nurse. There had been an upset with him, for the first nurse's milk had run dry and it had been necessary to find a second, and Prince James – the Duke of Rothesay, one must learn to call him – had been ill, but not for long. Duchesse Antoinette, who ought to have known, had written that that often happened. Now the child was growing fast enough to need new coats and shirts, made by the King's tailor. In short, the Queen had chosen Falkland because it was near St Andrews, and she might visit her son when she would. She travelled to Stirling for Christmas with the King, but did not ask me to accompany her, and was soon back with us again.

By February, however, she had given up travelling in the litter, let alone riding or walking. I myself used to relish the company instead of old Lady Maxwell, who was never deterred by the weather; on this day she had wrapped herself up in ancient moleskin furs, and brought a stick against the slippery frozen paths. With her was her grandson's bride – not yet, she assured me, his wife – who slid up and down like a child much younger than her age, which was about fourteen; her eyes started out of her head like a hare's, and she would give little shrieks of laughter when she came on a good slide. It occurred to me that she was not quite right in the head. However Lady Maxwell was talking about her own home country of Galloway, concerning which she had always something of interest to say; and of how it was never as cold there as here.

'There are flowers growing at Clary and Logan that are only seen in England, in the south parts at that,' she said, 'and some even from France. The Bishop has a walled garden at Carse of Clary, with all manner of flowers and herbs in it. That was on the pilgrimage road, in the days when they would go back and forth past the great willows on the river, at the ford.'

'Where was the shrine?' I asked, out of politeness. She looked round at me and then back at her granddaughter-in-law.

'Beatrix, do not go so fast, ye will end with a broken ankle, and then where are we?' she demanded of nobody. 'The shrine is St Ninian's at Whithorn. There is the cave where he landed, and the chapel he built. King James IV used to go down there often, but not this one.' She winked at me suddenly. 'It wasna, all folk ken, St Ninian alane that took the late King doun,' she said, 'but Janet Kennedy; she was a wild one.'

'But he loved Margaret Drummond.'

'Ay, but there's love and love. Beatrix, I'll take my stick to your backside if ye winna bide still. Ask Madame de Vouvray and she'll maybe teach ye French.'

I could not see young Beatrix concerning herself with French or anything else long enough to learn it, but smiled and said I would do what I might. Beatrix immediately nestled up to me and asked me the French for ice. When told, she went off into fits of laughter. Later I learned that the tocher, the bride-money, in her case and in that of her two sisters had been particularly large, because the King intended to take all of their father's goods, he being a Douglas, and an invalid. The third Earl of Morton had an issue in his leg, and was forever weak, so much so as to be excused military service. It would not have occurred to anyone then that by marrying one of his daughters, they were marrying a curse. The French disease, as everyone called it – it was Italian and Spanish as well – had been brought to Scotland by Albany's troops in middle-aged memories, and spread. All three of Morton's daughters carried its legacy of madness, two in themselves, the third in her heir. I did not know all of that when I looked at young Beatrix Maxwell that day, but I knew, for the old lady told me, that had the King been present in Falkland the girl would not have been suffered here. Her name was Douglas, like the rest: that was all that concerned him.

I taught her French, as best I could, a few words each day, until it was time for the Queen to take to her litter again for Stirling, where the King had decreed the coming birth in March. By then, the old lady and the young had gone their ways back to the warmer south places, where flowers grew that otherwise only grew in England.

This was Madame Marie's fourth child, and that it should again be a son was joyous. We heard the cannon thunder outside within the walls; we saw the King, too greatly filled with happiness to remember me, come in and bend over the cot; in it lay a baby with delicate features, like all the Stewarts; and this one was to be called Robert after the early Stewart Kings, and created Duke of Albany. The English, mistakenly, said that his name was Arthur; but that is an English name, though James IV used it once for a child who died, named after his Queen's brother.

The labour had been short. Presently the Queen was able to sit up in bed and take a caudle, but the March cold was still sharp in the room. 'Claudine, fetch me my rabbit-skin wrap,' she whispered, and I went and got it from where it hung; she would wear it always in the litter, and the fur was growing worn, but she loved it and it kept her warm: the outside was black velvet. She snuggled into the fur, and we listened to the people roaring with triumph outside; the King had gone to show himself to them. It was particularly happy that the birth should have taken place at this castle; Stirling was the place where as a boy James V had won free of the Douglases, having ridden across Scotland alone, a fugitive. It was his particular kingdom; the people here loved him, and he would make his way often in disguise down the Ballengeich Road as the Goodman, and folk must never show they knew it was the King.

So he had two sons now; and the Duke of Albany was christened three days later, in the Chapel Royal. It was less grand a christening than his brother's, as he was not the heir; but torches flared again, toasts were drunk, and there was the sound of piping, for Perthshire was not far off and the clansmen had come down to welcome the King's son, while the baby slept through it all, having been made a Christian.

Later that night Madame Marie herself could not sleep, and called for me to be with her. She said that she was troubled about the King.

'He was joyous today,' she said, 'but he still has his nightmares; that man –' she would not name Hamilton of Finnart – 'still comes to cut off his arms, and threatens to cut off his head. Otherwise he is low; I have often sent for herbs into France for him.'

'Maybe he will mend as he sees the boys grow,' was all I could say. The blue-grey eyes looked at me steadily.

'His uncle of England troubles him,' she said. 'He is a determined enemy now that King James will not forsake the Pope, and cleaves as well to Cardinal Beaton. King Henry hates Beaton, and will do him harm if he can. He knows that the Cardinal is committed to the French alliance, and will not see it broken.' She gave a little laugh. 'Why, I am here myself as a guerdon of that,' she said. I smiled.

'You have proved your worth, doubly by now. They say King Henry's only son is not healthy; he must envy you.'

Madame Marie shivered a little in her furs. 'His envy is dangerous,' she said. 'So many Scottish lords are in his pay that my husband dares trust nobody.'

'Except the Cardinal.'

She lifted her shoulders. 'Except the Cardinal, perhaps. He is not a man I like; but one must forget the man in the priest. Claudine,' and she stretched out her hand towards me, 'would you not be happy, as I am, with children of your own? Always you are solitary. It is unimportant now, perhaps, while you are young; but when you are old, that will be different.'

I cast my eyes down, in the way Duchesse Antoinette had bidden me. 'I do not need children, madame. I can watch over yours.'

Fear reached Stirling in the form of a messenger, on the seventh day of the rejoicings. He demanded to see the King.

'What is amiss?' said James. He was dressed in crimson, which he often favoured, and had Oliver Sinclair near him, and the latter's wife who had come for the christening from Tantallon, the Douglas stronghold in which there were now no Douglases left. James's thin eyebrows flew up, questioning the fellow who had come, splashed with mud from the March ways. The man fell on his knees.

'Sire, it is the young Prince. He is gravely ill, not like to live, even were ye to ride fast.'

The King's face blanched. He said nothing, except to give a curt order to be horsed; then he leaped as he was into the saddle, and was off to the east, not a man with him. Later we heard where he went; by the road he had taken on his first escape, by Stirlingshire into Fife, past Kinross and the place of Lochleven where he had had a mistress once, but did not think of her now; and at last to St Andrews, flinging the reins to a waiting groom who already knew the worst tidings, for he said nothing.

The King strode into his son's nursery, where he had so often come with joy; where beneath the crimson cut velvet covers there lay no longer the laughing child for whom he had made a whistle, for whom he had had a bear's tooth set in gold. There was only a small waxen figure there, like one on a tomb. It would never move again.

The father turned away; and as he did so another messenger came, giving no semblance to reality in this grief; it could not happen so. 'Sire, the young prince in Stirling was taken ill within the hour ye left; he is near the point of death; maybe if ye were to ride at speed ye would see him ere he goes.'

The King rode back; covering the dreaded miles with the swiftness of a born horseman; galloping into Stirling on the evening of the same day he had left it, making his way with a heavy heart to the second baby's nursery, newly fitted out only that week.

Prince Robert lived; but no more than that. He breathed for a little while, his father and mother watching over him sadly; then he died. There were now no princes in Scotland.

'Madame! Little Madame!'

I had not called her that since the days at Joinville, even the days at Bar; remembering that I was the older by almost a year, and for a time had almost had charge of the sunny-haired child who had never grudged me a share in her toys, a bite of her marchpane, for all she was the heiress of the Guises till her brothers came. Now, she was a child to me again; a child in sore trouble. Her women had all been sent away, and she was alone in the dark; lying supine, only the flicker of the dying fire outlining her long form, still clad in the rabbit-skin cloak. The gleam of her eyes came to me; she was awake.

I went to her and put my arms round her. It did not matter that she was the Queen of Scots, or queen of anything. I laid her head on my shoulder and knelt by her, saying nothing after the first.

'He is not with you?'

She knew I meant the King. She turned her head a little, and smiled weakly. 'I do not know where he is,' she said. 'There is nothing I can do for him. I have lost him both his sons, when all is said.'

'It was not your fault. Children die.'

'All my children have died now, except François; and I may not visit him. My mother sends me drawings of him; that is all.'

'There will be more children. This cruelty cannot happen again.'

'Life is cruel, Claudine. It has been cruel to you also. It was my turn, no doubt. I must write to my mother.'

I was certain Duchesse Antoinette would have some wisdom to send; but in the meantime I must comfort Madame Marie. I knelt on, and presently she dropped asleep; my arm grew cramped with the weight of her head, but I would not wake her.

The door opened, in the early hours of the morning, and the King stood there, his eyes red-rimmed. I raised my finger to my lips; no doubt others did not use familiarity of such a kind, but I did not care. He stared at me for instants, then turned away. When the Queen woke, I told her that he had come in. She smiled a little.

'He is like a child himself,' she said. 'It is impossible to help loving him. He has had a cruel blow. I fear it will not make his nightmares better; two arms cut off, meaning two sons dead.'

She began to shiver, and I asked her if she would like her women to come and wash her, and comb her hair. Presently they came, and I left her.

I caught cold at Queen Margaret's funeral that late autumn, and could not shake it off. It was a humid day and I rode in a press of black-clad people, beside me none other than Lord Maxwell, who knew me as a friend of his old mother. Nevertheless I deemed myself flattered that the Great Admiral of Scotland, Provost of Edinburgh, Extraordinary Lord of Session, and all the rest of it, deigned to talk with me when there were so many others ready to claim his attention. No doubt he found me restful after his demanding wife, who had had many husbands and was to have more. His beard was still grey and full, as it had been in France three years ago when he came across as the King's proxy to wed the Queen in Notre Dame.

We did not discuss the dead Queen Margaret. Her gross coffin was borne before us towards the Charterhouse of Perth, where the murdered James I and his beautiful English Queen lie buried. I reflected that there went the last we would ever see of the Rose, who could have asked anything she wanted of the Scottish people when she was left a widow after Flodden, with one child by the hand and expecting another. But Margaret Tudor had thrown away her honour and their respect, first with one foolish marriage, then with the next. As if I had spoken aloud, Lord Maxwell echoed me, cautiously as the King rode ahead alongside the young widower, with whom he had remained close friends.

'Now that his sister is dead, King Henry will invade Scotland.'

The dread sound of the words was like a passing-bell. 'You think he was only waiting for her death?' I exclaimed.

'For that, and other things. Lately he has been making much, they say, of his own right to rule north as well as south. Moreover, Angus now will have no scruples against leading such an army as may be called up in England. He is a widower, the Queen being dead, and it is like enough he will marry again to get himself a son, for Her Grace gave him none, only the young Lady Margaret Douglas.'

He looked about him cautiously, the black velvet of his mourning-gear hushing against its lining. 'He and his brother George have been pensioners of King Henry for long enough, since they escaped into England,' he muttered. 'They will needs do what he bids them, now. I doubt me there will soon be news.'

The news did not, however, come till late summer; but in general there was a feeling of unease, not yet due to the English, but to the King of Scots himself. He had grown distrustful, the more so since the death of his sons; he was still not certain that they had not been poisoned, and that by his own lords. He could rely on none of these, and they knew it; England would pay them more than he could. Also, fearing James' sudden vengeance, many went over to King Henry in secret, if not yet openly.

I myself knew little of it, for I was lying by then with a phthisis of the lungs made worse by a cold damp winter after the death of the old Queen; tended by servants and physicians, I felt at times as if I myself would die.

'You are a little better, Claudine. What you need now is sunshine and rest.'

I struggled up. The Queen was standing by my bed, and I did not think it respectful of me to lie still. The leeches they had clapped on my arms and legs still sucked at me.

'Madame, I have rested all these weeks. I have not thanked you for your Yule gift.' She had sent a little box of marchpane to me then, but had not come herself. I thought that she looked wan today, as much so as last year when she and the King had made a doleful visit together, in mourning, to Perth and Aberdeen.

'I would have come myself at Yule,' she said, 'but truth to tell I have been catching colds, and did not want either to give you mine, or to catch yours. Now listen to what I have to say.' She appeared to be her practical, managing self again, and I was glad to see it; but when I listened to what she had to say, was uncertain whether to be glad or sorry. Lady Grant had offered me a home for the summer, at her stepson's new castle of Freuchie, up in the north. 'You will be company for her on the ride, and will get well in the good air,' said Her Grace. 'They tell me there are fresh salmon in the river; I envy you.'

'Madame, I will be a stranger there; may I not stay? I am much better.' The thought of going away from her was more than I could bear, in my sick state; she was everything to me, family and friends. Lady Grant, kindly as her offer had no doubt been, was nothing.

'No, you must regain your strength; you have not looked at yourself lately. You are thin and pale, quite different from my Claudine that I remember. Go to Freuchie – *mon Dieu*, I cannot pronounce these names! – and drink their goat's milk and eat their salmon, and put on flesh. I will send for you at the summer's end.'

'You promise, madame?' I could envisage being left, forgotten, in a Highland glen, while the court moved elsewhere. She smiled. 'I promise,' she said. 'And now I must go.'

The tall figure moved away from my bedside, and I was left with the prospect, which should have been pleasant, of riding by Lady Grant and her escort to the north parts, on the banks of Spey.

It turned out to be pleasanter than I had foreseen, although I was taken aback at first to find that our sole escort consisted of two caterans who would lead our ponies barefoot. I had seen Highlanders occasionally in Perth, where their saffron-dyed shirts mingled brightly among the drab crowds; but it was a different matter to be alone with them, faced with a prospect of many miles in their close company. They were fierce in aspect, armed with short black knives and swords bestowed about their persons. The leader also carried a bag of silver gained through sales at the cattle market, for they had come down with a drove of beasts and were returning, with us, to take the laird his *airgead*.

'They will not cheat my son out of a penny,' remarked Margaret Grant, following my glance from where she sat astride her own pony, old as she was. 'He is Am Grantach, and they are entirely loyal. For the same reason you may be certain of arriving safely. A guest in the Highlands is sacred, and will not be betrayed.'

I moved a little in my own unfamiliar position in the straight saddle, which was the only one possible on these short-legged beasts; it reminded me of the way Duchesse Antoinette had travelled from Vendôme. I remarked that it was kind of Lady Grant to invite me, and she replied that the Queen had suggested it.

'I think that she herself needs a sojourn among us in the north,' the old lady added thoughtfully. 'She does not look well, and the King, of course, has long ago returned to his mistresses. Word of it even got abroad, they say, to Her Grace's parents, and her mother offered to send the Duc de Guise to Scotland to put matters right. But the Queen is proud, and wrote back to say that no such situation existed. Of course it exists; he was always so inclined, and the death of the boys has driven him back to where he was before his marriage.'

We were well out on the Ballengeich Road by then, so it was safe for her to speak above the clattering of the ponies' hooves; the caterans knew only enough Scots to bargain over cattle. I saw the *gille-sporain* bestow his silver carefully in the purse he wore of that name, and stride on. Perhaps stride is the wrong word; it was more of a smooth running motion, like that of a wolf. I did not comment on the behaviour of King James, which did not surprise me, but instead remarked, 'These men go swiftly barefoot.' They must have come down from the glens in such a fashion, I thought, with their cattle.

'Wait till you meet Alasdair Dorch,' she said. 'When he was a young man he walked to Carlisle with a boat on his back. Once there he cast it into the River Esk, and the folk threw coins into it. It was before my husband died, perhaps a dozen years ago, and I remember how he laughed. Alasdair Dorch brought the coins home and handed them to my husband, telling him to give them to me for pin-money.' She smiled reminiscently. Despite all her talk she was a reserved woman, with a good opinion of herself; I did not know whether I liked her or not. At any event, I must do my duty as a guest. I was beginning to find the gentle exercise, in the open day, do me good. The ponies did no more than trot, with our baggage behind the saddles and the caterans running alongside, and I was losing the weak, helpless feeling that had assailed me in my room in Stirling Castle, which had been small and damp. I raised my head and sniffed the fresh air, away from the town as it now was and bringing with it a waft of the hills, which we could see ahead of us. A mile or two on, we plunged into the ancient Caledonian forest, and here we had to go more carefully, for branches had grown in places low down across the only paths, which were those kept open by cattle-drovers. Evidently all the chieftains lived on the money they made from their cattle, and otherwise maintained themselves from their land. The Grant stronghold would have its salmon as the Queen had told me, and game from the hills.

I learned more from Lady Grant on the way. She had been married young, and, as she had already said, her husband had been dead now for a number of years. 'He died in the year the King escaped from the Douglases, for I remember he was beyond hearing of that, and it would have gladdened his heart,' she told me. She herself had married all her daughters well, except for one who was spendthrift. 'Christiania is my cross,' she remarked. 'I would not have brought her to Court for all the world; she would have run up debts at once for kirtles and jewellery. Then there is Ian Mór, who also is troublesome.'

She pursed her lips and fell silent, while the green shade of the trees engulfed us. 'Is he your only son?' I asked in sympathy. It was evidently the wrong thing to have said.

'He is not,' she said firmly. 'He is a natural son of my husband's; the only one, I may say. He is in a process of divorce at present which is a disgrace to all of us. My son James, *Seumas nan Creach* as they call him, James of the Forays, allows him houseroom. I would not do so, but I no longer have the right to speak. The castle itself is new; it was only built five years ago, and I myself am there on sufferance.'

I reflected that perhaps a guest of hers would not be too welcome either, but held my peace after what she had said about guests being sacred. Later I was to find that she had married her daughters into every clan in the Highlands, except that of the Campbells. I was intrigued by the title of James of the Forays; perhaps he would have a sword in his belt, like the drovers who escorted us, bending and twisting themselves in lithe fashion below the overhanging branches and guiding our ponies, and ourselves, to safety.

We slept in a bothy that night, with the clansmen lying wrapped in their plaids outside the door. It was empty, and I was to find that often one came across such a place, left for the convenience of travellers. A fresh bed of heather sprigs was spread for us to lie on, and it was more comfortable than many in which I have slept in palaces. When morning came I was hungry, but there would be nothing to eat till we reached Freuchie. I marvelled again at the endurance of Lady Grant, at her age, undertaking such a journey.

It was still daylight when we came to Freuchie, and I was amazed less by the castle – it was of ordinary dressed stone with lime cement still white between the blocks – than by the great river, with its rushing power and deep amber-brown pools. A woman was kneeling to wash by it, a plaid over her head; presently she stood up to trample the washing with her bare feet. I reflected that the water must still be cold at this time of year. She saw us come, and bobbed a curtsey to the laird's mother. I still thought of him as the laird, although it is a Lowland term; Am Grantach was on the other hand a chieftain, looked on as a king.

He was not in the hall when we entered, having first seen our ponies led away. I stared at the soot-blackened flare marks already on the new walls, from torches that would be lit at night. I was led up to my room, Lady Grant having handed me over to a young woman who proved to be the spendthrift Christiania; despite her grand name she was evidently not permitted to leave home. I reflected that her spending must be truly formidable.

She asked me, in pretty, lilting Scots, if I would care for my food to be sent up to me, or would come down. I replied that a drink of milk would be welcome, as I had eaten nothing that day, but that otherwise I would come down to the hall later on. I was anxious to set eyes on James of the Forays at his high board, and the members of his family. Water was brought for me to wash, and I made myself ready; my baggage contained only one other gown, and it was crushed, so I wore the one I was in, combed my hair and replaced my coif. Christiania had gone downstairs, and I was left alone in the room, which had heather laid on the floor instead of straw, making it warm. Otherwise, the air here was as cold and clear as the Spey itself; I went to the window, which was smaller than those in the south, and breathed it thankfully. The milk arrived and I drank it slowly; it was fresh and creamy, and abated my hunger.

By evening I made my way downstairs, and found the hall filled with the chief's family and his clansmen. The women sat separately from the men, their children with them. I glimpsed Am Grantach, seated by himself at the high table; he seemed a man of mild appearance, hardly deserving of such a name as James of the Forays. His costume was superb, consisting of a great plaid of a soft red colour, that I saw repeated on the heads of the women and the shoulders of the men; a shirt of fine smocked linen, that would not have disgraced the Court; a great round brooch, and the black knife, the *sgian dubh* that they all wore. He saw me come, and to my consternation rose up in all his splendour, past the clansmen who stood by the lit sconces flaring on the walls, and came to me where I stood in my shabby gown. His voice was gentle and he spoke Scots with the same lilt as his sister Christiania.

'You are welcome,' he said to me. He gestured to a woman

who must be his wife; she wore several silver rings, and a coif in the Lowland fashion. She came over, and I saw that she was a good deal younger than he; in fact she was a second wife, as I found out later, a Barclay from the south. Old Lady Grant remained in her own place; no doubt she was tired, but she never again addressed me if she could help it, and seemed to have withdrawn into a haughty state of her own.

'Christiania, this is Madame de Vouvray, who is to be our guest. Make her known to the other women.' Am Grantach smiled, bowed a little, and was gone back to his high table, where I noticed a priest dining with him in a worn plaid of seven colours. There was also a tall man by them who turned out to be Ian Mór, the bastard half-brother. They all bore a likeness to one another.

Christian Grant – her name must have led to confusion with that of her sister-in-law, except that they were quite different – bade me be seated on the common bench, and brought her children to greet me. They were all of them girls, except for one little son named Archibald; but Am Grantach had other sons of his first marriage. They greeted me in mannerly fashion and went back to their places. All of them wore the red plaid. I remarked on it to Christian Grant, who had placed me beside her; in the Highlands, I recalled, a guest is sacred.

'That is the clan tartan, which was not worn generally till the rule of the Lords of the Isles was ended,' she said. 'Before that it was seven colours for a priest as you see now, six for a king; and anyone else could wear what he chose. Now every clan has its own pattern. You will see two kinds here often; one for ourselves, one for the Gregarach, who are friends and allies, and more than that by blood. No Grant would ever see a MacGregor come to harm without aiding him or giving him shelter, and a MacGregor would help a Grant in trouble wherever that might be.'

'Why is that so?' I asked, knowing there was nothing of the kind in the Lowlands, or for that matter in France, although men might aid one another for the time.

She smiled, and spoke as if she were a born Highland woman herself. 'Well, now, long ago the three crowns on our shield were given us by three kings of the north. Also we are descended, both clans, one through the other, from the ancient Kings of Alba, *'S Rioghail mo dhream*. Do not ask me any more, but there is the friendship; if great trouble comes, there will be the aid.'

She continued to smile quietly, and picked at her salmon. Its flesh was delicious, fresher than any I had eaten in the south. It was followed by a venison pasty, also very good; and strong ale for the women, while the men drank whisky. 'You would not fancy a drop of that, to see you to your bed?' the wife of Am Grantach asked me, in sly fashion. I shook my head; I was already drowsy enough with the food, the heat of the torches, and the press of folk. The women and children began to get up and go, leaving the men still drinking to the sound of a small harp. I went to my bed to sleep dreamlessly, with the smell of fresh lime in my nostrils from the recently-built walls.

Part III

As the days passed I grew accustomed to the ways of the household at Freuchie, and helped with them as best I could. I was not entirely useless, for Duchesse Antoinette at Joinville, the Poor Clares, and Madame Sanserrato at Vouvray, had all of them taught me to bake and conserve and carry out other tasks. This was necessary, for one could not send out here to a shop or a booth for anything at all, though there was fresh food both from the moors and from the river. On the first morning I found Christian Grant herself with her face flushed over the ovens, her head wrapped in linen to preserve her hair from oatmeal flour. The maids were rolling out the dough and cutting it into small round cakes. I asked if I might be of use, but Christian shook her head.

'Go to see if the fish are rising in the river, if you care to, and bring word when you can,' she said. I knew I was being got rid of, as strangers are usually in the way, and did not hasten back; in any case I saw no fish, but was more than ever enchanted by the brown deep pools and rushing water, and lingered by them. There were no women washing today, as this was only done when there was neither baking nor brewing. I walked along a little way, and out of the trees sprang a lithe white creature, a little nanny-goat with fur bells on her neck. Her slitted pale-green eyes looked at me. I laid a hand on her neck and she did not back away; she was tame.

'Walk with me,' I said, and the goat did so; whether or not she was used to company I could not tell. I talked to her in a low voice in French. We were making our way along contentedly, when, again suddenly, I saw that we were being watched, had in fact been watched for some time, by an extraordinary man in a round bonnet, seated by the water. He appeared to be doing nothing at all; he was not fishing. I had never seen anyone like him; he was about forty years old, tall, no doubt immensely so when he got to his feet; very dark of skin, almost like a blackamoor, with no beard but with two long flowing black moustaches above his upper lip, and long hair. His eyes were small, black, and suspicious. He was clad as Am Grantach had been, but not in the same tartan, although the one he wore was like it, but with a white stripe, very narrow, through the plaid. Nor did he wear a round silver brooch. I could tell at once that he was not a chieftain, or anybody of great importance except, maybe, in his own estimation. However he rose to his feet in a courteous enough way. I had noticed that all Highlanders show courtesy.

'You will be the new lady, the guest from the south.'

I said that I was so, and as he did not vouchsafe his own name there seemed to be nothing more to say. I passed on with the little nanny-goat, who still followed me. As we went by the man's voice, which was deep and musical, with the inflections of the Gaelic although he spoke Scots well enough, followed me also.

'She will have taken a fancy to you. She is a maiden milker.'

I thanked him, and feeling that it was time I put in an appearance again at the castle, retraced my steps. He was still standing there, and I could feel the small dark eyes burning into my back as we returned. I stroked the goat's neck again, talked to her, and forgot him. I had decided that I must try to think of a name for her, and I remembered, for no reason at all, that Lady Drummond, before she died, had told me of two beautiful Queens of Scotland of her name so that my lords in council did not want a third. I remembered that the name of one had been Annabella.

'Annabella,' I said to the little goat. 'Annabella.' She had bells, after all.

She bleated, and when we came to where her herd were tethered returned to them. I wondered why she was not tethered also, but was glad of it; she had provided company on the walk. Perhaps she would come to me again.

That afternoon, I found Christiania spinning, and asked her why the white goat was free. 'They will be hoping she will mate,' she said. 'She is a law unto herself, that one.'

I asked, again, if I could help her. The shorn fleece lay in a pile on the floor, and the wheel was idle as Christiania was carding. 'I will show you how to card, if you like,' she said, 'and then I can get on with the spinning.'

She showed me; there was nobody else about, and I learnt that the priest who had been at the high board on the previous evening acted as tutor to the children, which explained the silence. The men were out on the hill. I set to with the carders and was soon fairly proficient. 'That is a help,' said Christiania. 'Another time I will show you how to spin; it is pleasant, and not such hard work.'

However I was doomed never to learn to spin; a voice sounded at the foot of the stairs and old Lady Grant stood there, having come down silently. 'Christiania, you have been given that task of spinning to keep you from being idle,' she said. 'You should not accept help from our guest. Put down the carders, Madame de Vouvray, and leave her to do as she was bid.'

I was sorry for Christiania, who had flushed a little, but said nothing. After all she was no longer a young girl, to be berated. When I returned to town, I thought, I would send her a small gift, perhaps a brooch. To ease the situation I put down the carders and then said aloud. 'I saw an extraordinary man on my walk today,' and described the personage in the round bonnet. Mother and daughter began to laugh, and the difficult moment was over.

'That was none other than Alasdair Dorch Gregarach, who carried the boat to Carlisle,' said the old lady. 'It is lucky that you should have set eyes on him so soon. He is far off in the hills as a rule, after the deer, or visiting his own folk, or going south with the cattle, like the two who brought us yesterday, Donald Gorm and Angus Dubh.'

I had noticed that all the clansmen's names were known and valued, as though they belonged to the family.

I forget when I was able to ask Christiania about Alasdair Dorch. I knew enough by now to know that the clans kept together; if Alasdair was a MacGregor he ought to be in their country, not that of the Grants. She laughed.

'He is a MacGregor indeed, but different, a little,' she said. 'His mother died in giving birth to him, as he was so large. She had come here among us, because as you know, the Grants and the Gregarach have always helped one another: not a word is spoken, but one will lay a hand on the other's shoulder, in the dark, and it is known then that there are men ready, down at the ford.' Like many Highlanders, Christiania tended to wander off the subject a little, but she came back. 'The poor woman died, and her man had to get back to his clan, and left the child with us to be nursed; my mother had an eye to him as he grew. He stays more with us, accordingly, than he does with his own folk, although he goes back to see them, and would not think of himself as other than one of them, and helps them in trouble. But he pleases himself, and when the salmon are running he is to be found here, and when the antlered deer are on the hill. If we were at feud, he would fight for us; and Alasdair Dorch is a grand fighter. He has been to the south many times with our cattle, even to England, and speaks Scots better than most. It is amazing to look upon him, is it not? He is a giant, and has a kind heart.'

I wondered if she was a little in love with Alasdair Dorch Gregarach herself, but if so nothing ever came of it.

On Sunday the priest said Mass at Freuchie, and I noticed one or two of the MacGregor clan, in their white-striped tartan, among the worshippers. Alasdair Dorch himself remained at the back, for if he had not done so nobody would have been able to see past him. Afterwards I went out to walk again and almost at once, my little white goat came running. 'Annabella, Annabella,' I called. She seemed to be growing accustomed to her name, maybe only if I were to say it. I reflected that she would have been the first creature of my own in the whole of my life, except that of course she was not mine, but the property of James of the Forays.

Her udder was heavy, and it looked as if nobody had taken thought to milk her; perhaps she would not allow it. I talked to her and stroked her neck, then presently laid my hands on the soft teats. They were not as sharp as a cow's. While I was at this I became aware of a presence behind me, and to be sure it was Alasdair Dorch. I hoped that he would not follow me everywhere. I looked at his tremendous presence and said, 'I should like to try to milk the little goat, as nobody has done so; can you find me a pail?' I hoped that he would follow my Scots, and gestured with my hands, while Annabella stood still, her head bent.

'I can that,' he said. 'Will you be knowing how to milk a goat?'

His tone was respectful, but practical. I said I could milk a cow; I had done so once or twice at Vouvray, when the milkmaid was ill. I closed my eyes; I did not want to remember Vouvray, and only had to do so briefly when my jointure-money came. The cousin lived there now, and so presumably, still, did Andelot and Madame Sanserrato. I heard Alasdair Dorch's voice as if it came from a different world. 'It is otherwise milking a goat,' he told me. 'You should put the whole hand on the udder, not only the teat. I will show you, if you will let me.'

Annabella did not seem to mind either his great hard hand or mine clasping her velvet udder, and presently he went away and brought a bowl from somewhere; I was to learn that he was always resourceful enough to procure whatever was asked for. I began to milk Annabella, and she endured it; the narrow jet of milk squirted into the bowl. Afterwards she was relieved; I could sense it.

'They should have milked her yesterday,' I said. 'They saw to the rest.' We did not, as a rule, drink goat's milk at Freuchie; that from the herd was used to feed the calves, while we ourselves drank cow's milk. Alasdair Dorch raised the bowl, brimming full, and held it out for me to taste it. I did so, and it was delicious; not tasting of turnips, as ordinary goat's milk will do. I said so to him.

'She is a different kind,' he told me, 'and that is why they do not heed her. Lady Lovat, the old *cailleach*'s daughter, sent an in-kid white goat to her mother two years since, and the goat died, but this is the kid. They say they came from across seas. I have never seen the like myself.'

We parted, and he said he would wash the bowl in the river and hide it in a certain place in the trees for me daily. I thanked him, but had no wish to make him my constant companion, and said farewell. On return to the castle I asked Christiania, with whom I had struck up a friendship, what a *cailleach* was. She laughed. 'An old woman,' she said. 'It is not a polite term.'

I blushed deeply; I could not explain to her that Alasdair Dorch had said it of her mother, but she knew. 'He cares for nobody,' she told me. 'He is certain that the Gregarach are descended from the Kings of Alba, and maybe they are, and us through them, so he think himself as good as anybody. My mother was an Ogilvy of Deskford, and that is upcome to him.'

'I thought he brought her coins from Carlisle, for pin-money; she told me herself.'

'That would be to show his cleverness. I must get away to my bidden task, or she will be after me.'

I remembered how I had been unsure, on the journey here, whether or not I liked old Lady Grant, and now decided that I did not; but being her guest I must not show it. Nor did I ever mention Glamis to her again, where we had first met. I was filled with guilt that I had been unable to help young Margaret Lyon and her brothers, in fact that I had made matters worse. If the King was with his mistresses, however, it was the less likely that he would take time for further revenge on them; or, for that matter, on myself.

At Easter we had had a great gathering of the clans, and all the daughters and their husbands and children rode over to Freuchie; Lovats, Camerons, Mackenzies, Mackintoshes, a Lowland family named Cumming, and, somewhat shamefaced, the *chère amie* of Ian Mór who was also a Fraser of Lovat. The old lady ignored her, but the rest were kind enough. The couple would be married in the following year, and meantime took their walks together, so that I was prevented from seeing Annabella most days and, for that matter, Alasdair Dorch MacGregor. The latter had elected to become my servitor, or whatever the term might be, and although he never troubled me with attentions he seldom failed to be present if I went outdoors. I wondered how he kept himself in food meantime; no doubt he fished in the Spey when I was elsewhere. He came to Mass on Easter Day, and I saw him kneeling reverently as the Host was raised, and the shining chalice. Next day, the visiting families prepared to go home; they would escort one another through the glen paths.

I myself began to be troubled that I had heard nothing from the Queen. I knew that she meant me to spend the summer here, but it was unlike her to send no word to me. Some weeks passed, and I happened to mention it to the *cailleach*, as I had never ceased to call Lady Grant in my mind. She smiled in a knowing manner.

'It is very early yet, but I heard in a letter from my daughter Margaret Cumming, whom you met, that the news had come to Erneside; the Queen is expecting another child early in

December. I pray that it may be a more successful outcome than the others.'

No doubt that was why Madame Marie had not had time to write; but I resented the superior way in which this old woman, mother of many living children, wished success to the Queen. 'Her Grace has a handsome son in France,' I said. 'It was misfortune, or accident, that killed the princes.'

'Well, misfortune comes to us all. I doubt, though, that the Queen will be needing you meantime. I only hope her husband pays her some attention.'

I hoped so too; the King's unfaithfulnesses must have irked Her Grace, even though she would say no word of them to her own mother. I ceased to expect letters, accordingly; but myself sent for pen and paper and wrote a line, to say that I was happy, and had prayed for her especially at Easter. It must have been about then that the child was conceived.

The weeks went on, and I walked with Annabella often; she showed no signs of being mated. The other goats pulled placidly at branches when they were let; they can soon destroy a forest. I had grown used to the shadow behind me that was Alasdair Dorch; I seldom troubled to talk to him. Sometimes, on the other hand, James of the Forays himself would talk with me, either in the hall, which was a great honour for a woman, or outside if he chanced to be returning from a day's stalking or fishing in the Spey. He had a wide knowledge of what was going on in the Lowlands, and even in England, which he called the old enemy.

'The only strong man they have down there to withstand the English King is Cardinal Beaton,' he said. 'As long as he is in a position of power, there will be less danger.'

I said that I thought he was a proud man, and that I did not like him, having seen him in France.

'Few do so,' said James Grant. 'He can play with nations – France, Scotland and England – as other men play chess. He is not liked because he is successful. He has many enemies, and he knows it well enough. I will join with him in any promised banding together of Scots noblemen; the King cannot rely on those in English pay.'

'The Cardinal, at least, is not among them,' I said.

'No. He will always oppose the Douglas faction, who are; who

have been for years. They say they are preparing to lead a foray
into Scotland, at the behest of King Henry.'

'They have been saying that for a long time. I heard it before I
left Stirling,' I said hesitantly; I did not want to appear to know
more than he did, as he was evidently well informed.

'Well, it will happen, sooner or later,' he said, and departed
with his fishing-line. I stood reflecting on it all, and stroked my
little goat's neck.

I still had heard nothing from the Queen, and I was beginning
to be troubled: by now, her pregnancy must be advanced and
certain, and she would have taken time to write to me. I wrote
again, and still there was no answer; and I enquired at last of old
Lady Grant, who seemed to know everything, if all was well. She
said that it was, as she had heard again from Erneside, her
Cumming daughter's house.

'Her Grace is at Peebles for the time, or was so. The King is
troubled by rumours from England, and is raising an army if he
can. Because he will not abandon the Church, old Henry Tudor
is angry. There is so much trouble that nobody will have time to
write.'

I felt myself troubled also, and greatly desired to be near the
Queen, to help her if I might; but how could I go if she had not
sent for me?

'That old *dhiabail* in England has tried to waylay the King to
carry him by force over the Border, because his own rights in
Scotland have not been confirmed and he is not pleased,' said
James of the Forays. Ian Mór, who had been with him on the
hill, nodded, his long arm swinging a brace of hare he had
taken. Their eyes were glazing, the blood congealing on their
soft noses; he held them by the feet. Beyond where we were, the
heather was purple; it was August, and the dust shimmered in
the heat. I heard what they had to say with consternation; if the
King had been taken, what would happen to the Queen and her
unborn child? There was nobody left to protect them, except
Cardinal Beaton.

I said so, and found both men's eyes fixed on me with an
expression I could not read. 'If that befalls,' said Ian Mór, 'you
will find that the clans will march.'

I must have looked bewildered, because Am Grantach said

gently, 'Ever since the days of James IV, who made himself loved among us, we in the Highlands have been loyal to the Stewart Kings. It is as it used to be in the time of the Lords of the Isles, but now they are no longer with us.'

'Except that Donald Gallda, the usurper, came and burned Glenurquhart in his time, and held it for three years,' grumbled Ian Mór, but I did not care to hear about that.

I went inside and took my pen once more, and wrote *Madame, if I may come to you, to be of aid in any way, I pray you send me word. If you do not want me to come, send word also, I beg. I fear that letters may have gone astray, as I have had none; and I hear that the news is very bad. If I may come, I will; if not, I will pray. Your ever loving and loyal Claudine de Vouvray.*

By the end of the month, a messenger came running. The King of England had armed the Douglases, Angus and his brother, and they had ridden into Scotland, and had been soundly beaten at Kelso, and chased back south. As for the Queen, she had walked seven miles in pilgrimage from Edinburgh to the shrine of Our Lady of Loretto, although her pregnancy was now far advanced. I was glad to hear that the King had ridden a part of the same way. But there was still no word from her.

The summer had come to an end, the trees in the forest thinned, the cattle were slaughtered and their carcasses salted for the winter, and hung up in the castle kitchens. I saw Christiania draw the neck of a good midden hen for us to eat; it was becoming more difficult to find food, and I felt myself a burden. By November, relief came; a letter for me at last, with scarlet seals. I did not know it at first was from Her Grace; she had always used, in private letters, a little signet her father had given her, with the martlet and the cross of Jerusalem, and she used green wax. This red seal flaunted the lion of Scotland, but no doubt Madame Marie had taken to using it now that she was Queen.

I opened the letter. It was short, and in an unfamiliar hand, no doubt that of a secretary. *Come south to Lady Maxwell at Caerlaverock Castle*, it read. *There will be more news here. Marie R.*

Even the signature looked different from the sprawling one I remembered, but I had not often seen her writing; there had been no need. The whole message seemed strange, but who would trouble to send me other than the truth? At least old Lady Maxwell was a friend; I looked forward with warmth to seeing her again, and to having further news of the Queen. The Grants had been kind, but I was after all a stranger among them. I thanked them for their hospitality and said that I must leave.

'It is a pity that you must ride the winter roads, but they would be worse in December or February,' said Christian Grant, with the slow certain foresight of the countrywoman. Christiania kissed me, and I remembered the promise I had made myself to send her a gift. James of the Forays, Am Grantach himself, did me the honour to escort me for the first few miles of my ride, and after that my bodyguard was made up of a single man worth many; none other than Alasdair Dorch Gregarach, whom nobody would have dared prevent from coming, certainly not myself.

We had progressed through the trees, and his huge height adapted itself easily to avoiding the low branches; every muscle in his body was taut, swift and ready, his strong legs covering the ground in the way they must have done on the walk long ago to Carlisle. The round bonnet sat on his head like a basnet, with a feather in it; beneath, his grim features made a fearsome sight, and anyone meeting with us would have hesitated to attack me with such a guard. The time came when I wanted to relieve myself, and also to eat some of the food Christian Grant had kindly provided in a package for the journey; eggs boiled hard, with a poke of salt to season them; a little new-baked bread but more oatcakes, for the latter would not turn stale; a cut of hind's venison for the time of year, and a bottle of Spey water. I said firmly to Alasdair that I thought we should stop, and eat; he had no sign of any food with him, except for a flask in his belt, and I could not let him go hungry.

He stood, however, holding the pony, while I excused myself for moments; when I came back he was rubbing in a circular fashion between the beast's shoulder-blades. I offered him food, but he shook his head.

'I am after making the drammoch,' he explained. I could not think what he meant, and proceeded to eat some of Christian's provisions, as he would not share them. Nor would he sit down, though I had invited him to do so; after loping all that distance beside my mount, a seat for a time would surely be welcome.

'I will be standing to take the drammoch,' was all he said, and began to mix the substance between the pony's shoulder-blades. I asked what in the world it was; I had never heard of it. The small black eyes looked at me consideringly.

'It is a poke of oatmeal I am bringing with me in my *sporán*, and a drop or two of *uisge-beatha*, the whisky yourself will be after calling it. A man can last all day on it, except that we in the clans do not ride to fight; I learnt the *cuilbheart* on the Borders, the time I walked there. They will take the meal out with their ponies, and a drop of whisky, and mix it as you saw me do, and last all day in a foray, then come home, driving other folk's cattle.'

He was scooping up the pudding-like stuff from the pony by this time, and eating it; nothing he did was gross or disgusting, and he somehow managed to eat like an aristocrat. 'I will not be offering any to yourself,' he said as he finished. 'It would not do if you were to take to the whisky, to be sure.' He spoke gravely, for the expression of his face seldom altered. Presently he disappeared into the trees in his turn, and on his emergence I mounted my pony, which had only a small light patch left between its shoulders, and we travelled on, occasionally stopping for Alasdair Dorch to refill my water-bottle at a river.

This kind of exchange lasted all the way down into the Lowlands, and by the time we had passed through Stirling I was on very good terms with the big MacGregor. Folk in the street stared at the sight of me, in my coif and kirtle, astride a pony led by a great Highlander of fearsome appearance; but they would not dare even call after us, let alone molest us. At one time we stopped, to buy some apples I fancied; and the woman at the stall told us that the news was bad.

'The King has sent a great army to the south against the English, and another is in the east, at Haddington, and the Cardinal with it.' She was well informed, as stallholders are, for they hear all the rumours that come. I stowed the apples in my baggage with a heavy heart, and a sense of urgency; that was why the Queen had wanted me to travel to Caerlaverock; she must have ridden to the Border country to be beside her husband, near her time as she was. I must reach her quickly; I took no more heed of Alasdair Dorch except to bid him hasten, which was unfair; he had wasted no time on the journey, even in the occasional making of his drammoch. As we went, I heard him say, 'If my King is to fight, I myself will be fighting beside him. I will see yourself to this place, and then I will go.'

'God go with you,' I told him. I knew nothing I said would stop him from fighting, and that he would fight well, even with the short sword that was all he had brought with him, and no targe.

Caerlaverock Castle was rose-red, set back in a green place of its own. All the way down we had encountered parties of armed men, riding to the Solway muster: but, again, they did not trouble me with such an escort as I had, though they gazed at us curiously, when we came at last to the castle. I did not see it to the best advantage, for an hour or two back it had begun to rain, with increasing heaviness. We had been fortunate in this way so far, but soon I was soaked; and having always loathed rain since the appalling time at Fontainebleau when I had been taken, newly raped by Andelot, to a room for King François' pleasure, I cast my mind back to that, and meantime forgot poor Alasdair Dorch, who was as wet as I. His voice recalled me.

'It is very wet you are, but they will have a fire at the castle to warm you.' His dark face was upturned to me, running with raindrops. I said, 'And yourself, Alasdair Dorch; they must let you sit by the fire also. You have come all these miles with me, and guided me safe here.' I knew one did not offer a Highlander money, and did not know how else to thank him. He turned his attention to the pony again, and said quietly, 'Do not be troubling yourself for me. I can wring out my *breacan* and sleep in it. I have done that many times before. Water in stuff is warm to sleep in.'

I wondered at his indomitable strength; nothing seemed to defeat him. 'Will you take the pony to battle with you?' I asked. 'I am not likely to need him.'

'No, I am best on my own two feet. It will frighten the English to see me coming, although I wish I had my good sword with me, and my *sgiath*. But they will maybe have weapons to lend, when I find them.'

'I will pray for you,' I said, 'that you come safe out of the fight.'

'It is myself will be glad of your prayers. If you are ever in trouble or danger, send word to me, and I will come, no matter how far.'

We had reached the small drawbridge, which was down. 'I promise,' I said. There was no time to say more, because the door had opened, as though we were expected. In the fading light I could see torches beyond, and the tall figure of a woman in a round coif.

'You are Madame de Vouvray?'

I said that I was so. She looked with disfavour at Alasdair Dorch, who still waited with the pony, the rain falling down on him; it had not slackened.

'Get away, fellow.' The voice was high and importunate. 'Take the beast with you if you are going to, otherwise get it to the grooms, and take yourself off. Come in, madame.'

I hesitated; I did not like her, or her speech to Alasdair Dorch. 'May he not come in and dry himself?' I said. 'We have come a long way, and he is hungry.' I knew that he would survive well enough on his drammoch; but I would not see him treated badly if I could help it. However she was adamant, and pulled me in as though I were a child, out of the rain.

'I must shut the door; the wet is flooding in.' She did so, and I looked round in vain, hearing the pony's steps led away; Alasdair Dorch had gone, with no warm food in him. I resolved to speak to Lady Maxwell when I saw her; she would not have countenanced discourtesy to a servant, and a Gregarach was no ordinary one.

But the tall woman, removing my cloak, put me out of countenance, saying, 'I am Lady Maxwell.'

She was extraordinary, in that she was not young, yet still had tremendous attraction, as I could well guess, for men. Her bosom was so fine and full it dominated her figure, yet was not loose or flabby. Her hair, when she was young, must have been very fair; it had darkened slightly, and sat smoothly under the coif. She had a trim waist, although, as I was later to learn, she had borne many children. Her mouth was full also and yet firm, as though she were used to having her will carried out. Her cheekbones were high, like a cat's, and so was her colour. She smiled at my evident astonishment.

'Ye were expecting my mother-in-law, without a doubt,' she said. 'She is in Galloway, with daft Beatrix whom she tends. This is my stepdaughter Margaret, who has never yet married; and this is my daughter Lady Fleming.'

Two women were seated by the fire, the one young, the other

not so. Margaret who had never yet married kept her eyes cast down prudently; Janet Fleming gave me look for look. She too was attractive, with the mixture of fecundity and magic that distinguished her mother. I was bidden to sit down with them, and handed warm ale. Glad as I was of it I hesitated to drink it, wishing that Alasdair Dorch could have shared it; by now, if I knew him, he was far away. I wondered why I had been bidden to Caerlaverock; no doubt, if I listened, I would be told. But Lady Maxwell – her name was Isabel, and she was the wife of the old bearded lord who had spoken with me at Queen Margaret's funeral after we had met earlier in France – showed no signs of enlightening me. Instead, she talked about herself.

'Where is the Queen?' I had asked, after we had sat for some moments about the great hearth, which blazed with heat despite the drips of rain that came down the chimney, hissing on the logs. My clothes steamed and I had begun to be warm; but I was filled with unease. There seemed no reason in the world why I should have been brought to this place; and now I was alone with these three women.

'The Queen? Ye may well ask me, for I have queen's blood in my own veins.'

I did not want to listen to her, for she had not answered me; but later I remembered her story, told as she stood there in front of the fire, her face composed, her gown hanging in seemly folds about her beguiling body. The others said nothing, and I realised with disbelief that if Lady Maxwell were Lady Fleming's mother, she must be old. Lady Fleming herself might have been thirty; it was difficult to tell. Margaret was younger, but not at that a very young girl. I learned afterwards that she was her father's only daughter, and kept at home. Beatrix, to whom I had once tried to teach French at Falkland, was married to one of the sons. I doubted if she would ever make him a sensible wife: all her family maintained this madness. The old lord was gone off to the army on the Solway, his son Robert to Lochmaben where the King was encamped; so the women were alone. I decided to listen to Lady Maxwell, at least with half my mind. It was a strange story enough.

She was the naural daughter of the Earl of Buchan, and he was descended from the second marriage of Queen Joan Beaufort to the Black Knight of Lorn. This had taken place after the murder of her husband James I, for as a widow she was unprotected. I reflected that Margaret Tudor might have been in such case after the death of James IV at Flodden. We must have spoken of it, because the old lady – I should not call her that, for she had no appearance of age, no wrinkles, no grey hairs – smiled, with a sly look on her face. 'He was a lovely man, the late King,' she said. 'He was my lover. He got Janet on me. She likes to be called Joan.'

Janet, or Joan, looked up and then down again. The other two were evidently used to the old one's stories; after all, few women have such stories to tell. Isabel Maxwell went on to talk of James IV; how he was kindly to everyone, but could never resist a woman, 'and that bitch in Galloway thirled him to her many a year'.. He would go on pilgrimage, walking miles northward to St Duthac in Tain, south to St Ninian in Whithorn. He would tie a bird's wings on a man to make him fly. He would practise surgery and alchemy. 'There was no new thing but he had cognaisance of it, and would try it. At the end, he had fine French armour, fine French cannon; but they availed him nothing, and all the ships were lost at sea. My lord lost many.' Her face twisted in scorn. 'A woman could wage war better, I believe,' she said. 'Women are not fools.'

Joan Fleming caught her eye. 'Mother, it is growing dark.'

'Why, so it is, and we must show Madame de Vouvray her chamber. There will be meat set out up there; we do not bring out the trestles when we are alone. I did not tell you of my two late husbands.' She was ascending the stairs, her skirts high in her hands, and I followed her, realising that I was weary. 'There was Bothwell, who fell at Flodden; I bore him the Fair Earl, as they call him; Patrick has my colouring. Then there was Home. I do not doubt that if my Lord Maxwell falls this night, I would take a fourth husband; I am seldom without a man in my bed.' She turned and smiled at me over one shoulder, and her smile was that of a witch. I saw my own bed waiting, but a serving-woman came, and she and my lady undressed me, putting a gown about me at last that lay on a chair; it was of satin lined with budge, and warm against the November night. 'We will dry your clothes downstairs,' said Lady Maxwell, and they departed with all my gear, even my shoes, leaving me naked except for the gown.

Food was there, as she had promised, and I tried to eat a little, but could not. I felt as if I had been enticed here, but for what purpose? There was no word from the Queen; my question about her had been turned aside. Tomorrow, when I was rested, I must insist on knowing how she fared, and why I was here at all.

There was a brazier in the room, for it had no hearth; I lingered in the chair by the lit coals, certain that they would be warmer than the bed. Their colours flared against the dark. I thought I heard a horseman: then a little later footsteps coming upstairs, but it was difficult to be certain because of the beating rain outside. I wondered how Alasdair Dorch fared, and if he had found the army. It might have been nearer for him to go to Lochmaben, but he knew his way to the Solway best.

The latch of the door lifted, and a red-bearded man came in, carrying a lighted candle. It was the King of Scots.

'Well, little nun? You see I have found you again.'

I knew that it was useless to cry out. The storm outside would deaden other sounds, or else the women below would pretend not to hear them. I remembered, in that moment, the glance Lady Fleming had given her mother to say it was growing dark; and the procuress had led me upstairs. But the King was upon me already; he had laid his candle down, and with his easy accustoming from many women took me, still in my chair, with the budge gown fallen as open as his codpiece. Then he peeled the gown off, and carried me naked to the bed. I struggled silently; it did not matter that he had taken me already by default; he should not have a second victory, and a third, so easily.

I kicked and bit; and James V was angry. He had laid me down, and stood there looking at me, his narrow eyes filled with cold rage. 'By God, if ye will not oblige your King, madam, I'll give ye over to the men-at-arms. That will force the prudery out of ye.'

Terror filled me, but I would not let him see it; instead I let him climb upon me in the bed, and do as he would thereafter. I turned my face away, and when he had done with thumbing my body and thrusting in it, he noted the fact and from being angry, laughed.

'That is of no avail,' he said. 'See, I will pinch your little nose, and your mouth will have to open; then –' He did so, and inserted his tongue, and made all manner of other caresses, if that is what they are called, leaving no part of my nakedness undiscovered or untouched. The great bed was rocking by then, and I knew that the women below, if they were still there, would note it, and nod and smile to one another knowingly. A great anger and pride grew in me; I would never, by word or look, complain or cry out; I would give them no satisfaction of that or any kind.

Satisfaction was taken by the Majesty of Scotland, however, to the extent that the dawn had come up before he rose from me. I let him go, not asking if or when he would return; later on fresh food was sent upstairs by the serving-woman, and water with which to wash myself. I washed, combed my hair, and wrapped the budge gown round myself while they lit the brazier and took away yesterday's ashes. No one else came near me all that day.

The next night, the King came again; it was possible he had been to Lochmaben, but I did not ask. I made no talk with him at all, and he seemed to desire none from me, only possessing me much as before, but if anything more urgently. On the following day, he came while it was still light, and made love again after his fashion; but he seemed absent and reflective, as though my body solaced him in place of some other thing he would rather have, and could not.

He left me at last, and I surveyed my bruises. Time passed. At one point I heard the latch, and thought it was the King returned; but it was Lady Maxwell, and her face was white. She carried my clothes and shoes.

'There has been a doleful defeat of the Scots army at the Solway,' she said. 'They floundered in the moss, and were lost; and many rode home before that, as the King was not in command of them, but only Oliver Sinclair. My lord is taken prisoner, and my son-in-law.'

She looked accusingly at me; I, her look said, had been the reason why the King had been elsewhere. 'Your pony is in the stable,' she said, 'and if ye will take heed of me, get on him quickly. Mounts are in short supply, and they will soon come foraging, and maybe the English likewise.'

I huddled on my clothes, and went and did as she said. The rain had stopped; that was the only comfort.

The released pony jogged briskly, for he had been well fed on hay. I was in no state to be solaced by any saddle, and thought that I would faint before we had even won beyond Caerlaverock; but I bit my lip, and endured it. What saved me was the sight of the path down which Alasdair Dorch had led me on the way to the castle drawbridge three days before. To the left of it, I would meet the fleeing army and possible rapine by the English. The only thing to do was take the road to the right, into the hills; to my mind, made stupid as it was by the happenings of the last days and nights, it seemed that in the end I would come out at the east coast, and find Madame Marie in one of her palaces; if she had returned to Stirling, I must go there as soon as I had rested at Edinburgh or Falkland, where they knew me. I had a moment's fear that I lacked money, but feeling in my cloak my purse was still there, and full; there had been little to purchase on the way down from Freuchie, and Lady Maxwell, whatever her faults, had not taken my coins. I was much comforted by their presence, but regretted the apples we had bought in Stirling, which there had not been leisure to finish, and my baggage was not with me, for there had been no time. Then I thought of Alasdair Dorch and wished he were with me now; the hills had closed in, bare and lonely, and the path wound unknown to me, but we travelled on.

I do not know how I accomplished that journey. Fortunately I was able to stop when I saw a haystack, and ask if the pony might have fodder, and offer to pay for that and a drink of milk for myself. I have learned since that man can live on milk alone, if he cannot live on bread. Sometimes the folk would not take any money; once or twice they glanced curiously at me, a woman riding alone.

'There has been a battle in the south,' I would say. 'Many men are dead', and would hope that they thought my own man was among them, and have pity on me; otherwise I might be attacked, and used as King James had used me, or worse, left for dead.

I reflected on King James, when I could bear to think of him; to have behaved as he had, in my own case and others, with such a wife as he possessed, deserved the utmost contempt. With me, I knew, it was partly a punishment; I had thwarted him on several occasions, and I remembered his Tudor blood, which made him nurse a grudge for a long time, then take sudden revenge. He had said certain things while he lay within me which made it clear that that had been his reason for the elaborate

affair of the letter sent with red seals; no doubt I was a fool to have
been deceived by it. I could not rid myself of the feeling that I was
soiled, more so than I had been even after the business of
Andelot. That, after all, had mattered to no one but myself; but
this, if she knew, would hurt the Queen. Perhaps when my bruises
were healed I could forget. If only Alasdair Dorch were with me
now! What was it he had said? *If you are ever in trouble or danger,
send word to me and I will come, no matter how far.* But I could not
send to him in the midst of a fleeing army, even if he were still
alive. The thought that he might be dead brought tears to my
eyes; it was likely enough, for he would have been in the front line
of the fighting, even with his short sword. I remembered the little
white goat, and how he had taught me to milk her. I remembered
many things.

The journey took several days. Once I slept in a haystack,
wrapped in my cloak, for it was growing dark and cold and we
could go no further. The pony pulled at the hay, and in the early
morning I was wakened roughly by the owner of the stack, taking
me for a vagrant woman and telling me to move on. The episode
did nothing for my appearance; my hair was full of hay, and my
clothes seedy, and when I tried to obtain a bed at an inn in Hawick
later they turned me away, so I rode on. It seemed as if I had been
riding all my life, and would ride on into eternity. Fortunately
there had been no one on the road; there are lonely places in
those hills.

I came down at last into the valley of the Teviot, then of the
deep-running Tweed; and in the end to a glittering town in the
distance, with watchmen on the walls. I knew this must be
Berwick, so turned away from the English prize and headed
north; and came at last, to my joy, to the sea. All I had to do now
was follow the coast, and it would bring me to where I desired to
go; but I was very tired, and so was the poor pony. I got off his
back and walked with him a little, and at that moment a horseman
appeared on the road. There was a rose-red castle in the distance,
much like Caerlaverock but larger; a fortress. The rider came
from there. He turned off on to the main path, and I saw that it
was the King.

I shrank back, hoping he would not notice a vagrant woman
walking with her pony; and he did not, for he was beyond noticing
anything. His lips moved, and he was talking to himself. He was
like a man who sleepwalks. I caught the words he was repeating,

over and over, as he passed by, not seeing me.

'Fled Oliver? Is Oliver ta'en?'

Oliver Sinclair had been in command of the men at Solway Moss. It seemed that news of the defeat had deranged the King's mind. I watched him ride on, and out of sight.

I was less lucky with the next encounter; a rough pair of men, met with about an hour after the King had passed by, whither I had no means of knowing. I was riding the pony again by then, and they came at me and pulled me off it; began to jest about women on the roads alone, and I knew what they meant to do with me, as well as stealing the pony. It may be thought that what had already happened to me made it unimportant what happened next, but I was still fastidious, and I struggled and lashed out at them, having tried in vain to tell them that I was going to Edinburgh, and would see the Queen.

'The Queen? The Queen'll no' see the likes o' you. Give her here, Geordie.'

Geordie had his eye on the ditch. 'No, I'll ha'e her first. I saw her first, and I'll ha'e her.'

It was then that I saw the glint of armour, and a streak of red against the dull distance. I began to scream aloud, and try to fight my way towards the riders; whoever they were, even English, they could not be worse than these ruffians. I had lost all sense of direction, or I would have known that they were coming from the north.

The man riding in front wore a close basnet, and shining armour beneath his scarlet robes. I knew him, through the continued pullings of the men at me; and screamed his name.

'My lord Cardinal! Cardinal Beaton! *Au secours! Au secours! A moi!*'

I called all the things I could think of, in French; how I had seen him in Paris; how I was a friend of the Queen. 'Aid me! Aid me! *Je vous prie! A moi!*'

They had let me stagger towards him; they themselves had fallen back, sullen resignation on their faces; Cardinal Beaton's name was known well beyond his diocese. He looked down from his tall horse and said, also in French,

'I do not know you, madame. How do you come to be here?' It was doubtful, I knew, if he would have remembered me, and my present haggard and dirty appearance did not help.

I told him. I said nothing of what had happened at Caerlaverock, except that I had ridden through the Border hills. 'We are seeking the King,' said the Cardinal. 'Since news came of the defeat it is not known where he may be, except that there is a rumour he was last at Tantallon.' He glanced ahead, shading his eyes with his hand, and I realised that the strong red fortress I had passed was the Douglas hold, now free of that clan. I remembered having heard somewhere, perhaps from Lady Drummond or old Lady Maxwell, that the King kept a mistress there in charge of Oliver Sinclair's wife. Evidently I had not sufficed him: or perhaps he had only ridden in to take news of the defeat to Sinclair's wife herself. But he had not had the air of a man taking news to anybody. Whichever it might have been, I spoke up, and told Cardinal Beaton the King had just ridden past.

'Then I am grateful to you,' he said, the dark eyes assessing me; I had the feeling that he would have known if I was lying or mistaken. 'We may have missed him where the roads fork.' He turned his head, and like any commander gave the order for a detachment to break off from the main party, and go to look for the King on the way I described. They caught up with us later, saying there was no sign of him on the other road, or on ours. Where he had gone was discovered later; meantime, the Cardinal signalled to one of the men-at-arms who rode beside him, and to a second in a black habit, without armour.

'You, Brother Melville, and you, Patrick, convey this lady to St Andrews. Tell Mistress Marion to prepare a bed for the night, and hot food. You need not return; we ourselves will retrace the way to Haddington, then home when all is clear.' The last words meant that he had been guarding the approaches to the capital under the King's orders lest the English advance north; but they had not, or not so far.

The pony was secured, and came with us, but I no longer rode him. I was carried behind Patrick the man-at-arms in the saddle, and truth to tell felt as limp as a piece of rag, and thankful for his leather coat to hold to. The brother in the black habit accompanied us in silence, on his own mount.

I do not remember that journey much more than the last; I believe I slept for part of the way, and was only prevented from falling off by whatever good fortune looks after sleeping folk. When I came to myself we had left the open country behind,

and were clattering through the streets of a town; then there was
the sight of the Forth, and the Queen's Ferry, which we crossed,
with our horses, having paid the tolls, with the water lapping
round the flat barge that carried us. I was too bemused both then
and earlier to ask why the Cardinal had sent me so far north, but
realised later that it was only the natural action of a man thinking
of his home, and that it would be the best place to send me,
especially as the Queen would be at any time in labour. I knew
this, and was in a frenzy of anxiety as well as all my other ills. It was
useless to ask the men escorting me to set me down in Edinburgh,
from whence I could have travelled more quickly to wherever she
was. They had their orders, and would obey them. It occurred to
me that had the Cardinal not been a churchman and diplomat, he
would have made a commander of armies. It was evident that he
was a man of many parts.

This was borne in upon me when I had recovered a little. We
had stopped for some food bought at a baker's, and I asked
Patrick, the man-at-arms behind whom I rode, who Mistress
Marion was. I had a notion, having seen her, I was certain, before;
but I wanted to hear what he would answer. He replied, chewing
bread,

'She comforts the Cardinal. They ha'e eight bairns.'

The matter-of-fact way he said it made me shake with laughter;
suddenly, after all I had endured, I could not stop laughing, in
the same way as, a short while previously, I had hardly been able
to stop weeping. The man in the black robe said quietly, 'Easy,
now, easy.' He had hardly spoken on the journey.

I was curious about him, and when we were mounted again I
asked Patrick in a low voice who he might be. 'He is an Observant
Friar,' the soldier replied. 'He goes about much for the Cardinal,
and helps him with his writings.' He cast a glance behind to ensure
that the friar did not overhear me. 'As to Mistress Marion, watch
her, if ye should pen any letters,' he said. 'She is a fair hand at
counterfeiting writ.'

I was consumed with curiosity to behold again Mistress Marion,
who comforted the Cardinal, had borne him eight children, and
could counterfeit writ.

The strangeness did not depart. We came to St Andrews, and I
saw with relief the castle jutting above the town; I expected that
we would go there, but we did not. The men drew up instead at an

unpretentious stone house in the street, and tirled at the pin which was fixed outside the door. We were admitted by a maidservant in a clean apron, and presently the mistress of the house came down. I could not envisage the Cardinal's coming here, in his scarlet finery and lace, and later learned that when he needed comforting, Marion Ogilvy would go up to the castle, and slip in by the postern gate. Meantime, I stared at her in some astonishment. Long ago, by the light of torches, I had seen her resolute face against the night at Prince James's christening here. It was a face one would not forget.

For a moment, I did not speak of it. She looked at me and said, 'What ye have need of is a good wash in hot water, and then a soft bed. I will see that both are made ready,' and she turned and gave orders to the maids. I reflected that she and the Cardinal were a well matched pair; both knew what they wanted, maybe had few scruples in obtaining it, and had no nonsense about either of them. But Mistress Marion had understood my need, and I was grateful to her.

I stayed in Marion Ogilvy's house four days, and a kind of lassitude stole over me, so that I could not even contemplate my duty to the Queen, though I knew I should go to her at once. When I left my bed and went shakily downstairs, I met the eight bairns, or most of them; they ranged from long-legged lads to a small girl clasping her wooden doll. All of them resembled the Cardinal, with sharp features and dark observant eyes; or maybe it was that the Cardinal and his mistress, as many married couples will, looked like one another by now after so many years together. Mistress Ogilvy had come and perched on the edge of my bed while I still lay in it, and talked to me; she had dark hair beneath a working mutch, and when she smiled two deep dimples appeared in her cheeks. She affected no rich dress, and in fact affected nothing. I forget how we touched on the subject of priests; perhaps Marion introduced it, her strong body erect and without shame or pretence. I could not but admire her honesty.

'A priest is a man, and men have their needs. Why should they not have them met, and still administer the sacraments and baptise bairns? That is what the Cardinal says, and he is as good a servant of the Church as any, and the Pope knows it, and excused him the journey to Rome to get his hat. He and I met when we were no longer young, and we deal well together; if we did not, we would have parted long since.' She smiled, the dimples deepening. 'I was the youngest of the family; my father had married four times, and he was past sixty when I was born to my mother, who was young. After he died she did not marry again, and it was a solitary life for me, till I met Davy; all my half-brothers and sisters were old enough to be my parents, and my mother and I lived alone for many a year. Now I am my own mistress, because I am his; and glad of it.' She raised her head proudly. 'You must see my house in Arbroath, one day; it is larger than this, but I stay here most of the year to be near the Cardinal.' She was punctilious in referring to him by his title, except for that one slip when she had called him Davy, and I liked her the better for it. Shortly after that I went downstairs; and noted one of the girls, about fourteen years old, named Margaret, who was the image of her mother, and carried the same air of assurance and of getting what she wanted, in whatever fashion. When I said that I must travel to the Queen, who proved to be at Linlithgow, Marion Ogilvy said that I could not ride the whole way, as I was not yet well enough. 'You must go by litter, at any rate as far as the ferry, and Mag shall go with you and come back in it,' she said. It was kind of her; the litter was comfortable, with cushions, and Mag told me that in stark cold weather they put a brazier inside to warm it. It was not, in spite of being early December, cold then; once away from the east coast, the air grew warm. I lay on my cushions and thought of seeing Madame Marie again. I would say nothing to her, nothing, of what had passed. She must be left to think that I had taken longer than expected in coming down from the Highlands; I would not mention the letter. That was the best tale I could think of, and I hoped that it would serve, as she was shrewd. I hoped also that she would be glad to see me again.

Linlithgow loch was covered with a skin of ice by the time I made my way there with the party of travellers for whom I had waited, for safety's sake, at the South Ferry inn. The hired jennet I rode was gentle enough, and Mistress Ogilvy, whose kindness I would never forget, had lent me money for the journey which I would repay as soon as I could reach my own. I entered the palace at last, shabby but clean; I felt tired, but that was due to the journey; and my face, when I caught a glimpse of it in a wall-glass, was white as chalk. I pinched my cheeks and bit my lips, to redden them; I would not come upon Her Grace looking ill. I reflected, not for the first time, how she preferred that form of address, whereas the King insisted on Majesty, like his uncle. I could think of the King as someone remote, hardly known, again by now; what had happened might have been an unpleasant dream. But the defeat was not a dream; I had heard it discussed at the inn, and folk saying how it was a worse disgrace than Flodden; at the latter almost every noble in Scotland had fallen fighting bravely behind their King, whereas now at Solway Moss there had been no fighting, only withdrawals, floundering in a bog, and prisoners taken to England, with few dead.

I had almost made my way to the Queen's lying-in chamber, for Alan Leboeuf her servant knew me well enough; and lest she be already in labour drew back the curtain softly, prepared to go in. I could see her seated, heavy with child, before the fire; she wore a furred robe and a light linen coif. Her long hands were idle in her lap and I could see the firelight glint on her rings. It was as if she had nothing on her mind but to wait for the birth; and yet she must have heard of the battle, and its sad outcome.

I hesitated; and as I did so the further door opened, and the King stood there. He had lost flesh since I saw him on the road. His mouth still worked, as though he continually talked to himself; he seemed not to know where he was. The Queen turned her head, but did not rise and make him obeisance; there was her state to prevent it, besides which they thought they were alone; that is if he were capable of thought. It was she who spoke.

'Take heart. Nothing is the end. There are more loyal men in Scotland, who will fight if they must. When our child is born, that will console you.' She reached out a hand to him, then let it drop; he might not have heard her.

He began to talk. It might well be the last meaningful speech he would ever utter; and yet, at that, it was the maunderings of a schoolboy. He spoke of vengeance, always vengeance; on his own lords who had betrayed him, preventing him from fighting when he would; he swore that he would capture as many as had fled from Solway Moss without a fight, as some had; and last of all he blamed Cardinal Beaton. 'It was he who was the chief procurer and setter forward of the matter,' I heard him say. The Cardinal had advised him to muster troops against a possible English invasion.

'He is your friend. He is the friend of France, who may send aid,' she said. 'The King of England fears him for that reason, and because he will not change the Church in this country. That is your guerdon; you must cleave to it, and soon there will be help from abroad, never fear.'

But he turned away; and before I could go into the room I felt a hand clawing my elbow. I looked round; it was Lady Rothes, a poor soul whose husband was a philanderer, and who hung alone about Court. Behind her was young Marion Seton. They pulled my sleeve, and I had to go with them; my last memory of the Queen was of her still figure as I had first seen it, waiting, waiting for the birth.

'Her Grace has asked to see no one,' hissed Lady Rothes. 'Ye must come away.' Marion Seton said nothing, but stood between me and the door.

I was shaking and doubtful; would she indeed have seen me, of all women? The sight of the King, the very sound of his altered voice, took me back again to Caerlaverock. I followed Lady Rothes with trembling knees, and in the end shared a bed with her, as there were no orders yet given for me to be lodged at the Palace. But she saw that I was fed, and shared such news as she received; the King had ridden to Hallyards, the house of old Lady Grange, and had supped there.

'Take the will of God in good part,' said the old lady uselessly.

'My portion of this world is short,' replied the King. 'I shall not be with ye fifteen days.'

His servants came to ask where he desired to keep Christmas, and he smiled bitterly. 'I cannot tell; choose ye the place. But this I can tell ye; ere Yule ye will be masterless, and the realm without a King.'

He would say over and over again the words I had heard on the road by Tantallon. 'Fie! fled is Oliver? Is Oliver ta'en?'

He went at last to Falkland, and took to his bed, saying he would rise from it no more; and he did not. 'A horrible dread has taken hold of the people, they are saying,' was how Lady Rothes put it. I was more concerned with listening for sounds from Her Grace's chamber; there had been footsteps treading to it lately which I knew were the midwife's. I prayed that my little Madame might not die in labour after all the sorrow she had undergone; but she did not, and the labour was short, in fact earlier than expected. In time, word came to us who waited; the child was a girl, very beautiful. It was hoped she would live.

The King did not. In ballads one hears of men dying of a broken heart, of confusion of the mind; but I would not have believed that it could happen in everyday life. Perhaps James V had never been of everyday; there was as I have said an enchanted quality about him, the only one left of many children, the Gudeman of Ballengeich, the poet who had written *Christ's Kirk on the Green*. Now he willed himself to die, for he felt he had no reason to live. There were certain lords with him; Sir George Douglas, his own old tutor Sir David Lindsay of the Mount, Cardinal Beaton himself, who had ridden to Falkland, and others. The Cardinal alone tried to obtain sensible direction from the King, without result; James V was in delirium. They blamed the Cardinal afterwards for guiding the King's hand to sign a document naming Beaton, Moray, Huntly and Argyll as regents for the infant Princess, news of whose birth did not cheer her father. 'It cam' wi' a lass, and it will gang wi' a lass,' muttered the dying man. The crown had come to the Stewarts long ago through Robert the Bruce's daughter Marjory, who had died as her heir was born. What they call the Sight, in the Highlands, had come to James V; or perhaps, like his father, he had always had it. At any rate, the Cardinal seized him by the arm as he was sinking towards death and said close in his ear, 'Sir! Take thought for your realm!' But the King was beyond it by then.

Just before midnight on December 14th he roused himself from his fever, turned over in bed, knew all who waited, gave what was described as 'a little rise of laughter,' kissed his hand to them, and died.

The child Queen of Scots was six days old, left without a protector except for her mother, Mary of Lorraine.

No such news had yet reached Linlithgow when I contrived to gain admittance to the Queen's chamber. Great care had been taken in selecting a wet-nurse for the baby, as Prince James, who had later died, had been said to have been taken ill somewhat earlier because of a change of these women, so that the milk was different. I waited about the passages, knowing that there must come a time when the woman would have to come out; and when she did, waylaid her.

'If you will tell the Queen that Claudine is here, with Lady Rothes, you will be rewarded.'

I was not yet in a position to reward anyone, having not had access to my money. However the woman bobbed, and her reliable high-coloured face convinced me that she would do as she was asked. Nobody else, evidently, had thought of making use of so humble a creature, but in my case it worked well enough. Word came down at once, by one of the chamber-women, that Her Grace would see me immediately. I picked up my skirts and ran towards the lying-in chamber.

She was in bed still, but recovering. She extended her hand to me, and I kissed it. I heard her murmur, 'Ah, Claudine, Claudine! It is good to see you,' but absently, as if many things had come between her and myself. She gestured towards the cradle, and I knelt to look at the little creature lying there asleep. She was a most lovely child, with the fine features of her two dead brothers. Her hair was reddish gold.

'Stay with me, Claudine. I did not know you were in the palace. When did you come? Lady Grant kept you over long.'

I was prevented from answering; there was a servant at the door, less seen than heard in the shadows.

'Madame, it is the Cardinal. He would have speech with you.'

I was frightened. 'Madame, madame, the Cardinal must not see me!' I recalled my own harried, shabby figure on the road from Tantallon, rescued from further rape by the Cardinal and his men. It was possible that he would not know me again here, but with his sharp eyes that was unlikely.

The Queen did not question me; no doubt the matter did not interest her greatly. 'Go in behind the curtain,' she said evenly, and I obeyed. I saw Cardinal Beaton come in, his scarlet skull-cap on his head, his face grave. At first the Queen was joyful to see him; perhaps she thought he brought news of the King, and of how he had received tidings of the birth.

'Welcome, my lord!' But the gravity of his face told her more than his tongue could have done. I heard her speak, still in a controlled voice, still without evident emotion.

'The King is dead, is he not?' She spoke in French. The Cardinal inclined his head. He then told her gravely of what had passed at Falkland. The Queen listened patiently. At the end she mentioned what later proved to be a matter of great concern.

'Who is to be Regent; you, myself, or the Earl of Arran?'

I grew stiff with waiting behind my curtain. It was not decided then. It was not to be decided till many stormy debates in council had been lived through, amid the accusation against Beaton for having, they said, forced the King's hand to sign while he was dying, naming the Cardinal himself as Regent, and no other except a handful of lords who would obey him: Moray, Huntly and Argyll.

The Cardinal would never be Regent. There is no doubt that he was not liked among my lords, especially those who favoured reform; besides, those who know what they want, and as a rule get it, are resented by those who do not know and who therefore achieve nothing. However the shadow of power was meantime in the hands of the irresolute, by a decision of the lords in council who promptly disallowed Beaton's paper, allegedly signed by the King. The result was that a very different man came to power, for the time.

I have said already that Lord Maxwell had lost a number of ships long ago at the time of Flodden. However the commander who had lost the entire Scots navy then, causing defeat by land and sea, was the Earl of Arran, the next heir to the throne. His son, to whom they handed the power now, was like him, or like his father must have been; a weak agreeable creature, unable to make up his mind, switching from one party to the other and then back again; twitching his face by habit and regarding his feet, or else flying into a sudden temper as uncertain persons do. He could be violent at that; he had once been prevented forcibly from drawing his sword on the Cardinal in council. Maybe he had reasons for his own lack of strength; his parents' marriage had been doubtful, and it enraged Arran to be called illegitimate; he was married to a Morton girl, a sister of mad Beatrix Maxwell and her two mad siblings, and they had a small son who meantime seemed handsome and promising; in manhood he also was to become quite crazy, and had to have his estate handled for him. It was as well, at that rate, that Arran's plan to marry the boy to our baby Queen came to nothing, any more than Henry VIII's same plan for his son Edward, a notion whose setting aside involved much dolour for Scotland. A child in the cradle, who might not live! Madame Marie remained cool, pleasant, outwardly agreeable to everyone, playing them like fish: both marriages would be an excellent thing, no doubt. I heard it all. Afterwards she said to me, 'Claudine, the only thing to do is agree with whoever comes. Otherwise there would be an invasion from England, and Arran would snatch the child from my arms.' She turned tenderly towards the baby, whom she kept in her own room. The little creature's eyes had opened and were hazel, like her father's, set obliquely so that they appeared narrower than they were. What was to become of her was already perturbing nations; Scotland, England, France.

They buried her father meantime with great pomp in Holyrood. Yards of mourning stuff were bought, and torches lighted for the procession to escort the body, which had lain all this time at Falkland. Trumpets and pipes sounded about the catafalque, and the people mourned in their hundreds in the streets; they forgot past cruelties, such as the burning of Lady Glamis and the infamous betrayal of Johnnie Armstrong on the Borders; they remembered only that James V was the poor man's King, the Gudeman of Ballengeich who had often come among them, and as his effigy passed, they wept. He was buried in the same tomb as Madame Madeleine, which would have contented both him and her.

The Queen was not present. She had had the baby christened Mary in the chapel at Linlithgow, where once a strange man had appeared with a warning to King James IV not to march south to Flodden; and, herself, again wore dule. I sat by her, remembering the time we had waited together at Amiens after the death of the Duc de Longueville, and she had played with little Duc François to console herself. It was as if everything had spun back to its beginning, like a wheel.

One thing I did achieve. As soon as I might, I spoke to Her Grace about the two Glamis boys in prison in Edinburgh. She gave the order to release them at once. It was a time when her orders were still obeyed.

'Madame, would you not consider returning to France, perhaps in a little while, when the Queen herself is older?'

I was thinking of all she could enjoy once more; the company of her son, the places she loved; Châteaudun, Amiens, Joinville, Tancarville, the Court, although they said that had changed its nature since King François had become an obedient son of the Church and was persecuting Huguenots. She had had little joy of Scotland; an unfaithful and moody husband, dead children,

quarrelling lords. But she looked at me from under the
dule-hood, smiled, and shook her head.

'How could I leave my little daughter? She would be like a
lamb among wolves. Arran is the heir to the throne after her; is
he likely to let her live? The King of England would hardly take
care of her, wife to his son or no. I must be here to guard her,
and insist that they let me do so. Also, I was crowned Queen of
this land; I cannot abandon it, poor Scotland, and its people.'

'The people will not be grateful,' I said crossly. I was out of
sorts; I had been troubled with sickness lately, and did not feel
well. I heard her say that one could not expect gratitude; it was
not in human nature, but one must do one's duty.

My sickness continued daily, especially in the mornings, and my
periods had stopped. I was filled with terror, and wondered how
to tell Madame; but at least I need not break it to her yet. To give
birth to a child of the late King's was an honour, no doubt, but I
would far sooner that the necessity had not been forced upon
me. Fortunately the mourning gowns were cut full, and it would
be some time before anything would show. At nights in my bed I
would think what to do, and wonder if and where the child
could be secretly born; could I perhaps hide it, then send it out
to nurse as they did in France? But I was left with the Queen
Dowager – the title came strangely at first – so constantly, as she
craved my company, that to escape even for a little while would
be difficult. I decided to bide my time; it was the only thing to
do.

I cannot describe, or even clearly remember, the squabbles and
hardships that afflicted us all as winter slowly gave way to spring.
First of all Arran, naming himself Governor of Scotland, made a
show of strength and moved into Edinburgh Castle and also the
Palace of Holyrood, keeping a few apartments there for the use
of the Queen Dowager, if only for the look of the thing. As for
Cardinal Beaton, he called again at Linlithgow, surveyed the
beautiful healthy baby with some doubt, and said no woman, in
especial no child, could rule Scotland; he suggested not Arran,
whom he despised, but the Earl of Lennox, descendant, like the
Governor, of a Stewart princess, as King. Lennox was in France,
an officer in the Scots Archers of the Guard, and said to be
handsome. 'His brother is a half-wit,' murmured Her Grace

after the Cardinal had gone. Gradually she had slewed the
churchman round from such a point of view; she was skilful
enough to match Beaton at his own game, and had caused him
to leave with agreement in his mind that they should both
dissemble concerning the English marriage. To refuse it entirely
would precipitate war.

There now returned to Scotland a man who would do great
harm; the Earl of Angus' brother, Sir George Douglas. I heard
much more of him later, but he came with King Henry's blessing
and the instructions to do whatever he might to overthrow the
Cardinal. He boasted – and it may have been true – that a
thousand horsemen were waiting for him as he crossed the
Border. He had not dared set foot in his native country since the
dead King's boyhood, and had lived in England, on an English
pension, ever after. He had also – and for this reason alone the
Queen Dowager would have viewed his coming with dread –
embraced the reformed religion in England strongly, after
reading Tyndale's Bible. He was a rough, unpleasant, devious
man, and his son James Morton was worse. At first Sir George
tried to see Governor Arran, but the latter was with us at
Linlithgow, paying court to the Queen Dowager and pretending
to admire the little Queen, whom he would gladly have seen
dead; but for her life, he would be King of Scotland. He
twitched and grimaced and made bland courtly talk which
meant nothing, and at last went away. 'It is impossible even to
bribe him,' said Madame. 'He will take the money, then fail to
carry out the promises. He is a man of straw.'

She bent over the baby's cradle. The wet-nurse who had
admitted me to the Palace was still with her, seated in her chair,
her good red face content. The child gave no trouble, and had
sucked amiably. Now she was asleep after feeding, her face
already showing the oval shape it would finally achieve, like her
father's; the red-gold hair beginning to curl a little at the ends. A
single ear showed exquisitely, like a tiny shell beneath her close
cap.

Meantime, Sir George Douglas had at last been received by
Governor Arran, who made him swear that he and his brother
Angus had come back for the good of the realm of Scotland. For
what it was worth, George Douglas swore. He was then admitted
to Council, but shortly put out of the room; on return the

Cardinal drew him aside. The report of their talk I remember hearing.

'Are ye a good Christian man or not? Are ye given to the new learning after the fashion of England or not?'

Sir George replied that he had been christened. 'If I am not a good Christian I pray God to make me one. I wish that in the realm of Scotland there are no worse Christians than there are in the realm of England.' This was the kind of answer he would make.

The Cardinal, sighing deeply, then gave him twenty thousand crowns and promised to be his friend. However he told the Governor afterwards to take heed to himself; the Douglases would do him a shrewd turn if it lay in their powers. Arran then told Sir George what had been said, and they made a pact that as soon as Angus himself returned to Scotland, together they 'would lay hands upon the said Cardinal and pluck him from his pomp,' sending him prisoner into England. Later, Arran made a fool of himself by handing the Cardinal the wrong paper out of his doublet; it was no less than a setting out of the above plans for Beaton. 'This letter speaks of a special message touching myself!' cried the Cardinal. Later, explaining everything to Sir George, Arran admitted that he 'had overshot himself.'

On hearing all this, confused as it may have been by then, Her Grace made an instant decision; she must leave Linlithgow and travel to Holyrood, where she might influence events. 'It is not only Sir George Douglas I fear, but Angus himself; he is expected at any moment, and will certainly be there by the time I reach them all; and Governor Arran will be wax in his hands as the King's mother was once; even King Henry pleasured Angus by the end, and made his stay in England easy enough. He may be easy here on his own estates if he wills, but he shall not misguide the fate of my daughter.'

She was already directing her women to pack her gear, standing tall and commanding as if she had never lain in childbed. I glanced towards the cradle where the baby lay; what was to happen to her in the meantime? She could not travel to the bitter capital in January.

As if she had read my thoughts, Madame Marie turned to me. 'You will not accompany me, Claudine,' she said. 'I want you to stay with the Queen day and night; do not leave her for an instant. There are so many, so many –' her voice broke – 'who would do her harm, even by subtle means, when I am not with her. I can trust you as no one else. Have a care to her.'

I promised that I would do so. I watched the small cavalcade leave for Holyrood; the bundles of gowns and cloaks, for Her Grace must make her appearance royally despite mourning still; the great black litter with its gilded thistles and fleurs-de-lys in which I had so often travelled opposite her; the mounts of the escort and of the few ladies-in-waiting. I felt solitary in Linlithgow when they had departed, and it was cold; the cherry trees where James IV had walked with Margaret Drummond were bare of leaf, skeletons against the sharp wind. Such cold must not be allowed to harm the little Queen; I ordered a brazier to be lit, and brought near her cradle, as well as a fire in the hearth. I sat by her all day, sewing or else doing nothing; it was a pleasure to watch her unfolding like a flower, reaching up her long-fingered hands that were like her mother's, and laughing at me. She had been put into a little embroidered bonnet which fitted closely against the cold, and the covers on her cot were plentiful. I hardly found myself taking time to wonder how the Queen Dowager fared in Edinburgh, or whether she had contrived to beguile both Arran and Angus. She would do everything, I knew, not by complaints but by guile. It was the only way to defeat these noblemen and pay them back in their own coin. As for Cardinal Beaton, Her Grace did not exactly like him, but he would be her ally, strong for France; the King of England hated him, accordingly, for that and for his religion.

When Madame returned, however, it was in haste and alarm. She came straight to the chamber, stripped off her gloves, bent over the cradle, then turned to me, her expression grim.

'The Cardinal has been seized by them,' she said. 'Those ruffians may have sent him to his fate in England.'

'Let me send for mulled wine, Madame,' I suggested. 'You are frozen. Warm yourself, and tell me of it.'

She sank gratefully down by the fire in the hearth. 'Poor man, I do not know where he is,' she said. 'They took him by force in Council, set him on a horse and led him away; a priest came running after him with his crucifix. I would not trust the Douglases not to murder the Cardinal on Henry's orders. That Angus! He is most plausible still, in old age; no wonder he cozened Queen Margaret into marriage after Flodden. He has gained complete control of the Governor, and that in a few days. He and his brother Sir George –' she laughed a little – 'have set it about the town, and from there no doubt the whole country, that my father Duc Claud is coming with a French force to rule all Scotland. I only wish it were true.'

So did I. The mulled wine came, steaming hot; I set it by the fire, poured it carefully into a stoup, and handed it to her; she drank gratefully. 'This is good,' she said. 'I was in too great an agitation to eat on the journey. I had to come back to see what had befallen here to *her*, but she is safe, thank God, and thanks also to your care.' She smiled at me, and I could not but notice how her face, formerly so serene, was beginning to wither a little; and she was only twenty-seven. The tilted eyes, the witty mouth, were the same; her long throat was hidden by the mourning.

She set the empty wine-stoup aside, and continued to smile, more broadly this time. 'I have perjured myself,' he said. 'I decided – the Cardinal and I, poor man – that we should have a rival claimant for the throne here beside Arran, one who is his great rival; both say the other is illegitimate.'

'The Earl of Lennox?' I asked, for I knew a little.

She nodded, the folds of the wimple creasing. 'Lennox indeed. They say he is not to be trusted either. Who is, except yourself and poor Cardinal Beaton? However that may be, I have promised to marry the Earl.'

'*Madame!*'

She laughed outright. 'Have no fear, my Claudine; that part is the perjury. It is a bribe to bring him over to Scotland, having abandoned his place with the Archers of the Guard and its uniform of white and gold, which will be becoming to him if he is as handsome as they say. Once he is here, I can delay the marriage; for Arran to be discomfited, and the Douglases, is the main intent; and the English marriage for my daughter may be as long delayed as mine.'

She rose and began to walk up and down, as if her energy could not be contained; she was like a she-wolf in defence of her young. 'If only we could save the Cardinal!' she kept saying. 'Without him, my right hand is gone.'

I wondered how Mistress Marion Ogilvy in St Andrews was taking the news that her Davy was a prisoner, but held my peace.

Time passed. I myself was no longer suffering from the sickness that had troubled me in the mornings, and hoped to hide my condition for some time yet; but it afflicted me with a sense of great unease, in particular as the third month had passed, when one may expect miscarriages. That had not occurred, and the child increased daily within me; I was already thickening, and my breasts grew full. But in the events which were happening, my business was not of importance to anyone, or, fortunately, noticed by them. I would walk out when I could, by the loch, which was full of jumping fish that supplied our daily needs. I stood one afternoon, wrapped warmly, watching them with Joanna Grisenoir, who was now Madame Delareyneville and had travelled among others with the Queen Dowager to Edinburgh. Joanna was more friendly than formerly; no doubt considering that it was worth improving acquaintance with one so constantly about the Queen. She told me several things Madame had not.

'She was very much frightened when the affray broke out in the Council chamber, and the Cardinal was taken; she screamed aloud, which is not like her. She said afterwards that she thought they were all at one another's throats. The Earl of Angus came up. He is a personable man still, and persuaded her roundly.' Joanna smiled beneath her coif, as if any man could persuade Her Grace if she were not so minded. 'He said all they had done was to arrest a false, lying fellow. He did not say it was the Cardinal. They say Beaton has been taken not to England, but to Dalkeith, the Douglas stronghold. How wise the late King was to banish the Douglases! They have caused nothing but trouble since they came home.'

I agreed absently, but was already thinking of the other things which had chanced meantime; the return of some of the Solway prisoners, whom King Henry had released after forcing them to swear support for the English marriage and to work for the reformed religion in Scotland. Alasdair Dorch Gregarach had not been among them, as far as I knew; though why I should know was doubtful; he would have made his way straight home, and in any case would not have taken King Henry's oaths. I feared he was dead; he would not have been foolish enough to have sunk into the boggy ground with the rest, knowing his way to Carlisle already and having a feeling for the lie of any land. No, he was dead, his great powerful body lying among the slain, despoiled by the Borderers as had happened after Flodden. It was useless to pursue the matter, or to hope.

*

'We are no longer safe here, Claudine. This place was not built to withstand a siege; it is a pleasant palace, which is why I love it. But we must win out, I think to Stirling, which is mine by right of dower. I can protect my child there: it is strong.'

She spoke to me in a low voice in her own chamber, where the baby Queen was still kept; it was the only safe place. The palace had been invaded by servants, who were suspect, less those few from the late King who did not care to serve Arran, others perhaps however sent by him; and there lay the danger. How could a woman, two women, protect a little child from murderers? With the Queen dead, Arran would be King of Scots.

Madame Marie showed swift determination in the matter. Laden horses, with hair trunks on their backs, set out in charge of Leboeuf, and sixteen others carrying pots and pans. Our beds went to Stirling; we slept on the floor; even the chamber-pots were bundled into baskets and sent off. We were bereft of all comfort, but that mattered nothing; we waited only for word to start, and beasts to mount. Instead, the Queen Dowager came to me with two bright spots of anger on her cheeks.

'We are not to be permitted to leave,' she said. 'The Governor forbids it.'

I was aghast. 'But the Governor gave his consent.'

'Have I not said already that Arran is a man of straw? He told Sir George Douglas of my intent, and Sir George, if you please, cozened him to say quite other; putting it to him that the King of England would be angered if we went to a strong place. We are to be subject, evidently, to Henry's whims.'

'So we are prisoners.'

'Only till I have worked my will, in some fashion. I am less of a fool than Arran; it will not be hard, though it may take time.'

So we continued in our uncomfortable camp, eating fish with our fingers, drinking wine from the bottle as it came from France. Fortunately there was no shortage of food at Linlithgow, and never had been; the French sent dried fruit, Marshall the baker performed his duties, and there was butter and milk from nearby. Madame Marie laughed at me one day, for she continued with a high heart despite all hardship; but it dismayed me.

'Why, Claudine, you are growing fat. It must be with eating too much butter.'

I smiled, blushed, and hung my head down; what else could I do? Daily it was growing harder to conceal my state, and now we were out of mourning, and into lighter clothing, my thickening belly began to show beneath the folds of my summer gown. I would keep my hands, in their wide sleeves, across it to hide that and my breasts, which were already swelled like a matron's. What was to become of me? I was in the same situation as my mother had been, except that my child's father was no longer alive. Would Madame Marie act as Duchesse Antoinette had done when I myself was born? If that should happen, it would destroy the love between us; and rather than have such a thing happen I would die. Yet Madame had changed; she had been forced by events to do so; she was no longer the happy and serene girl I had known in France. She was a subtle woman now, a diplomat, even, when the necessity arose, a liar on behalf of her daughter. I could no longer predict how she would meet my situation. It was unimportant, in any case, to everyone except myself.

The common people were discontented with Arran. It was not only because of the Queen's wrongful holding at Linlithgow, but because of other things. He had had brought into Scotland large numbers of Bibles, and priests went about their duties in armour for fear of such treatment as the Cardinal himself had received. Ordinary folk can think for themselves; a party of citizens came to the Governor with the request that their Queen be put in charge of four Scots noblemen till she was of an age to marry, also that Cardinal Beaton be set free; and that the clergy might continue to say Mass in peace as formerly, despite the insistence of England and the promises extracted from the Solway Moss prisoners that they would promote the reformed religion if set free. 'Give us the primer and the psalter,' the folk said, speaking of the age-old books many knew by heart, accompanying as they did the age-old faith. But the Earl of Angus and Sir George Douglas, who had already wrecked so much, intervened, and the people's request was ignored by closing Parliament. By then, it was mid-March.

Part IV

There was a great brushing and shaking out of furniture returned two months before in a crushed state from Stirling; Her Grace had commanded Sir Ralph Sadler, the English envoy, to visit her at Linlithgow. He had already been to Edinburgh and had met Governor Arran walking in Holyrood gardens as if he owned them, and they had talked together. Sadler saw, of course, Sir George Douglas also, who regaled him with the story of how he himself and none other had saved the kingdom. Angus, Sir George's brother, was engaged elsewhere; he had an understanding, now that the old Queen his first wife was dead, with the douce unmarried daughter of Lord Maxwell whom I had briefly met during my three days' ravishing at Caerlaverock Castle on the Border. Angus was old now, but to do him justice he had entertained no thoughts of a second marriage earlier despite the divorce, because it would have put his daughter by the Queen, the Lady Margaret Douglas, in danger of bastardy. She was still at the Court of Henry VIII, said to be a close friend of the Princess Mary and a convinced Papist. So they all came and went. Angus evidently hoped now for a male heir.

Sir Ralph arrived bowing and scraping. The English have suave manners, but when it comes to bargaining are as hard as stone. We knew that he had been sent north partly to find out if the little Queen were healthy; reports said that she was not. For that reason, Madame had put me in charge of the child, dismissing the wet-nurse; as he would not know that I understood French, I could overhear anything she and Sir

Ralph had to say. 'Claudine, you could make play to suckle the Queen yourself, my friend, from the look of you; it is the butter, I still believe,' Her Grace observed merrily. She was at her best before a battle of words; she knew very well what she would say to Sir Ralph, and lead him to accept.

They came in together, after a few words in the outer chamber. The Dowager did not make me known to him; I was the wet-nurse. Instead, she bade me undo the baby's clothes presently and show her naked. 'As you can see, and may tell your master, she is healthy enough, and I will believe be tall like myself,' Madame said. Certainly the baby had grown, and was long in the body and limbs already. Sir Ralph swore he had never seen so goodly a child. I dressed her again, as it was still March, and set myself to rocking the cradle while they both talked on. The envoy was expressing his pleasure that the Queen Dowager agreed to the English marriage. I kept my eyes down, not to show my surprise.

Madame sighed. 'Indeed, sir, England is the only safe place for my daughter; dangers beset her here on every side. I thank God that after taking my sons from me, he has given me this guerdon; Mary, Queen of Scots may accomplish the union between Scotland and England. I myself will be advised by the King of England in all things.'

She then proceeded to demolish Governor Arran. 'Whatever pretence or fair weather he made,' she said, 'he is not for the marriage. He has advised me, in fact, to keep my daughter with me till she comes of age, by which time your master will in nature be dead.'

Sir Ralph looked pale; a world without Henry VIII would surely fall apart. The Dowager's tilted blue-grey eyes grew knowing. 'This is why I had to see you in person, my friend,' she murmured. 'I can trust neither Scots nor French here, for none of my own are about me. Arran has filled the palace with his own men; we are in constant danger, therefore, but I believe that perhaps he will not have my daughter killed, as he wants her for his own son.' She sighed. 'If only the Cardinal were free! He would see to the carrying out of the English marriage.'

Sir Ralph gave a perceptible start. 'Cardinal Beaton aid my master? They have been enemies from the beginning. You deceive yourself, Madame, and perhaps hope to deceive me also, Beaton hates the English, and the reformed religion. He can do no other, being a Papist.'

The Dowager raised her hand delicately to the gold cross at her own breast. 'The Cardinal is a wise man,' she said slowly, 'and can better consider the benefit of the realm than all the rest.' It was not often I had heard her blunder; she knew it herself, and came swiftly back to the theme of Arran and his weaknesses. 'The moment you, sir, have left us, he will come hurrying here, and will endeavour to find out what you have said to me, and I to you.' She summoned up her charming smile. 'When he comes, I shall, as is my custom, make as though I were not well willing to this marriage and then – he is a simple man, you understand – he will tell me his whole intent on that part. If I do not listen, he will keep himself the more covert and close and tell me nothing.'

'And Lennox?' said the bemused Sir Ralph suddenly. He had been particularly instructed to find out if this tall subtle woman intended marrying the absent Earl, or not.

Madame laughed. 'There is no truth in such rumours. Now, since I have been a King's wife, my heart is too high to look any lower.'

It was a good answer. My eyes closed for an instant, remembering the avid lecher in my bed at Caerlaverock. He had, after all, been royal. When I began to listen to them again – they still spoke in French – Madame was scotching the other rumour, the one that had said Duc Claud was to come here with an army. 'My father's army will be turned against the Emperor, not Scotland. Any certain information from France will tell you as much.'

Sir Ralph sighed, as though certain information was proving difficult to obtain from anywhere at all. They talked on for some time, by now about the baby Queen, who again slept, her breathing clear and even. 'To give her in charge of the Governor is to court certain danger,' said Madame. 'He is the next heir; what man would not take the chance to harm her? He told you, when you were with him, that she was unlikely to live; now that you have seen her, do you think he spoke truth?'

The Englishman agreed that Arran had not, and departed. We were to see him again.

As soon as he had gone Her Grace came and kissed me. 'Claudine, I have told a great many lies, and I must confess them,' she said, 'but it was only to take refuge in the further danger from the nearer. Arran dare not offend England, and if we have England's protection meantime, as long as they hope for this marriage, then we are safe for a little while. But it shall never take place; that I swear.'

She began to walk up and down in the way she had, as though the room could not contain her. 'I know who I shall see next,' she said. 'We must grasp at every straw. This man, maybe, is not of straw; they say that while others take bribes, he must be bribed more than most. Is that a good thing or not? I swear I do not know. How well she sleeps! She is growing fast.' She smoothed the baby's coverlets gently, not to disturb her, and her glance roved over me also. She said again cheerfully, 'You, my friend, are too fat.'

During the days that followed, I was somewhat diverted from my misery by the sight of the various noblemen upon whom Her Grace called to help her escape from Linlithgow and its dangers. The first was the Earl of Moray, whom I had never yet seen; few had, as he kept himself to himself, generally in his estates in the north. He was the son of Janet Kennedy, the vixen of Galloway, and James IV, whose ghost, unburied in England as he still lay, seemed to walk unceasingly. But the sober man in his forties who came, wearing the collar of St Michael about his neck, bore no likeness to what I imagined of the dead King, or of Janet either. His appearance was in no way notable, nor was his converse; although having spent part of his youth in France he was able to speak with Madame fluently, and I longed to join in the talk; but, again, I was the wet-nurse, minding the cradle.

The Queen Dowager tried to persuade him to see Governor Arran and so handle that personage with words that his changeable mind would at last permit us to go to Stirling. The Earl promised it, and might even have achieved it; but, again, Sir George Douglas, everyone's evil genius, intervened and said it must not be allowed. He was more nearly the Governor of Scotland than Arran, 'the most wavering and unstable person in the world, and the soonest altered and changed with every man's flattery or fair speech.' So were his words reported to us by Sir Ralph Sadler later, when he returned to see us. As for having the Cardinal set free, that was more than ever unlikely; even Arran refused outright.

The next nobleman interested me more than Moray had done. He was the Earl of Huntly, whom James V had loved well,

for Huntly was his nephew on the wrong side of the blanket.
James IV and Margaret Drummond had had a daughter, and
she was Huntly's mother. He was a young man with an open and
friendly face, fond of manly sports of all kinds. He at least had a
plan to suggest concerning Cardinal Beaton.

'Place him with Lord Seton, away from the Douglases, and he
will soon be free,' he said. Madame clapped her hands.

'Splendid!' Lord Seton had married Mary Pierres, her
lady-in-waiting from the early days, and was our friend; he lived
mostly at Tranent, although the imprisoned Cardinal would be
transferred, it was planned, to Seton itself. 'How is it to be
achieved?' cried Madame. 'How can anyone persuade Arran to
it?'

'Without the viper's tongue of Sir George in his ear, many
things may be accomplished. It is likely, and I shall put it to him,
that the long holding of the Cardinal at Dalkeith is unpopular
with the common folk, who would think more of Arran were he
to connive at a change of prison; one, maybe, that would lead to
freedom, which Dalkeith will not.'

'Arran said to Sir Ralph that he himself would surely go to hell
fire were he to set the Cardinal free.'

'He will maybe go there anyway,' observed young Huntly
drily.

We saw him ride away with great hopes, which this time were
not disappointed. James V had loved Huntly; from what we
heard, the young Earl swiftly made Arran love him likewise. Sir
George Douglas later called him the falsest and vilest young man
in the world, which meant that he had been successful; the
Cardinal was taken out of Dalkeith, doubtless saying farewell to
it with no regrets, and brought with an armed guard to Seton.
From then on there were growing rumours that he would soon
be set free. It was a triumph for Madame, and a triumph for
Huntly. Perhaps there would be others to follow.

The last nobleman of all was the Earl of Lennox. He arrived at
Dumbarton with French ships, and a promise of aid.

I shall have more to say about Matthew, Earl of Lennox.
Meantime we were diverted by the confusion of poor Sir Ralph,
who was duly berated by his monstrous master concerning the
Cardinal's removal to a less secure place. It was obvious that it
could not have happened without the knowledge of the

Governor; what was Arran about? Arran himself had burst out laughing when the envoy suggested that the Cardinal be sent to England, saying he had liefer go to hell. On the other hand he stated that he himself would surely go there if he were to release Beaton. 'Surely he is the greatest dissembler that ever was,' said Sir Ralph sadly. The dissembler meantime warned him that no matter how often he might visit us at Linlithgow, he would find the Queen Dowager nothing but a Frenchwoman. This was natural enough. 'They tell me he says I am both subtle and wily, with wit to work my purpose,' said Madame cheerfully. 'In that he does me, perhaps, too much honour.' But she told Sir Ralph smoothly next time he came into her presence that she was certain that, were the Cardinal freed, he would go at once into England to offer his service to the King's Majesty: a less likely situation than which could not be imagined. 'And still she labours,' muttered Arran, 'by all means she can to have the Cardinal at liberty.' Meantime the Queen Dowager persuaded England's envoy that Sir George Douglas was the wiliest and craftiest man in all Scotland; a statement with which Henry VIII could hardly quarrel, as he had entertained the Douglas brothers at his Court for years.

Meantime the Queen's plans began to bear fruit. By some means, the Cardinal was allowed to ride under escort from Seton to his own castle of St Andrews, not noticeably cast down, his bright robes flapping in the late spring wind. Once there, Lord Seton's servant disappeared mysteriously; in other words, the Prince of the Church was left to his own dignities and his freedom. I was glad for Marion Ogilvy's sake; no doubt she hurried to her lover. The King of England was furious, as was to be foreseen, and blamed Governor Arran, who swore that he would thrust a sword through his own heart if he had known of any such possibility.

One way and another, Madame and I continued merry enough; matters were easing. Also, one day soon, a rider came to Linlithgow; a tall fair man who would stand out in any crowd. He was announced to us, and to the royal baby kicking in her cradle.

It was the Earl of Lennox, whose presence meant that we were no longer such prisoners as we had been. He was the enemy of Arran.

Before I set eyes on him, and guessed at a certain two-faced quality, I had sympathy for Matthew Stewart, Earl of Lennox. As a small boy he, with his younger brother John, had been hustled out of Scotland after the murder of their father by Hamilton of Finnart, at the skirmish near Linlithgow which was to have rescued the young James V from Douglas custody, but failed. Thereafter, the two boys were reared in France, and no doubt Lennox almost thought of himself as a Frenchman after his appointment there to King François' Scots Archers of the Guard. He must have made a handsome sight in their white and gold livery, but at the time we saw him he arrived in an ordinary hauberk and mail. He bared his head repectfully, showing hair that was thick and golden. He might have been twenty-eight. Then and later, Madame was to encourage him in his allegiance by repeated half-promises to marry him; she did this to the Earl of Bothwell as well. Later she even promised to marry Lennox to the Queen. She would say anything in her battle to keep the baby girl alive, and out of England. I believe – it was after I had gone elsewhere and I did no more than hear tell of it – that there was dancing and lute-playing and much singing and mirth about the Court while Lennox and Bothwell contended for a royal bride, Bothwell meantime having divorced his own wife in order to enter the lists. He, as it happened, was the son by a previous marriage of the strangely beguiling woman who had received me at Caerlaverock Castle, so that I am glad I did not come across him. He was known everywhere as the Fair Earl.

Lennox and Governor Arran were hereditary enemies, which was why Madame had called the former home. They met in Edinburgh, quarrelled, and met again; but when Arran demanded to be recognised as heir to Scotland Lennox refused, and told the Governor to his face, in effect, that he was no more than a bastard. Later Lennox refused to render up Dumbarton Castle, on its high rock, to Arran; this on the advice of Cardinal Beaton, who had again begun to play a part in events. What the Cardinal did not then know was that Lennox kept for his own use a large sum in silver money which King François had sent across to help the Queen Dowager. That is the manner of man Matthew Stewart was. His presence in the end got us out of our prison, after two near-battles when the palace itself bristled with Arran's guns after his twitching, evasive face had briefly shown itself at Linlithgow. But in the end – perhaps one could hardly blame him – Lennox tired of promises, promises, from

Madame, with no performance; she was no Margaret Tudor. He himself had for some time been prudently courting, by letter, the Lady Margaret Douglas, Angus' daughter, who was kept at Henry VIII's Court almost as a hostage. Lennox married her much later by consent of the old King, who wanted the bridegroom's services for his planned invasion of Scotland, as the baby Queen was not forthcoming for his son, Prince Edward.

In its way, the Lennox marriage was a love-match. Margaret Douglas had been neglected and abandoned by both father and mother, though Queen Margaret had written once when her daughter was in trouble over a forbidden engagement to a Howard. Although nearly thirty by the time of the marriage, Lennox's bride was said to be beautiful, with flaxen hair. The couple lost their first child, but the second was Henry Lord Darnley, who lived, and that was a pity. But, as I say, I was far away by the time all of it happened. In the meantime, events pursued their course.

'Now that the Cardinal is freed we may hope for better things. Also, Arran's half-brother the Abbot is home from France. He has worked on that man's weak mind so much that King Henry has had to offer his bastard daughter Elizabeth to Arran's son as a bribe.'

Madame was playing with her own little daughter, who was sitting up, laughing and reaching out her hands for a coloured ball of wool tied by a thread, which the Queen Dowager held. I marvelled at the gaiety between them; a child would know nothing, but had the guns upthrusting about Linlithgow begun to fire, they could have deafened or even killed the baby with their thunder. As yet, they had not been fired; it was like Arran to fortify the palace and then leave it.

'The King of England need not trouble himself,' murmured Madame, swinging the thread in circular fashion. The baby's long fingers grasped at the gently whirling ball and pulled it. 'There, now, you have it, my lamb,' said her mother, and carefully disentangled it from the Queen of Scots' grasp; chewed or swallowed by a baby, wool is dangerous. She began her swinging and cajoling with it again; it released the anxieties within her, and entertained the baby.

'The Cardinal gathered all the clergy together at St Andrews, but they can do nothing except to agree that where Lennox supports France, Arran will support England. If either were to change, the balance would shift; in the meantime, the Scots folk do not like the late treaty. To me, it has the advantage of gaining time; to wait till my daughter is eleven years old before being sent to marry in England, and to return if Prince Edward should die childless, is reasonable, at least for the moment; and in time many things may change. But the people, as I say, do not like it at all.' The thread swung.

I thought of what I had heard, from Madame and others; the people liked the English treaty so little that they had fired a shot at Sir Ralph Sadler, which fortunately had missed him, and had broken into his garden in Edinburgh and demolished his precious archery targets, in shooting at which he had been in the way of passing much of his spare time. That was the least of it; Madame learned many things through her spies, whom she paid well and promptly and who could come and go secretly. Lately she had sent a man galloping to Cardinal Beaton, who was now in Stirling joining forces with the supporters of France, to tell him of our plight, and of Arran's guns. I guessed that as soon as he heard, Beaton would march east to Linlithgow with many horsemen, like a seasoned soldier. I had begun to admire him.

It happened. Within two days we heard the tramp of approaching men and the sound of horses. They passed by where we were, and surrounded the palace, the Cardinal's bright figure leading the rest in shining mail, with swords, with pikes; but Madame struck her hands together in despair.

'They have no guns! How can they overcome what has been made ready here? It does not matter that Arran has gone away; his lieutenants can fire if the order is given. Why did they not bring guns? Why did they not bring guns?'

'Madame, had they done so the palace would have been ruined, ourselves perhaps killed or injured, and the Queen also.'

'It is interminable. This war goes on and on; and it is not a war of fighting but of words, words and dispatches. In a day or two, you will see, the two armies – their leaders are at least acquainted – will send emissaries to one another, and argue the matter; that at least is hopeful; we must pray for it.'

We prayed, in the little oratory Madame used for her private devotions; we carried the baby there with us, for she was never left without the presence of her mother or of myself. We knelt for a long time, while there was silence beyond, and no sound within except for the baby's gurgling.

Then news came, late as such news often does. A French fleet had been sighted off the coast, there had been talk that it had come to take the Queen to France, and so Arran had taken fright and had fortified the palace; but now the fleet had gone.

Madame was right. There could be no battle, because one side had the strength and the other the artillery. Our would-be rescuers encamped outside the palace for a day or two, and there was much movement and some half-hearted skirmishing. We hardly slept, awaiting we knew not what, surrounded always by Arran's spying servants who had been in our midst for weeks; fortunately they did not all know French, and we could talk together in low voices. In some manner, the Queen Dowager kept herself informed of events outside; she knew, slightly before it happened, that the leaders were at last arranging a meeting and what the Cardinal's idea would demand. As before, the child who was Queen of Scotland was to be given in charge of four Scottish lords, which in practice meant nothing. Arran himself was to rule with the advice of a council, not that of the Earl of Angus and his brother Sir George, who were spoken of without flattery. If the Governor refused all this, he was to be forced to resign. As for the Douglases, they must absent themselves for a season from Court. This seemed a beneficial demand, but was hotly argued over; in fact, an offer was made to fight it out, which was never accepted. In some manner, possibly due to the unsleeping wiles of the Cardinal, all was sudden friendship. Everyone shook hands, embraced, and talked together, even Angus and Beaton. Possibly the old Earl was in a good humour; his new wife Margaret was pregnant, and he hoped for a son.

My own pregnancy troubled me increasingly, not that I was in ill health with it; but I knew I was almost at term. There seemed no alternative to my being forced to give birth to James V's child in his widow's palace, for I could not escape from it. To myself I seemed huge, but Madame had noticed nothing; possibly she was too greatly preoccupied with present events. I found her one day standing by her child, who had been fed lately from a bottle, having been weaned. Madame's tilted eyes brooded and seemed dark; her mouth was pursed with reflection.

'There should be relief for us, but is it so?' she said. 'Lord

Glencairn is riding here, to dismiss Arran's men. I am thankful for that, at least; but Glencairn himself is not to be trusted any more than the rest. He was taken at Solway, released on payment of a large ransom and a promise to make King Henry Protector of Scotland and to promote the English marriage, as they all were. They tell me also that Glencairn said he would guide an invading English army from Carlisle to Glasgow without harm. How can I trust such a man?'

'Madame, it is that or nothing. At least we will be able to leave, and go to Stirling, where you may then make all safe.'

'It seems so,' she said, 'but on every step of the journey I shall look for betrayal. Henry of England is demanding my separation from my daughter. You will be with me in the litter, Claudine; carry the Queen.'

So it was that I carried Mary, Queen of Scots home to the ancient capital of her ancestors, her warm and tiny bulk resting against my heavily pregnant body and hiding it. It was late July, and the curtains were drawn back; all along the way the common folk lined the roads to cheer the Queen and her mother, released from an imprisonment lasting almost eight months. I let the baby be seen, holding her up a little from time to time; she was her customary placid self, her cheeks a little rounded in the small oval face, her eyes bright and as always seeming narrow, like her father's. I reflected how strange it was that I should be here, carrying the King's daughter in my arms and the King's bastard in my womb.

As to that, disaster struck when we reached Stirling at last, and were borne up the great slope to the Castle, where James V had ridden to free himself from the Douglases long ago. When we had crossed the drawbridge away from the milling people with their shouts of joy, I had to climb out of the litter immediately after Her Grace, who had taken the baby. She had turned, smiling, to watch me come before being greeted by those who waited from within the castle; and I caught my gown on one of the points of the gilt fleurs-de-lys which studded the poles. It was pulled back sharply, revealing my pregnant belly. I could hardly hope that Madame had not noticed: but matters proceeded as usual until we were inside, alone in our own rooms, and the twenty-four horses bearing our great beds had been unloaded, also the baby's cradle, the larder from Linlithgow, the baker's stuff, the pots and pans, the wine cellar and all the rest we had sent ahead the earlier time Arran had forbidden us to follow.

I waited, eyes downcast; I knew I must submit to whatever came. I heard her speak, but I could not look at her. Her voice was even.

'Claudine, you are going to have a child. Who is its father?'

I raised my eyes then. They were full of tears. The tears spilled down my cheeks and on to the bodice of the gown which had briefly betrayed me. I stood silent, weeping still, for there was nothing I could say concerning a man lying dead in his tomb. One does not discredit the dead. I could never describe to Madame Marie what had happened at Caerlaverock.

She understood, however. The two bright patches of rare anger flared in her cheeks, and the Guise hauteur chilled me.

'You will leave here at once,' she said. 'You will no longer be in my company or in that of my daughter. The disaster of Solway Moss was due to you and none other; in the King's absence they would not obey a lesser commander. Nobody could understand why he himself was not with the army. While you were in dalliance with him, Scotland was lost.'

'Madame –'

'Do not speak to me. You may stay here tonight, for I have no wish to be hard on you after the long journey; but you will sleep elsewhere. Tomorrow you will take what money is owing to you, and your gear, and go. There are lodging-houses; there are inns. I recommend you to return to Vouvray when you can: you have your jointure to maintain you. Possibly you will find the steward more to your taste now than formerly. Without doubt you encouraged him also. I have been mistaken in you from the beginning, and I do not want to see your face again; my mother was right about you from the beginning. Now go.'

Madame Marie was not a cruel woman. She would not have sent me out into the town looking for a lodging in my state had she herself had experience of finding lodgings, even in France; and France is not Scotland. As it chanced, Stirling was crowded with people anxious to see the little Queen pass by, with word of her crowning soon; and having seen her pass, they went to make merry with drink because her imprisonment was ended, and because, in any case, the Scots drink deep. The long street was noisy with songs and bagpipes, thronged with beggars, riff-raff and pickpockets, as I realised too late. I had hired a boy to cart my small baggage, not knowing where I was to go; he walked behind me, while I tried first the inns, which would not take me because they were already full, then lodging-houses. These were often dirty, and my experience of them was summed up by the sight of one woman in a grey linen apron, with greasy hair straggling beneath her cap, who opened the door. She looked me up and down, saw my state, and said belligerently, 'Where's your man?'

I said that he was elsewhere; this was true enough. 'Ye'll pay afore ye come in,' said the woman, and I reached for my purse, only to realise that it had been cut and emptied on my journey down the street. I had no money at all.

'I have been robbed,' I stammered. 'I will pay you as soon as I can.' I was sure, even now, that the Queen Dowager would meet my expenses till I could reimburse her; this accident she could not have foreseen. But the woman, with a coarse gesture, spat.

'Like enough,' she said. 'The likes o' you can mak' mair; awa' wi' ye.' She shut the door in my face. I turned, my knees almost giving; and saw that the urchin with all my gear had vanished in the crowd, knowing he would not be paid. I had nothing, neither money, goods, nor a friend. I was forsaken. I did not know what to do. I could not go back to the Castle with my abject tale; nor could I go further down the muck-littered street. I stood there, helplessly; and said a prayer.

Prayers are answered, often very quickly. Along the street, towering above the milling folk, came a tremendous creature in a round bonnet with an eagle's feather. I could not believe my eyes, and ran forward, crying aloud, elbowing my way between the crowds which separated us.

'Alasdair Dorch! Alasdair Dorch Gregarach!'

I reached him at last, and cast myself against his hard, muscular body; I could feel its substance through the plaid. I was sobbing, while all about me they were laughing and jeering; a wanton had called for a man, and got one; they cast epithets at me, but Alasdair quelled them with a look and they fell silent. He had put an arm about me for support, for without it I would surely have fallen. His mouth was grim; dishevelled as I was, he saw my state.

'*Leatromach*,' he said gently, and laid a hand on my belly. 'Why are you alone?'

I did not learn, till after we were married, the full story of what

had befallen Alasdair Dorch after the defeat of the Scots at
Solway Moss. He had fought valiantly, unlike many who turned
and retreated, or else gave themselves up; and would no doubt
have been killed except for his notable size, which attracted the
attention of the English commander and caused Alasdair to be
pinioned by the arms – it took four men – and taken south with
the rest. Once there, he was put with certain others in charge of
the Duke of Norfolk. This was the uncle of Queen Katherine
Howard and the kinsman of Anne Boleyn, who had seen both
his female relatives perish on the scaffold while contriving to
remain a trusted servant of the English King. To divert his
master, therefore, Norfolk did not demand a ransom for the
return to Scotland of Alasdair Dorch, nor did he try to extract
the promises from him which the rest gave. 'They knew well
enough they would get none from me,' said my husband. 'When
they asked me, I told them so.'

He was escorted at last into the presence of Henry VIII in
London, who stared in amazement at a man the size he was
himself; possibly he had not seen such a one since the time long
ago of the Field of the Cloth of Gold, when he and King
François had measured up to one another and the King of
France had thrown his rival at wrestling, but King Henry did not
like to have that remembered. 'He came and felt the muscles of
my arms,' said Alasdair. 'He is an old man with a white beard,
and has an ulcer on his leg. This means that he cannot ride as he
used to, and he will not take to a litter. He would stump about
the palace with myself by him, and wish he was on a horse so that
I might run by it in the way I do. I pretended to understand less
of their language than I did. At times he would play his lute,
with myself and his *cleasaiche*, his jester, Will Somers, standing
by. His Queen is a sad soul. It will be a hard life for her when she
remembers what happened to the other five.'

'How did you escape?' I asked. I was eating an apple he had
bought me in Stirling; we always seemed to be buying apples
there. For the time, I was in no great discomfort, although the
pony he had hired for me to ride did nothing to ease me. In fact
the child was born sooner than it ought to have been, for this
reason, a little later; but meantime we travelled pleasantly
enough through the forest, with Alasdair leading my rein.

'I bided my time, and waited till he chose after all to ride, for
he loved to hunt, and would not admit that he was too old and

lame. He went into Oxfordshire, and I dived into a river from his
horse's side, and swam across it behind the shelter of some
willows. There was nothing he could do about pursuing me,
except shout in his squeaky voice: and there was nobody to hear
him, for he had left his gentlemen far behind, even being crippled as he was. After that I hid myself till they had gone, and
made my way north by night: and then a strange thing happened.
There are folk in England who live always in the dark, and are not
seen by day at all. They are the ones King Henry has been after at
one time and another, and if they were found he would hang
them or else cut their heads off, as he has done to so many. Some
are for the Faith –' he crossed himself – 'and they give or receive
the Sacraments in secret, for the King killed his saintly bishop,
and the Carthusian monks, and any who disagreed with him in
the way of religion. Others were from families he had decided to
wipe out, like the Poles and the Buckinghams; it is not known that
members of them are still alive. They have banded together, and
know one another by a sign when they meet; and by good chance I
fell in with them, and they sheltered me and set me on my way,
handing me from one to the other all up the length of England, so
that the King's men could never find me. And so in the end I
crossed the Border, and here I am.'

'Have you money?' I asked him, adding, 'I have none. It was
stolen from me, but there will be more sent from France when
they know where I have gone.'

'They gave me money which I will return later. You yourself
will be in a *bothan* in the Grant country, or else at Glenorchy. It
will not be grand living such as you are used with.' The expression
of his face seldom changed, but he looked for an instant like a
rueful little boy. I put my hand across in the saddle and touched
his cheek.

'I was more thankful to see you come up the street than I have
been for anyone in the whole of my life. I am proud that you have
married me, being as I am.'

'I will guard and bring up the King's son as my own,' he
promised, for I had told him of the child's father, though not
everything.

We had been married in the Church of the Black Friars of
Stirling, where I had sat in some apprehension while Alasdair
went to find the priest. I stared at a painted recumbent effigy by

the wall; it was that of a man with yellow hair and beard. After we had taken our vows I asked the priest who he was. He cast down his eyes, not approving of me very greatly; heavily pregnant women do not make suitable brides. He thought, no doubt, that the child was Alasdair's, and probably considered us a wild pair.

'That, they say, is Richard the Second of England, who is reputed to have been murdered at Pontefract Castle, but others say he escaped, and became the jester of the Lord of the Isles, and after many years died in prison here, and was buried. Nobody will ever know the truth of the tale. I wish you good fortune; God go with you.' He turned away, glad no doubt to be rid of me.

I told Alasdair of it, and he had already heard of the story; he had heard of most things of that nature. However, he was not particularly interested in it for the time; he was looking at me.

'It is God, no less, who has brought us together,' he said. 'I have known that you were the woman for me ever since I saw you walking towards me by the running river, with the white goat by you.'

I was assailed by fear, for the thought of lovemaking in the state I was in wearied and frightened me; but I need not have troubled myself. Neither then nor later on our journey did Alasdair touch me, sleeping a little way off in the trees at night while I lay down alone, and wrapping me first in his great plaid so that I would be warm. He himself never seemed to feel the cold. The hidden men's money – the English would have given some to him, with the rest of the prisoners, and the offer of a horse which he would not take either, although he admitted later he could have sold that – had bought us provisions in Stirling, and he made up his drammoch between the pony's shoulder-blades as before. Altogether I almost felt as if I was coming home; except that with the jolting, my labour pains came on in the middle of the forest, a shameful flood of water soaking the pony's flanks to begin with, and afterwards much straining and groaning in the shelter of the trees.

Alasdair proved better than any midwife; he knew exactly what to do. He told me afterwards that he had never before helped bring a human baby, but had calved a cow and a mare, also a pig. The comparison was perhaps not flattering, but my own sounds

resembled a sow in farrow; I could hear them myself, and hardly
knew the tearing agony as belonging to the woman I had so
often seen; I was beyond myself, hearing the crying grunting
creature I had now become, and feeling Alasdair's great
leather-hard hands solacing me. At last, after many hours, the
head came down, and it had red hair; and he pressed on it, as
midwives do, and presently brought out a boy, a month
premature with having been shaken down in the saddle.
Alasdair laid him by me, wrapped in a corner of the plaid; he
had already cleaned the mouth and nose with his shirt-sleeve,
and I could see the resulting stain on the linen, which would not
come out if it were left to dry. 'Go and find water for your shirt,'
I said weakly. He tucked the plaid more comfortably about me,
and went away. 'I will be finding water for yourself,' he called
back, and I knew I would be glad of it; meantime, still lying
where he had left me, I looked at King James's son.

A certain likeness struck me at once. I had seen the splendid
little prince to whom Madame Marie had first given birth after
she came as a bride to Scotland. This child was the image of
Prince James, Duke of Rothesay, who had died at a year old. I do
not know if a plan was born in my mind then; but I know I felt,
from that time, that I had not after all severed every link with
my Queen Dowager; that there was hope in that way for me yet.

I have never known any man as resourceful as Alasdair Dorch
Gregarach. For some days after the birth I was too weak to ride,
and our provisions from Stirling became exhausted except for
his drammoch. I could not stomach that, although I was very
hungry by now, nursing the baby with my breasts full of milk.
Accordingly Alasdair would disappear for long periods,
standing for hours in a burn with his hands cradled under the
stones, catching young trout, which he hit on the head with
another stone, and when he had caught enough brought them
back, lit a fire by rubbing sticks together, and cooked the fish, so
that we ate them with our fingers, without salt. On other days he
would stalk the little roe deer, as here were none of the larger as
yet in our part of the forest. I was sad when I saw him carrying
the first, like a small dead dog, holding it by the legs, and he was
regretful at once.

'I did not mean to hurt you,' he said. 'I will take her and
gralloch her out of your sight,' and he did so, returning with the

venison cut up into steaks with his knife, and turning it over the fire, which by then I was able to tend with fallen wood, keeping it lit all day. I will say the flesh made good eating. He said himself that he did not like killing the little *fiadh*, but it was a question of ourselves and whether we starved or not. 'It will not be long now before you are drinking the white goat's milk,' he said gravely.

'Annabella? Is she well?' I felt as though she were a person. He nodded. 'I have not seen her since I left with yourself, but had she not been well I would have known it,' he told me, and I realised, as I should have done earlier, that he had his share of the Sight and that there was nothing I could not ask him. Nor was there anything I could hide from him; I left a good deal unsaid, but the small dark eyes were shrewd, and I was certain he knew far more than I had told him. However it might otherwise have been stupid of me to ask about the goat; he could not possibly know in the ordinary way of things, for the last I had seen of him had been with the rain running down his face at Caerlaverock Castle, when Lady Maxwell would not let him in, and he had travelled on alone to Solway Moss.

As far as that went, I had thought of a name for the baby. I did not want to call him James, for the name had unpleasant memories for me; nor would I call him Alasdair. The Grants, when we returned, would undoubtedly take him for Alasdair's child, as we had both of us been away for so long; and I had the feeling that to name the boy after a man not his father was both unfair and unlucky. I had thought, and remembered my first husband, Jean de Vouvray. He had been kind to me, as far as he might; I had borne him no son; and in his memory I decided that I would call the boy Jean. When I spoke of it to Alasdair he said at once that that was a girl's name.

'It is French,' I said, laughing. His expression grew strict.

'We have no Frenchmen at Freuchie. If you will be calling him John, like the beloved apostle, the folk here will call him Iain Ruadh, because of his red hair. That will mean that he is at home, and not a stranger.' So Iain Ruadh it was.

One thing more I remember about those days, which were strangely happy, though midges troubled me – they did not bite Alasdair Dorch – and I had a constant task to keep them from the baby. 'Stay near the smoke,' said my husband, who had a remedy for everything. He himself was busy with an object I did

not at first recognise, made out of the bones of one of the deer
he had slain. I was unkempt, for the boy who ran away with all
my gear at Stirling had taken my comb, which was among it; and
as far as I might do so I had had to comb my long hair with my
fingers. Now, Alasdair brought me a comb he had made, most
beautifully shaped and slotted out of the resistant bone. It was
far better than the one I had lost. He called it a *cír*. I flushed with
pleasure, reached up and kissed him on the cheek.

'You are kind to me,' I said. 'I will try to make you a good
wife.'

It was not so easy as it might have been with the Grants. Of
course the women gossiped; the sight of me arriving back, after
so long an absence, and Alasdair likewise, with a baby between
us, made them certain that he had not been in England at all, but
sojourning with me in some love-nest. They might have known
him better, and James of the Forays did; often enough he would
come to our *bothan* and sit outside it on a bench my husband had
made, while I busied myself about the tasks to be done, which
were new to me but with which Alasdair at the beginning helped
me greatly. However old Lady Grant would not acknowledge
me, and stared in a haughty manner through me if we chanced
to meet, which we did not often. No doubt an Ogilvy of
Deskford could afford to look down on one who had married a
common clansman, even though he was a MacGregor. I had lost
my standing, not a doubt of it; but Christian Grant, the chief's
wife, was kinder. The day after we had arrived at Freuchie a
young maidservant came to the door, leading the white goat.
Lady Grant had said I was to have her; it was a marriage gift.
'She has been mated,' said the girl. One would not have known,
to look at Annabella, that she was in kid; she appeared the same
as usual, and once free of her rope stayed near me, and bleated
with pleasure whenever she saw me from afar off. There was
one order from the great house which disturbed me; if the kid
proved a billy, it was to be destroyed. More than one in the herd
would make for fighting.

I did not know when Annabella's kid was to be expected, but
one day she went to the back of the *bothan*, without fuss, and
next day I found her there with an enchanting white baby,
wagging its short tail and sucking at her. I thought it was a
female, and was glad, but in a little while I saw an arc of urine

come out of its middle. Alasdair was hunting, and I did not tell him; but he asked about it later.

'Do not take him away from her,' I begged. 'They are happy.' I recalled the kid's contented draining of her milk; it reminded me of Iain Ruadh and myself. I was carrying him in a fold of my *breacan* that I wore by then, and he was growing heavy.

Alasdair said nothing, but he fetched a wooden tub we used for washing and filled it with water from the river. I did not long watch what happened next, but he took the kid, put its head in the water and a flat piece of wood over its neck, then sat on the wood. It was not many seconds till it drowned, and its body grew limp like the roe deer's had been. I would not cook or eat the flesh, and Alasdair took it to the couple in the near bothy, who were glad of it.

Annabella was never quite the same again; I know she felt that I had betrayed her trust. She let me milk her, and did her duty in this way for a long time; then one day I went to look for her behind the *bothan* where she was tethered, and found her lying dead, of what cause I do not know. I am glad to say Alasdair did not make us eat her; he buried her for me. By that time a great many other things had happened, both north and south.

Am Grantach had more than begun to earn his name of James of the Forays, and it is a wonder that we ourselves did not meet him on our journey, for he had ridden down, with a great party of men, to sign a bond with Cardinal Beaton on behalf of the Queen Dowager and against her enemies. The chief one of these was England, for Arran was now in so wavering a state that he could hardly be feared on his own account, though Henry VIII still sent him offers of the hand of Anne Boleyn's daughter Elizabeth for his son. All this Am Grantach told us on our bench, as the summer days lengthened into autumn and the whisky stills bubbled slowly in the bothans. The two men would sit with quaichs of it in their hands, as I still did not drink it. When my tasks were done I would come and listen to Am Grantach's quiet voice; I was beginning to pick up the Gaelic from speaking it with Alasdair.

'The lords who were to have custody of the Queen's Grace came to Stirling to carry her off, but they never managed it. The Dowager took their baggage and they could not get away.' There was laughter, in which I joined; Madame Marie was resourceful in such ways. 'My lord Erskine, who is her friend, keeps the keys, and none will pass him; and in any case the castle is hers. The old King of England sends orders that mother and daughter are to be separated, but that is what he tried with his first wife when she would not do as he said.'

He downed his whisky, and held out a wrist for more. I poured it from a jug, and listened. Madame had sent an urgent message to Huntly saying she feared Stirling Castle might be besieged by the Governor; Huntly had assured her that should that happen, he and Lennox would route Arran's force. Sir Ralph Sadler had been summoned again, and reassured of Madame's eagerness for the English marriage. I wondered how long she would keep that pretence up. In the meantime, Arran's half-brother the Abbot of Paisley, Beaton's good friend, was working on the weak member of the family, and King Henry made a fool of himself for once in a letter. 'He offered Arran kingship of all the lands north of the Forth, but Arran owns far better land already south of it,' grinned James of the Forays. His grin vanished swiftly. 'No man can trust Arran,' he said. 'He was at High Mass in Holyrood, celebrating the English treaty the Scots do not want. They had music at it, they say.'

'Was the Cardinal there?' I asked, and Am Grantach looked at me as if he realised for the first time that a woman could have a mind.

'No, he was not,' he replied. 'The Cardinal is very careful where he is seen, and with whom. He would not receive the Governor when Arran rode to St Andrews to him.'

Later we heard that Arran had quietly left the capital, saying his wife Margaret was ill in childbed. He went from her to Falkirk, where the Cardinal did see him privately. 'There were friendly embracings, they are saying,' remarked Alasdair. 'These are changed times.'

Times were changed indeed. Publicly, the Cardinal and the Governor rode side by side, with a train of men, to Stirling. I wished that I had been present to see their reception by Madame. Further, the repentant Governor was made to swallow both his words and his actions; he did open penance in the very Black Friars where Alasdair and I had been married, and where I had seen the effigy of the yellow-haired man who might have been a king. Cardinal Beaton gave absolution to the Governor of Scotland who had been importing Bibles and English

Testaments at the behest of King Henry; then the Fair Earl and the Earl of Argyll assisted Arran at Mass, which he heard kneeling, at last receiving the Sacrament he had so often betrayed.

Next day was the Queen's coronation, and the baby wore a cap and wide ruff. The repentant Arran carried the crown of Scots gold to place upon the tiny head; Lennox bore the sceptre, Argyll the sword of state. Her Grace cried throughout; perhaps my lords saluted her roughly. There was dancing afterwards, plays before the Queen, who must have been sleepy by then; a banquet, and much merrymaking, with the fool Senat, who had never left Madame, and her little dwarf Jane, still about her.

I looked at my son's red hair, and thought how but for him I would have been among them; but I must remember that I had a good husband here, and was well treated.

We seldom went up to the great house of Freuchie except for Mass on Sundays, and the feast of Christmas, or if anyone killed a king salmon. When that happened it was cooked in a silver fish-kettle old Lady Grant had brought with her from Deskford on her marriage. My son was three years old when Alasdair killed one, a great beauty weighing more than twenty pounds. We took it proudly up, Iain Ruadh toddling sturdily alongside by himself; he had grown strong on the good Spey food and the milk of poor Annabella. When we reached the house he clung to my skirts; he had been told to behave respectfully while there.

The hall was full, and the salmon much exclaimed over; I looked up, and beheld old Lady Grant, whom I had not seen close at hand since my return after my marriage, nor had we spoken. Contrary to her custom, she paused; but there was no friendship in her eyes as she looked down at Iain Ruadh.

'That is the King's son,' she said in a low voice, in French. 'I was with the Queen in St Andrews, and I saw the young prince as often as anyone. Can Alasdair Dorch not get sons of his own? See you to it.'

I was as red as fire, and as she moved away I spat at her, 'They call you the *cailleach* here, and they are right. Do not address me so again.' I was no longer the humble clansman's wife, but as good as she was. She turned her shoulder, and I knew I had made an enemy; but in any case she had been no friend since my first coming.

I sat with my son in a corner, and we ate our share of the salmon. As we were going home I said a thing to Alasdair that should have been said long before.

'It is time that I bore you a son of your own, with the blood of the Gregarach in him.'

In all the years of our marriage he had never touched me. He had grudged me nothing, only helping me with the work, with rearing the boy, collecting eggs from the chickens, preparing meat, taking washing to the river. He had treated me like a queen, and I had given nothing in return. At nights, I slept on a bed of heather stems, which was comfortable, by myself; Alasdair slept on the earth floor near the door of the bothan. I had once asked him if he would not share my bed, for the comfort of it; but he shook his great head.

'I can sleep anywhere,' he replied. 'I can sleep on stone.'

The matter had not arisen again between us except that I knew the other wives bore children yearly and would have thought it a reflection on the strength of their men had they not. I had let Alasdair endure all this, and knew it; and knew why. I was afraid. I had been raped by two men, and wanted my body to myself. But out of gratitude for his devotion, and after the old *cailleach*'s taunt, I must give Alasdair what he had never demanded, never used force or persuasion to obtain. Now, when I said what I said that day on the path, I saw a deep flush spread over his face and neck; he smiled a little, and kept silence.

That night – it was to happen on all our nights together – he threw away the old heather bed, cut fresh shoots, brought them in and laid them. I put Iain Ruadh to bed, and once he was aleep undressed myself. I felt shyness overcome me, as if I were a new bride naked; I covered my body with my long hair. When he came in, it was dark; I heard his movements as he took off his plaid and shirt, sensed the warmth of his great body as he came near me. My heart was beating with fright, and he must have sensed it; in the darkness, I heard him say, 'Do not be afraid. *Tha gaol agam ort*,' which means 'I love you.'

He lay down, and gently took me in his arms. I have never known anyone so strong and yet so gentle. It was as though he held back nine-tenths of his strength because of my fear, and even so I was crying already, the tears spilling out of my shut eyes, and making sounds women make who are in sorrow, not joy. It troubled him, and he tried to soothe me, but presently I sobbed aloud; and in the end, being a man, he did as men do, and entered me fully, then murmured to me in his own tongue as we lay, made one flesh at last. I had stopped trembling, but was not yet willing, not glad; I made him a shabby bride that night, and the other nights, and he was very patient with me. 'They have not been kind to you,' he said once, and I knew that he understood. At least I could answer that.

'You yourself are kind. You have been kind from the beginning. Take me when you will. Do not heed my folly.'

'Then I will not.'

It took me four months to conceive his child. Had I been eager, it would have happened sooner.

I could not complain of neglect by the castle of Freuchie, or most of the great folk there, as my child came to be born. Christian Grant herself, the laird's wife, ministered to all the women of the clan, seeing to their wants as Madame Marie had done long ago to her poor folk at Châteaudun while she had leisure, and would have done the same for the Scots had they let her; as it was, she had contrived a little even there, calling at poor houses with comforts when she could, in Stirling and Edinburgh. I remembered her while Christian's gentle hands helped me with the birth; by now, she had much experience, as well as children of her own. Christiania did not visit me all through my pregnancy or after; possibly her old tyrant of a mother had forbidden her, or maybe Christiania still envied me Alasdair. I was sorry for it, as I would have liked to make a friend of her; in a way, we had been kindred spirits.

The labour was short and easy this time, the child, to my relief, small; but it was a girl, and I feared Alasdair would be disappointed. However he came in when he was let do so, his great bulk blocking the light from the door of the bothan, and came straight to me, kneeling down to ask how I was, and if I felt rested now. Then he saw the baby, like himself dark of skin and hair. A smile like that of a delighted child broke out on his face. '*Leanabh beag*, little one,' he said softly, and almost fearfully touched her with his great hand. 'Hold her,' I said, laughing. 'She will not break.' But he would not lift her up then, though in a day or two he began to do so, and would also watch shyly while I fed her at the breast. I think he was happier and less solitary than he had ever been in his life, although he was a man who by nature craved solitude.

I called the child Mhairi, which is the Gaelic form of the Queen Dowager's name and the Queen's. When Mhairi's eyes opened they were water-green, like mine. It made for a curious enchantment in the darkness of her face.

That was the birth, and after that our life went on as it had done, but with more joy for a while. Am Grantach came almost daily and had his dram with us, and ruffled the red hair of Iain Ruadh, who was growing fast but would never be very tall. Mhairi, I thought, would outstrip him in the end; she had her father's height to grow to, and the tall legend of the Guises. She would be a formidable woman, a true MacGregor. She showed signs of having a mind of her own before she could walk. Alasdair loved her; in ways, more than he would ever love me. She was a part of him, his true flesh. Maybe he remembered being a lonely boy brought up by a friendly enough clan not his own. I do not know; we did not speak of it; I watched, and was happy for him, and got on with my tasks; having two children to care for left me with little time. I knew I was becoming like the other women of the clan, occupied solely with their men and their children, and their prayers. Now and again, this made me discontented within myself. I liked to be at the centre of affairs, and was so no longer. No doubt this accounted for what happened afterwards. I was, as they say, a fool for myself; I should have known when I was fortunate.

Iain Ruadh was growing in other ways than in his body. He already spoke French as well as the Gaelic, for I taught it to him myself. In many ways the languages are similar, for there had been an exchange of words and terms in the days of the Lords of the Isles and their courts, which were famous, and much visited. Iain observed things out of his narrow eyes; he was never talkative. This led to an episode I cannot forget. More than a year after the birth of Mhairi, when she was well past weaning, Alasdair tried to have a son by me. He would cut new heather shoots and I would know that the begetting would be attempted that night, and would prepare myself. I still wept, like a fool, when he used me as his wife, although he had every right to do so and had no doubt accustomed himself by now to my tears. He was never hard on me, as most men would have been in such a case; but he wanted his son. That night, as always, I had put the children in their corner to sleep, but it was summer and not dark. Alasdair came and lay with me on our heather bed, his great bulk on top of mine, his buttocks duly jerking; and the tears ran as usual down my cheeks. All of a sudden a voice piped up from the trodden earth floor; Iain Ruadh stood there in his own nakedness, watching us.

'*Tha mathaír*, what is it that he is doing to you?'

His narrow eyes missed nothing; he might have witnessed everything for some time. Alasdair rose from me, went straight to the boy, bent him over and gave him three smart blows on his backside; the child began howling.

'Go back to your bed, and stay there.'

It was the only time I had ever seen Alasdair angry with any of us. He returned, and I expected him to enter me again; but he turned over on his back and slept. I stayed awake, and for the first time was aware of resentment against my husband. My son was the son of a king, and he was being reared like a kern. He would grow up to be no more than another of the clansmen, living in a bothan, drinking whisky, maybe driving cattle south or running behind his chief in time of war. By rights he should be at Court, like James V's other bastards who had been given Church preferments and a fat living. I myself had been neglectful, too greatly taken up with my own affairs. I must do more for my son.

For whatever reason, I did not conceive another to Alasdair Dorch; possibly had he forced me harder I might have done so. He always considered me before himself, however, and had I done the same for him it would have been better for us both. He was never angry with my boy again, except once, and that anger was terrible, and he was angry then also with me.

When I have a thought it does not cease to trouble me, and gives me no peace till I have carried out some plan. It was not long before I was walking up to the castle, my children with me, to ask for pen, ink and paper to write to Her Grace. Alasdair knew nothing of it; he was out on the hill, which was why I had chosen the time to come. I thought that I would wait for Madame's reply before putting the matter to him at all; perhaps none would come, in which case no harm would have been done by anybody.

Christiania was at her wheel, and dared to stop to take Mhairi on her lap; surely, I thought, the old woman would not mind that, if she came down; she kept mostly to her room nowadays with rheumatism. I saw Christiania smooth the baby's dark hair, and the thought crossed my mind that, extravagant or not, she would have made a better wife to Alasdair Dorch than I did. I remembered also that I had not had the leisure, with the events that had taken place one way and another, to buy her a silver brooch in Edinburgh as I had planned. If Madame answered, and agreed to let me visit her with Iain Ruadh, I would send one then. Perhaps Christiania would look after the baby.

At Freuchie, 2nd May, 1545

Madame,
   I dare to write after so long, in the hope that you are not still angry. I would like you to see my son. He is the image of Prince James, who died at St Andrews. He has red hair, and the Stewart features, and is forward for his age. I think that you would love him. He is being reared here as the sons of clansmen are, and will be no more than a cattle-drover and fighter if matters continue so. I would like him to be at court, if you will have him there (after all, as I did not add, there were the others).
   I myself am married, to a good man, a MacGregor. He looks after me very well and we have a small daughter. I have called her after Your Grace and the Queen. I hope Her Grace fares well; we hear little here, and not till long after it has happened.
   May God be with you, and if you do not want to see me or my son, pray remember the times we knew in France.
   Your ever loving and loyal half-sister,
                    Claudine de Vouvray.

After the letter had gone off I wondered if I had been forward. No reply came for many weeks, and I had ceased to expect one, but in the end it was brought; and, this time, it bore the Cross of Lorraine and the green wax seals. This heartened me; Madame was not writing as the Queen Dowager, but as my dear sister who shared our proud Guise blood. I tore open the letter; Alasdair was playing with his daughter, whom he adored and used to carry on his shoulders, and later lead about on a pony.

At Stirling. 3rd August.

To Madame MacGregor,

My dearest Claudine,

   I was heartened to have your letter and to hear how you fare. Certainly I was angry, as you say; but anger does not last, and so many worse things have happened.

   I should be glad to see your son, who you say resembles mine. His tomb, and that of his little brother and also my husband, were destroyed and the Abbey burned by the English the year before last. There has been much other burning of towns, and destruction of the poor folks' crops everywhere; also treachery in council, some of whom will forever pretend to aid me while still taking money from England. I can tell you more when you come.

   Do not come yet. Matters here are unsettled, to say the least, and it is not safe to travel anywhere, so I bide in my Castle; even priests go about with a coat of mail and pikes. I am fortunate in having friends new come from France, who aid me truly; but my lords do not like that; you know the Scots.

   When you hear that the land is at peace, come. I will welcome you with joy, and your son and daughter, and your husband also; I heard how he fought at Solway, and made his way back from England. Such men are rare, and the Queen can use their service.

   Your ever loving friend and sister,
                                        Marie R.

I wondered how she had learned of Alasdair Dorch, or knew that he was my husband; but James of the Forays had been south again, and sooner or later the Queen Dowager heard everything.

I have said that Alasdair worshipped his small daughter. As Mhairi grew, he was to be seen more and more with her in his company, on the pony as often as walking. She was a child of courage, afraid of nothing, neither animals nor water; she loved to splash and paddle in the Spey, held by her father, while I trod the washed linen a little way off. Iain was quieter, and did not laugh so much; he generally stayed by me. I hoped that when he was older Alasdair would take him out stalking, and teach him to shoot and use a sword and targe. But meantime it was Mhairi, Mhairi; it was almost as though she had replaced me in Alasdair's love now that I had been a useless wife to him and had moreover borne him no son. At any rate, it was pleasant to watch him happy with his child, his big dark face content, his hands ready to catch her before she fell, for she darted about like quicksilver as soon as she could walk. Everyone loved her; Am Grantach would take her on his knee when he came to drink our whisky and talk of the affairs of the day, and Mhairi had been taught to bide still for once while the chief held her. Her green eyes would dance, however, as though all the movement of her body had been poured into them for the time. I do not know what I myself felt about her; all my pride was for Iain, and no doubt I thought of my daughter as only belonging to her father.

When she was three years old the tragedy happened. Am Grantach was with us, and was telling us as much as he knew of the terrible burnings and destruction in Scotland. I was with the men, seated listening, because after Madame Marie's letter I wanted to know more. The children had wandered off together, Iain leading his little sister by the hand. 'Look after her,' I called, but he did not turn his head, and they went together out of sight.

Am Grantach proffered his wrist again for another dram, and I reflected that our whisky must be better than his own. Alasdair Dorch used a recipe that his own folk had given him in Glenorchy, and none of the Grants had it. The laird was speaking about the unrest in Edinburgh, where he had lately been.

'It is better now, but they say five or six thousand men were out in the streets, swearing to destroy every monastery and convent in four days,' he said. 'That is the fault of the English, and of Arran; they have spoilt many of the folk by now with their Bibles and the new religion. But the Queen's Frenchmen came, and they were dissuaded.' He did not say how.

'What of Arran?' I asked, remembering that personage from Linlithgow. 'How long will they suffer him as Governor? Her Grace would be far wiser than he.'

'Maybe, but they will not suffer a woman,' said James of the Forays gently. 'To be sure it is time they hanged Arran; he has spent, they say, all the King's money, and that was a vast deal, for the King was careful.'

I thought how Madame Marie could have used the money.

'Lesser men would have been hanged for less,' I said, then realised that I was talking too much; if I was suffered to remain, I must be silent.

'The English envoy, Sadler, has left for England, vowing he will never return. They say the treaty with England will itself be torn up, because their old King seized our Scots ships at sea. Myself, I think that if they would not harm our Queen, and take the land for themselves, the godly marriage, as some call it, would be a good one; but a child can die easily.'

Those words should have been a knell. I took no heed of them, but went on listening to him speak of Madame and of how she had walked again to the shrine at Loretto, as she had done before the little Queen's birth, and prayed there the space of twenty days for peace between England and Scotland. 'If prayer can accomplish anything, she will surely have her way,' said James of the Forays. 'But the Earl of Angus, he who was married to the old Queen before, was angry, and set up an army against the Cardinal, but they all ran away. Then the Governor, and you will hardly believe this when you hear it, said he would divorce his wife, who is maybe daft like her sister, and marry the Queen Dowager.'

We laughed immoderately at this, even Alasdair's face splitting into a wide grin; then we heard of the Cardinal and Arran marching west to besiege Glasgow Castle, to try to capture Lennox who was supposed to be inside; and of how Arran had bribed the garrison to surrender and then when they came out, hanged all twenty-eight of them. 'As for Lennox, they never took him,' said Am Grantach. 'He is a fox, and is long ago in England. All of this news is old.'

It was at that moment that I heard a child cry out. Alasdair turned his head.

'You should go to them,' he said to me. 'They are maybe harming each other.' They would fight, like puppies, but only in play; yet Iain was the older, and could do harm.

I went, and found Iain running up from the river, his face white. 'Mhairi has fallen in,' he said. 'I cannot reach her.'

'Fetch your father,' I told him, and ran to the place. There was a deep brown pool further out from the bank than the rest, beyond the stones. The child's body lay floating face down, and I knew at once that she was dead.

I waded out, but Alasdair was already before me. He lifted up the limp dark shape that had been his daughter, and carried it ashore head downwards; once there, he laid Mhairi on the ground and knelt upon her, pressing her chest with a regular motion and trying to breathe into her mouth. Her dark hair was like weed, lying wet on the grass. Her eyes were open.

Iain had hidden his face in my skirts. 'What happened?' I heard myself say. He muttered that they had been playing; that he had held Mhairi the way the *athair* himself would do, but she had broken away from him and clambered to the deeper water. He began to cry. Alasdair turned a ravaged face to us at last, his efforts at revival useless.

'You may save your tears,' he said harshly to the boy. 'There was no play between you. You are dry. You have never been near the water.'

'*Cuíle* –' I began, using the word he had taught me for husband; but he quelled me.

'He thrust her in, I say. Take him out of my sight. If yourself had been in your rightful place, minding your children instead of hearkening always to men's talk, she would be alive still. You wanted to take your King's son south to the Queen; *gu math*, take him. I do not want to see his face again, or yours.'

Am Grantach had come down to us, his expression full of grief when he saw what had happened. He tried to reason with Alasdair whose words he had heard; it was only a little child, he said, who could not have thought of such a thing.

'It is only a little child who is dead,' said Alasdair Dorch. He picked Mhairi's small body up and went away with it. I did not dare to follow. Later it lay in the hall of the castle, with candles at its head, and was assoiled with many present. Before the crowds came out, Alasdair had gone. I knew that he would maybe travel to his folk in Glenorchy, at least for a space: or maybe not. I did not know if I would ever see him again.

Meanwhile they were speaking of an English invasion by the old dead King's will, and the soldiers disembarking at Leith. Like everything else we heard, it had happened some time ago. For once, I did not think first of Madame Marie.

How can I tell of the bitter time that followed? I was alone, lying at night in the heather of the bothan with Iain Ruadh beside me for warmth. For a time I hoped that Alasdair would return, and even prayed for it, using the prayers they had made me recite long ago at Pont-à-Mousson with the Poor Clares, and for which I had cared nothing. They did not bring him back. I was past weeping; one day I caught a reflection of my face in the water and it was the face of an old woman, brown with outdoor living, hair unkempt. I stretched out my hands and saw that they were red and rough. It did not matter.

Christian Grant had a seeing eye, and everyone knew that Alasdair had gone. One day she came to the bothan and said, 'Claudine, you must come to us at Freuchie, and sleep in a bed; this is not a life for you alone.' She knew that Alasdair had helped me with all manner of things, the carrying, the finding and cooking of food and scouring the pan afterwards with ashes.

I obeyed, and they gave me a soft bed to lie in in one of the upper rooms. The walls still smelt of damp plaster, but it was private and no one shared it except the child. For some days I lay in bed with my face to the wall, shivering, and they brought us food. Then one day Christiania herself came, with a bottle of rosewater. She said nothing and handed it to me.

'There is ill news from the south,' she said presently, when I had unstopped the bottle and inhaled its sweet pampered smell, reminding me of my days at Court and in castles, of Madame Marie. I knew it would make my hands smooth in time, and my face, and set it aside. Then I listened to the news from the south and forgot about rosewater.

'The old English King before he died left word to come to Scotland and burn everything with fire and sword, and they are at it now,' she said, her mouth drawing into the hard line of acceptance her strange life had given her, making her seem forty years old when she was not yet thirty. 'My father is making ready to go with the men to fight. They have put man, woman and child to the sword as they were told, and they have burned Edinburgh; they say they called it a jolly fire and smoke. Many are homeless. The English commander, Hertford, stood on a hillside and watched the flames grow high in the east wind and heard the women wailing. It is all because they would not marry the little Queen to the young King of England, and now they never will.'

I sat up. I heard later that Cardinal Beaton himself had fought with the Scots army. News reached us in a hotchpotch of time, earlier events confused with the later, and back again and forth; but that there was desolation and rapine and war was certain and I knew that if Am Grantach was marching south, my husband would go too, either with his clan or by himself.

'I will speak with Am Grantach before he goes,' I said. Christiania glanced at me in silence; she had never grown used to my habit of speaking as a man might, without fear or favour, to the chieftain himself. It had lost me my daughter and my husband, and I would do it again. I tidied myself and used some of the rosewater to smell sweet, and combed my hair with Alasdair's little comb that he had fashioned for me out of the deer's bone. Then I went down.

Am Grantach was occupied with the clansmen, with targes and broadswords which had been kept in the heather thatch, and was making ready to ride. When he saw me, he was impatient and his fine eyes flashed.

'Tell it to the women,' he said. 'We ride in an hour. They have burned Leith, the ships in the water and the towns all up that coast. They have not dared come within six miles of Stirling, but it is said that the little Queen is to be sent to a place of safety.' He turned back to his targe and other business; since Alasdair left, he had not visited me.

'I will ride with you and the men, and my son,' I said. 'I will seek my husband.'

The chief made a gruff sound, went on arming himself and did not look at me. 'You took little enough heed to Alasdair Dorch while you had him by you,' he answered. 'It will be a hard ride, and as swift as the ponies and the running men can go. There is no time for women with us.'

'I am coming with you, or I will come behind you,' I said. 'Take me as far as Stirling, at least to the Queen.'

James of the Forays made an impatient sound and no doubt cursed all women. 'Be ready, then, you and your son, in half an hour. Donald Gorm will take him on the saddle-bow and my son himself will bear you at his back. We will leave you at the castle drawbridge and then you may do as you please. Now leave me.'

I thanked him, and left. There was little to prepare; a cup for water, a black knife in my bosom to cut meat. Although it was summer I wrapped Iain Ruadh in warm clothes for the cold night, though he grumbled at it.

'You are a soldier,' I said. 'Soldiers do as they are ordered.' He asked me if I was a soldier too, and I gave a wry smile. 'Maybe,' I told him. I saw his hazel eyes narrow suddenly, like the King's.

'Women are not soldiers, *tha mhaithír*. They cook the food. Aonghoís told me.'

'Well, I will perhaps do that.' We rode off, and I hardly had time to bid farewell to the Grants, or to Christiania. I had the bottle of rosewater with me thrust in my bodice along with the knife, such is the conceit of women.

I need not describe the ride; I have done so already. I hardly heard the skirling of the pipes or the soft tread of the men who ran by the ponies. I kept looking through the trees for the narrow white stripe of the MacGregor tartan, for I knew the other clan would ride with ours. But the swift men who had come from Glenorchy had outstripped the softer Grants, though I would never say so; a man who could carry a boat on his back had hard kingly ancestors. We rode on, and once slept overnight on the ground, and I lay wrapped in my woman's plaid with Iain Ruadh cuddled against me, and at last he was glad of his warm clothes. Although I was tired with the jogging of gentle John Grant's pony, I lay awake for some time, and planned what I would do with Iain; I would take him first to Madame Marie, and hope she would receive him and keep him with her as a solace in her troubles. Then I would search for my husband. If Madame would not take the boy, if she rejected both of us, he would have to come with me, but he would be a burden. I no longer had any fear of travelling as a woman alone. What must be, must be. I heard the quiet breathing of the Grant men who slept, and smelled the fresh manure from the ponies and the fragrant tartan damp with dew, close by. Not one of the men came near me, and we had not spoken on the way. A woman going to war is like a woman on a ship, and brings ill fortune; but they had not used me as a camp follower on the long journey, nor did they, for a Highlander is a gentleman.

I had never yet seen desolation. I had never yet seen the abomination of desolation: black shells of ruined houses, charred trees, bleak fields in May. There were no people; they had fled, perhaps to the towns. We marched, with the running feet of the clansmen hardened to a steady tramp, tramp, while the pipes still skirled, and the grim-faced men saw what had been done by the English within six miles of Stirling Castle, no nearer; maybe they were afraid, or maybe their commander, having his instructions, was prudent. The Sassenach is so; they are said to make bad lovers. They had not loved Scotland. They had not loved a single man, woman or child in it; some of the corpses were along the way. Six miles precisely towards the town, where Hertford had been told to stop, they had stopped; the places were green again, although without the living folk who were afraid. In the town, they thronged the streets, huddled in doorways, frightened and smeared with smoke, children crying against their mothers, babies at the breast in the open street. The men had gone. The women and children and the shopkeepers, their booths bare, stared incuriously at the marching men in tartan, hearing the pipes. They had heard them before. They had heard them in times of joy and sadness and the day the King's body was buried in Edinburgh. They had heard them in peace. It was not peace now. It was war, and it would go on for years.

We came to the Ballengeich Road and, still marching, ascended to the Castle. The drawbridge was down, as the English had gone and there were men-at-arms on guard inside, and lounging ready in armour in the sunshine. Am Grantach had escorted me himself, causing his men to wait, and before I left him I took his hand: there was no need for words of farewell between us.

'I will send Aonghaís in with you and the boy, then he may return,' he said briefly, and I knew that, with his usual courtesy, he wanted to see me safely to the Queen Dowager's presence and to be sure I was not molested by the men. Aonghaís carried Iain Ruadh and we were not asked who we were; they had seen James of the Forays and knew him. I went through the familiar rooms and as I did so, saw an old bearded man, very handsome, come out of the presence-chamber. It was not the only time in my life that I was to set eyes on the Earl of Angus, the late Queen Margaret Tudor's husband and formerly Madame's forthright enemy. If his time-serving Douglas loyalties had veered in her direction far enough to seek her presence, it was good news: nothing now amazed me. He looked at me without interest, a travel-stained Highland woman with a plaid over her head and followed by a servant and a child, and passed on.

'Wait here with the boy,' I said to Aonghaís. I went in, and I do not remember crossing the room; here was Madame Marie, and her eyes red with weeping, which had never happened before. not even when Longueville died. I forgot my curtsy. I went to her and took her in my arms.

'Claudine,' she said. 'Claudine, you know already they burned the chapel at Holyrood where the King's body lies, and those of my sons, and Queen Madeleine. Of all the things they have done that was the most cruel, the most terrible. I am filled to this day with a hatred and grief I never knew, and now there are all these poor folk, here and along the east coast and in Edinburgh.'

She seemed to have forgotten her earlier lack of forgiveness to myself, and I was glad and thought of it no more. I said aloud, 'Madame, I think I have someone here who may console you; if not, he shall be taken away.'

'Nothing will console me,' she said, 'but I will fight. I, a Guise of Lorraine, will fight with my last breath. Arran has failed. He is of use to neither man nor woman. It is a woman, now, who is defending this realm. That may be better, as long as the woman is I.'

I had left her, talking as it were to her own mind, and I took my son from Aonghaſs, bade the latter wait lest he should be required, and led Iain Ruadh by the hand and brought him in. For moments Madame stood, her hands as by custom stiffly at her sides with the upholstered breadth of her sleeves; then her whole body grew less rigid, she moved, her eyes filled with fresh tears; and she held out her arms. Iain went into them at my thrust, a trifle bewildered, perhaps in some awe of this tall lady in black. I saw his red head held against Madame's dark satin kirtle, smothered tightly in the folds at last.

'He is like my son,' she said, 'so like. Prince James would have been so, had he lived. Leave him with me. As things are now, I may have to part with my daughter soon.'

Later she herself took me to the Queen in her nursery. The little girl had grown, and was taller than my son, as Madame herself had been taller than the King. Iain Ruadh stared solemnly for moments and the small Queen stared back, on her side with curiosity and some mischief; she was used to strangers, though perhaps not to boys of her own age. I knew they would play together soon and that it would be good for them both; after all, Iain Ruadh could not have forgotten his dead sister. The Dowager was watching, her harried face once again serene.

'He will stay with us,' she said. 'You also, for a little while, perhaps? I do not know how your affairs stand.' We were talking in French, and I did not ask about the Earl of Angus, or at that time probably know who he was; it remains in my memory from later on. I looked Madame squarely in her tilted eyes and told her that my husband was missing, had gone to the war, and that soon I must follow and find him wherever he was. She looked grave.

'He may be dead,' she said. 'Many are so. The Cardinal and the rest had to flee back again to Linlithgow from where they were drawn up to fight. Stay for a little while, Claudine; sleep in a soft bed. We still have that here.' As always, she thought of others; she seemed to have no further resentment against me in any way. Later she saw that I received food, clean linen sheets and warm water in which to wash, and I was glad of all of them. She sent me shoes and a gown, and I put them on to please her, but would not wear them long. I would go as a Highland woman to look for my Highland husband, wherever he might be.

There was however one occasion when I wore the gown; it was shortly before I left. Madame sent for me; when I went to her, her face was no longer weary but strong. I have never known such courage in a woman's face, although she was never manly except for her height and her courage. She stood looking at me and then led me to the little Queen, who was playing with Iain at a game where they counted beads. 'I want you,' Madame said, 'to carry Her Grace behind me into Council. It will be on the twenty-ninth of May. Arran is coming. There may be trouble; if so, take the Queen and go immediately out of the chamber. A great many will be here, including the Douglases.'

A great many were. The notion of a woman who could summon a council in time of war was strange, and no doubt intrigued them; there were still memories of Margaret Tudor and her petulant summonings for no reason at all when she had been, briefly, Queen Regent in the dead King's infancy. They were there, seated close-packed, in armour with their heads bared, and as we entered they rose, in a sudden confusion and clashing of arms, cap in hand, as it were, staring in silence at the beautiful child Queen. Arran, the Governor, looked at the floor, his irresolute face twitching, the jocose expression that endeared him to certain men gone for the time. Everyone else surveyed Madame's tall erect figure, beside the Queen of Scots borne in; I felt the latter's warm weight against me and she made no fuss. She was no ordinary child and kept silence at this tense moment, watching everything from behind her eyelids. It was as though

she understood what was happening, although few others
seemed to. Madame was seated, with a rustle of her black skirts,
and I stood behind her. The Governor stood up suddenly and
began to bluster; nobody listened. He tried to explain that he
had ordered the Council to take place on the previous day, at
Linlithgow.

'It is perhaps preferable here,' said Madame. I saw her cheek
curve in a grave yet coquettish smile, beguiling them if it could
be done; she had great charm, and they already knew that, but
distrusted it still. She made a pleasant and practical little speech
in which the presence of the Earl of Angus, and his brother Sir
George, was mentioned. 'With two such able helpers present in
Stirling, how could we fail to take advantage of that? Together,
my good stalwart lords, we may defeat this enemy who invades
our land. That is all that matters at present. What now, my
hearts, do you suggest?'

She left it to them, while subtly insinuating her own ideas so
that they thought they had thought of them themselves; it is
what one must always do with men.

It was not the only Council, but Arran sneaked off next day,
riding to the east. I had begun to believe that Alasdair Dorch
must be there, for the English attacks were generally in that part
when they came, at that time. I said this to Madame and she
looked at me considerately, in the midst of all her troubles.

'Claudine,' she said. 'If you will wait till these noblemen,' – the
wry smile flickered – 'have finished arguing and threatening one
another for the time at least, I have already asked the Earl of
Angus if he will escort you as far as Tantallon, and perhaps
permit you to stay there for a time while you make your search
to the east. He is returning shortly; his young wife will soon take
her chamber again, and he is anxious to see a second male heir. I
do not know what the Lady Margaret, his royal daughter, who
was always in expectation of the Angus title, thinks in England.
However one cannot but admire the Earl; he is not young, but
he persists. He is a forthright man; I enjoy his company.' She
brushed a fly from her sleeve fastidiously; it flew away and came
back. 'His brother Sir George is different; do not trust him, in
fact trust neither of them; they are Douglases. The Earl had my
husband the King in charge in his boyhood as you know.' She
said no more of that, but I had heard that the boy James V had
been done little good thereby when he became a man: it

accounted for a great deal. 'It will be better for you,' Madame was saying, 'nevertheless to have the salamander vert, the device of the Red Douglas, above you than for you to ride alone.'

She was right, and I thanked her for her trouble; but the salamander vert sprouting its flames was already all over Stirling, in the packed hall of the castle and in the streets and the inns, with Douglas men-at-arms in their livery swearing and dicing and clashing noisily with everyone else and waiting for the order to ride off. I myself made ready. Meantime a proclamation was issued to the effect that Governor Arran had destroyed the realm, broken the truce with England, and must resign his office forthwith into the hands of the Queen Dowager. There was no mention of the fact that he had left her with no money, having spent it assiduously on his whims. I do not say Arran was a bad man; at least, he was better than some. However, as many things in council do, the whole thing came to nothing meantime. I left my son with the Queen Dowager – by then it was June – and rode east among a jostling press of Douglas horsemen, carrying in my bodice, to be sent as soon as I could contrive it, secret letters from Madame to the King of France, who had once tried to ravish me at Fontainebleau.

'The Dowager is but a frail woman, like yourself. She has taken my advice, and I have urged her to be very circumspect in her dealings with Council matters.'

I could still, despite some days by now spent in his company, be amazed at the complacency of Sir George Douglas, the Earl's brother, who was known by everyone to turn and twist between English and Scots as it suited him, but still contrived to be heard in Council. He rode beside me as usual, and the rattling clamjamfrie of men-at-arms with their gear in the saddle rode all about us, and the banner above, and the Earl himself in front, his grey head bare in the heat and his basnet perched ready on his crupper, to be clapped on in case of trouble. At present, there was none. The horses jogged solidly eastwards while Sir George talked on. He liked to hear the sound of his own voice and I answered him absently, knowing he was by far too pleased with himself to note my lack of attention. I was praying for Alasdair and that I should find him alive. It seemed so long since I had seen or heard anything of him that it seemed like another life when I had known him, as indeed it had been; was it I,

Claudine, who had lived in a bothan, not unlike many of these poor blackened cottages of the south parts, and now slept between sheets on the way? Now that the King was dead the Earl of Angus, and all his kin, could be received openly again in Scotland, their exile having been ended by decree. Even in his outlawed days there had always been a secret welcome for Angus, for he was a taking old rascal; like Madame, I could understand how in his youth he had cozened Queen Margaret Tudor into marriage. Anyone riding in his party was also made welcome now openly. We stayed at such castles and abbeys as were still strung by then across the land; it was before the worst of the burnings, and the poor folks' dwellings had meantime suffered most. Sir George told me, however, that Tantallon itself, from the attentions of the English, was a ruin by now with the wind whistling through it, which he said it had always done in any case. The young Countess had been placed in a rented house for the time.

I listened; I did not care whether I stayed in a rented house or a castle. I thought briefly of what I had heard of the Earl and of his daughter Lady Margaret Douglas in the old days, when Angus was put to the horn in Scotland; and of their wanderings, when they had had to live the life of fugitives all along the Border. Margaret Douglas had stayed with her outlawed father and had supported him through everything, although she was a queen's daughter and could have lived with her mother in palaces. I agreed with Madame that she might, from where she was kept in England, resent the birth, by a new marriage made in old age, of a healthy male heir to her father. The present one, about three years old now, Sir George said, was sickly. I recalled Margaret Maxwell, Angus' present Countess, as I had met her before her marriage at Caerlaverock, a demure young woman mocked for her single state by her stepmother. I remembered many things there, and Alasdair driven off in the rain beyond, and the dark, and my eyes filled with tears. I closed them and the horse jogged on, and Sir George went on talking, having noticed nothing. When I opened my eyes again his glance was fixed on my breasts. I was used to that, and hoped the secret letters did not show. Sir George's son James Morton, who rode with the party, was worse than his father in this way. He was married to yet another sister of Beatrix Maxwell, already they said half mad; to do Morton justice, madness was in that family from the beginning. Morton himself looked like a pig, with red eyes. I would be glad when the journey was over.

Sir George had been reading his Bible, copies of which were now flooding by demand into Scotland, he said. He had been used to read it at Hampton Court and even in Henry VIII's presence chamber while he himself was waiting for audiences with his brother. I maintained a brief interest while he tried to instruct me in the Reformed faith, but I said I was a Frenchwoman and had always been a Catholic, or a Papist as Sir George called it, and he said 'Ay,' glanced again at my bodice and fell silent for a while. He then told me I would need to feed myself up, I was too thin; I would have a rest, maybe, when we reached where the Countess was. 'I do not desire a rest,' I said. 'I desire my husband.'

'Ay, women need their husbands. It is an unnatural thing to shut them away in convents, and the men in monasteries, the way they do, but all of that is changing in the south, and shortly here also, despite French aid if it should ever come.' I felt the letters rustle against my over-thin breasts and hoped again that he had only noticed the latter and not the former. It was perhaps by chance that he should have mentioned French aid, but I kept silent and he went on talking about other matters to which I did not listen. Madame had said Sir George was unstable as water but saw to his own weal, and she was right. He resembled the Governor in that way, but Arran talked less and probably thought less with such wits as he had. I hoped Madame had by now achieved some accommodation with him. I had lost count of how long we had been on our journey; all I knew was that it was still summer and that at any moment, the English might come again. There were at first no campaigns in winter; they would come when the corn was getting ripe, so that they could burn it and starve the ordinary folk. Later, they would come in winter as well, so that anyone driven out of burning places would perish in the bitter cold. I have never taken to the Sassenachs, as Alasdair would have called them; they are complacent, like Sir George Douglas, in their cruelty.

The young Countess had given birth prematurely, and whether it was a boy or a girl I know not, for by the time we arrived it was dead. The Earl, though cast down, went up at once to his wife, of whom he seemed fond; I stayed downstairs in the rented house, while Sir George hummed and hawed with his Bible and presently the Earl came down again, his face decently grieving.

'We must trust in God that He will mend your fortunes speedily,' said Angus' brother, who was known to be forthright as well as sly. Later I went up to see poor Margaret myself, leaving the brothers staring at one another in the hired room, with rain running down the walls from where the roof leaked. It was not a comfortable place, and the gaunt bulk of Tantallon rearing in the distance must have reminded the Douglases of better days. The English had battered it, but it was said not to be beyond repair, and workmen were already at it, mending gaps in the great stones.

The Master of Angus, a child of perhaps three, who looked less, had a turnip head and could not yet walk, was crawling aimlessly about the upper chamber near his mother. To look at him I thought he probably had worms, but in fact the Earl's heir by his third marriage never thrived; maybe Angus had caught the pox during his years in London, or there might have been a weakness from the Maxwell side. In any event, the pale girl lying on her bed and I made talk, forgetting Caerlaverock, if indeed Countess Margaret had been aware of everything that had happened there: she was prudent enough, if so, not to make it evident.

I was anxious to start the search for my husband, and did not accept with any eagerness the Earl's invitation when he said I should stay on for a while. 'Ye cheer my wife by your company,' he said, 'for she is low in spirits, in the nature of such things. I will give ye a horse and two Douglas men, and ye may search, but maybe not over far; I am in close touch with events, and will send word, or bring it myself, if I should hear aught of battles or of Highlanders.'

There was a twinkle in his eye, and I reflected that in his youth the Earl of Angus must have been hard to resist, even though one suspected that he was never sincere, and might like all Douglases be rough; but he was certainly preferable to his brother and nephew. Without doubt I might show wisdom in allowing him to help me in my searching rather than attempt it alone; and the offer of a horse was kind. I said that I would stay, and had the honour of the Earl's company for the next few days at the table, while Sir George went off on one of his mysterious errands; he was forever coming and going, and as usual imagined himself of great importance, but everyone knew that what he did with his left hand was not known to his right. The days passed and the Countess came shakily downstairs. The Earl told us that the Queen Dowager had written to old King Henry before his death to ask him to leave the Scots in peace, and to send ambassadors. I knew that Her Grace would have rendered it more tactfully, but in Angus' unpainted way that is how it was put. He also told me that Arran himself had veered about, collecting forces of his own, proclaimed abroad that he was after all Governor of Scotland despite the request made in full Council that he resign, and that Mary of Guise, as he called her, had no right to call false parliaments. Lest Her Grace should hold more, he then fortified Holyrood against her, and declared worthless the bawbees she had minted, called as they were after the baby who was Queen, and showing the latter's smiling head in her crown, cap and ruff. Arran now said these coins were without the law, and forbade their use.

The Countess recovered slowly from the birth, and while she was doing so I was permitted – I soon came to realise this, and that the Douglases had for their own reasons become my gaolers – to ride on small, useless searches, flanked always by the same two men-at-arms who rode in scowling silence except when they murmured to one another behind my back. No doubt it did not suit them to escort a woman.

We contrived places such as Auldhame and Scoughall and Whitekirk, once Kingston, and saw Berwick Law jutting against the sky like a goat's soft nipple. That is not a Scottish mountain; I cannot think how it ever came there. In the small towns the streets were strangely quiet, most folk having fled to the larger; except for some, most of them old, maybe set in their ways and mending their roofs as if there never would be another English invasion. I could find no word anywhere of Alasdair, or of any Highlanders; by this time I was certain he was alone, and not with his clan, but he would have been remembered had he passed by. I began to wonder if the east parts held him at all and if he had, after everything, gone home; this was not his country, in the Lowland places.

Meantime, the Douglases fed me well. There was milk and butter and pork and cream from Auldhame, where by some means or other a woman had preserved two cows and a litter of pigs. I found in a little while that chickens had been obtained by some other means, no doubt filched from across the Border; and were picking, scratching themselves and laying occasional eggs in what had once been the great wine-cooling chamber to the rear of Tantallon. The Countess and I, when she was able again to venture out of doors, used to go for douce walks there daily to gather the eggs and bring them home in a basket. Afterwards she and I would wander in silence, for her health, round the great earth ramparts James V had dug when he was angered with the Douglases in his boyhood, after his escape from them; and also those dug earlier by James IV when he had been angered likewise. We stared into the hall where old Angus Bell-the-Cat, our Earl's grandsire who in his time had hanged a King's favourites, had also hung his huge sword which no other man could wield. We once climbed carefully, despite the danger of loose stones, to the windy upper chambers overlooking the dizzy rock down to the North Sea, and watched that in its constant strife and moaning. 'My husband and his daughter the Lady Margaret escaped down here in the bad days, and took to a boat,' said the young Countess. It was one of the few interesting things she ever said, and I wondered how Angus's earlier bride, the pampered Queen Margaret Tudor, had fared in this storm-buffeted place when she stayed here, briefly, with the Earl himself after their disastrous marriage following hand on Flodden.

Angus came and went, and once the rumour arrived before him that he had won a great victory over the English at Ancrum Moor. He arrived home flushed with triumph, and I hurled myself at him at once: had there been Highlanders in the fray? 'Na, lass,' he said, and looked at me kindly enough. I was beside myself; even Madame had assumed that any action would take place to the east, which was why I had stayed here; now, Alasdair could have been in the fight, wounded or killed, and I elsewhere! But there was nothing I could do now; and it did not sound as if he had been present. I heard the men-at-arms carousing over the victory, and wept alone in my bed; through the wall, I heard Angus trying to fashion himself a third heir.

I was worried all this time about my failure to send off Madame's letter to King François. It was not forgotten, but there was nobody I could trust, for all the Earl's and Sir George's victories and new allegiance. In the end, when I could obtain materials, I enclosed it, with one of my own wrapped about it, to Duchesse Antoinette at Joinville. Although I was not in the habit of writing to Madame's mother, nobody here would know that; and a letter from me to her might travel innocently without being opened. Also, the Duchesse was loyal and practical, and would see to it that the inner letter reached the King. I prayed that it might reach her; and it must have done so by the end, because other letters, urgently sent by the Queen Dowager to France by means of the Sieur de Bauldreul, did not. His ship was boarded off Scarborough by Sussex fishermen, and in haste he foolishly wrapped the letters in a linen bundle, weighted it with coal, and dropped it in the sea, where it was at once seen by the fishermen and hooked out again. They sent the soaked but still legible contents straight to the English Council of the North, and so Madame's plans were known in England before the French ever saw them. She had to endure a great deal, being a foreigner and a woman.

I myself endured other things. Despite my continued failure to obtain word of my husband – he was beginning to resemble a dream of long ago – I was rested at the leaking house, and put on flesh with the good food, fresh fish from the sea, the occasional chicken we ate after its neck had been drawn when it became egg-bound, and the steady flow of milk and cream. The Countess gave me rosewater. Seeing myself in her glass – women, no matter in what tribulation, always look at their own reflections if they can – I could observe that I was again not unlike the young creature who had lived with Madame Marie at the Court of France; though perhaps not quite, as my dress was plain, like that of a peasant. I no longer wore the tartan *arisad* over my head meantime, as it was still summer, though such trees as were left by the English were beginning to turn their colour by then.

After Ancrum Moor the Countess thought herself again pregnant, which was good news for her. I forget when the little turnip-headed Master of Angus had died; I think it was in February. I knelt while the priest, a Douglas uncle though not, as would have been customary, a bishop, said Mass for the repose of the child's soul, and saw him buried. Then I went to collect the eggs alone, leaving Countess Margaret lying on her covers, anxious, no doubt, this time, for success.

The castle was strangely deserted and I could hear the whistling of the wind. I had put the tartan arisad over my head and wrapped about my shoulders again for warmth, and with the basket over my arm went and collected several eggs in it; the chickens knew me by now and scratched on placidly. I scattered some corn for them, and went out. At the great door, I encountered a figure I did not welcome there; Sir George Douglas. I had not seen him for some time and I wondered if he had followed me to empty Tantallon; there was no other reason for him to be here unless he wanted to read his Bible by himself; he kept it in his bosom as always, bulging a trifle. He smiled now, in his ingratiating manner.

'Ye do well enough with the eggs,' he said in homely fashion. I replied pleasantly enough and would have passed him by, but he moved to prevent me, and took my arm.

'It is sad to see the hens scratch where in our great days the wine used to sit,' he said. 'Have ye seen all Tantallon? There is much still to see.'

I was off my guard, which was foolish; but what interested me, not for the first time, was Sir George's curious voice. He prided himself on having learned to speak as the English do, owing to his long residence in England and his friendship, as he put it, with Henry VIII, though that monarch no doubt regarded him less as a friend than as a pensioner, to be made use of as and when advisable. I replied absently that I had not in fact seen all of the castle, then regretted saying it; but he at once said that he would show me, and I could hardly draw back. We went through one chamber after another, saw the ruins of grandeur, and at last, in one of the inner places, where the rose-red stones had tumbled down, Sir George put out a hand and fumbled my left breast. It was fuller than it had formerly been with all the cream and milk I had been fed, and evidently gave him satisfaction.

I drew back then, remembering that between my breasts, where it had lain with Madame's letter, was Alasdair's black knife, his *sgian dubh*, which I had brought away with me after he had for some reason left it behind in our bothan, and had since always carried with me. Meantime, the doughty Douglas was opening his codpiece to reveal his marvel, ready erect.

'Come, now, ye have had much hospitality from my brother,' he said, as he saw my expression. 'Ye owe us something, maybe.' His English had deserted him and he was back again in Scots, but it would have been the same in any language. He thumbed my wrist and went on to say that I was a comely lass now, with the right feeding, and that he would continue to take care of me, as I pleased him greatly. I took little enough time to consider how they must have fattened me up for him deliberately, like a pig brought on for bacon; the Countess knew of my past and no doubt thought I would be willing. Sir George's own wife had been a heiress and had brought him much land, and James Morton: I did not know if she was alive or dead. All this passed coldly through my mind while I first struggled with him, then, when he had finally rummaged his hand up my skirts, kicked out with all my strength at the place where it hurt most. He staggered back, with an oath, this time certainly in Scots: and I threw the basket of eggs at him with one hand and drew out the *sgian dubh* with the other.

'If you and your sorry clan, neither Scots as you are nor English, think that I am your whore because you fed me, you may take thought again,' I heard myself saying. I saw his jaw drop when he had finished his cursing; his face was covered in egg-yolk and it dripped from his beard to his doublet, which was no doubt new. I kicked out once more, freed myself with a whirl of my plain skirts, and fled: out of Tantallon, down the long approach, plaid flying, and back at last to the hired house, which I did not enter. I ran into the place where the horse I rode was kept; its stall also leaked and I remember the damp stains on the wall, but the Douglas grooms were elsewhere; at such times Providence aids us. I saddled the beast quickly, threw myself on his back, and galloped like the devil away from Tantallon and all Douglases and the memory at last that came to me of the poor King, his mind deranged, ambling along this same road muttering 'Fled Oliver? Is Oliver ta'en?' after Solway Moss, when Sir George and Angus and their like had been on the side of England. I did not then recall the similar way in which I had myself escaped from Vouvray; afterwards, I was to compare one with the other. But I had to sell my horse this time for food when I became a whore.

It is difficult to think of a way in time of war in which a woman alone, without food or money, can obtain either for long without soliciting. No doubt it may be asked why I did not turn back when I grew hungry, placate Sir George, and become his kept mistress, living in docile fashion on cream and pork, instead of giving myself for lesser sums to whatever honest man wanted to buy me. The answer is that that is what they were; honest men. They were most of them soldiers, at such places as Haddington and Dunbar; I did not go near Edinburgh. That was for the future; meantime my horse galloped on and I did not know where we were going, for it was beyond the confines of my late searches. Presently I saw a great grey keep rise, and when I drew nearer and made out the device on the banner floating above, it was again the green salamander spouting its flame. In other words, I had hastened from one Douglas stronghold the next, and I suspected that it belonged to Sir George himself and that this was Dalkeith: it could be no other.

I walked my horse then, for he was beginning to tire. I did not know what to do. For some reason the tale of a brave woman floated at that moment into my mind, perhaps to sustain me; I covered the distance on foot thinking of her. Lord Borthwick's wife Isobell was seldom at Court and I had never met her, but the Countess of Angus, aroused briefly from her torpor, had told me not long since of what she had done. At that earlier time when Her Grace was being wooed without success by the Fair Earl of Bothwell and the handsome Earl of Lennox, encouraging both and succumbing to neither, the Fair Earl himself was maybe growing despondent. He had gone so far as to divorce his wife, who was a Sinclair and the mother of his heir, in the expectation of marrying Madame, and now Madame would not marry him. In this despair, he fell in love with Isobell Borthwick. He was unstable, and moreover the son of the procuress of Caerlaverock; no doubt his affections veered with the wind. Unfortunately Isobell loved her own husband dearly. At this moment, Sir George Douglas chose to imprison Lord Borthwick at Dalkeith. By this he hoped to please Her Grace, but did not. Borthwick himself had been a supporter of Arran, and Sir George was in process of changing sides.

I stared at the nearing banner as it waved above the keep. There was nowhere else to go; but at least I knew Sir George could not be at home. It was unlikely he would be in any shape to ride for a while after the kicks I had given him; but one could never be certain of a Douglas. I thought of Isobell Borthwick again. She had thought out a plan to rescue her husband, lured the Fair Earl by means of a love-letter all the way to Borthwick itself, a long distance, but no doubt he considered his stoop-shouldered charms irresistible – and when he was there, and in her very chamber, caused him, as the Scots say, to be handled and kept. Lord Borthwick was thereupon returned to his wife by Sir George and both men, never ask me how, were transformed by that same personage into ardent supporters of Her Grace.

However, all this would not help me if I were to encounter Sir George with a hurt groin and still scraping egg from his beard, and I was glad to see the stable for the sake of my poor horse: I had almost had to drag him up the approach, and was in no state to travel further myself, and much in need of a meal. If I could sell the horse to the Douglases, and continue my journey on foot, it would be a jest; he was after all their beast, but maybe the groom would not know they had paid for him twice over. I decided that I would try; horses at that time were hard to obtain, owing to the war.

There was in fact a lone white jennet in her stall, and she whinnied at our approach. The sound brought out a groom, a middle-aged man dressed roughly, but not in armour. No doubt he was one of those excused from military service for duties at home, a state which makes men either smug or crestfallen. He was the latter, and kept casting furtive glances at me while he fed and saw to the horse, as I had not yet told him I had no money. When he learned of that, he was angry, as might have been expected, and knew the horse as a Douglas horse and himself as a Douglas man. He then told me that his wife was dead, that there were no women here and that he often had to pull himself. I had not before heard the term, but understood. 'You are in as sad a situation as I,' I said, hoping to excite his pity. 'I have lost my husband, and have searched everywhere.'

The tears came into my eyes. I was tired and hungry, and I had begun to be certain by now that I might never find Alasdair Dorch, or that if I did, he would still be angry with the slow deep Highland anger and refuse to take me back. This man's anger had been lighter, different; but he was still a man, with a man's need. I agreed to let him use me if he would pay me, but first asked, saying I was not commonly a whore, how much those persons took for payment.

'I have fed the horse,' he grumbled, 'and my lord will ask concerning it, for he keeps close watch on the corn. I could take ye now, without siller, for I am strong despite what they say, but I am a merciful man and –'

'There is no such thing as mercy here,' I said, with truth, and haggled again about money, backing away from him. The French have shrewdness in such matters, even the first time. He named a price and I doubled it, and he grinned suddenly, showing square yellowed teeth.

'Ye be a fine lass,' he said. 'I can give ye a warm bed if ye will stay.'

I said I dared say he could, and the thought was welcome in its way, but I feared Sir George's return. In the end he shared a flagon of ale with me and we lay down together. I can remember its bitter taste in my mouth and the glow it gave on an empty stomach, which helped matters. The man assured me that he had never caught the pox, and I was grateful for having my attention drawn to the matter. He then did the same to me as other men had done, and it was no worse to endure as I turned my head away and closed my eyes. At the end, he counted out the sum on which we had agreed, but the ale had somewhat fuddled my wits and by next day, having slept under a hedge in the cold with my plaid wrapped round me, and washed myself in a burn, I saw that he had had the victory. He had in fact paid me in Madame's bawbees, which were no longer accepted in the country as legal tender. However, he had at least had the courtesy not to leave Douglas seed in me.

I knew now what to do, at any rate, and thus my calling began. I was fucked by men from Haddington, Berwick, Dunbar, Dirleton, Gullane, Aberlady and halfway along the coast. Most of them were men-at-arms following one or other leader, including the Cardinal whom I never again saw, but he was much spoken of among them as a fine commander and a brave man. Between custom, and as I could, I would try to gather news, no longer of Alasdair – that was past – but of the state of affairs. The men gave away certain things in their mutterings, and there were other women at the same occupation as myself; in fact, they swarmed, owing to the times, to homelessness, hunger, cold and widowhood. They varied in attraction, or its lack, and there was much envy among them, as well as some friendship. I was in demand among the men, so many women disliked me; but one I am grateful to in certain ways. She was old, and could remember, when she was a child, seeing James IV ride out to Flodden. Her name was Agnes Heron and she came from the Border Marches. She told me how in those parts, a woman carries her riches on her body for safety: gold necklaces and chains, gold stomachers, gold rings. Anything else, comfort, furnishings, a peel-tower even, will be stolen away or burnt sooner or later, then other raiders ride out on their short-legged ponies and steal from the stealers, and bring the gear back. I knew sadness at mention of the raiders, because I remembered that it was from these strange twilight beings, said to be descended from a fairy and a bear, that my own lost Alasdair had learned to make his drammoch.

One thing Agnes Heron told me, while we were sitting having our breakfast on the shore at Dunbar; it was possible by now, after the night's work, to have a good one, and eggs and ham were frying in a pan on a fire we had made with gathered driftwood, so that the salt in the flames turned them green. Agnes came of a tribe which were known since Flodden as tinklers, because their name, which had once been noble there, and their houses had been ruined both by Scots and English since the battle. They were different from the Egyptians who had come to Scotland a generation since, nobody knows from where, and had been made welcome by James IV who had heard their dark-skinned fiddler play, and had listened to their unforgotten stories. These tinklers had to take to the same outdoor life as the gypsies did, and Agnes found it better in the end to be a whore; she tried to get me to set up house with her in Edinburgh, but I would not go as near as that to Madame. Agnes Heron spoke then of Angus's victory that time at Ancrum Moor over the English, and mentioned that Governor Arran had kissed him twenty times for it. 'Your husband may have been at that fight,' she said, her gap-toothed mouth grinning. 'Why did ye not go doun?'

I thought of myself as I had been when the news came, and how I should have left at once and walked, if need be, from Tantallon to the forsaken battlefield; but it was too late. Agnes began to comb her hair, which was grey and full of lice; later, in the summer, she would perhaps wash it.

'He was not there, he was not there,' she said, and I wondered why she should have said the first thing to me and then the second; I turned away from her, shivering not only with the morning cold but with the certainty that such folk have a foreknowledge gained in their wanderings. When one of them dies, they know of the death across the mountains. Did Agnes know where Alasdair Dorch was now? If so, she would not tell me. She looked at me with a certain sly enmity, which I had seen before in the other women. After all, we were rivals for custom, and I made more money than she did, or they either.

'Ye will see him again, oh ay,' she said, and then 'To be sure, ye will see him again.' That was all, and she would not tell me when or where, but after that, despite everything, I hoped for it.

In Haddington I was not well. It was not a pregnancy; thank God, I never conceived in all that time. Whores are kept busy enough nightly to shift an embryo from its moorings, otherwise they can take to herbs or hooks. I had tried the herbs once when I was uncertain, and they made me queasy, but I never had to use them again. No, it was not a pregnancy, but it was a fever, and I know what caused it. In the end it defeated me and made me unfit for custom. It was not the pox – I always made my customers open their codpieces before we began, that I might see the contents for myself, and if there were boils I told them to go elsewhere. My fever, I believe to this day, had been caused by one fellow with enormous parts, who boasted aloud that he could stretch me wider than any man in Fife and Lothian. He had been after me for some time, and in the end I let him try, if only to be rid of him; but it was true enough that he stretched me, so hard and so forthrightly that he made me bleed. I could hardly stand after it, and for days I limped and staggered and could do no work, and the other women laughed. In fact, for some time I was never again the same. I had been able, by then, to choose my custom a little, for although sin makes some women haggard it made me plump, and by this time I had put on a quantity of creamy flesh men liked to handle. One of the ways in which they did this was too much for me, and I would not permit it to the sailor who asked for it, though he would have paid me double; there are limits to one's endurance, and a woman is a woman. Otherwise, it is a matter of opening one's legs, no more. Sometimes I was able to afford a lodging to sleep in all of next day, though there was little lodging to spare then, in Scotland. After that time with the wide man, though, I was not the same, as I say, and my customers fell off.

It may be asked why in all of this affliction I did not return to the Queen Dowager, who had been seen by all in Edinburgh, kneeling at Mass before Cardinal Beaton himself with Governor Arran beside her, the same who had lately drawn his sword in her presence and that of the Cardinal, as well as fortifying Her Grace's own strongholds against her. The Fair Earl of Bothwell was here, as well as the Campbell chieftain, Argyll, in his dark tartan. Campbells always know which side to support and it is always the winning one, and I reflected that Madame must have done a good deal more than wait helplessly in Stirling to manage to bring them all together. Of that I had no knowledge except hearsay, but I myself had in fact avoided Edinburgh from the beginning, though I could have made much money there and as Agnes suggested, set up a house with it. The fact is that I knew Madame was pure, whereas I was so no longer; she had always been chaste, and in my present state I dared not appear before her. Also, she had better advisers than I, the chief of them being God.

The Cardinal had been useful, but nobody could trust him and I knew that Madame herself would not do so. He had ridden untiringly between Stirling and the capital to try to mediate, but on the whole supported the Governor while matters remained uncertain, as if this would have added to their certainty. I wondered how much time he had to spend nowadays with Marion Ogilvy. I had not forgotten her and was to see her again.

Meantime, I wandered weakly about Haddington, shivering with fever, and considered going to the St Mary's nuns to get them to cure me, but I did not want their mortifications. I stared at the stone gargoyles spouting rain into their gutters and remembered those in Paris at Nôtre Dame, then turned away, refusing a customer who passed me and went elsewhere. I was in no shape for him or anyone, though I needed food. They say one ought to starve a fever and so I was perhaps my own physician. I do not remember how, but in an hour or two, while it was still dark, I found myself in the great abbey, which used to be known, till the reformers smashed it, as the Lamp of Lothian. I had not previously gone in, as my trade, and with it such convictions as I still retained from my upbringing, had prevented me. Now, I scarcely looked at the wonder of the gilding and the carven saints, and the bones in reliquaries from early times when kings came here to be crowned. The stained glass, with the light of coming dawn, was already casting its colours on the floor. I stretched myself out prone on the floor itself, by a pillar, in the way those in despair often do; my cheek was turned against the cold stone, and I felt near death. I was tired, sore in my parts, and ill. The nuns no doubt would have taken me to their infirmary, cared for me for a day or two, then sent me to the priest to confess my sins; but of what avail was that, as I must go back to them again? I found I could not pray, but help was sent. When I rose up at last, it was to see a group of young men with fair hair wandering about, uncertainly; they were no doubt wondering in which chapel Mass would be held, and nobody else had arrived for that as it was still too early. Joy welled up in my heart at sight of them, for they wore the white-and-gold livery of the Scots Archers of the Guard of France, and I knew that Madame had after all obtained French help from King François, perhaps by means of my letter.

I went up to one young officer and touched him on the shoulder. 'Monsieur,' I said in a low voice in French, 'I am one of your countrywomen, Claudine de Vouvray. I am glad in my heart that you have come. If I may aid you in any way except that to which, as you will see, I have grown accustomed, tell me, for I know the Queen.'

Another might have thrust me away in alarm or contempt, especially in that place, with the relics and the Host in its tabernacle which he no doubt hoped shortly to receive. But he was grateful, told me his name – it was none I knew, for he came from Touraine – and his rank, which was that of lieutenant. He admitted that he had difficulty in understanding our Scots tongue, and so did the rest who had come, and they needed an interpreter. I said 'I am willing to travel wherever I may with you, if you will buy me a meal. That is all. I have eaten nothing for two days,' and then I swayed and collapsed on the stone floor at their feet, and knew nothing more for some time, except that they stayed with me and did as I had asked, with courtesy.

I am not accustomed to swoon. No true Guise would countenance it. Madame Marie did so only once in her life, when a disgusting thing happened in front of her. That was the only time that I know of, and it was later and I will tell of it in its place.

Part V

The man George Wishart screamed, darkened, writhed and charred at last in the high flames fanned upwards by the March wind. It was not a wind such as had flattened and delayed the burning of the earlier reformer, Patrick Hamilton, turning his execution into a long-drawn-out agony bravely endured. This wind whipped the flames as it should, flinging them against Wishart's face, reducing him soon to nothing but a long greyish twisted cinder, dead and hanging motionless from his chained stake. All about were crowds, standing back from the intense heat and the quivering air it sent above, making vision impossible beyond the stake itself. Knox said afterwards that the Cardinal had sat at his castle window gloating, but nobody could see as far. Some in the crowd told their beads, from habit; others read from the Bible, daring the authorities by now to come in and stop them. It was for that, and for preaching Luther's heresy in Dundee and Montrose and Kyle and the east parts of Lothian, and also maybe for being privy to a plot by Henry VIII, that Wishart had been arrested by the Cardinal two months before, while my Frenchmen and I were riding back from the west parts with messages from the Queen to Beaton. Knox, in his history, says that the Cardinal was by then Madame's lover, but like many other things he says that is not true. As far as that went, I was in my woman's clothes again and beside me stood Marion Ogilvy. She stood impassive, watching, her strong face pale, as I had first seen her stand long ago – it was not so many years, after all – at Prince James's christening, when the torches

182

burned by night here at St Andrews as the wretched reformer had burned lately now, while we watched.

I had travelled north with my Frenchmen dressed as a boy servitor, no doubt a somewhat plump one, but men's coats of the time were padded and I bound my breasts with linen to keep them flat, and had cropped my hair. This was because it had been decided by the French commander, M. de Montgomery, Seigneur de Lorges, that it would not be seemly for me to ride among the proud and ancient Scots Archers as a hired woman and a drab. Nevertheless they were glad of my French, also my Scots and my shrewdness in bargaining at the booths in towns we passed. They took no more from me than I had offered them. A Frenchman understands such matters, and they remained courteous and distant. Besides the leather jack with its padding, the hose and the sword I carried, they gave me money to buy myself a new mutch and gown. I was glad of the mutch, as it would pack flat in the saddle, which a coif does not do, and hid my cropped hair when required. I had briefly, as my brown locks fell to the floor once again, recalled the Poor Clares at Pont-à-Mousson and my early punishment, but the hair had grown again then and it would grow again now. I had been unwilling to come so far north lest I miss tidings of Alasdair now that I was no longer about my shameful trade, but none had come; yet Agnes Heron had promised I should see him again. There was nothing to do but go on from day to day. I did so, bargaining for rooms and food for the men in the towns we passed, and at times, asking the way, for roads are foul in winter and cart-tracks can bewilder horsemen in search of a town. I also, riding behind the Archers' white-and-gold backs, thought of France, then of myself as Jeanne d'Arc with my hair cropped in time of war. That was a brave woman, but the story is confused; there is perhaps some truth in the tale, whispered even now in my country, that the Maid of Orléans was not a peasant girl, but the secret daughter of Louis d'Orléans himself and Isabeau de Bavière, Queen of France. There is a tomb, with the Maid's portrait on it, where she was buried beside her husband, Robert des Armoises. She was married to him, and sent into the provinces afterwards, because she had abjured her oath. In any case the final part of the plan for which she had been reared, the rescue from the Tower of London of her father Louis d'Orlèans was never accomplished, though the Maid raised the siege of Orléans itself and drove out the English, crowning Charles VII whom of course she knew already by sight as he was her half-brother. It is perhaps only a tale, but it disposes of the mystic voices; I am a sceptic about such things. Some other woman was burned at Rouen, and died bravely.

I looked now at Wishart's dying pyre and at the ashen thing chained above it, and by now I could see across the lowered ashes a man in black with an open Bible in his hand, from which he was reading aloud while the tears streamed down his face. There were several so engaged, for Wishart had been much loved, especially in Kyle where he had stayed for some time; in the first place he had been a schoolmaster in Montrose. The weeping man's face was familiar, but not notable enough for me to recall where I had previously seen it. I stared for moments, then felt Marion move beside me as if she was ready to go. I followed her silently, as while my Frenchmen were housed in a tavern for the night she had kindly received me in her house. It was merry with coming preparations for young Mag's marriage to the Master of Crawford, and there was much satin stuff to be sewn, spilling with everyone's haste about the floor. I had helped with the stitching and did not say how I came to be in St Andrews again, and no one asked any questions as I was by then seemly in my gown and mutch.

Presently, as things will do when one has stopped thinking about them, I remembered where I had seen the weeping black-clad Bible reader. He was none other than the friar who had accompanied Cardinal Beaton on that ill-fated ride to search for the dead King while he was still wandering near Tantallon after Solway Moss. The friar's name had been Brother James Melville. He had evidently abjured his habit, and turned reformer.

It happened that I was left behind at Marion's house, while M. de Lorges and the rest galloped without let to Madame in Stirling. There was no further need of interpreters concerning the evil news from the south. Hertford and the English had come again, as everyone had foreseen. Thereafter began, or rather continued, the pitiless destruction known, in the macabre Scots wit, as the Rough Wooing. The English were under orders to destroy the abbeys. They burned the one at Melrose, and Melrose town. They burned Dryburgh and the harmless houses round about, where folk did no more than mind their sheep and spin the wool. They burned Jedburgh. Of all the beauty of the fertile Border lands, the beauty kings and saints over the centuries had raised in stone and glass and gold to God, there was left only stark ruins and a shell, and burned fields before harvest. Even the skeletons of the springing arches of the abbeys are beautiful; they will endure, as no more can happen to them in such a way. Hertford reported to his master, the old King who was to die at last in bitter January for the flames of hell to warm him, that not so much damage had been done in Scotland for a hundred years. I myself would call it a thousand.

I could picture the distress of Madame Marie, but did not plead to be allowed to go to her, the Cardinal meantime having seen his daughter married with royal splendour at Edzell. Mag made a happy marriage and would bear six bairns, but she was left with a shrewd Campbell mother-in-law. However, this is nothing to do with my story, and Marion returned home filled with triumph at the noble wedding and some amusement at Countess Catherine's dealings and instructions over the profitable use of money and land.

She seemed pleased enough to have me with her, and I in my turn was pleased to let my hair grow again; it grows quickly. The town became quiet once more after its timely restlessness at the burning of Master George Wishart, although I cannot say what was happening further afield. The Cardinal returned, riding in with proud splendour, for I saw him pass. On the last night of his life Marion went up to the castle and spent it with him. I know that she was glad of this for as long as she lived, and she has lived very long alone. Sometimes I hear from her.

There had been no further disquiet in the town. We heard rumours – there were always these – of a quarrel at Stirling in the Queen's presence between the Cardinal and M. de Lorges, who had as quick a temper as David Beaton himself and shouted that the Cardinal had lured the Earl of Lennox, an Archer, to Scotland under a false promise to marry the Queen. Beaton raised his hand to strike, and de Lorges drew his sword. Madame, in her cool way, demanded that the two men be separated, which happened; then she ordered the Cardinal back to St Andrews and De Lorges I know not where.

It was certainly the old English King who, before he died,

arranged the Cardinal's murder. Beaton had been a thorn in that ulcerated flesh for long enough; diplomatic, shrewd, courageous in leading armies and advising the lone Queen Dowager: and, through all of it, a churchman, in spite of his bastards; after all Popes have had them also, and why should it not happen? A man is a man; Marion said as much to me afterwards, her face stony and her eyes dry; she was too strong a woman to weep.

She had slipped out of the castle postern early in the morning, after spending the night with her lover, and comforting him for the late trouble. They had been together for twenty years and for all Beaton's self-importance he was still glad of her. I am glad that she was there, also that she did not witness what happened next. Certain men – their names were known later – burst in after she had gone into the castle by overpowering the garrison, by means of one man who was not yet fully awake: set fire to the Cardinal's chamber door, smoking him out, for he had had his man drag a weight across it when he heard them come; and, reaching him, and without allowing him time to say a prayer, stabbed him again and again, despite his crying out 'I am a priest, I am a priest.' The last murderer – I had reasons for knowing him later well enough – made a sanctimonious speech before the *coup de grâce*, when he plunged his sword three times in the dying man's body till the blood gouted on the floor. I did not like the Cardinal, nor did many maybe; he was proud, hot-tempered, pleased with himself, but he was a supporter of Her Grace, at least till near the end; and he died bravely. His last cry was a great 'Fie! Fie!' All is gone!' which left his mouth open as his soul left it. In cold blood, they dragged his corpse to the castle wall, beneath which a crowd had already gathered, fearing what they had heard, that men had broken in; and though they did not love the Cardinal, they knew that, while he lived, they were safer than if he was dead, as he was without doubt now. The murderers – I saw it for myself by this time, for I had run out – lifted by an arm and a leg the bloodstained thing, exposed it, and one of the killers pissed into the open mouth. Afterwards, I heard that they salted the body and thrown it in a coffin into the castle well. By that time I had run back to Mistress Marion, who I knew must not be allowed to come out of the house and see what I and others had seen. It had all happened within an hour, or perhaps moments. I stood with my back against the door to prevent her going out to the street, stared at her, and told her; but there was in any case no need.

'David is dead.' Her voice was strangely calm; but she had not seen the horror. Later, after asking a few terse questions, she walked away, back into the room, and sat down alone. Presently she called 'Come in, Claudine.'

As I have said, Marion Ogilvy shed no tears. She said aloud 'I always knew this would happen; that at some time, they would kill him; but not like a dog, without the sacraments. They should have allowed him that, and Christian burial.'

'Perhaps they will allow that last,' I said, to comfort her. Many men had died unburied and without the sacraments lately, in Scotland; but it was strange to think of David Beaton doing so, as whatever they said of him he had been a high prelate and had always done his duty by the Church. Perhaps, for that, God would have mercy on his soul. 'He and I,' said Marion slowly, 'met when I was thirty, as I told you, past marriage for no one had arranged it for me. He was a thought older, not by so many years. I knew he was lonely; so was I. It was never adultery between us, which is all Christ forbade.' She raised her head and smiled at me and I saw her almost as she must have been when a young girl, alone with her mother, as she had long ago stated, the only child of a fourth marriage to an old Scots lord who shortly died. 'All of my half-brothers and half-sisters were like uncles and aunts, married long since and away. My mother did not marry again, as I told you; she had maybe had enough of it. She taught me to keep a house and to cipher, and manage accounts, and I can forge anyone's writ if I choose. That might have been of use to Davy, maybe, but he never asked it of me. He never asked anything but that I would comfort him and bear his children. He was often away, in France and far parts, on great matters, and he warned me of that before we might agree when I should come to him. Folk talk; oh, ay. I have been known as the Cardinal's whore these twenty years, and pointed at in the street, both here and in Arbroath, for I seldom went to Edinburgh. I'm glad we had wee Mag's wedding together, lately in the north.'

'What will you do now, Marion?' I asked her. She had risen to stand by the window, where a man with a plum-red mouth was already haranguing the crowd through his long sparse beard, his hands thumping a Bible. His name was Knox, and he had joined the murderers later, not before the death; he had no open hand in that, at least. Marion turned away, so that the light from the window was behind her face.

'I shall go to my house of Melgund Davy gave me,' she said. 'It's quiet, and I will take the bairns with me to the green places and the hills. We can live there without being pestered. If you should want to come, Claudine, you are welcome. I would not say as much to everyone. I lived alone for long, and I can do so again, till I die. Let us pray now for his soul,' and so we did, and if the Cardinal's passing was marked no more than by the sound of a great bell, we heard it toll. It tolled, maybe, for the true faith in Scotland.

Marion went away with the younger children, and I stayed behind to help clear the house and send such gear as she needed on to Melgund. I was waiting to hear from M. de Lorges if there was any word of my jointure, which had stopped meantime owing to the war; accordingly, Marion had lent me money. She would have given it to me, but I insisted that it be a loan and that I pay her interest. She said I was like the Campbell woman in the north and I replied that I was certainly no Campbell, but I had some reason to be grateful to that clan, as will presently be explained.

Once in the clearing of the St Andrews house I found a letter from Her Grace to the Cardinal, left by chance and, no doubt, not intended for my eyes. I scanned it idly in case it was still of importance in any way, but it was not; it concerned a meeting between them at Stirling. I noticed that certain of the writing was slightly different between lines, altering the arrangement in a way I cannot fully state, and remembered Marion's saying proudly that, as I have already been told, she could forge anyone's hand she chose. There might have arisen some misunderstanding between Her Grace and the Cardinal over this as well as other things, and it was possible that Marion was a trifle jealous of her lover; Madame Marie was, after all, a beautiful woman, and later on the regrettable Knox wrote that he had once espied, or someone had, the Cardinal's red shoes peeping out from behind Madame's curtains and that he was surprised at her. If this was true, and it may have been Knox's fertile invention, I am certain that it was because there was some matter of state the Cardinal needed to overhear, not that they were, then or at any time, lovers. The Queen Dowager was like steel, entirely devoted to the service of her daughter: she had known love with her first husband Longueville, had been compelled to leave her son by him in France, and now gave all her strength, all her love, to the young Queen Mary and to Scotland. Some years later, Marion Ogilvy was in fact arraigned for interfering with the Queen's writ, but I had destroyed that particular letter.

There arrived one for me, at last, from M. de Lorges, who had taken time to write from Stirling. The commander of the Archers had always treated me with courtesy and respect, and now I had much reason to be grateful to him. He had obtained no news of my jointure – he had very little time – but thoughtfully enclosed a note of hand, which I could exchange for money if I needed it. He also thanked me for my services. I wrapped the note of hand in my bodice round Alasdair's *sgian dubh*, with which I had never in all my adventures parted: and there was news, at last, of Alasdair himself, or rather news of a kind.

There is to be an array in the east, near Musselburgh, to which we hope to ride with the Governor, de Lorges had scrawled in great haste, adding that Argyll had come down from the north for it with his clansmen and was it possible that my husband was with them? It was not, but I knew that, if the Campbells were to fight, so would the Grants and the McGregors. *It is thought that we may confront the English commander there; say a prayer for us, good madame.* He professed himself my humble servant. I said the prayer and while I was doing so I completed the sending off of Marion's stuff, put on my tartan arisad with which I had never parted, and rode south on a horse hired at great expense, for they were in short supply, but by now I could afford it. Attendants I had none; what might happen to me on the way was no longer of importance, although as I had made my confession and received the sacrament I had no wish to have to become a whore again, in particular as my narrow parts had healed.

I can remember crossing the Queen's Ferry with my short hair blowing in the wind; it no longer looked like a boy's. I longed for Alasdair with all my heart and soul and hoped that perhaps when he saw me, he would not be angry any more. After all he had not known where to get in touch with me; perhaps he had tried and I had not known. I switched my thoughts away and briefly contemplated Saint Margaret, Queen of Scotland, who early travelled by the ferry and gave it its name, and whom I have always disliked faintly; she seems sanctimonious, but perhaps that is the teaching.

Once south of the water, there were many on the way. There were the Queen's men and the men of Governor Arran, men riding and men walking. I did not see the Scots Archers, or the clansmen of Argyll, or hear the pipes. With regard to the Frenchmen, Arran disliked them because there was a suspicion, later proved true, that the little Queen was to be married in France, and he wanted her, or said he did, for his son. Meantime, there was still talk that she was to be sent to some secret place for safety. The Governor might kill her, for all his protestations, for he was the next heir to the throne by his own descent from a Stewart princess; the English would almost certainly do so if she fell into their hands; and a child's life is in any case delicate. I thought for the first time of little Mhairi and of how she had been brown and strong, and promised myself that if God gave me the chance I would bear Alasdair more children and tell him nothing. This may seem deceitful, but it is not always advisable to bare one's soul totally; one must consider that of the other person. This is one reason why it is useful to have priests, to whom one may make confession.

Arran made his will on the battlefield, as it was to prove, near Inveresk where they had encamped, at a place named Pinkie Cleugh. It was a curious thing to do at the time, and I heard later that he had left his son, and his widow in the event, to the care of the King of France. This was by now not old lecher François, who had died in the same year as Henry VIII, and no doubt they met one another in purgatory if either were permitted to enter it. The new King of France, who continued to aid Madame, was shy Henri, who had been crowned after his brother died and was devoted to his elderly mistress and neglected his wife. I shall have more to say about her, and about him, and about that other.

We saw the English army under Hertford, now Earl of Somerset, drawn up in the September sunlight across the clear fields of autumn, and it glinted on their spears. I had drawn back with the other women who were there, and could see what was happening; the land there is flat. For three days they skirmished, while we shared our food; we always thought it was the main attack, but neither side seemed to know what to do:

they would send out small parties, who forded the Esk, joined, clashed and retreated again across the river, without much harm or much spilled blood. I had by now made out Argyll's Highlanders in a solid mass of dark forest green, but could see no MacGregors. It was possible that they were not near one another of purpose, as the clans did not deal together. There were, in the main, three phalanxes; Arran led one, old Angus himself the next, his grey beard sprouting below his flushed face in the sun, and I reflected that for all his faults and his former friendship with England, he was a man of tough resolute courage and probably, by now, loyal: after all he had been harshly treated by James V. His basnet sat on the back of his head, almost gaily: he looked ready for anything. Huntly, whom I did not know and whom Madame had caused to replace the Cardinal as Chancellor of Scotland, commanded the third division. I prayed for every man in the Scots army; how I prayed in those three days! I could see something else, jutting dark in the sunshine like a wall of death; Somerset's English cannon.

It should have been a victory. The disgrace of Solway Moss was not to be repeated; all the commanders were noble, so there was no question but that they would be obeyed, unlike the King's unlucky favourite Oliver Sinclair, whose fate I forget. There was to be no more floundering in an English bog; this was firm ground, in Scotland, near the coast. The clove-pinks, which gave the place its name, still bloomed here and there in the salt air in early autumn, pallid against the green grass, trodden by many hooves to give out a spicy scent. It drifted to our nostrils as we waited, we women; all of our senses were sharpened, so that we heard Governor Arran shout to the Earl of Angus to go with his division across the River Esk. The old devil refused, no doubt on the grounds that he was not to be ordered by anyone; Arran, his face twitching more than ever, then sent a herald to order the Earl to advance on pain of treason. Flushing bright red – he was troubled with a skin rash, which in the end killed him – Angus led his men over, making a great splashing as they crossed the ford. There was a moving among the Englishmen and they leaped to horse and charged, but the Douglas spears defended themselves, if not much more. Then the English cannon began to fire; they fired from the hill, as our own had done at Flodden, but these were sited better; and they fired them also from the

English ships close by at sea. It was the noise that frightened the
Campbell Highlanders, a great thunder the like of which they
had never before heard; they flung down their targes, their
swords, and fled in a great swirl of confused dark tartan, for
they had not taken time to strip themselves as a Highlander will
do in war, hurling himself on the enemy with his weapons, stark
naked. I saw it, then saw little more; clouds of dust were rising
from the stubble in the gleaned fields over which the battle now
raged. The Campbells could see nothing either, and they were
like men who have gone mad with fear. They fell in great
swathes, while the cannon thundered on. Afterwards, we found
the bodies.

The English meantime charged against the old Earl, who
decided to be prudent; he retreated to Huntly for help. Huntly
in his turn, half blinded with the dust, thought it was the English
who had come, and attacked his own countrymen, all of them,
Gordons and Douglases, hacking unknown at one another,
falling half-dead in the dust and trampled on by the English who
followed swiftly behind, killing any who still remained alive on
the ground or on foot, or in the saddle; the poor horses
screamed. This was the time when, as long ago at Flodden, the
flower of the Scots nobility fell; Madame's friend Lord Fleming,
the Master of Erskine, Lords Livingstone and Ogilvie, Methven
and Ruthven and many more; and Huntly himself, the
Chancellor of Scotland, they took prisoner. I saw a man with a
twitching face ride hard out of the fray and make in a stir of dust
for the north-west; Arran, who should have died like a dog with
men who were better than he. I knew he was riding to Madame,
and that she must greet with respect this dangerous fool who
presumed to call himself her superior because he called himself
a man, and to hear of yet a third Scots defeat in the unhappy
century. Pinkie Cleugh, a name a child might have uttered in
play, a place where flowers had lately bloomed, was worse than
Flodden, worse than Solway Moss; it left us without defences,
without armour, without aid, without anything except hope and
courage still.

I did not feel all of that then; I could not. When the
marauders had retreated it was growing dark, and I and the
other women crept across the twilit field among the white,
already robbed flesh of the dead; already, also, though it was
evening, waiting kites wheeled about in the dusk; they would be

back by early light. The English had taken armour and swords, but they had not, as the Borderers do, stripped everything; and, thank God, they had gone back again to their own place, wherever that was. I searched till it was dark, and then lay on my face among the dead, whoever they were; and early next morning, before the kites had pulled their fill of ribboned bloody meat, I went on searching; searching, till at last, where I should have known I would find him, at the forefront of the battle, I found the body of Alasdair Dorch, my husband.

I knew him at once; he was larger than anyone else, and the kites had not yet begun to tear at him. His great body, with the tangled black hair, sprawled forwards well towards the English lines; when I examined it gently, he had wounds to his chest, his belly, and his heart; the front of him was red with blood, therefore, but never his back. Soon he would be bones, picked clean; the angry kites wheeled above me and dabbed at me as if they wanted me soon gone, but I did not yet go. In other parts of that field there must have been other women seeking, searching, perhaps never finding, as I had done, their dead. They meant nothing to me. Nothing meant anything, except that I could hear myself give, at last, the grieving and ancient wail of the bereaved Highland woman, the coronach, over the body of my husband.

'Woman, you should not be here. The Lord will raise him up again on the last day. Until then, come away with me.'

I heard myself fall from wailing into silence. There, in the dawn's light above me, was a gaunt black-clad figure in a gown and bands, holding a Bible open at two flat pages. The grotesque appearance of such a creature, still living among all the dead, was in itself a part of the horror and the despair, and his words ridiculous; to go away with him, to follow him, as the apostles had followed Christ, or was this another kind of following? It was on my lips to utter blasphemy. The kites tore, a little way off, at other dead men's flesh, and but for our presence would be now at Alasdair's. How could he be raised again at the last day? He would be nothing by tomorrow but clean, giant bones.

I heard myself say so, rising with difficulty from my knees and facing the man. He quoted the Book of Ezekiel at me: the Lord had raised bones from a dry valley and clothed them in flesh. I looked down at what remained of Alasdair Dorch, at all I would have to remember him by; forgot my skirts dabbled with blood where I had held his body close, and felt, maybe, that wherever his soul was now, he had forgiven me, was perhaps already with Mhairi, and that we would all meet again: but for myself, for the present, there was only emptiness. I no longer cared what became of me. I was like a rag in the wind, blown on and about, twisting and whirling not by its own will or direction, until it is caught on thorns and falls, at last, to bleached threads, then to dust.

That is why I followed James Melville, whose face I had last seen beyond Wishart's fading pyre; and, before that, riding by Cardinal Beaton himself, in the friar's habit Melville had lately put off. Many who knew on which side their bread was buttered did so, these days: but I think that that man believed in his true conversion. He told me, with pride, as we walked, that it was known of in Rome, and that the Pope had sent instructions that he was on no account to be allowed to rejoin his Order. 'I am in any case done with those sons of Belial,' he said proudly.

I did not look back at Alasdair's body, or at the hovering kites. There was nothing more I could do for the dead man who had loved me in his lifetime. I followed James Melville, and for my sins in the end became his wife.

Before I forget to mention it in relation to all that followed, Sir George Douglas, in the turmoil of events still to come, offered the English Protector Somerset, who had been in command as Hertford in the time of the Rough Wooing, his services as the leader of yet another invasion into Scotland. I forget whether or not the offer was accepted, but maybe if I had become Sir George's kept mistress and beguiled him at Tantallon, he would have stayed at home and caused no further trouble. However perhaps I overrate myself.

The courtship of Mr Melville, as he was now called, was respectful. He had guided us both back across the dreadful field, stumbling as we did over the corpses of men and their beasts. His hand under my elbow steadied me, and when we won out towards Musselburgh he continued to support me as we walked, quoting aloud from his Bible. We had to go on foot, as we could not ride; every horse that was left alive had been taken already by those who had fled when it became clear that the battle was lost. Dead horses, their guts gaping, were less troubled by the kites than by carrion crows, thick as black flies on the slashed bellies, pulling the livers out and shaking them. Horseflesh is less delicate than man's flesh to eat, but a crow knows its master and will not face a kite. The smell of corruption had come with the day, and I was glad to be gone.

I expect we had been joined by the others by now, for I can remember the sound of plodding feet on the road. My shoes were soaked with the dew and with blood through which we had waded, which was drying out to brown; as it dried the leather made a nagging blister on my toe. This occupied me to a greater extent than anything Melville might be saying; even now I do not know what it was, except that at one point I heard him explaining why he had gone to the stricken field, as he called it, in case there were souls to be saved of men or perhaps of women. Afterwards I learned from him that some are saved and others are damned in any case, according to Calvin; so I do not know why he troubled to be there. He then looked at me, and admitted that he knew little of women himself. In his monkish life he had lived as a virgin, and to put it bluntly would be glad of instruction in the habits of marriage. A minister of the new religion ought to be married, and most accordingly were. I took it that I, as the first lone woman he had noted among the rest, would suffice. I did not speak of my past, in fact of anything. I was not, as I soon found out, expected to do so; the wives of ministers of the new religion keep their mouths shut, there being little opportunity to interrupt the flow of the evangel.

This was made evident at a house to which Melville eventually took me as I by then was, limping, filthy with dust, bloodstained, and wan with lack of feeling of any kind. Grief was with me still, but no longer memory; and grief is like a drug from an apothecary, shutting out feeling, not in fact a sensation of itself. There was a kind enough woman of the house who took me in, and gave me goose-grease for my hardened shoe and water to wash myself. Afterwards we all sat together at a table by the fire, eating thin porridge with bowls and wooden spoons; I was glad of it. There was no other man present except Melville, who was treated with great reverence and addressed as the minister. An old woman, maybe the mother, sat nearby, having put aside the sark she was sewing to eat, then take it up again; her eyesight must have been good for her age. Both women wore mutches and plain gowns, so I was not in bad company. Melville had said a long grace before the porridge. After it I felt sleepy, and would willingly have lain down in a bed, but alone; yet it was incumbent on me to sit up, out of courtesy, till I was shown where to go. After the meal Melville said another long prayer out of his head, then read aloud some more from the Bible. The two young sons of the house – I never found out where the father was, but no doubt he was dead, or with the lords' army – were made to bring out their books and get on, on the cleared table, with their schooling. 'Master Knox would not be pleased if ye were to neglect it,' said their mother. The name aroused an echo in my mind.

'It is a pity Master Knox could not have married us,' said Melville to me. It was the first time he had addressed me in company, being too greatly taken up with himself and his prayers. I was to be reminded of John Knox very often; he was, I found later, the man I had once seen in St Andrews after Beaton's murder, with his red plum of a mouth, his short stature, broad shoulders, and wispy black beard and hair. I asked now what had become of him, and everyone began to talk at once.

'He joined us in the castle after it was all over,' said Melville, and I did not ask more then; no doubt I should have done. The two women, young and old, praised Knox, who had evidently set up as a kind of tutor after the murder in St Andrews and otherwise had instructed the young as he went about the country; I saw the boys at the table raise their heads, an expression of some awe on their faces. 'He was arrested by the Frenchmen,' said one, 'and sent to the galleys.' 'Mind your books, George,' said his mother sharply. 'The Lord will release good Master Knox from bondage in His time.' I remembered hearing how the French had taken the castle of St Andrews, and had no doubt retrieved the Cardinal's body from the well and buried it in seemly fashion; but did not ask. The old woman by the fire spoke up in a piping voice.

'It is a pity Master George Wishart could not have married them, he knowing foreign parts, for this lady is French,' she said. Her daughter-in-law – I think after all that is who she was – rounded on her.

'Master George Wishart is burned long ago by the Papists; do ye not mind it? Good Master Patrick Hamilton was burned by

them likewise.' She closed her lips firmly and Melville said the time
had come when God's preachers could speak out freely, without
fear either of the flames or of cardinals, let alone the Pope. He
sounded smug and I did not think I liked him, but it could not be
helped. They showed me, at last, to my bed; and they told me that
Mr Melville would preach tomorrow, it being Sunday. That day
the battle had been fought was always to be known in Scotland as
Black Saturday. It was the longest day of my life.

On the following morning we all walked to the preaching.
There was at that time no such thing in Scotland as a Protestant
church, and so it either took place in the open air, in a field, or
the street, depending on the place and the weather; or else in a
ruined church the reformers themselves had knocked to pieces
or the English set on fire. Wishart, Knox and Melville himself
attracted many followers, for interest was growing with the
determined influx of Bibles over the years from England, the
murder of the Cardinal and, before that, the burning of
Hamilton and Wishart at the stake. In any case it made a change
from the rumours of war and the fact of loss. Whether the folk
were edified by Melville's rantings I know not, but he was the
first of his kind that I had heard, and soon stopped listening.

We were married by the first minister of the reformed faith
we met; they were to be found mostly in the towns, in their long
black robes and bands for preaching, wearing round gathered
flat caps on their heads like schoolmasters. Having not yet fully
assured themselves of what form their marriage ceremony was
to take, ours was a handfasting; we promised to take one another
as man and wife, then Melville was asked for the ring.

'She is wearing one,' he said petulantly; he had a high voice
with a whine in it. 'I saw no need to buy another.'

'Take it off and turn it the other way up,' said the minister
practically, and with a surge of regret I slipped off Alasdair's
gold ring he had bought for me that time in Stirling, and which I
had worn faithfully through all that had happened to me since. I
had thought it would never leave my finger until death, but
meantime Melville slid it on again the other way. We received
the good wishes of the minister and witnesses and went on
westwards, judging by the sun, still walking. By the evening we
came to a place where as it happened there was an inn which still
had its roof. Here, after a meal of sorts, I was bedded by Mr
Melville, erstwhile friar and, as I discovered later, rather more

or perhaps less. Neither fact made him easy of instruction in bed. He was inept, as might have been expected, at the first, but afterwards almost as futile, though not quite, as my first husband the Comte had been; but neither was he as kind. I heard him grunting through the performance and at last discovering his own ecstasy, which was by its nature separate from mine as I had none. That, for the wedding night, was the end of it for me, and the beginning for him. I need say no more.

All this time, the country being in confusion, there was no news of Madame or of how she had received news of the defeat, though I could picture to myself her bitterness and anger at finding Arran, out of all the brave lords who had gone, still alive with his tidings, and useless as ever. There were also rumours that the little Queen had disappeared, even that she had died. I did not believe it, for I thought it more likely that Madame, being practical, had sent the child secretly somewhere out of danger. Perhaps Iain Ruadh had gone with her, or perhaps he had been permitted to remain, to comfort the woman they now spoke of as the old Queen. Madame was thirty-three. The English were back in Leith. This I ascertained from a man who had come from the east, with many others fleeing from the burning towns along the coast; he must have had friends to receive him, as he seemed in no distress himself. Most of those who assembled to listen to my husband's preaching seemed unaffected by events and assumed that Scotland, in the nature of things, would be absorbed into England shortly. There seemed no word of further French help, although I did not doubt that Madame continued to solicit it. More I did not know yet, but learned later.

Meantime I myself was discontented, although sheltered and fed. My husband and I were made discreetly welcome in the subdued reformed manner, wherever we went, with much Bible reading, exhortation, prayers sent presumably by God straight to folk, and saying of long grace composed of whatever came out of Melville's head while the meat grew cold. It must not be thought that I am against the Bible itself or knowledge of it; it is a record of the life of Our Lord, of the prophets, and of wisdom; but to open it at random and rely on oneself not only to interpret it, but to do so aloud to crowds of ignorant listeners, seems rash in my estimation. However, this was the evangel, as they call it. It was spread all over Kyle, where Wishart had preached before Melville ever came there. The dead man's memory was still as green as the hills; he must have been a rare spirit; everyone who had heard him loved him. The folk listened with commendable patience to my husband's ravings instead, which after the first is more than I did. I do not recall a single coherent thought Melville ever had that had not been preached by Catholic priests long before him, but perhaps I am not one of Calvin's saved. My task, as it turned out, was to go round discreetly with a leather bag during the sermon and collect silver offerings for our maintenance. We thus made enough money to live, and for me at least, it was easier work than being a whore. As far as that went, Melville seemed to derive prior inspiration for his sermons by copulating with me particularly on the previous night; whether he thought them out then, or at all, I know not and did not ask. He made some prowess, and why I did not conceive by him I do not know, but thanked God for it. We moved down out of Kyle into Galloway, where the folk are different. They were once an independent fief, separate from the rest of Scotland, and have never forgotten it. One of their clan, a McCulloch by his marriage, kept his own private fleet, having raped the heiress of a castle situated high up by the coastline. The daughter she unwillingly bore him took in her time a fancy to a young man at Orchardton, on the other side of the bay, whose family were not willing for him to marry a freebooter's child, so Eppie McCulloch borrowed the fleet to try to kidnap the young nobleman, and was herself killed in the resulting battle. The place was full of such stories and had we lingered longer, I would no doubt have heard more of them.

I did not myself linger, for this reason. One night while we lay in a borrowed bed Melville began, during his completed urgings within me, to babble. Whether he knew what he was saying or was merely borne away with himself and his physical achievements, I neither know nor care; but this is what he said. He had been with the others in the castle that time the Cardinal was attacked and they had already wounded him. Melville felt himself called to administer the *coup de grâce*, not once but three times. 'This work of God ought to be done with greater gravity,' he began unctuously. The rest was conveyed in murmuring. *Repent thee of thy former wicked life, but especially of the shedding of the blood of that notable instrument of God, Master George Wishart, which albeit the flame of fire consumed before all men, yet cries it in vengeance upon thee.* A thrust here. *I protest that neither the highness of thy person, the love of thy riches, nor the fear of any trouble thou couldst have done to me* – a second thrust – *moves me to strike thee; but only because thou hast been, and remain, an obstinated enemy against Christ Jesus and His holy Evangel.* 'And then I gave him the third thrust with my stog sword.' The poor dying wretch called out as I have said 'I am a priest! I am a priest! Fie, fie! all is gone!' and on the last great cry died, with his mouth open. They had piddled in it that time when the Cardinal was dead, flung out on the parapet before the crowds.

Melville then explained how he had, some time before, seen the Gospel light despite his previous false occupation, which led him to act as he had done then, and no doubt to act as he was doing now. He had gone further with me that night than ever before; under the harsh comfortless rucked-up folds of the sarks, or night-rails, he caused us to put on to cover our nakedness during the long preliminary prayers he always said before we went to bed, my thighs were wet with his semen. There was starlight outside in the clear night, and by it I could see Melville's mouth gaping in his thin unshaven face; some of his teeth were bad and made his breath stink. I had heard him out, meantime resolving in my mind to leave him. While he finished I thought of generous Marion and of how she had been a friend to me, and here was I lying with her lover's murderer, though not by any intended design. I resolved not to do so again. How I would have achieved this in the ordinary way I do not know, for Melville had come to rely on it; but with the aid of Providence my courses came upon me next day, during which time the Old Testament says a woman is unclean and Melville therefore left me alone at such seasons. I lay by him three nights thereafter with a linen rag stuffed between my legs instead of his member, thinking of ways and means of escape, but there seemed none; wherever I walked he would find me. At the next preaching, however, I decided at any rate to secrete some of the silver for myself; after all, I had earned it. Further than that I did not plan, except to say, as I lay by my sleeping murderer, a prayer to Our Lady. That there would never be more danger for me from Melville thereafter I was certain; the Mother of God, whom the reformers have from the beginning insulted, never fails to answer prayer. I knew that I would in some way soon be free of that man who had drawn a priest's blood, but could not himself have engendered a mustard seed or considered a lily. I would leave as I had come: myself still, but better fed.

That was the reason why I did not linger in Galloway. There was an outdoor preaching once at the edge of a wood, in the cold. When the inevitable sermon started I went round surreptitiously with my bag, as I did sometimes early. I had made no plans for what followed and if I went into the wood, it was with the intention of quietly relieving myself, or at least pretending to do so, for sermons go on and on and I had heard enough of hell fire and God raising dead men's bones, and the saved and the damned, and the elect. Melville was evidently one of the latter, and by now he believed it himself. I looked at his thin earnest face spouting forth damnation and other probabilities and suddenly could endure it no longer, and went away and wandered about in the leafless wood till he should have finished and I could hear the crowds go. I made water and shat behind a blackthorn bush which by then, with the closing year, was beyond its early creamy blossom and its later blue fruits, from which the Galloway folk make wine. Then I became aware of a good smell, for variety; it was rabbit stew with herbs, and I was hungry. I still held the leather bag, and had no compunction in intending to use it to pay for food if whoever had made the stew would give it me. I worked for my keep, and even a horse needs corn.

I went on, and Melville's voice was by now a drone far off behind me and presently faded. I came to a fire, a cauldron, and women sitting round it, with thin brown children playing by themselves or sitting idly, not speaking much together. There was a lean dog too, I remember, which bared its teeth at me, but I am not afraid of dogs and extended my hand, and it sniffed at my palm and subsided. One of the women looked up, and said something in a language I did not know. There were carts in the distance, with round hoods and painted wheels. Evidently these people lived in them.

'Will you give me some stew?' I said, pointing to the cauldron. I dipped my hand in the bag and brought out silver, and the woman smiled, revealing yellow teeth with gaps; she might have been forty but it was difficult to tell her age. She ladled me some stew, took the coin, and I sat down by them tailorwise to eat it, my legs crossed.

'We may not sit so,' she said in Scots. 'The women of our tribe must sit with straight limbs, except in presence of a man they do not know, when they cross them for chastity.'

I was eating the stew with my fingers and it was good. 'You are fortunate to be chaste,' I said bitterly. 'I myself have not been so.' I felt already that the woman knew all about me, and her dark eyes regarded me with understanding, perhaps compassion.

She then told me, while I ate, an extraordinary story. King James V in his wanderings had come across these Egyptians, to whom his father had been hospitable but who had since been driven out. No doubt he thought that as they were vagabonds, they were without principle and need not be considered; at any rate, he tried, in his usual fashion, to rape one of their women. The men of the tribe came and set upon him, tied an immense bundle of cut wood on his back, and beat him, still carrying it, out of the forest. The King of Scots did not trouble them again, and did not mention the matter to anyone; no doubt his Tudor mind had festered over it, but by then the gipsies were gone. They had ways of disappearing without being seen to go, and would travel back and forth over the Border in a way no one else could do.

I had no desire to cross the Border, but asked if they were going north and if, with more silver though I must keep some for myself, I might travel with them. They were vague as to direction, but I did not think they were going into England; there was to be a wedding and a funeral later, in what I now believe to have been Perthshire. Time and place are confused in their reckoning, and the story about King James would go down among them as if it had happened yesterday. They put me in one of their wagons, where a very old woman was lying in the dark on some straw; perhaps it was to be her funeral, as she was clearly dying, but in great peace. Later I heard the men come home from their occupation, no doubt, of taking more rabbits, mending pots or whatever else they do, using their lurchers who slink by them and can also disappear. I lay in as much peace as the old woman who was dying, clutching my leather bag, for Melville if he searched would not be told I was here; and before dawn the carts began to rumble off, leaving a charred fire and nothing else. I was comforted by the sight of an ikon of the Virgin on the wooden wall of the inner cart, below which a lamp swung in oil, moving faintly with the cart's wheels. They had brought the ikon with them from India, or Egypt, or from whence they had come: which country that was no one will ever know. I left them at Stirling, and went straight to Madame Marie.

There was no difficulty in gaining access to her presence. I might be dirty, as gipsies of necessity are, with my hair unkempt though I still kept Alasdair's comb. It did not matter; Madame was accustomed to strange messengers of all kinds by now, and no doubt the Castle guards thought I was such another, and let down the drawbridge. They were different men from those I remembered, and wore on their livery, a good many of them, the Erskine clenched fist carrying a cutlass. Lord Erskine himself was with Her Grace, a grave-faced man, not young. His father had been killed at Flodden, his heir at Pinkie Cleugh. He was Keeper of Stirling Castle and also of Edinburgh. Madame could rely on at least one friend, besides myself. She had put on weight and looked older. She came forward to me in all my dirt, holding out both her hands.

'Claudine,' she said. 'Claudine.'

She gestured to my lord, who bowed and went. When he had gone she began to talk as if we had never been parted, almost absently, as if it were a release. 'He is good to me, and gives me advice,' she said in French. 'At times I still feel a foreigner here and that is how they think of me still, despite everything. Lord Erskine's daughter was the King's mistress after her marriage, and bore him the Lord James. I do not know whether or not that young man still calls himself Prior of St Andrews, and it does not matter. Everything is changing. Claudine, what happened to you? Did you find your husband?' Her eyes searched me and she knew by my face that I had not, or at least not alive. 'So many are dead,' she said, 'so many. The English are in Leith and by now also at the River Tay. I have sent the Queen away for safety.'

'We heard that she was dead,' I said, 'but I knew she was not.' Her Grace smiled, a sudden mischief lighting her face, as in old days sometimes when we were children.

'By no means, God be thanked,' she assured me. 'She is on a small island in a lake; they do not even call it a loch, as is usual here, I do not know why. Lord Erskine's second son is still Commendator of Inchmahome Priory, though he will have to resume the world now he is heir to the title, his brother being dead. Your son is with my daughter there. Both have grown and are well. I ride there sometimes, when I can. You must come with me.' She had spoken in a low voice, so as not to be overheard by anyone but myself; none except a chosen few must know where the Queen was, even in loyal Stirling Castle. I nodded, and said I would come.

We sat down presently together, for Madame had always allowed me to be seated in her presence when we were alone, and she sent for wine. 'Thank God, M. d'Oysel sent cases from Bordeaux, so there is that, if nothing else yet from France,' she murmured.

I did not yet know who d'Oysel was, but meantime Madame's fastidious nose wrinkled. 'My friend, you need a bath. I will see that they obtain hot water. Tell me of all that has happened; I have talked all the time of myself.'

Simply, I told her what had happened, or rather not quite all; only that I had found my husband dead at last, like so many others; and that I had married again, and disliked my second husband and had left him. I hung my head at this; Madame had perhaps not greatly liked James V, although she had tried in duty to love him; wives do not leave their husbands whom they have sworn to cherish. But I made clear that Melville was a reformer, although I did not say he was a renegade friar, and that I had let him marry me while in despair after stumbling across the battlefield and had, without much delay, grown sick of him and his beliefs. She could perhaps guess the rest, and the blue-grey eyes fixed them steadily on my face.

'You must stay here, Claudine,' she said. 'For the sake of your soul you must not listen to such people any more. I still have Mass said here daily, and can pray before the Sacrament. That sustains me, and it will sustain you also. Do not go away again. I will send for the bath to be filled now, and then food.'

She rose, called the servants, and I saw with the sweeping of her black robes that her tall body had grown majestic, a ruler's; but she was not yet permitted to rule. During the days that followed I observed the snickering Arran enter once or twice, and others; and noticed that whether they knew it or not, the foreign woman they still called Mary of Guise was beginning to guide them. In time, I was certain, she would rule them, and Scotland. Meantime the Queen was safe, I had had my bath, and as before Madame obtained me clean linen, shoes and a gown. I combed my hair and felt better, and one day we rode together,

with a few trusted attendants, to the island of Inchmahome, to
visit the Queen of Scots.

It is assumed by most, if they think of it at all, that the time spent,
by the little child who was Queen Mary, on the island in the Lake
of Menteith, for one of the few times in her life was peaceful and
happy; certainly this was so. It is not, however, correct to assume
that the Queen's stay there took place near the water in fine
weather, perhaps in spring, with the osier buds bursting among
the branches where she played, the lake itself blue and clear,
primroses on the ground, moorhens on the water, and the
surrounding hills protective and calm. It was in fact a winter's
day when we rode there and the north-west wind blew in our
faces. We rode by the crazy twistings of Forth in that part of the
country and at last came to the Goodie Water, and Madame
smiled beneath her hood. 'They think of strange names, the
Scots,' she said. I thought of how names began and how the
strawberry growers, the *fraisiers*, Madame had brought with her
from France as a bride had had little chance to grow their
strawberries, but had otherwise multiplied exceedingly and had
given rise to the name Fraser, despite what anyone may claim to
the contrary. The wind died as we rounded the shelter of a hill.
Madame then drew near to me in the saddle and spoke very
quietly, out of earshot of the attendants.

'This is most secret,' she said, 'and even in the Castle and the
Priory precincts I dare not speak of it yet. There is a suggestion
– it is at present no more – that my daughter shall be sent to
France, there to be married to the young Dauphin François. He
is a little younger; that does not matter. As Queen of France she
will be secure, and France and Scotland can then control the
ambitions of the English, which never seem to die. Perhaps
French and Scots together might even invade that country in
their turn; after all they have done the same to us time out of
mind, and it is all they seem able to understand; the sword and
the flame, blood spilt and poor folks' crops ruined.' Her mouth
set bitterly.

I reflected that, for once in her life, Madame was wrong. An
invasion of England for the sake of France and ourselves was
what had been attempted at Flodden, and all of James IV's fine
French brass cannon had been fired too high on the hill and had
been later captured, and many lords killed, foremost of all the

King, leaving only a child to inherit. However, I held my peace, and Madame went on talking, intense now in her hate; Lennox, who had once with unction wooed her, was now marching north with an English force to destroy what he could against Arran, leaving his Lady Margaret, who was again pregnant, in London. On all sides there was treachery, and no doubt it would be a good idea, if it could be done safely, to send the little Queen into France; but the Scots, being stiff-necked, would not readily take to such a plan despite the earlier alliances. I said as much, and Madame made a wry mouth.

'What else will they take to, apart from the English marriage?' she asked. 'Many of their misfortunes stem from themselves; they are unstable as water except for their feuds, and have no other loyalty, at least not to me.'

I murmured that it took time, and that Governor Arran was now generally admitted to be of no account; and I remembered our recent ride to Edinburgh, where I had stood once more behind the Queen Dowager in Council, this time without a royal child in my arms. Madame had made a magnificent speech, and had rallied my lords, at least as much as it might be done. Some were loyal, no doubt.

'Here is the place,' said Madame now, and I saw how her weary face had brightened at sight of the water, grey and whipped into cold waves as it was today. We were rowed to the island, and the neatly kept Priory buildings; but before that a small figure ran down, bright skirts whipping, through the wind, without her cloak, and waved and blew kisses, her red hair flying beneath her close hood; and behind her a boy, also with red hair. I forgot that he was my son, and later disliked his closed secret face, which resembled his father's. However he would be handsome enough, and provided the Stewart misfortune did not overtake him Iain Ruadh would do well, perhaps in the French army. I watched Madame embrace her daughter, lifting the little creature from the ground; they laughed and kissed and kissed one another, then took hands and walked together up the path, like any mother and daughter, to where the Prior waited in his robes by the arched door. He resembled his father Lord Erskine, and was grave. No doubt he had preferred his life in the Church, and now must leave it and breed heirs. He had in fact already achieved a certain amount of this, and had two natural children, a son and a daughter; likewise his brother, dead in the battle, left a bastard son David, a boy already in orders who would succeed to the Commendator's office at the Priory in due course and waited now to bow over Madame's hand, behind his uncle.

We entered, and there was a fire and food and wine; they had caught fish in the lake that day and now roasted them for us. We laughed and ate and talked together, and I tried to address Iain Ruadh in Gaelic but he had forgotten it, and answered, courteously enough, in French. The visit was over all too soon, for we had to ride back in the dawn, having stayed overnight; more time with her daughter could not be allowed to Madame, lest news come out of the east or west, from Broughty or Leith or France or from Arran. There were tears in her eyes which had not been brought there by the wind, and I thought how she, like myself, had been denied joy of her children, though I had loved mine less well than I had loved myself. She, on the other hand, could have lived long ago in company with her small son Longueville in France, and could have left this savage land and its untrustworthy lords to go to the devil, or else to England, in their own way; but she would not abandon her daughter. Also, she was herself a Queen and had vowed to rule: and rule she did in the end, though her gifts were never given full rein; she was never permitted to rule Scotland in peace, only in war, and so history has judged her.

Governor Arran was meantime discovered to be making advances to England again, as French help was tardy in coming. Madame accordingly wrote to Henri II himself, in reply to one of his to her full of promises, to persuade him to flatter Arran and keep him if possible on our side; it was suggested that, in addition to the Châtelherault dukedom, a French heiress should be offered to Arran's son. To do Madame justice, it was not yet known that this handsome boy would become an idiot; in fact, for some years he showed promise in that refuge of noble Scots in France, the Archers of the Guard. However Arran had already agreed to send the boy there as a hostage and the situation irked him. It was in fact impossible to be certain of his intentions at any time, and Her Grace proceeded without him in her resolute fashion. At any rate, Arran accepted the dukedom.

Musselburgh was burned, Dalkeith captured, and Arran rode out to besiege Haddington, which the English had taken, but failed to retrieve the town. Meantime, we waited in the capital, and Madame strode up and down the room with impatience at the French delay; if only they would come! 'I have prayed,' she said, striking her hands together. 'Surely God has not abandoned us!' I soothed her, being evidently unable to help her with my prayers.

At that moment, or perhaps the next, there came a rushing of feet. Informers burst into the room, joy on their faces, forgetting their obeisance; Her Grace drew herself up. Immediately they were repentant, and bowed. 'Madame, forgive our haste, but it is the French fleet! It has been sighted off Dunbar; a hundred and twenty sail, they say, sixteen galleys and a brigantine, and three great ships. It is our salvation! We know you will rejoice,' and they fell on their knees, and kissed her hands; they were every man devoted to her.

Madame thanked God, and on the seventeenth of June the French commander, the Sieur d'Essé, came to seek audience, saying there were five thousand Frenchmen, as well as mercenaries from Germany and Switzerland and France. They had landed at Leith; the situation was saved; the famous soldier Strozzi, who had fought in the Continental wars, was there, and his brother the Count Rhinegrave, also a careful personage named Jean de Beaugé who wrote down, in clerkly fashion, everything that then happened and every word Madame said.

I spoke with De Beaugé afterwards; it was a relief to hear the French tongue again. He was concerned with the state of so warlike a people as the Scots, who always seemed to be defeated. 'It is not because they are less belligerent than the English nation,' he said cautiously, his long face considering the matter. 'It is because they will fight among themselves, brother against brother, clan against clan. Accordingly, God is angry, and before aiding them is concerned to prove to them the error of their ways. Perhaps now the French have come He will relent, and allow us to conquer.'

Madame held a council, and as usual I stood behind her and saw her tall dark-clad figure, standing erect in its dignity and strength. 'I cannot ride at the head of armies, my lords,' she told them. 'However, when you have finally taken Haddington and made it no longer a centre of attack by the English, I will withdraw from Stirling, for I need no longer remain there for my daughter's safety now that you are present. I will be here in

Edinburgh, if you should need me at any hour of the day or night. There are perhaps some who will not fight the English, but I will do so.' She smiled a little, mentioning no names, and in that smile was the resolve to pay in full coin for the burnings, the ruined crops, the starved and homeless people, the constant danger to the little Queen. I remembered how the old King of England had once been hot to marry Madame, and took leisure to wonder how that gross flesh would suitably have encountered such steel in a velvet glove. At any rate, it had not happened, and by now such a prospect would be impossible. Madame, although a Christian, loathed England and the English for what they had done, and would reply in full measure. Thereafter she rode into the camps, to encourage the men; but before that the Sieur d'Essé was able to report that the mere sight of his advancing army had made the English scuttle back like scared rats into Haddington. 'They fear the French before they even see them,' he boasted.

However, a number of French were found to linger in Edinburgh itself, in the taverns and no doubt among the whores. There were also, sadly, Scots who had drifted away from the army, discouraged by the lack of events. Madame made a decision. 'You will come,' she said to me, and instructed me to tell the members of her household likewise. 'We will go out into the town, stop at every door where they may be, and I myself will speak with them.' She was afraid of nothing, but I reflected that even yet, her spoken Scots was still that of a Frenchwoman; yet as the Holy Ghost came down on the apostles at Pentecost with the gift of tongues, so no doubt He would do for Madame, for her cause embodied truth.

This happened, and Her Grace and the rest of us walked on foot down the Canongate and the Cowgate, the High Street and the Grassmarket, stopping at every door and every booth behind which renegades might lurk drinking ale. 'My hearts, every man who can bear arms,' she addressed them, and they stared in amazement at this tall royal lady in her summer coif and gown, who had come to them to make them ashamed, and to make them fight. 'Go, I beg of you, to the Scots camp outside Haddington, which we must take,' she said. 'Every man can help. Take with you a gift for those who are already fighting; if you can buy none I will help you, but you have enough money for ale.' This made them rise to their feet, and swear to go; I saw no man deny her. Madame called her servants then, and gave them bread and wine and meat and barley, and sent it to the men at Haddington. 'This is not payment for what I hope you will achieve,' she said in a message. 'The merits of each and every one of you will be rewarded when the time shall come. It is not unfitting to urge on men of courage with promises of reward. A prince –' she described herself as though she were a man, her child a son – 'is the more dearly loved by his soldiers when he shows appreciation of their striving.'

Then she mounted her horse, and we women mounted ours. In a clatter of calm hooves we rode out again and down into the High Street. I recalled again how in times long ago, during her first marriage, Madame had gone out from Châteaudun to help the poor, house by house; now she did the same in Edinburgh, but for a different reason. She called at every door to ask for soldiers who might be hiding. She spoke to each man she found, and De Beaugé wrote down her words afterwards, having heard them from me.

'Is it thus, my friends, that you support the French? Is it thus that you set them a good example? Before God, if I had not seen you with my own eyes and if anyone had told me that you were like to forget your honour in this way, I would not have believed them. I should have thought such a thing incredible, having praised you so much all my life for what I believed and still do believe to be true, that no nation on earth would equal your courage. I think it must be that you have come to this town to equip yourselves with arms and horses rather than in order to escape from combat with our enemies.' Her clear eyes surveyed them. 'All the same,' she continued, 'because I believe you would not wish to fall into some unforgiveable fault, I am warning you that we shall have a battle at Haddington within two days.' The men stirred. 'I am sure you would not want to live to regret that you had not been in the right place to wreak vengeance on those who have injured you in so many ways, to avenge the deaths of your relatives and friends, and to take redress for the damage to your goods and property.'

Again, I do not remember a Scotsman after that who did not set out for Haddington. But there were still the lounging French. With them, Madame was at home. 'The English are coming with four or five thousand horsemen in the hope of raising the siege of Haddington,' she told them. 'However things have been put in such order that, with the help of God, we should manage to foil their endeavours.' There was scorn in her voice for those who had deserted their duty already, having struck not a blow; most of these were mercenaries. 'Even if you do not take their part, there are enough brave men in our camp to vanquish our enemies,' she told them. 'But in this way, the prowess of the soldiers already there will be plain to see, whereas the infamy of the deserters will be published abroad by the whole world. However, regardless of what I say, do as you please.' Again, she shamed them; they went back, and fought, and the siege in the end was raised. We heard of it in Madame's closet. There had been skirmishing, as a result of attack by the French at once, and many English prisoners were taken; several hundred English also were left dead on the field. Madame turned to me with sparkling eyes, her face bright as it had been in youth. 'We will go to them,' she said. 'They have fought as brave men will, and we must go.'

We set out before dawn, but the summer light came soon. Madame went round every soldier, clasping many by the hand. 'Since the state of this realm and my service depends only on you,' she said, 'it is only right that your praise should come from me myself.' She offered them, again, gifts. 'The greater the dangers and the hazards of war, the greater will be the fruits of victory.' I remember her words well, to this day, and the way she looked as she said them.

We could hear the French cannon pound from where we waited in Edinburgh, like distant thunder which did not come close. The dead began to be brought in for burial, in carts. One young man – he resembled the one like an angel, with fair hair, who had rescued me that time I was in despair in the Lamp of Lothian – lay dead in all his finery, great chains of gold about his neck and arms, and his hose embroidered richly. There was solemn Mass said for him and I saw Madame weeping; perhaps he reminded her of her brothers.

All this was very well, but suddenly there was a slowing of the war; the French are shrewd. They were giving their strength and their young men, and we had not yet signed the treaty to ensure that France and Scotland would be allies as of old, and that the young Queen would be married to the Dauphin. Accordingly, Madame and I rode out. The treaty was signed in the cool of a stone-built nunnery near Haddington, and ensured that Mary, Queen of Scots, would not after all be Queen of England but Queen of France. That done – it had taken but a stroke of the pen, and Madame signed with a flourish – we refreshed ourselves, for it had been decided that the camps must be visited again, while we were there; a concourse of ladies and lords of the household were with us, and Madame's position must be made clear. She, and not Arran, would henceforth govern Scotland; the sooner it was realised by all men, both Scots and French, the better.

Arran did not show his face while we made ready to climb St Mary's tower. Madame had expressed a wish to view the whole campaign, the whole battlefield, spread out beneath where a soldier's daughter could sum it up from that height. We went with her, all of us. The guns still fired. Madame rode up to the back of the church and prepared to dismount.

At that moment there came an explosion like thunder. The English had fired a cannon from the town, having watched us come. I myself was choked with the smoke and saw nothing, but felt as if a blow had hit me in the stomach and fell to the ground. When I rose up, it was to see amid the clearing smoke a frightful spectacle. Many among us were dead; limbs and other bleeding parts lay about, not all of them belonging to men; sixteen of these, of Madame's household, were afterwards found to be dead, and some women. Others were wounded, or lacking a limb or an eye, or both eyes, the blood running down their faces.

It was cold, deliberate carnage. Undoubtedly they had hoped to kill Madame. I went to her; she had fainted, which I never saw happen before in all her life. I held her in my arms, and they fetched water to her presently; by that time, she had sat up. I could see the expression in her eyes, deep with horror. There was also, and still, resolution.

'They are dead,' she said, 'and we will say Masses for them. My daughter, thank God, is alive still. She must not be exposed to this evil. She must leave the country. She must go to France. I did not want to lose her, but she must go, perhaps even with the French ships when they return.'

I heard her decision amidst the sight of the dead bodies of her friends, though they were already being removed; sixteen is not so great a number when compared to the losses on the field. The rest were bandaged, soothed, conveyed to shelter;

afterwards, Madame visited them. Following that she left the French commander to conclude the siege of Haddington, and herself, with me, rode to the west, to Dumbarton, alongside the useless Arran and his train and hers, to arrange the departure, as soon as might be, of the Queen of Scots out of her realm. It was no longer safe for the child to stay in it.

I did not at that time meet M. d'Oysel, as he had sailed by then to France with instructions. No doubt, I thought, he was like other ambassadors, charming, urbane, shrewd, and giving nothing away except perhaps a few cases of Bordeaux. However he had disturbed the English, who described him as a Frenchman of fair words that had altered the mind of Her Grace and the Governor with regard to their former resolution. This of course meant the English marriage, which had in any case never been in Madame's mind, either former or to come. As for Arran, his mind veered in so many directions that it resembled the tail of a weathercock. In case I should forget to mention it, he was eventually rewarded, or rather kept quiet, with the French dukedom, that of Châtel-herault. It was no doubt less prestigious than the Crown of Scotland but, as Arran's heir proved an imbecile in the end, perhaps more peaceful for all concerned.

Meantime, the child Queen was removed in great secrecy from her island on the lake to Dumbarton Castle, the more easily to take ship for France. All this was made the more necessary by the advent of yet another English commander, Lord Grey de Wilton, who arrived with troops to invade the east and may have meant, had his prey meantime not deserted him, to relieve the garrison up at Broughty and, with them, encircle Madame at Stirling and also capture the Queen. This is only my own surmise, but my father was after all a soldier and I can read maps. As regarded that, Madame herself showed me a letter from Duchesse Antoinette, trusting that the course her daughter was now taking would hinder the enterprises of her enemies. It certainly seemed, for the time, as if it might; though Henri II was still cautious until the child bride was in his hands, and meantime sent no real relief.

Iain Ruadh had been conveyed with the Queen to the gigantic rearing rock which resembles a pair of human buttocks, with the castle perched on top like a clyster. I demurred to Madame Marie; would not she keep the boy to comfort her, as I myself offered him gladly? She looked me straight between the eyes.

'Once I was glad of him, for he reminded me of the son I had lost. Now I need no such comfort. My daughter is going, and my sons also must go,' and I knew she was thinking of the little Duc de Longueville left in France, whom she had not seen for thirteen years and, who, though he could not have remembered her, had lately written a letter wishing he were old enough to come to her side, and fight. No doubt Duchesse Antoinette often talked to him of his mother and at first she had sent drawings and measurements of the Duc's height as he grew. Such things by now were less important. However Madame and I agreed that the close company of a boy as playfellow might, as the children grew, be less than proper for a Queen of Scotland and France. It was decided – Madame had thought of it for herself, not I – that several little girls, all of them named Mary, should be chosen as the Queen's playmates and, later, her companions. The choice was carefully made by Madame. There was Mary Fleming, whose father had been most loyal and had fallen at Pinkie Cleugh. Unfortunately his widow was that Janet, James IV's natural daughter who liked to be known as Joan, whom I myself had earlier encountered at Caerlaverock. She, of all people, was to be the young Queen's governess. No doubt Madame thought of her as a motherly soul. Besides young Mary she had seven other children, most of them old enough to look after themselves, who were to be left at home. Perhaps their grandmother had an eye to them; that would do them no good. Lady Fleming herself later, in the French records, was spoken of as a young fair maid. History is full of such errors.

A second Mary was the daughter of Lord Seton, also loyal, perhaps more so than any; he had formerly had a hand in letting Cardinal Beaton escape back to St Andrews from his imprisonment. He had taken as his second wife Marie Pierris, whom I had never much liked either; she was to accompany her stepdaughter to France. My lord was a fine falconer, and I have met him at times with a hawk on his wrist, riding near Falkland. He had earlier been for the English marriage as the best thing for the country, but like many was sickened at the burnings and slayings, in particular as the English marauders burned down his own great house and, more importantly, the collegiate church founded in honour of St Catherine by his pious mother, the Lady Johanna. Lord Seton could long since be counted Her Grace's firm friend; his daughter Marion was one of her younger ladies and I had come to know her fairly well since she had once tried to keep me out of Madame's presence shortly before the Queen's birth.

The third Mary was Mary Beaton, some kin of the Cardinal's, and the fourth was Mary Livingstone, whose father, along with Lord Erskine, had been the young Queen's guardian and would come with us and the children to France. All four little girls were pleasing to the eye, and also of necessity the ear, for the little Queen loved to sing. They would be taught to join her in French madrigals and also, perhaps, learn to play the lute. In all ways Madame chose them well, for every one stayed loyal through many dark years, even Mary Fleming, who in the end married the treacherous secretary, Lethington.

As for Iain Ruadh, we discussed his future with the rest. It was decided that Madame herself should recommend him to the King of France, which accords with her kindness to James V's other bastards. King Henri II had loved King James and would do all he could for his son. More I will not say, except that my boy became at last an honoured officer of the Scots Archers of the Guard of France. I left it to others to rear him; after all, I had not asked to bear him. I fear that in any case I am not by nature maternal. Had I been so, Alasdair's Mhairi would not have died.

I had not expected to return to France to live. I do not know whether I had expected ever to see it again. It had become for me a place from which my jointure was conveyed regularly, paid by Andelot the steward at Vouvray, who also looked after the new Comte, my first husband's cousin, evidently an imbecile. Once I had had word from the steward, other than a demand for receipts; his mother, Madame Sanserrato, was dead of the stone. I had written my formal regrets, but could say little as I had not liked the lady, and both Andelot and I myself knew well for what she had tried to be responsible when my first husband the Comte had died; but that was, naturally, never mentioned in the correspondence.

Some days before the Queen's departure Madame herself had sent for me. I found her standing alone, looking down at the summer sea where, far below the Rock, the sun made the waves dance in little points of silver. 'I trust that it will be as smooth for the voyage,' she said. She seemed rocklike herself in her calm; but after it was all over, and the beloved child had gone, I knew that Madame would torment herself with weeping alone, when nobody else could see or hear. She said nothing of that.

'Claudine,' she said, 'I want you to go with the Queen to France.'

My heart sank. To leave her, again, with all that might happen amiss? Leave her alone, to face unsleeping enemies, without comfort, without a single one of her own kin to whom to turn? Besides Iain Ruadh, who had been like a son to her, two more of James V's nine bastards, a fair and a dark, the Prior of Coldingham and the Prior of St Andrews, to both of whom Madame had been goodness itself, were to sail. I did not like the elder young man, Lord James, who feathered his own nest from the beginning, took everything Madame out of her kind heart gave him, and then at last betrayed her. However it was not my concern. Now, Madame explained the rest to me, while I thought first, God forgive me, of my clothes; others were better prepared than I to be in fashion at the Court of France. Madame smiled, as if she had read my mind; that is not difficult in such ways between women.

'There is a chest prepared to go on board for you,' she said, 'and it is filled with all you need; gowns, linen, ruffs, sleeves, hose, shoes, kerchiefs, caps, and I will give you money until you can receive your jointure from Vouvray. You need lack for nothing, therefore, but you will be Madame de Melville, a widow close about the Queen, as much so, perhaps, as Lady Fleming.' I cast down my lashes; had Madame, who was shrewd, perhaps already a suspicion of distrust? As far as that went, Duchesse Antoinette herself would have an eye to the Queen's entourage when they reached France, and dislike me as she might, would arrange matters as Madame herself requested them.

'All her life my daughter will have to walk in a quagmire, even as Queen of France,' Madame said now. 'There is enmity for her both here and in England, but, please God, she will be sheltered in our own country. Yet she is only a little girl of scarce six years, perhaps frightened, homesick, seasick if there is rough weather; and separated from her mother. I have tried to be a mother to her; she loves me, but how long does love last if two beings are separated?'

'You still love Duc François, your son,' I said, to cheer her, and she smiled a little. 'It is true,' she said, 'though I know him only by his letters. He will be waiting, with my mother, to greet the Queen. He will be a new brother for her, like your Iain.'

She extended her hand. 'I know that I can trust you with all my heart,' she said, and I fell on my knees, setting my cheek against the long white fingers. 'Madame, I will not fail you,' I promised, and during all that happened afterwards I do not think that I did so, in that way.

We went on board on the twenty-ninth of July, 1548. Madame had already said farewell to her daughter. The great ships had their rowers waiting, but we had to rock out at sea for a week, while we waited for a favourable wind. During that time I and the others played watchdog, letting the little girls romp about the decks in the sun, seeing to it that the little Queen did not tire herself or, as nervous children will, grow too greatly excited. The rest I left afterwards to their mothers, stepmothers, and the other ladies. The crew amused us and gave us timely assistance often, when the ships swerved at anchor. Royal weather is always bad; till then, it had been sunny and calm, but as soon as we were on board the gales came, and continued until at last we left with filled sails on a fair wind for France. I looked back at the frowning Rock of Dumbarton, but I knew Madame had long gone, riding back to the east; she would not have been able to endure the sight of the idle sails, knowing her child to be on board and out of reach. There was, also, the ever-present threat of capture by England. But the little Queen stood on deck with her cloak clutched round her, and appeared like a much older person in her calm; she appeared to understand that great things were required of her. Nevertheless the voyage itself was a terrible one, and Lady Fleming begged to be set ashore early on the coast of Brittany, but the captain would not. We landed, after a fortnight's rough weather, at Roscoff, and the English had not sighted us. There was a great welcome for the Queen of Scots, and the lesser nobility from miles round had ridden to meet the child and catch sight of her in her litter; at the Te Deum of thanksgiving for our safe arrival the church was packed, and afterwards there was a disaster when a bridge collapsed owing to the press of riders. It could have been taken as a bad omen, but no one was hurt. We went on, and soon Her Grace was conveyed at last to the arms of her grandmother, Duchesse Antoinette. That lady had hardly aged at all. As the hooded eyes met mine over the child Queen's red-gold head, I knew that Madame's mother was fully informed of my position, unofficial as it might be, and would respect me despite everything; no doubt she was grateful for the safe arrival of the letter requesting aid from France.

We reached St Germain-en-Laye at last, and my clearest remembrance of the concourse in the late summer garden of the old palace is that it was made up mostly of children. The King and Queen were absent in Burgundy; few of the Court were in residence; and our five little girls, leading them the tall Reinette – they had begun to call her that in Brittany before we had even set eyes on the little boy she was to marry – advanced across the grass under the careful eye of Duchesse Antoinette, Lady Fleming, myself and the rest; and there was bowing and curtseying, even though some of the little creatures had only just learned to walk. Among them was a tiny dark-haired girl, very pretty, who smiled at our Reinette and was soon at ease with her; this was the King's daughter, Madame Elisabeth, aged about three years. The Dauphin himself was a pale backward boy a year older, weak in the legs, not very tall; he made his bow shyly, and was told to kiss his future bride, which he evidently did not mind doing; his eyes followed her about wistfully afterwards, as if she were already too bright a star for his pale sun. It is easy to look back, and remember; how much of what happened could be predicted then I do not now recall, but I thought already that François the Dauphin was not as strong or as handsome as Madame's own son, that other François, Duc de Longueville, our own Queen's half-brother, a fine lad of almost fourteen summers, who had already met her and, despite the difference in their ages, was her firm friend, although but for her birth he would have known his own mother.

My father Duc Claud and his wife had had many splendid sons. The second of these, who was nine years younger than Madame, was Charles de Guise, later to be known as the Cardinal of Lorraine. At the time of which I write he was still an archbishop, tall, erect, slender and yet steely of build, fair and with the proud Guise features. I have a clear memory of him, some years after our arrival, bearing La Reinette on the crupper before him up to the great entrance of Blois, where the statue of Louis XII on horseback prances forever over the doorway, his housings flowing blue to the ground with their gilded fleurs-de-lys. The Cardinal took La Reinette by the hand, having dismounted, and led her in to the King. She looked up and chatted to her uncle affectionately on the way; they were always close to one another, as the father might have been whom La Reinette had never known. As for King Henri, he adored her; so did everyone at Court, I believe, except the Queen of France, the Pope's niece Cathérine de Médicis.

That woman's history is well known, but I must repeat some of it briefly. I was sorry for her then, as few people even so early dared to be; in any case etiquette at court was strict and feelings were not shown. This was largely the doing of Madame Diane, Duchesse de Valentinois, the King's mistress; matters had not been so in King François' day. Madame Diane – she had been born Diane de Poitiers, and still signed herself so although she had been married in youth to an old man, a minor nobleman from the provinces – was about twenty years older than the King, and had enslaved him in youth, before his marriage, when he was still no more than a shy boy returned from Spain with a certainty, which perhaps remained with him, that he was inferior to his dead brother, the brilliant Dauphin who should have become King. Henri II went to Madame Diane, perhaps, for reassurance. She gave him confidence, as Agnès Sorel had done for Charles VII. Certainly Madame Diane gave no evidences of outward passion. Nobody could read her; she was most beautiful, with a beauty I cannot describe and which was independent of age, like that of a statue, and she had a flawless skin and they say never used cosmetics. What her secret was no one ever discovered, not even Madame Cathérine, who tried: after her wedding night, which her husband admittedly passed with her, he ignored her, and for many years she was assumed to be barren. At length Madame Diane, and the King's advisers, counselled that Henri II cohabit occasionally with his wife to produce an heir if this might be achieved, and in extreme embarrassment he did so. The Dauphin, who was to marry our Reinette, was the result of such a sacrifice. As is known, he later became François II. He was a pale unhealthy child as I have described, prone to boils, but our little Queen was kind to him and he doted on her like the rest. There were by now other sons of Henri II and Cathérine de Médicis, their begettings duly prescribed, at suitable intervals, by the urgings of Madame Diana and her advisers. None were healthy, but in due course there was a younger daughter, Marguérite, who was so, and dangerously beautiful as well. Between all these births King Henri returned with relief to his mistress, and Madame Cathérine, it was said, bored a hole in the ceiling of the lovers' accustomed chamber so that she could lie above on the floor and watch; I never observed her to do so, but that was the gossip at Court. She never in any case learned Madame Diane's secret, because nobody did, not even that lady's daughters. The King was kind to his wife in all other ways, and no doubt grateful for the heirs she bore him. He used at times to sing Huguenot hymns with Madame Cathérine, while she plucked at the virginals with some skill.

Madame Cathérine never liked our Reinette. Undoubtedly she was jealous of her charm, her beauty, the fact that she would one day become Queen of France, and the way everyone else, including King Henri and all his sons, adored her. I make an exception of the Constable of France, Anne de Montmorency, who did not; he thought the marriage between France and Scotland was an expensive mistake, and said so repeatedly. He did not remember conveying me out of the forest of Fontainebleau years since for the expected pleasuring of François I, and I did not remind him.

To return to Madame Cathérine, she subsequently, after the King's death, when she herself was in power, became la Reinette's enemy, secretly at first and then openly, as far as that word can ever be applied to her. Madame Cathérine herself was not ugly, although with frequent childbearing she grew fat. Her eyes were unreadable, her nose long, and her expression discreet, as in fact was that of Madame Diane. The whole situation would have been disbelieved had it been written as a romance. I should moreover have mentioned that, long before becoming Duchesse de Valentinois or achieving the favours of King Henri II, Diane de Poitiers had slept with old François I and caught the pox from him, as many did. She then passed it on by way of King Henri to that monarch's sons, who were without exception spindly, irresolute, and mostly infertile. Poor little François II with his pallor and boils was probably unable to consummate the marriage with La Reinette when they were both old enough; but, again, nobody was ever certain. Meanwhile, we lived.

Although I remembered my promise to Madame Marie and did not flag in my duty of watching over the little Queen, I could take a respite when she visited her grandmother. Duchesse Antoinette naturally did not care to see me at Joinville, and I was accordingly free at such times to do as I chose. On one occasion this happened while the Court was at Amboise, and I took the opportunity to ride from there to Chinon. That castle, which used to be the fortified residence of the Kings of France in the days when the English occupied our country, was by then in bad repair, and neglected; but I was anxious to see for myself the place where the Maid of Orléans had encountered the Dauphin.

There was nothing left but a bleak space of stones with grass thrusting through where the roof leaked, but what interested me was not the thought of a young woman with cropped hair in a boy's clothes, making her way through amused courtiers towards the future Charles VII. It was, rather, a portrait I saw there, which somewhat resembled myself. It may be recalled that owing to force of circumstances, both earlier in my life and now, I was made to behave as a nun. The King of Scots himself had called me one while he ravished me, at least at the beginning. The woman in the portrait might have been one, but for one thing made cruelly evident. She wore, in the fashion of the time, a great filmy wired gable headdress beneath which her light-brown hair was almost hidden; under it, her eyes were cast down chastely so that one only saw the eyelids. Her dress was black, should have been laced up, and partly was so; but at the top it had been deliberately unlaced to reveal one perfect breast, quite naked. I cannot describe the temptation of this picture. Her aspect made it clear that she was available, not to any man, it is true, in her case, but only to the King. She was Agnès Sorel. Her beauty is still remembered and she died of poison. In the days before that happened she had changed Charles VII from an ugly, uncertain, incontinent – he still wet his breeches, they say, at twenty – spurned and irresolute young man whose own mother had publicly denied his legitimacy, to the later statesman and ruler he became after there was peace. It is true that the Maid saved France; but Agnès Sorel saved France's King. Without his father's policies, Louis XI could never have become the ruler he was, the last great ruler of the house of Valois.

I never forgot the sight of Agnès Sorel's portrait; the memory is with me yet. It was worth the ride to Chinon, which otherwise was disappointing. I returned to my duties when the little Queen came back from her grandmother's, and said nothing to anyone about my journey.

Part VI

To Her Grace the Queen Dowager, at Holyrood.

Madame,

I write this to you from our new quarters, having been moved here from St Germain-en-Laye with the Court. Her Grace our Queen does well and is loved of all here, especially by her little fiancé, M. le Dauphin. They are being taught to dance together by one Paul de Rège, found by the King. They danced together lately before both their Majesties, and pleased them greatly.

It seems that you may be hearing shortly from the nurse, Janet Sinclair, Kemp's wife of the chamber who is not pleased with Blois and has already made complaint to myself, to the Lady Governess, and finally to Madame your mother, saying that she is kept short of her proper allowance of wine, fire and candles, and is being made to eat with Frenchwomen. She threatens, being a Scot, to write to you yourself if her complaints are not met, so I warn you of this in advance.

Otherwise, I am overjoyed to hear of the progress in Scotland, both from your gracious letter to myself and from the astounded talk about Court, where you are much spoken of. It is magnificent that after the difficulties with the Frenchmen in Edinburgh, ending in a poor man's being hanged, the Earl of Huntly managed to make his escape from the English with great dexterity, and was with you in time for last Christmas.

As for Protector Somerset and his boastings, nobody takes them seriously. The English have laid claim to Scotland since time out of mind, whereas in sober fact it was the Scots who in the first place owned Northumberland. *The Ambassador told me of all this when he returned, with a worried face, but I laughed at him.*

M. le Duc de Châtelherault, lately our friend, was here to receive that honour from the King, with his face twitching as usual. I hope that he will become less troublesome to Your Grace as a result. It was splendid news that you had recaptured the island of Inchkeith; it is quite right that the English would have used it as a foothold to attack Leith. Sometimes we women see further than the best commanders. I heard of your speech to the assembled army on the day of Corpus Christi, and how it heartened them. It was right, as they recaptured the island on that day, to rename it L'Ile Dieu.

I hear also that the English trapped up at Broughty are complaining about the cold winds and salt meat. If they would go home, they could have fresh meat. It is good news that they are at last out of Haddington. I recall what happened there as well as you do: we will not soon forget.

The English garrison in Boulogne here are being attacked by the French. This no doubt will ease matters in the north, as even that nation cannot be everywhere. Already a peace treaty is spoken of, which must include yourself. You have endured enough with the wars and the extravagance of Arran — I crave his pardon, Châtelherault. Unfortunately he was told by the King here that he might spend as much as he liked before resigning the Governorship, and as usual did so. If you yourself were here, you could persuade His Majesty that you, and not he or another, are best fitted to govern Scotland now that there is a prospect of peace.

I myself am well, and carry out my duties as you commanded. This will always be the pleasure of

Your obedient and devoted half-sister,
Claudine Melville

I sat back. I had not included, for Madame's sake, the other thing that was in my mind. The Queen of France had great faith in astrologers and soothsayers, and a man named Michel de Notredame, who liked to call himself Nostradamus, had been consulted by her about the child Queen's future as the wife of her son. The man was a Jew by birth, and a clever physician; he had earned great praise because of his labours among late sufferers from the plague at Aix. He looked gravely from Madame Cathérine, who had called him in, to the royal child playing nearby with her friends and her future husband who was, being younger than she, and delicate and pale, inclined always to be backward in their games; whereas Her Grace had astonished everyone by dressing a hawk herself, without assistance, lately; that, and the dancing.

'What do you predict for her future? What do you see round her head?' the Queen of France enquired, her secret eyes fixed on the floor; one felt she did not in any case wish to hear anything good about her future daughter-in-law, for her own reasons. Nostradamus looked at the bright-haired child, then at Madame Cathérine, and said three words only.

'I see blood.' I did not repeat this to Madame in my letter. Perhaps he is mistaken, as prophecies are not always correct. But I will remember.

Madame replied to me briefly in due course, because by that time she hoped to see me. She told me that her younger brother Claud, who had been sent as hostage to England at the time of the peace treaty at last, was to be permitted to visit her in Edinburgh: I pictured their joy at such a reunion and wished myself present. Nearer home, there was however bad news of our father Duc Claud himself, who was ill. I prayed that Madame might come to France in time to see him alive. As often, my prayers were in vain. My father, Duc Claud de Guise, died shortly before her visit, and he never saw her again, or myself either. His wife Duchesse Antoinette, who had nursed him with devotion, was present at his death-bed, and his eldest son and his youngest, my half-brother René. The Cardinal of Lorraine was not there, nor was the second Cardinal of our family, Jean de Guise: he died on the way, they said of poison, but they always say that at a sudden death. Madame Louise was dead, Mesdames Renée and Antoinette in their separate convents. Madame Marie was with young Claud, in Scotland, I myself at Blois. I would of course not have been welcome at Joinville. I stared at the palace ceiling with its entwined F's and C's for François I and his Queen Claude, poor Claude de France who had borne his children and been neglected by him, and thought of the passing nature of all things, love and hope; and waited for the news of my father's death. Later I heard that above the great white scars left from Marignano had been found still, on his body, the spiked metal armlet he wore always in penance for his sins. No doubt my begetting was one of them. When he had finished with purgatory, perhaps my magnificent golden father, whom I had hardly known, would again be permitted to encounter my mother, in that place where there is no sin.

I have said very little about King Henri II or about my brief chance to become his Agnès Sorel. Like many people, I had remembered him as the shy Dauphin, overshadowed by the memory of his dead brother who should have reigned. By now, no doubt owing to the ministrations of his mistress, Henri had gained confidence, and was an urbane and adult man, aware of the world and of what it might bring him in his position. Madame Marie – it was rumoured that he had been in love with her in their youth – watched him carefully; she knew he was not entirely to be relied upon, and she made a practice of communicating with him frequently, discussing policy privately with him, and keeping herself in his view as an ally and as someone whom he could trust to govern Scotland better than Châtelherault. All this I left to her, as she knew what she was doing; but in other ways the King had on certain occasions addressed me for myself, and I knew that he found me attractive; many men at court did, despite my discreet behaviour on all occasions.

I forget why I had been invited to Chenonceaux. It is a mistake to say, as most do, that this pearl of a château was erected by King Henri for his mistress Diane de Poitiers, Duchesse de Valentinois. It was originally built by old King François I on the probable site of an earlier castle, for the river runs broad there and the arches of the bridge reflect gracefully in the water, and in the autumn the brown leaves float in melancholy fashion down on its moving surface. Madame Diane had certainly made suggestions, and directed whatever Henri II added on for her; her device, of a horned crescent moon after the goddess Diana, began to be seen everywhere, chiefly in the plasterwork, and she herself was constantly in residence when the King visited the place. My invitation came from her, and I was too wise to refuse; she had great influence, and I knew could help Madame. Accordingly, I went, and admired the new additions and the ceilings, and the staircase, and His Most Christian Majesty one day took me by the arm and showed me a particular view of the river available from a certain window, high up; then he squeezed my upper arm through its sleeve. In the room was, unavoidably, a bed. I knew that, although I could not hope to rival Madame Diane, I could at least join her in certain mutual exercise did I desire to do so; but I did not. King Henri was a personable man, and I had not had one in my bed for a long time; but I had no wish to catch the pox, and having seen his sons I was fairly convinced he had it, having as I have already remarked got it through Madame Diane herself who had slept with his father, and everyone knew King François I had been riddled with it, having in turn caught it from Madame d'Etampes. Accordingly, I backed modestly away.

Henri II was not like his father, who would certainly have pursued and taken me in such a place, as King James V had long ago done. The King of France however was at heart still a diffident man, and I saw hesitation in his eyes and spoke up boldly. 'Your Majesty would not force an unwilling woman,' I told him, and his eyebrows flew up; kings are accustomed to be flattered, and I had to think quickly of something else. 'If my heart were not given,' I said, 'it would be my pleasure to oblige you, but I am in the expectation –' I cast my eyes down and blushed, which was not difficult as what I was telling was a downright lie – 'of receiving the addresses of M. Péquillon.' This was the seneschal, a crusty old widower who had hardly looked at me either here or at Court, but one must use what material comes to mind, and I could think of nobody else who was unattached enough to be convincing.

'Péquillon?' The King was stunned, and not a little shocked. 'He is a servant,' he said. 'I can arrange a better marriage for you. After this, perhaps –' But I was adamant, and protested my growing affection for Péquillon and that, because of his modesty, we had had to keep our attachment secret until now. 'He desires no promotion,' I said, 'as he is happy in the service of Your Majesty.' I did not add that I was already married, if I was so, to Melville and that he was still alive, as most people assumed I was a widow: that would only have complicated matters. I smiled, curtseyed, letting King Henri escort me without embarrassment downstairs again, and thereafter allowed him to treat me in courteous fashion, but took care never to be alone with him any more, and left Chenonceaux as soon as possible. In view of what happened afterwards with Lady Fleming it shows that the King was not as totally enchanted with Madame Diane, to the exclusion of all others, as he was said to be. He was a man like other men. I had, in any case, no wish to incur the enmity of Madame Cathérine, who was not present on that occasion. As for the question of Péquillon, it was forgotten, thankfully, in the pressure of other matters.

It was by now certain, as far as human affairs can ever be so, that Madame herself would come to France; young Claud de Guise had already returned and had brought me loving messages from her, both to myself and to her daughter, which Madame Parois the new governess would hardly allow to be conveyed. King Henri was also anxious for Madame's arrival, not only to discuss affairs of state: Madame Cathérine had given birth to yet another prince, and His Most Christian Majesty wanted the Queen Dowager of Scots as godmother. However, affairs at home delayed her. The Earl of Huntly, who had so cleverly escaped from England and whose presence at first had greatly cheered Madame, was hot-tempered like all the Gordons, and having been granted the favour of lands and an earldom in Moray in the Queen's gift, had become by this means the feudal superior of Clan Chattan. This is no more possible to explain than if one had become superior of a separate part of the entire human race, all of it different from any other on earth, mostly at war with opposing clans since the time of Robert III, and requiring tact to control them, which Huntly did not possess. As a result, Huntly himself fell out with the chief of Clan MacIntosh, the largest sept of Chattan. In some way Lord Cassilis, an equally hot-tempered Kennedy out of Galloway, was also involved; I never found out clearly how, but it ended in the execution of the unfortunate MacIntosh in the month before Madame was finally free to sail. In the meantime, the new French prince being delicate like all the rest, King Henri found a different godmother and the christening proceeded without Madame.

I have mentioned the governess Parois. She was of course strict in her morals, as after Lady Fleming's indiscretion, which I shall relate in its place, a more careful choice had to be made; but Parois was not a pleasant woman, and she was mean. What is worse, she made the little Queen appear so, and that child was the most generous creature on earth, who would have given away her last coin and her last jewel if there was need. Madame Parois did not let Her Grace part with so much as a pin. There were other things; I myself did not deal well with the lady, and

by degrees resolved to ask Madame, when she came, to let me
return to Scotland with her. There was no need for two of us to
perform the same task at Court, and Parois was already jealous
in ensuring that I myself was superseded wherever possible. I
held my peace, for the little Queen's sake, and awaited events.

It was Parois, I believe, who evolved the stupid necessity of the
child's making a formal speech of welcome to her mother on
first meeting, as if they would not want to fly at once into one
another's arms. Madame would in due course arrive with a great
train from Le Havre, including her brothers, and the Earls of
Huntly and Cassilis whom she had somehow reconciled to one
another. There would follow the Earl Marischal, ponderous in
his great chain and no doubt forgetting for the time his mad
wife out of the Morton tribe, whom he had left in Scotland.
Home and Fleming and Maxwell would be there, all known to
me; and also known, and much less welcome, but no doubt
Madame desired to keep an eye on him, Sir George Douglas of
old days at Tantallon. I may say that when he did come, he
either did not remember me or else made pretence not to, which
suited me well enough. I remained outwardly a nun, as always,
with my eyes cast down.

In fact, after arrival at Le Havre Madame spent a few days first
with her young son, the Duc de Longueville. They had that little
space to know one another, apart from letters over the years. As
I was not present I do not know how they passed their time,
except to talk together. Duc François was still very young, and
had been carefully brought up by his grandmother. I saw him
often about the Queen afterwards; he was a well grown lad,
resembling his dead father Duc Louis. I was glad Madame had
been reminded in this way of her early love, the days of her
happiness. By the time her train rode into Rouen six days later
she was rested and well. The child Queen waited, her bearing as
calm as two years' residence at the Court of France could make
it, but her eyes danced. She had been made to commit her
speech to memory and it was long, and she was disciplining
herself. I, on the other hand, could scarcely contain my
excitement; it was two years since I had set eyes on Madame.
When the concourse rode in I had no eyes for anything but her
face, unchanged, the eyes a trifle wistful; I forgot the great
Abbey of the Good News rearing behind us, the Court all

about us, the triumphal arches, the elephants and contrived unicorns and nymphs in the procession of welcome. Madame's body had stoutened a little; a tall regal woman, in black for her father, she was worthy of all the homage poured on her, for her deeds in Scotland were known and admired even by the crowds who gaped in the street; even had she not been the daughter of Claud Duc de Guise, newly dead, they would have cheered her for herself. There was a sudden silence, as the eight-year-old Queen of Scots began to recite the prescribed speech in her clear low musical voice; and then Madame broke through all etiquette, ran forward, seized La Reinette in her arms and covered her face with kisses. Some were shocked, others understood and smiled. La Reinette laughed, hugged her mother, then, unperturbed, went on with the edifying speech till it was finished. Young François de Longueville, his cheeks flushed with pride, stood by his tall mother and his growing sister, himself unforgotten; Madame smiled at him with her heart in her eyes. He wore his ceremonial panoply as Hereditary Grand Chamberlain of France and Seneschal of Normandy, but he was still no more than a boy proud of his mother. When it was all over, Madame gathered both her children close to her, and the three talked happily on their way as though they had never been apart. That was the welcome; it was one of the pleasant times, after the years apart with stormy seas between.

Madame was to stay in France for a full year with her daughter, and what I am about to relate began before her arrival and continued, in its way, after she had gone. It was more evident when she was present, as there was, unavoidably, a certain amount of crowding between her ladies and those of Madame Cathérine when we travelled together to Paris, Blois or Fontainebleau. It had already been decided that selected pairs of us should share a bed at each of these places, have our baggage carted all together to avoid confusion and waste of space, and generally live as one. It fell to my lot to have to share with Joan Fleming, which hardly pleased me. However it gave me more opportunity to study that lady than I had had at Caerlaverock, which place was never mentioned between us. I am convinced that she thought herself the image of her ancestress, the beautiful Joan Beaufort, James I's Queen. That unfortunate lady had had two long plaits of golden hair, seen in effigy on her tomb in Perth Charterhouse till the reformers smashed it. Lady Fleming could also boast golden hair, but unfortunately had to hide it under a coif like everyone else by day. When we were alone, however, in our chamber at one palace or another, she would sit and comb and comb at it, as though the exercise gave her some inner satisfaction. It made a long shining veil, certainly, and Joan Fleming was a fine woman still, despite her age and much childbearing to her late lord over the years. One day she smiled at me behind her hair and reminded me that her half-brother, the Fair Earl of Bothwell, had had the same colouring as she. 'Both of us got it from our mother, a King's love,' she said. I did not remind her that I had heard that same mother boast of her own charms at Caerlaverock, or that I had heard enough about the Fair Earl already at Court, thrusting his round shoulders in the way of that other golden-haired rival for Madame's hand, Matthew, Earl of Lennox. The latter was now never heard of by us, having long since thrown in his fortunes against France, being constantly with his half-royal Douglas wife in England when he was not raiding the Border.

This fact may have given rise to one of the ugliest happenings of our stay. La Reinette had a pet monkey on whom she doted, called Gris-Gris. He had a long gold chain and she would feed him nuts, and he also had a passion for marchpane. He was a swaggering little creature who knew when he was well off, and used to leap on one's shoulder, whip his long tail round one's neck, and chatter engagingly out of his skull of a face while his small eyes surveyed the world with melancholy. The little Queen was fond of animals, in fact had a passion for them; a tame hare, pigeons, even hunting dogs, but especially the monkey. Years later when she was in an English prison I heard she had sent her young son one as a gift, but that he had not been allowed to receive it. Meantime, she was given for herself, as many people who adored her gave her little presents from time to time, a box of marchpane, and fed some first to Gris-Gris. Something mercifully called her away, perhaps her mother who wanted her company for an hour; and on return, Gris-Gris was found to be no more than a twisted lump of grey fur, dead, having writhed thereto in agony. The little Queen burst into horrified tears, and cried for days after; but the rest of us were both shocked and wary. To poison a child – that had been the intent, and the wretched monkey had been unfortunate – had been a deliberate careful plot, and who could have wanted such a thing? There were two possibilities, in the main; Châtelherault, formerly Arran, who wanted the Crown of Scotland still despite the French dukedom Madame had persuaded Henri II to give him, and his unstable son's proposed marriage to a French heiress which never took place. There were also the Lennoxes, who as far as that went had an equal claim to the throne; both descents were from Scottish princesses, and both were suspect. The Lady Margaret Lennox had some years since, after the death of her first infant, given birth to her second son, Lord Darnley. He was said to be a prodigy of learning, handsome and well grown, with the Latin of a scholar, pleasing to Queen Mary Tudor to whom he wrote an eulogy in that tongue at the age of nine. Undoubtedly the Lennoxes, who were kept in poverty, saw him as their hope and had great ambitions for him, maybe even thinking of him as King of Scots by the end if his father could not be so. They may have been innocent of the poisoning plot, but the man who had doctored the sweetmeats, one Robert Stewart, an Archer, escaped to England, where he was captured, questioned at Greenwich and returned under arrest to France. He was questioned again, admitted that he admired the Earl of Lennox who had been an Archer also, and was eventually executed. After that nothing was given to La Reinette that had not first been tasted. Madame aged visibly after that episode, and in fact fell ill for some time with anxiety. Could she not leave the child safely even in France?

Lady Fleming continued to comb her hair. By that time it was summer, and the bed we shared in our chamber at Fontainebleau looked out over a planned court and garden to be named after Madame Diane. That personage glided with her accustomed smoothness through the passages, evidently undisturbed by any happening, forever serene, superbly beautiful and ageless, without many words for anyone, even the King. Words do not always enter into the matter.

I had been on some business, and during the day returned to my room, expecting at that hour to find no one there. I had decided to write a letter to Vouvray, for reasons I shall relate. I had moved towards the place where we kept quills, ink, paper and sand in a small box, and glanced at the bed in passing; its curtains were closed. In summer they are generally left undrawn day and night, because of the heat. At first I thought Joan

Fleming pehaps had a headache, and wanted to be in the dark; the smell of lavender told me she was in there. I went over very gently, and drew the curtains aside about half an inch to see if I could be of help, then dropped it again quickly. In my bed was indeed Lady Fleming, and with her was the King of France. I remembered that she had been importuning him for some time about the fate of her son, who was held prisoner in England; and this was the end of it, or perhaps the beginning.

They say, of course, that Madame Cathérine had arranged the whole thing, to beguile her husband from his timeless allegiance to Madame Diane. Even knowing the King's penchant for mature ladies, I doubt this. Certainly the favourite must have known of it, and decided, with her customary prudence, that a loose rein is the best. No one ever heard a word pass her lips on the subject and her expression remained unperturbed. As for Madame Cathérine, she was no fool. Perhaps she had hoped, despite everything, that such a liaison would last; but she must have known in her heart that it would not. There was, at any rate, no need for her to bore a hole in our particular ceiling at Fontainebleau.

I forget how long the affair lasted. It seems in my mind always to have been summer, while the Court travelled about as usual. It is connected in my mind with the time Madame departed for a visit to Joinville, but I may be confusing events. It was, naturally, embarrassing for Her Grace when the Scots royal governess's waistline grew compromising even below the loose surtouts then temporarily in vogue. This may have coincided with the sating of the King's brief lust, for Joan Fleming was there one day, and the next her things were gone and so was she. I understand that she was quietly removed to a convent, and there gave birth to a son of the King's who was later known as Harry de Valois, Bâtard d'Angoulême. In due course he received preferment at the Court of France, and it is instructive to reflect how much of the blood of Scottish Kings is in fact to be found there. As to that, Joan Fleming no doubt had a double share of the Stewart magic; her father James IV had mated his own cousin, the disturbing lady I had finally met at Caerlaverock.

The *succès de scandale* caused, of course, some sniggering, especially among the enemies of Madame Diane; but it was brief. The Duchesse de Valentinois having been restored to her former eminence, Lady Fleming returned in due season doucely to Scotland, without the Bâtard, and was absorbed once more into the bosom of her already large family.

It was, of course, unsuitable for her to have retained her place as governess to La Reinette, which is why the lamentable Parois was chosen instead. At least that rigid and firmly Catholic personage would never go to bed with a king, or anyone else. She caused La Reinette a great deal of unhappiness.

I had not wanted to accompany Her Grace to Joinville. I think she was hurt by my request for permission not to go, especially with our father so lately dead. Duchesse Antoinette maintained deep mourning, and thereafter kept her own coffin waiting outside the castle chapel as a reminder of mortality. I had had enough reminders already; and fairylike Joinville, with its pomegranate and lemon trees, its towers and staircases, was after all the place where I had been whipped like a dog. I remembered why, and wondered if the sin Madame Philippa and Duchesse Antoinette swore existed in me had yet been driven out: the witness of recent happenings, perhaps, had excited it once more. Also, I had spent long and dutiful years with Madame, in whom there was never any question of such impurity. I did not know; but I felt, and persuaded her at last to agree with me, that as certain others had meantime taken leave to return to Scotland, I should perhaps journey briefly to Vouvray, to see for myself how matters sped there. When I mentioned it to Madame she looked at me gravely.

'Remember what happened last time, Claudine,' she said. 'You have kept on the same steward.' It astonished me that in the midst of her great affairs, she should have remembered Andelot and that I had continued to employ him.

'That is past, and he has sent my jointure regularly,' I said, as if this mitigated matters. At last she agreed that I should go, but that it must be with as strong an escort as possible, and not alone. To my somewhat annoyance, she took the trouble to arrange all this with Lady Seton, who had formerly been Marie Pierris and, in early days, scarcely my friend. She regarded me askance even now; but as she herself had relatives near Troyes, and meant to visit them, she could not help but agree to take me with her. She supervised me all through the journey, as though I were a wayward child lacking in its wits; and at the end would even have made me stay with her and her relations, visit Vouvray briefly by day and return, but I quelled her by that time, as I can do on occasion.

'I intend to visit my own château for as long as is convenient to myself and Her Grace, and I will inform you when I am about to return, madame,' I told her, and Lady Seton had no choice but to agree and perhaps was relieved; a nobleman named the Seigneur de Bryante, whom she was afterwards to marry on Lord Seton's death, was already paying some attention to her, and she was one of these women who cannot endure to have one about if a man of any kind is in sight. In fact, the Seigneur gallantly offered to escort me to Vouvray, which was not far off, himself, which drove his lady-love almost demented, except that she was by nature too cunning to let him guess it. In the end, as she must have established her rights in some way, he left me at the fork, which is near enough to the château to see its pitched roofs rise. Not much, granted, could happen to me between there and my journey's end, and the Seigneur took himself dutifully back to Lady Seton.

I rode on by myself, savouring the pleasures of the summer day. I was aware of a languor, a lazy expectancy of the body. During all of Madame's visit I had done my duty and had behaved myself as I should, and in fact before that; and hesitant as I had been in my youth owing to circumstances, I was now ready for adventure. I will not say that I consciously planned it, but I certainly did nothing to prevent it when it came about.

I rode into the cobbled yard at last, handed my horse to the waiting groom, and made my way past the dovecote and the stables, where a black litter stood, into the house. They had been forewarned of my coming and I had made it clear that I anticipated no formal welcome owing to the Comte's condition, but that I expected to find everything provided for me for a short stay. This was so, no doubt; the place was silent except for the remote quacking of ducks. I crossed the hall, went into the dais-chamber behind it, and perceived a man standing there. It was the steward, Andelot.

He had not greatly changed. I had last seen him clearly, perhaps, the day before he raped me prior to my youthful flight from Vouvray. In course of that act it had been dark and I had been smothered in the sheets. Now, I could observe Andelot

separately from my feelings, which had grown more tolerant with
the years and my experiences. He was tall, broad of shoulder and
had kept his waist, unlike many men who enjoy drinking. I could
tell that Andelot enjoyed such things; food, women, wine. I
myself had been forced to live like a nun for years. Now, my knees
had already turned to water, I felt my mouth grow dry, my palms
moist, and my nipples begin to prick. I was aware of all these
things while surveying him, and also aware that he knew of them
in me. Out of the corner of my eye I saw the bed, and Andelot
began to move towards me like a cat. I do not remember a word
spoken between us, even a formal salutation to the owner of the
house, which after all, except for the imbecile upstairs, I was. In
the ordinary way Andelot was punctilious about such things, as
otherwise he would have lost his living. I recalled, I think, again
that he was a servant; also that he was the bastard son of my first
husband and resembled the De Vouvrays. Then I remembered
nothing more, except that I felt my clothes being slipped off me,
whether by him or myself or both of us I do not know. We fell,
thereafter, naked on the bed, where we began immediately to
make love. I call it love, for lack of any better word; in fact, it was a
furious copulation, and we were at it off and on for a week. I
suppose food was sent and that I must have eaten it, and drunk
wine also, as when our bodies were separate, which was seldom, I
remember moving unsteadily to the close-stool, and I expect that
my voided waste was taken away by someone and that Andelot
also spared some time for his official duties. But in my memory, it
goes on and on; I can feel him thumbing me yet in every
imaginable part, entering and finally possessing me. I can hear us
pant together, mouths joined, tongues touching, the great bed
jerking to our timely groaning; I did more of this than he, for in
such ways a man, if he is a man at all, is the master. Each day,
perhaps oftener, he would procure me the full response peculiar
to women, which is not always achieved. I had in fact never
experienced one before, for the occupation in which I had briefly
indulged does not bring on as much as a tickle in the tail, very
often; one earns one's living, that is all. I cannot describe this
response as other than complete delight. One is borne in some
way heavenwards while still in the body, remaining nevertheless
fully aware of which part causes it; the womb itself, tautening at
the man's held thrust to make a great tent, a pyramid of fulfilled
desire, flowing with the consummation in a manner I cannot

express, then one comes down again at last to earth, exhausted
and complete. My cries of delight must have filled the château
each time it happened, but that did not trouble me. I indulged in
this unique pleasure for as long as it lasted, and I think it was
only stopped at last by the awareness, one day, that Andelot was
addressing me by my given name, which is over-familiar for a
servant.

'Claudine,' he was saying. 'Claudine.' He must have said it
more than once. 'You are by now a little plump white pigeon;
formerly, you were too thin.' This, or something like it, had been
said to me already by Sir George Douglas, which brought back
unwelcome memories, and perhaps for this reason my flow of
desire dried up, being in any case by then, in the name of God,
satisfied. I closed my eyes and informed Andelot that in future I
would be unwilling to receive him, and would lock my door. He
was incredulous, which is perhaps not surprising; in fact we tried
again at his insistence, but there was, for me, no further
enchantment. I dismissed him finally and coldly, and I can
remember his snarl of rage as he turned at last, his fingers on
the latch, and looked at me. He could say nothing, being a
servant.

Next day, as my legs were still a trifle weak for riding, I had
the maids pack my gear, sent for hot water, washed myself, had
them comb the tangles out of my hair, borrowed the imbecile
Comte's black litter, and returned in it to Madame.

There was a portrait painted of her about this time for the King
of England. I am confused in my memory as there are several of
these, but it was certainly after the drawing done by Clouet,
which shows Madame as still hopeful, with innocent, almost
pleading eyes and soft eager mouth, a small cape being worn
formally over her shoulders. This other portrait must have been
taken after the parting with La Reinette, because of the papingo;
and before the visit to the young King of England, because by
then Madame was in deep mourning for her son the Duc de
Longueville. It shows a wary-eyed woman in a flat lily-starch
coif, her gown stately as became a Queen and diplomat, the
underdress red, like a churchman's, its rich colour shown up
close against the green body of the bird. The overdress was
black, as always. Later, in the more widely known painting by
Corneille de Lyon, done in Madame's forties, the face has

hardened and begun to wither, but is still humorous and shrewd, a true Frenchwoman's, even after all that had happened by then. But at the time of the papingo painting there had been too much horror with the attempted poisoning for Her Grace to seem other than on her guard, even in paint.

The parting with La Reinette had to come, though it is not true to say, as some did, that Madame outstayed her welcome in France. King Henri continued to consult her, and to take pleasure in her company; she was not always with her daughter, nor yet with her son. The Duc de Longueville had grown into a handsome boy, a true Guise in courage and promise, and we saw him often at Court in his position as hereditary Grand Chamberlain; he and his little half-sister loved one another, for of course Duchesse Antoinette, having brought the boy up, saw to it that her daughter's two children were not strangers to one another even before the arrival of Madame in person. Be that as it may, Madame his mother had promised her son Duc François that before she departed, she would pay him a special visit to his château of Longueville. The farewell before then to La Reinette would, of course, be formal and public, as had the reunion of necessity been; but that would not be the private farewell. That was when the little Queen brought in the papingo, which had been given her as some compensation for the loss of Gris-Gris, but which she had not yet contrived to teach to talk.

'*Madame ma mère.*' I was present, but withdrew into the shadows: and saw the shining fairylike child, nine years old, the green bird on her wrist, come to Her Grace, who held out a hand gently. 'Marie,' she said. 'Marie.' It was, after all, her own name, and the name of the Mother of God. When others were present they must call one another Madame and Madame, both Queens, and make the correct depth of curtsey: but not now.

'I know my father had a papingo, for you have told me so, when he was a little boy, and that it could make all manner of noises and imitate any other bird. Perhaps this one will in time, although I have not been able to teach him a single note. Perhaps he is stupid.'

Madame's hand reached out and caressed the bright hair, for once not contained in a bonnet of lace, but curling free about the child's fair oval cheeks. The parrot moved restlessly. 'I want you to have him to remember me by,' said the Queen of Scots. Her eyes, already secret like her father's, looked down at the small green feathered head and her fingers stroked it once. 'He is my gift to you. There will be letters, of course, and one day you will perhaps come back to France, or I will come to Scotland.'

She took the bird gently by the feet and detached them from her wrist to Madame's sleeve. The parrot turned its head from side to side, its beady eyes bright and uncaring. 'I would have given you Gris-Gris, but he –' and the tears rose, and Madame hastily gave the papingo to me and took her child in her arms.

'Gris-Gris will perhaps be waiting for us in the place where we all meet, your father, Duc Claud, the King, and everyone we have loved,' she said; I noticed that she did not mention Louis de Longueville, her first husband whom she had loved so well. He was no part of this child's life; but La Reinette had been nourished on tales of her own father. I thought of James V as a small boy before the Douglases debauched him, and pictured him at Stirling with his papingo, teaching it to talk and whistle so well that his tutor Sir David Lindsay of the Mount had made a poem about it to comfort the little King when it escaped and was found later torn to pieces by the wild birds on the Abbey Craig.

Madame had herself painted with the papingo, at any rate. It was like flaunting the banner of loyalty, and perhaps some love, for the man who had left her the bitter legacy of Scotland, also his royal daughter. The papingo died later of the northern cold. By then, Madame could accept his loss with the rest.

I had, on returning from Vouvray, had myself admitted to her presence: as always, this was easy for me. I found Madame seated at her table, writing, a quill in her long white fingers, the little flame for sealing the green wax lit close at hand, and by it her cipher. That diplomat, Sir George Douglas – I could have done it myself, from experience – had warned her of the dangers of careless or imperfect seals. I knew, in any case, what the present correspondence concerned; the present endeavours of Anne de Montmorency, Constable of France, to prevent the marriage of the Dauphin and La Reinette and to have her married instead to some French noble now that she was available. The argument of that formidable personage was that Scotland was a poor, remote, savage country, and that it would cost more in French blood to keep it than it was worth. He may have been right, but for Madame's sake I could not agree.

I said nothing of that, which I was not supposed to know in any case. I merely asked Madame if I might accompany her back to Scotland, as Madame Parois the new governess and I did not deal well together. I would have gone on to explain further, but Madame put back the quill in its holder, struck her hands together, rose, and came to me, her black skirts rustling.

'I will be glad of your company, Claudine,' she said, and took my hand. 'As to Madame Parois, she is strict, I know, and there is little joy to be found in her. She is however trustworthy, and since that affair of the monkey –' she turned her face aside for moments – 'I can trust few, even here. I will leave Parois, therefore, in charge of my daughter: she is steadfast in the Catholic Faith, and in these days, and in time to come, there may be trouble from Geneva and such places in that respect. The man Knox, of whom you already know, was freed from the galleys last year on the plea of the young King of England, who has promoted him since then to an important place about Cranmer, and may offer him a bishopric.'

'Knox would not accept one,' I ventured, remembering the plum-red mouth, the grey beard, and the way the reformers held forth on their own notions, independent of any liturgy. Madame smiled.

'Maybe not,' she said. 'At any rate it is arranged by safe-conduct for us, yourself with me and the rest, to visit England, and together we will see the young King. They say he is a prodigy, but they say that about all monarchs. I will visit my son for a little first, alone, then you may join me, and we will go, all of us, except my poor Longueville, to London. I have heard much of it from Sir George and others; it is time I visited it for myself, and we have the safe-conduct, to avoid the long voyage back by sea. Brrrr! On the way here, they had dressed the poor wretches in the galleys in white damask for me, so that the sight of their scarred straining backs would not offend my eyes, or my ears the crack of the overseer's whip. But I have heard and seen it all before.'

I myself heard her out, then went to order my gear to be set out for the journey. As to Madame Parois, it was wondered by many that Madame should ignore her daughter's pleadings over the years to have her replaced, as she often made La Reinette extremely miserable with her meannesses, also her greed and insolence. But Madame could trust her; and there was never a recurrence of the poisoned food, or any further sign of the attempts of the Lennoxes, or others, to do away with the child's life, if indeed that had happened.

Madame set out for Amiens with her son in early October. It was long enough since he had had her sole company. Mother and son were together for a little while, and then in her presence the young Duc took a fever, and in a few days died in her arms. I will say no more, except that it was evident that good fortune, as a happy woman, would never attend Madame Marie. She was in deep mourning when she rejoined us, and we also were warned to wear black hoods with tassels, and great dule cloaks, for the visit to Edward VI. Madame had worn black for her state visit to France, but informally; on the advice of no less than Madame Diane she had not openly recognised our father's death. Queens, said the Duchesse de Valentinois when consulted, mourned only for their husbands: otherwise, they lowered themselves.

I left my son Iain Ruadh in charge of the Dauphin's tutors, happy in the assurances of Madame that she had induced King Henri to promise him an appointment with the Archers when he should be grown. Two other bastards of James V had accompanied us, both having been given French abbeys: but I did not want this for Iain Ruadh. Times were changing, and the fate of Cardinal Beaton was still in my mind; there were other careers than the Church, where one could rise high and fall low, even dead into a well. The eldest bastard, Lord James, as he by now liked to be known – in addition to his Priory of St Andrews he had now acquired that of Maçon in France, and the promise of three other benefices by dispensation from the Pope – him I did not trust, as I have said. I can remember his cold grey eyes watching us depart, for he would not come with us, though I doubted whether Scotland had seen the last of him. Madame bade him an affectionate farewell, for she was grateful to him for, already, having repulsed an English party invading Fife; also, he had been cautious not to offend her. However I myself could see only his mother in him, and that lady I had met. Her husband Douglas of Lochleven had been killed at Pinkie Cleugh. Long before, Margaret Erskine, as she was, had married him unwillingly. She was still, when I saw her, a dark-browed handsome woman, despite having borne six children to her husband after James V had had his pleasure on her, for he seized her away after her marriage and kept her till it was satisfied, and the Lord James was the result. They say the King of Scots would have married Margaret Erskine himself, but that was not feasible. She reared her Douglas brood eventually in a frowning castle in a loch, and Madame reared her bastard for her and was kind to him.

Our crossing, made with an escort of ten ships, was not as rough as that I had made coming over with the little Queen, but I took it badly, and was thankful when we put in at last at Portsmouth, having missed Rye due to such storms as there were. Madame sent word of our coming to the young King, and as soon as it was known, many English lords and gentlemen came in haste to greet us and to offer us hospitality. I best remember, out of them all, the Earl of Arundel, a big bluff man with whom I felt at home. Madame gave his daughter, who was very beautiful, a piece of embroidery worked by the little Queen, of the Crucifixion. We went on. There were castles and new-built country houses, for England by now was a place in which to live graciously, free from attack, and the comfort was that of France and, in places, perhaps better. We made our way across the October shires to Guildford, where none other than Lord William Howard waited, and we parted with our escort of Sussex gentlemen with some regret. Before day closed I could see the fabled chimneys of Hampton Court rise above the grey water of Thames, and amid the throng of marquises, earls, gentlemen pensioners, men-at-arms and ushers who now surrounded us, we approached the place which had been filched from Cardinal Wolsey by Henry VIII a generation since. Cardinals do not always prosper to the end.

The marquises bowed and handed us to the marchionesses, who were waiting as it was now night. We had met Lady Northampton and her husband already at Boulogne. Our lodging had been hung with fine new tapestries, and there was dancing and a return later on of the gentlemen, as though Madame herself held Court. Next day, they hunted the deer and we watched; then, on the water, we saw a great array of barges waiting, gilded and filled with cushions, and an awning for Madame. They accompanied ours later down the river like great fish, the rowers' oars dipping evenly in the smooth autumn water. We came to the Bishop of London's palace and lodged there. The Lord Mayor had sent gifts of provisions; rounds of beef, mutton, veal, sucking-pigs, loaves and game, bottles of wine and ale, quails still in their feathers, sturgeon, which stank a little, and fresh salmon, as well as wood and coal. The food lay about on the great tables in the Bishop's kitchens, raw and untended, the pigs' flesh glistening, the parcels of spices with which to cook everything unopened still. The sight made me feel sick, and I returned upstairs.

We travelled in carriages to see the young King, from St Paul's to Westminster. I was interested in watching the company that got in with Madame, for my carriage followed close behind hers. There was the Lady Margaret Douglas, who had married Lennox in the end, and was said to be a devoted wife to him, and besides that a close friend of the Princess Mary and a zealous Catholic. She was fair, simply dressed in a flat coif, with three brooches on her bodice from which were draped narrow chains, in the English fashion. She was handsome, and seemed placid outwardly; I reflected that she did not look like someone who would have abetted the vicious plot to poison our little Queen, but one can tell little from appearances. Lennox himself was elsewhere. In their carriage also rode Henry VIII's niece Frances, Duchess of Suffolk, a big overbearing woman, and her daughter Lady Jane Grey, a tiny subdued creature said to be a prodigy of learning and beaten often. What they talked of on the journey I do not know, and Madame said nothing of it later. As always, crowds lined the streets to see us pass, and it was a fine day, without the heavy fog so prevalent in London at that time of year in especial.

Two men received us and led us in to the King. One, Frances Suffolk's husband and Lady Jane's father, was a small wispy-bearded creature of no account, with a mean look. The other was no less mean, and so history has placed him: Dudley, recently created Northumberland, who had caused the late Protector Somerset, our persecutor, to be clapped in the Tower. I had seen its white bulk rise from the calm river by its fabled ancient bridge, and had thought of everyone that had been imprisoned there and might be still: two of old King Henry's wives, perhaps later on his daughter Elizabeth, though I do not think that had happened by then. Certainly we never saw her, or her half-sister the Princess Mary. A chattering woman in my carriage said that the Lady Mary loved fine clothes, but the Lady Elizabeth plain ones, and kept her hair straight and parted in the middle, like a nun, and her eyes cast down. It is a refuge resorted to by many of us. Elizabeth Tudor has certainly learned by now how to curl her hair, and bedizen herself and look upwards. I think that she would not meet Madame, young as she was and cautious. Even then there was a breath in the air which rumoured that both King Henry's daughters were again to be declared bastard – it had happened on and off several times, naming them Lady or Princess according to which wind blew – and our Reinette the lawful heir of England, through her grandmother old Margaret Tudor, long dead.

The present heir was waiting; the son Henry VIII had longed for and, at last, obtained by a third wife. King Edward VI was a thin pale-faced boy with secret eyes, and for some reason, although he was not by then ill, I knew that he had not long to live. Madame, in her mourning blacks, swept a magnificent obeisance, and the boy he was a year younger than her dead son Longueville – bowed, and raising her hand in his between the long line of waiting guards, led her to her chamber. They met again at dinner. We women were put at three tables, and I could hear nothing for the whispering of the rest; but Madame and the young King were deep in talk where they sat at meat before their cupboards of gold and massy silver, beneath their canopies. I heard, though, one thing as they passed by after dinner, to hear some music. Both were on good terms by then, and I heard King Edward ask Madame courteously how she liked England, his prim mouth, which resembled that of his father, curved in an unaccustomed smile. He had not known enough laughter, that boy. With fewer solemn preceptors, and fewer sermons from John Knox, he might have been joyous in youth, like his father before him; but there was one story I heard later which told me that Edward was after all a Tudor, and had he lived might have been cruel. He had evidently grown angry with his treatment by rapacious lords and governors, and one day called them to him, his hawk by him. He took the hawk, plucked its feathers from it in handfuls till it was naked, and scattered them on the floor.

'That is the way you have used me, and the way I presently will use you,' he told them, and did not live to do it; but I pictured the poor hawk, the poor faithful hawk, trained, shivering, bleeding and naked, with no reprisal for its accepted master. Things of that kind are evident to me, and are perhaps unimportant, but I remember them. At any rate, the King asked Madame that time how she liked England. She replied in her courteous way that she liked it passing well, but that of all she had seen therein she was best pleased with its King.

'Yet ye would not have me to your son,' said Edward VI reproachfully, and I thought of the long wars there had been over that steady refusal. Would it have been better to have allowed the godly marriage, as some of our lords called it, and thereby saved much blood and many harvests and fine abbeys? God knows, but it had happened otherwise.

Later Madame told me that the King had tried to persuade her to relinquish the arranged betrothal to the Dauphin. 'He spoke like a grave minister of Geneva,' she said, 'and told me, who might have been his mother, that it was most meet for the union of both the realms, Scotland and England: the stanching of blood, he said, and perpetual quietness in time to come. They should have thought of that sooner.'

'What did he say when you told him so, Madame?' I asked her, trying to control the queasiness with which I had throughout endured this London visit; I did not feel well, and I thought it must be the foggy air; it would be better when we reached Scotland, but I did not anticipate pleasure on the journey.

Madame was looking out of the window at the flowing Thames, with its barges and little boats plying, and the late autumn night coming down. 'The King said then,' she told me, ' "I assure you that whosoever marrieth her shall not have her with kindness from me, but I shall be enemy to him in all times coming." '

She whirled round, her heavy skirts twisting about her. 'Is there always to be enmity for my daughter?' she said. 'I told him that if she had been sought by humane and gentle behaviour, if I myself had been consulted as her mother, something might have come of the English proposal; but he was still not content. I had to promise to mention the matter to King Henri when I shall return to Scotland.'

'It is arranged, Madame,' I said. 'You cannot alter it now by mentioning it. In any case there is the engagement of King Edward himself to the King of France's daughter, Madame Elisabeth.' That was a pretty dark-haired child, one of Madame

Cathérine's brood, who was already a close friend of our Reinette. She was later to marry King Philip as his third wife. A good deal hangs on the lives of children.

However King Edward might resent the lack of his Scottish bride, he sent Madame a gift of two horses, one of which I rode, and a diamond ring, which Her Grace put on her finger. We never saw the King again. He died less than two years later, they said of poison, but it may have been a fever, or inheritance; his father was not healthy when he was born. The body lay in a room alone for days with the stench growing so bad no one would go near it, then finally, in some manner, they buried Edward VI. There was more trouble after that in England, and the taller of the two mean men, Northumberland, put the smaller man's daughter Lady Jane Grey on the throne for nine days and in the end she was executed by Mary Tudor.

We ourselves were home long before that, having been met by the gentlemen of Middlesex, all the gentlemen of all the English shires as we went, and we encountered Sir Ralph Sadler, Madame's old acquaintance the Scots envoy, in Hertfordshire, and later that famous Dowager of Suffolk whose mother had been a close friend of Catharine of Aragon. We travelled north by stages to Berwick, where none other than the Fair Earl of Bothwell awaited us, anxious as he was to end his exile. He did not look well. Madame regarded his hangdog appearance with as little comment as I myself gave to anything at all by then, for I had discovered the cause of my malaise, and it was not the fogs of London, nor the Channel crossing, nor anything which might not have been foreseen, except that I had of course not foreseen it, or not in time. I tried to obtain herbs on the journey north, but it was not possible while in close attendance on Madame, who needed me constantly to discuss affairs, as if she was glad she had someone she could trust: also, I was controlling King Edward's gift of a spirited nag, and hoped against hope that the effort would dislodge something in me. It did not: nothing availed; and by the time we reached Stirling at last I faced the truth. I was pregnant, sealed with child at last by Andelot, and nothing now would rid it.

How was I to tell Madame, a second time, that I was in that state? True, it was not, this time, a pregnancy by her husband, but that by a servant was worse, and argued a looseness in my nature which Madame would be the first to abhor, especially after the behaviour of Lady Fleming in France, and her eventual dismissal. I reflected that Madame, despite all our childhood ties, would be justified in dismissing me likewise; and where was I to go then? I could not travel abjectly back to France, to Vouvray, and give birth to a child by my steward there. Nor, for similar reasons, could I return to King Henri's Court. Once again, I was cast on the world, and through my own fault. I pondered the situation night after night, lying on my bed, not sleepless as I no doubt ought to have been with guilt, but drowsy, as if the child sucked away life in me; I ate like a horse after my early sickness had departed. Presently, though not at once, the changes in my body would begin to show; my breasts were already tender; I remembered the ordeal that time in the Queen's babyhood, when I had carried her little bulk well up to hide my stomach, in the litter from Linlithgow to Stirling. Now we were in Stirling again, and I had time to reflect on my faults, and decided to go and confess them, and perhaps ask advice of a priest. I made this excuse to Madame, who was the first to understand this necessity as she herself confessed regularly, though compared to myself she lacked sin: it would not have been difficult. I got my cloak, for it was winter by then, and walked over the open drawbridge of the Castle and down the street, which was quiet, towards the Black Friars of Stirling, where long ago I had been married to Alasdair Dorch Gregarach.

I did not know what to do. There was no priest in sight in the church, and I went and knelt in the chapel of Our Lady of Pity where I sometimes used to go, and asked her again to help me. I remember staring across at the recumbent painted figure with the yellow hair and beard I had been told long ago was that of a lost King of England. The strange story haunted me, but it was no stranger than my own. As before, I could not pray. They say that it is at such times help comes, and it came in so extraordinary a manner that no doubt it will not be believed. It was drawing near to the hour of vespers, and despite all the efforts of the reforming brotherhood some folk still liked to come in. There were one or two that night, I remember; mostly women, and one soldier with his arm bound up in soiled linen. We waited, and presently the sound of chanting was heard and the Abbot, with the tall gold cross borne in front of him, entered in procession, followed by the black-clad friars. Last of all, in the dress of a lay brother, came in none other than James Melville. He seemed pale and wan, as well he might, and was muttering at his beads. He was last of all in the procession, and the least among them: I recalled his saying proudly that the Pope had given orders that he was not to be admitted again to the Order as a friar, but they must have let him start again from the beginning. I rose from my knees and went to where he was. He looked up, saw me, and turned his face away in horror.

'Woman, have mercy on me and go,' he murmured. 'I have made my confession and received absolution. Do not tempt me any more. I abjure the marriage. It was not made through the offices of Holy Church, whose obedient son I once more am.' He crossed himself, and moved on before I could strike him across the face.

'I too abjure the marriage,' I called after him. 'For two pins I'd walk beside you to God's altar and tell them of your preachings and before that, what you did to the Cardinal. If you will swear by the Host that we are divorced, and you will trouble me no more, I will go as you ask.' The rest were turning their heads at the noise I made, but I did not care. I saw Melville nod, and promise.

I marched out into the street, uncertain of what I had meant to do or of what I was going to do now. There was one thing; I took off Alasdair Dorch's gold ring that I had used at that mock wedding when Melville had been too mean to buy me another, and put it on my finger the other way round, as it had been in the first place. Then I walked back up the slope to the castle. I do not like telling lies, but I could say with truth to Madame Marie that I had encountered my husband and that he had insisted on his rights. I need not say which, and it would solace me for the thought of the coming child and the memory of Melville, double renegade and murderer, in a lay brother's habit again among decent men.

I told Madame that I had met with him, and let her think what she would. When, a little later, it became clear that I was expecting a child she looked at me with her blue-grey eyes in great pity and laid, very gently, her hand on my sleeve.

'My poor Claudine,' she said, and that was all. 'My poor Claudine.'

* * *

That birth took place eight months later, in Stirling Castle, in Madame's own chamber. It was assumed to be premature owing to the shock I had sustained. Through the pregnancy, it had been discreetly circulated among the others that I had encountered my husband on one occasion. He was in any case judged undesirable as I never visited him in the ordinary way. Everyone retained their discretion in my presence at any rate, and what they said when I was absent did not matter, as I was generally with Madame when she was there at all. She did not allow me to go out again into the town alone; all through the months she saw that I had such food as suited my fancy, though food was short then and worse later; and although she had to be away on rounds of justice ayres with the fool Châtelherault to try to win him over, she spared time to sit with me, especially towards the end. By then I was a sorry sight; swelled up like a frog, so big I could no longer see my feet, and short of breath; I waddled about unlaced at the last, feeling as if a troop of horse were inside me, and my breasts hung like cow's udders. The waters burst all over the floor in the Chapel Royal when we were hearing Mass, and Madame took me and made me lie down on her own bed, and I began to groan with the pains, but nothing came. I grunted and strained for many hours, and Madame could not be with me all the time; when she could come she did, and at last held both my hands when I clung to her, still gloved as she was from riding in. I pulled in agony at the leather, which must have hurt her slender fingers, but she did not draw away.

'Aaah, Aaahh. Madame, Madame, do not leave me, aaahh. Do not leave me. Aaahh. Aaahh.'

The tears were streaming down my face and I howled like an animal. I have never known pain like it. Time went on and she would murmur soothingly 'It will soon be over now, Claudine, my poor Claudine. It will soon be over,' but it was not, and I was straining like a sow in farrow and swearing that never again would I lie with any man, and that all the evils in the world came from men, whereas, as at that time Master John Knox must already have been thinking in his head, they have most of them come from women. At the end, when I was almost torn apart, twins spurted out one after the other, which was why I had grown so big: the second had the cord wound round the neck of the first, which accounted for the delay, and by some marvel it had killed neither themselves nor me. Both were boys, torpid but still alive, and both were the image of Andelot. Later, we put them out to nurse with a woman who lived below the Abbey Craig. I did not care if I never set eyes on them again.

Madame spent much time thereafter with Governor Arran, or Châtelherault, the Duke as everyone now called him, on the justice ayres. They were held both north and south, in the Highlands, Aberdeen, Elgin, Inverness, Banff, and later the Borders; long rides for a woman and a hard task. On the whole, Madame and the Governor endured one another; her charm won him over so long as she was present. As regarded justice itself, it was generally coming to be agreed that James V's widow was as capable as he had been, or the Governor now. Certainly she had shown more mercy, and there were no such occasions as that when the late King had hanged Johnnie Armstrong, the Border reiver, as soon as he laid hands on him after promising him pardon.

I myself should no doubt have taken to my beads, but did not, after the boys' birth. If my father Duc Claud had worn a spiked bracelet for his sins of the flesh, without doubt I should have worn a spiked chastity belt. After that memorable week with Andelot I resolved to be prudent in future, for my own sake and Madame's, but it was not always easy; however, I subdued the clamour in my tail for her sake rather than my own.

The next few years I spent unwillingly as a mother, if not a wife. Madame insisted that my sons be retrieved from the Abbey Craig as soon as they were weaned, and brought up at the Castle under her guidance and mine, for what that was worth. She was still occupied with binding the feeble Governor to her, and I know she had it in mind to take his governance from him in the end: but useless as he was he would not yet part with it, for all her flattery and example.

Once when my children were about three years old she rode home. The young King of England had died, and his sister Mary Tudor, though a Catholic like ourselves, still permitted raids to take place on our Border, and naturally we responded in kind. Madame dealt with it all as best she could, and finally sat with her feet up on a stool in Stirling, pale and exhausted. 'My right leg troubles me,' she said, 'it is swollen from so much riding. Rub it for me, Claudine.'

I peeled up her petticoats and rubbed the leg, which was indeed slightly swollen. It comforted Madame, and she suddenly turned her head and looked at me and said 'Claudine, I am beset on all sides. They are at me to press for the French marriage to take place soon for surety to themselves, and how can I importune King Henri further? Besides, my daughter is still far too young for it.' She talked on, then smiled suddenly and asked for the twins to be fetched. 'I do not know their names yet,' she said, 'with being so long away.'

I was ashamed of myself, for truth to tell I had left the boys with their nurse for the most part and had not had them christened, although I visited them daily in their chamber and, when the weather was fine, took them out about the ramparts or below in the park. They staggered in now, and I sent the nurse away. I muttered that I had not yet had them baptised, as they were healthy, and that I had been waiting for her return to think of names. She looked reproachfully at me, not deceived. Her features had sharpened a little and she looked older than she was, which is not surprising. I said that I thought of names of saints now and again, and what about Cosmas and Damian? I knew nothing about them and it was not their feast day as far as I was aware, but they are always mentioned together.

'I have never heard of anyone called Cosmas,' said Madame, 'but Damien –' we spoke in French – 'that is agreeable. Let us call one that, and the other, perhaps, after St Gilles? I am fond of him; he was the patron of the poor, the crippled, and blacksmiths, I do not know why. He also lived on the milk of a hind which he afterwards saved from hunters' arrows and which joined him in his cave. His arm-bone is in Edinburgh. Do you think that that would be a good name?'

Anxious to hold my own, I suggested that the Scots version, with one l, was better, and then one twin could be Scots and the other French. So Giles and Damien they became, and during Madame's sojourn they were christened by her chaplain in the Chapel Royal, where my waters had burst and where the little Queen had been crowned. Afterwards I took them out oftener in the park. James V had once fallen from his horse there and, they said, had never been healthy again. The trees in summer were pleasant. Madame was once more elsewhere.

* * *

In the end, while I left my twins at Stirling, Her Grace won, for the time. She won with flattery, subterfuge, wiles, bribes, letters to France and England, and riding from end to end of the country seeing justice done. She was also able to say, with truth, that Châtelherault had spent the royal revenues so liberally on himself from the first that he had by now left her in debt for £30,000 which she could never repay. Unfortunately King Henri had promised Châtelherault the reversion of Madame's debts if he would resign the Governorship: she herself promised him all money due to be uplifted by taxes since the death of James V. Châtelherault signed, as when all was said it left him still with the money, and no work; also, even he must have felt the tide of opinion against him among my lords and commons, who no longer cheered him when he rode out. They cheered Madame instead: she was the best-loved personage in the land by then. Their cheers sounded at last outside Holyrood House in Edinburgh, when with a great fanfare of trumpets the Queen Regent of Scotland entered in Council, a crown on her head and the sceptre of rule in her hand, her tall figure in robes of state. Later we all rode through the April day to the Tolbooth through the tumultuous crowds, cannon firing, Her Grace with the crown and sceptre borne before her. Châtelherault looked foolish, as well he might, for he had signed his formal renunciation with a drab countenance. He could hardly bear, at the last, to relinquish power; in fact, we had not even yet heard the last of him.

Now that we were domiciled in Edinburgh I was able to carry out a long intended good deed of my own. I went to the Tolbooth and found a small silver brooch to send to Christiania Grant at Freuchie. It was in the shape of a heart and, I learned later, often exchanged by sweethearts as a betrothal gift. I hoped, remembering her feeling for Alasdair Dorch, that I had not ended by hurting her. I never heard whether or not she received the gift, but that might have been due to the times.

I did not think then, and I do not now, that despite the constant need to placate Henri II Madame should have given far-flung posts to Frenchmen. The Orkney Islands had only belonged to Scotland since the time of the late King's grandmother, Margaret of Denmark, Norway and Sweden, when they were

given over to James III in lieu of part of his bride's dowry which
was never paid. The three northern kingdoms were no longer
one, and the folk of Orkney hardly knew yet to whom they
belonged; they spoke a tongue different from those on the
mainland, and how could they understand M. Bonet or he them?
That was a disaster; and nearer home, the King's Seal was given to
M. de Rubay as Vice-Chancellor. M. Villemort, whom I knew well
as he was in the household, was made Comptroller, and dealt as
best he might with such incoming goods as were taxed, and M.
Roytell was created master mason, which appointment aroused
jealousy among the Scots. I murmured about it to Madame, who
in those days did not allow the matter to perturb her.

'I cannot trust a Scot,' she said, and it was true; that nation,
apart from the Highlands, has a peculiar sense of honour, or
rather none; if a side is winning, they will join it. This was
proved again and again by those who swivelled between English
and Scots, Catholic and reformer, Scotland and France, as it
suited their purses. 'Done like a Scot!' old Henry VIII had
thundered long ago, when he heard that the Earl of Angus had
deserted his wife Queen Margaret and their daughter near
Morpeth; later, the King became as fond of Angus as of his own
sister. On all sides there was similar shifting and changing.
Madame had moved her household to the capital, now
Châtelherault had gone from it. She was in charge of Stirling as
always, but to this was added her own palace of Falkland,
Linlithgow, Holyrood, Dumbarton and Edinburgh Castle.
From it, or at Holyrood itself, she now attended Privy Council
meetings, often with myself in attendance, so I learned much. I
heard Madame, for instance, order the Earl of Argyll to pacify
the Isles, which were again turbulent; and held my peace about
sending Campbells there. Huntly in turn was sent to quell the
north, but this order was not carried out, the Gordon came
swaggering home, Chancellor of Scotland as he might be,
boasting that he had not been able to raise enough Lowland men
because they were unable to be mounted, or the Highlanders
because of the rising of one John of Moidart, and his wife was
involved in some way connected with the Clan Chattan, and
neither Madame nor I were clear who these were. Madame
marched Huntly to the Castle and put him in prison, for all she
was fond of him and had been glad when he escaped that time
from England to join her at Christmas. Later, instead of

banishing Huntly, she decided to fine him instead; he could well afford it, for men called him the Cock o' the North. Still later, when he was restored to favour, she spoke of a dukedom for him to rival Châtelherault's, but old Angus spoke up against it. 'By the might of God, if he be a Duke, then I will be a drake,' he said, and the matter was not pursued.

The Three Estates met in the summer of 1555; it was June. Madame attended each meeting all through the hot days, and at first things went well. The liberties of Holy Church, she told them, must be preserved intact; there was to be no more murdering of cardinals. Smaller matters came up; the way to summon a malefactor to judgement; the way to transfer property from one owner to another – they still do this more skilfully in Scotland than in England, thanks to Madame – and the need to guide a man's hand at the pen if he could not write and must nevertheless sign. Tenants, Madame made clear, were to be given a set number of days to leave their land, or rather their owners'. Methods were worked out of proceeding against murderers and fugitives, and no man might call himself a notary without qualification. Any man likewise found guilty of perjury was to have his tongue pierced and his goods seized: I thought of the number of lies told everywhere, and did not think they would contrive to pierce every tongue.

An assembly was set up to make weights and measures uniform, as had already happened in England. The exporting of wool and hides to that country was forbidden; in King James's time the royal uncle had sneered at his nephew for keeping too many sheep, but now there were not enough, because of the wars. For the same reason, no meat was to leave the country except for long sea voyages, when it would have to be salted; and no lambs were to be slaughtered, or sold in the market, for three years from that time, to give them a chance to breed. Poachers and stealers of beehives and fruit from trees were to be made to suffer penalties, and the young trees at Falkland were protected, for almost all the timber of the land had been cut down to make masts for ships and hafts for spears. As for goldsmiths, they had their own mark for the first time. Privileges were issued under the Privy Seal to the burghs and those folk who supported the Regent: she encouraged loyal folk.

Madame at this time was happy, despite the loss of her daughter and the fact that she herself was not well. I had once asked her why she had returned from France; surely she could have retired there, to Châteaudun or Amiens, and had the young Queen's company on occasion, and let a French governor rule Scotland? But the Regent had shaken her smooth head, smiling.

'When I became Queen of this land, I took a vow,' she reminded me. 'I would not abandon it now, or any promise of mine. Besides, I like to rule. It gives me pleasure to think of bringing this land over the years back to what it used to be, in the time of the old kings, before Edward I marched into Berwick and made the massacre there, and started the long wars. Before that Berwick was as fair a town as any port, and as rich. We have goods here; wool, the gold from Crawford, when I have leisure again to mine it; lead, iron, coal. Other countries will trade with us when they find that their orders will be promptly met. I have hopes of leaving Scotland prosperous for my daughter, even though she herself never visits it again.' She gazed far away beyond the room, and I knew she was thinking of the royal child in France, with the even younger child who was to become her husband. 'Bonds of manrent, agreements of men to protect one another and their goods, will no longer be needed here soon,' Madame said aloud. 'There may be murmurs against me soon, I know, because of the French; but there were greater murmurs formerly against the English. Soon we will be our own supporters, and can stand alone.'

Nevertheless she relied too much on French help, in the event. She herself rode north again on a further long justice ayre, having in the previous year tried thieves along the Border. She told the clan chiefs in the Highlands that she would uphold their feudal policy, where the chief is like the father of his clan, and the clan follow him in service to the King. They obeyed her; it was about then that I heard the name of Am Grantach again. James of the Forays had died two years before, and it was his son John the Gentle who was now chief; John I could not conceive as doing the thing that followed. It must have been the younger sons William or Duncan, lone wolves of the first marriage, or maybe even young Archibald grown to be a man. They were to hunt down two criminals, and being unable to catch these without killing them, did so, and sent their severed heads to Her Grace. The Regent received them with horror. She had much to endure in this way, remembering the cannon ball at Haddington and the flying limbs and maimed parts, and the blood. Indeed, it is astonishing that she contrived to remain a woman, gentle and humane; but she was unchanged in this way, and always showed mercy when it was possible. One man was beheaded instead of being strangled and burned as the law prescribed; another banished instead of being executed; yet a third, who was very young, but who had desecrated a church and stolen its chalices, was permitted to be drowned at his own request, a fate usually kept for women. I never knew Madame to torture anyone, as happened in the south.

She had been dealing with the fixing of prices in Elgin and Forres, and fining folk for crimes in Aberdeen, Dundee and Perth, when she came home to bad news at last in Edinburgh. I had been watching for her coming, for I knew what the news was; and my heart was heavy in me, for the young Queen had fallen ill in France, and by now she might well be dead.

Madame paled when I told her of it. 'If only I could go to her!' she exclaimed, and I thought how she had scarcely taken time to seat herself after the long journeyings, or take food. She asked the nature of the Queen's illness and I said that as far as I or anyone knew, it was a fever; word had come by letter, written from Court some weeks before. Christmas was approaching, and it was a gloomy one; everywhere now there were turned heads and averted faces; what if the young Queen should die abroad, and they left under the rule of foreigners?

'The King of France will claim our country for his son,' they growled, and it was maybe true. By Yule, better news had come of the Queen, but her betrothed, the Dauphin, who was always near her, had caught the fever. If he should die in turn, what was to happen? Should not the Queen come home, and the Frenchmen go back whence they came?

Some of the French troops were withdrawn then, by order of their King; but instead of being pleased, as they should have been, the Scots were enraged. There was in fact no pleasing them one way or the other. On the Border, raids again grew heavy, and Madame struck her hands together in anger and despair. 'We must raise money,' she said. 'There must be further taxes. They will not like that, but they do not like anything. Every day I find them more jealous, more suspicious. Also, when it is a question of meting out justice or punishment, they find these things insupportable, thinking always that one wants to give them new laws and change theirs, which in fact have much need of amendment.'

She wrote to our brother, the Cardinal of Lorraine, in this way, for I sealed her letter. She was in some distress about the lack of any fortifications against the English. There was no money to build these, and no French troops for garrisons, and the Scots knew nothing anyway about this form of defence. 'My lords agree, but the lesser folk do not, and suspect a tax in perpetuity,' she said. She struck her hands together again in the way she had, having given up her earlier walking up and down; these days, she tired easily. 'How weak I am! How far from their hearts!' she burst out. 'Everything takes so long; they are as they say themselves, doubtful under which lord they will fall. If only they would trust me, but they will not!' Matters were worse, she confided to me, than they had been since she came to Scotland. 'Once I led them as I wished, but now when I am a little severe, for the sake of law and order, they will not endure it and say these are the laws of the French, and their own laws are good, which they are not. This is the cause of all our discord.' She let her hands fall apart suddenly. 'God knows what a life I lead,' she said, in some defeat. 'I can safely say that for twenty years past I have not had one year of rest. A troubled spirit is the greatest trial of all.'

I suggested that once the young Queen and the Dauphin were married, matters would ease with the Scots. 'Will they ever ease?' Madame said doubtfully. Her mouth had acquired its customary wry twist nowadays. 'I will speak to them again,' she promised. 'I will speak to them when Parliament meets.'

All this time there had not been the whisper of any man in the Regent's bed; she remained as chaste and as pure as snow, nor, since the days of Lennox and Bothwell dancing unrewarded attention on her, had there been any talk of her remarriage. In fact, she had long ago known love, had bidden it farewell, and was now concerned with power; as I have said before, she was no Margaret Tudor. I myself subdued the occasional clamour in my tail, as I have related, partly in order the better to serve Madame, and also because prudence dictated that I dare not risk a further Vouvray adventure. Nevertheless my lords did not respect the Regent, wise and gallant as she was; they insulted her at last in Parliament, making a great clamour and demanding that she go to France at once to see her daughter married, and make no more delay over it. Madame was outraged. She had spoken to them reasonably and they had not listened. 'The Queen of England is wed to the King of Spain,' they shouted, 'and we lack a master.'

What was anyone to say to that? 'The future of Scotland is not at stake,' she assured them. 'My daughter will marry the Dauphin when the time comes. As for the King of France, he will never forget to assist the Scots as though they were his own people.' But silence greeted that, and a sullen silence. Reason from a woman would never convince them.

'What am I to do with them? What am I to say?' She had withdrawn to her rooms in anger; in the old way, despite her sickness, she was walking up and down. 'How can a young boy, a delicate foreigner, rule Scotland if I cannot, even if he becomes my daughter's husband? They have no reason in them; they demand now that I send an envoy abroad if I will not go myself. Whoever I send will be resented by them; nobody can persuade the King of France if I cannot, but I must not on any account leave this country at present. The marriage must however take place, too soon; my poor child! Whom can I send?'

'Myself, Madame,' I said quietly. 'Nobody will suspect me, and I can perhaps persuade the King.' I remembered Henri II at Chenonceaux, that time; I was still attractive, and he liked mature women. It might be necessary to catch the pox.

She had stopped in her tracks and was staring at me. 'You, Claudine?' she said, as if seeing me for the first time. Her gaze grew considering. 'Now that I think of it, you could see our brother, the Cardinal of Lorraine; he will help you with King Henri. There are things that letters cannot accomplish. Go with God, then, when you can. I will make all ready.'

I left Scotland in the late summer of 1557, carrying a tactful letter from Madame to the King of France. As it turned out, my journey crossed with one from him to her, saying that France was at war with Spain and that Scotland's Regent must again make an incursion into England, Spain's ally since poor Mary Tudor's marriage to Philip II. I knew that Madame would not want to make war and that the Scots would resent marching south at the order of the King of France. I knew, in fact, precisely what would happen, though to Madame it must have been incredible. She did herself march, with the army she had somehow raised with the help of M. d'Oysel, her constant adviser in such matters; and at the Border the Scots refused to obey orders and caused d'Oysel himself to withdraw to Eyemouth with his men, returning home themselves and making the Regent look foolish, but without any blood spilled. I knew that Madame would be very angry, but perhaps relieved that there was no war, and that King Henri would see that she had at least done her best. It was an unfortunate situation, and I decided that before going to the King himself, I had best consult our younger brother Charles, Cardinal of Lorraine.

I have had small occasion to mention him, as he had been little more than a boy when we first left for Scotland; he was the second Guise brother, nine years younger than Madame. He was said never to forget a fact or a face. He had already made a name for himself at the Council of Trent, which had been called by the Pope to halt the abuses which were spreading by reason of the beliefs of Luther, Calvin, and John Knox, also the Huguenots; and there was much reform needed within the Church itself. I rode to see him at Meudon, where his mother Duchesse Antoinette often sojourned with the young Queen of Scots; but to my disappointment, neither were in residence. However the Cardinal received me without delay, which last was in any case foreign to him; in all his dealings he was punctual. He wore lay dress, and it was difficult at first to imagine that this slender, fair-haired and elegant young man controlled so much destiny; that he would shortly be in charge of civil and financial matters in France; that when he had visited the Pope, the latter had given him an apartment next his own and had surrounded him with a guard of eighty gentlemen; that in the early part of the Council of Trent, called as I have said against the growing menace of Lutheranism and the cult of Geneva, this young man had had a compelling voice. Moreover when he raised his hooded eyelids now the eyes were cool and appraising, the colour of pale water; I felt that he knew all about me, had assessed me already, and would make use of me as he might. That, after all, was why I had come.

He had indicated a chair, in which I sat, spreading my skirts. We were alone in the room, which was the Cardinal's study. A marble statue of Our Lady with the Child, both wearing crowns, was behind him; he himself wore a small gold crucifix above his tunic. His long fingers played with a quill.

'How may I serve you, Madame Melville?' He did not call me sister, though no doubt he remembered me at Joinville: our father's peccadilloes were however not his. I said nothing, but handed him Madame's letter, which he perused carefully.

'My sister is in sore straits,' he said presently, 'and nobody knows it more than I. If I may aid her, I am happy to do so.' The cold eyes stared at me. I launched forth into my story; how the Scots were pestering Madame to force on an early marriage with the Dauphin, but that Madame herself did not feel she dared press the King of France further. 'As for myself,' I said, 'there are ways: but I do not greatly care to employ them. I will not deceive you, Monseigneur; if it is necessary, I can seduce the King.'

His lips twitched. 'You overrate yourself, perhaps,' he murmured. 'Others have been there before you.' The Duchesse de Valentinois was still powerful; her power would in fact end only with the King's death.

'Then what do you suggest?' I asked my half-brother, taking no offence from his tone; we were both diplomats. 'Can you persuade him, Monseigneur? Can Madame de Valentinois herself perhaps do so? There is little money for bribes, and what there is comes in any case from France.' I looked at him between the pale eyes steadily; when he saw that he could not overawe me, his manner eased. He smiled, reminding me a little of Madame when she was young. How golden she had been! Now, it was different.

'I suggest that you leave this letter with me, and that I do what I can in my own way,' he told me. 'There is one powerful advocate for the marriage with my niece; the young Dauphin himself. François is much in love with her. The sooner the betrothal is made final, the better he will be pleased.' He looked down. 'As to my sister the Regent of Scotland, I think that my brother Aumale should be sent, to aid and cheer her, soon, perhaps after the marriage.' That meant that he was at least confident of a ceremony. 'Meantime, she is in some danger.' He reached down into a little drawer, and drew out an object I did not yet see, for he kept it between his hands.

I was alarmed. 'Danger? You mean from my lords? They are rough, but she has friends among them. I am persuaded that they would not do her physical harm.' I thought of Huntly, who despite his late imprisonment and fines would defend Madame to the death; of Erskine of Dun, loyal from the beginning; and others.

'I did not mean the Scots lords,' said the young Cardinal drily. 'I meant the gathering danger from the so-called reforming movement, led at the moment by a man named Knox. He is at present, for a brief visit, in Scotland, I believe, after five years in England; preaching, like his forebear Wishart, in the west.'

'Knox will not risk another spell in the galleys,' I said scornfully.

'He continued to hurl an ikon of Our Lady into the Loire while he was chained in them,' replied the Cardinal. 'He is a man who attracts followers, converts, whatever they call themselves. He can rouse crowds to a frenzy. I have seen for myself the harm Huguenots have done here, and will doubtless do more, to our churches and cathedrals, our sacred vessels and images. All that may well come about in Scotland. My sister has neither the strength nor the forces to prevent it, though she is a devout woman and a brave one. I hear also that her health is not as good as it was. If she were to die, it is possible – I am not trying to alarm you, madame – that she may have to do so without the comfort of the last rites of Holy Church. For that reason, His Holiness the Pope, at my request, has sent her a consecrated Host, to be taken in the hour of dying. I have it here, and I trust you to keep it, preferably on your own body, till it is needed. If you yourself should be in danger of death before my sister, give it to somebody you can trust. I only regret that, in the urgency of the times and my commitment to His Holiness and the King, I myself am unable to attend the Regent in Scotland. You may convey my blessing to her, and my heart.'

He stood up, and I rose to my feet. The Cardinal took the small flat locket on its black cord, and put it round my neck; I thrust the concealed Body of God, in its pyx, beneath the square neck of my gown. I was aware of a deadly sense of purpose; whatever else my unworthy body might contrive, it should guard in the meantime the holiest gift of all, that which Madame's ruthless enemies would almost certainly refuse her, at the end, when at last it came. But, by the mercy of God, that would not be yet.

I left the Cardinal of Lorraine, and rode back to Paris.

He must have acted in his own subtle ways. Also, in January of 1557-8, our eldest brother Guise wrested back Calais from the

English, a town which was their last foothold in France and which they had held since 1347, in the time of their Edward III. Its recapture, it is said, broke the Queen of England's heart, but raised the fortunes of the Guises; there was no longer any doubt about the French marriage, and La Reinette and the Dauphin were formally betrothed at the Palace of the Louvre in April, in the ninth tower. I was able to write this glad news to Madame, but did not then see her again; she had ordered me to remain privately in France till the wedding itself, which she would of course not be able to attend in person.

The reasons for my remaining as a private person in Paris were twofold. In the first instance, to have appointed me to a place about La Reinette would have cost Madame money to maintain me, as she had always had to keep her daughter at the Court of France out of her own revenues, and these were sadly depleted. The other reason was that the Guises were in the ascendant, Duchesse Antoinette was much at Court and would preside at the marriage in Madame's place, and my presence as a reminder of Duc Claud's long-ago sins would not be welcome. It did not trouble me: my jointure arrived regularly, and I found comfortable lodgings above a pastrycook's shop near the Place du Pavé. The food was good and the man's young daughter, Justine, who was saving money to be married, acted as my maid and laced me up in the mornings and also washed my linen. I was able to go about as an unremarked woman of the citizen classes, and to observe the wedding preparations with great ease, for King Henri had decided to have the entire ceremony in full view of the common people. This pleased them greatly, as they adored La Reinette. I did not go near Vouvray.

Nôtre Dame de Paris was transformed inside and out. At first I used to slip in to one of the side chapels, for I did not forget that I was carrying Christ for Madame, and I would pray for her, the coming marriage, and myself: then workmen moved in, and erected a *ciel-royal*, where there would later be a cloth of gold carpet and cushions placed, before the altar. Outside, scaffolding twelve feet high was already being hammered together from the house of the Archbishop of Paris to Nôtre Dame itself, for the bridal procession to walk upon so that the crowds might see them advance above their heads. I think this may have been the suggestion of my eldest half-brother, the famous soldier, François Duc de Guise, Le Balafré: military commanders are used to survey heights and distances. He himself would be the master of ceremonies, magnificent in frosted gold; but I anticipate. Already there had been, in the customary way, bad news from the Scots lords who were voyaging to France. Two ships had been lost in the February storms; one contained all my lords' array for the wedding, and when they came, as they did, they had to spend money in Paris to make themselves fine enough. The second ship fared worse, and all on board perished off Boulogne, except for the Earl of Rothes and the Bishop of Orkney, who were rescued by fishermen. Unfortunately, the Lord James was saved from shipwreck; I saw him ride in later, with the Archbishop of Glasgow in close talk, also the Bishop of Ross, by then Secretary of State for Scotland. Their horses tossed their heads in the crowded street, for folk had already assembled to gape; the older among them remembered James V himself when he had come to France to marry Madame Madeleine, and still spoke of him with affection, *le beau roi d'Ecosse.* The Lord High Treasurer, and Fleming the Lord Chamberlain, the rescued Lord Rothes, and Lord Seton the fowler, young Mary's father, rode behind; and I was glad to see Madame's friend there, Erskine of Dun. They travelled through Paris and went on to Fontainebleau. I heard afterwards that they made their best endeavours to see that La Reinette received fair treatment in the matter of money from Henri II; but secretly, she was made to sign an instrument gifting him and his heirs, should she die with none, the succession of the realm of Scotland as well as all her rights to the throne of England through her grandmother. Also, the King claimed the sum of a million crowns of gold for the supposed expenses of La Reinette's residence in France, which had in fact been met all these years by Madame. He cloaked it by describing the outlay as his aggression against the English on behalf of the Scots. All this was related to me by Madame afterwards, as I had no means of knowing at that time.

I made my way daily about the booths and markets, hearing the buzz of preparation and the bargaining over the prices of gold thread and bales of silks and lawn. Milliners were creating airy head-dresses trimmed with lace; embroiderers were working designs of flowers and beasts on rich stuffs to be worn by the Court; goldsmiths were hammering at lockets and rings, jewellers setting their gleaming wares in silver and more gold. The Scots spent such money as they had, in the way King James had done before them, running up and down; I heard their rough accents again, but did not reveal myself. All this went on while the March winds turned to spring, and the day of the wedding approached; by then, the scaffolding had been covered with green boughs, some natural, some contrived. There had been a great ball at the betrothal, and the King they said had opened it with La Reinette; but we saw nothing of that. All the folk who waited to see the wedding itself were there by early morning, some having slept all night on the street, wrapped in their cloaks. As for the bride, she and all the royal family slept in the Archbishop's house, and by dawn trumpets sounded, and the beat of drums. The crowd began to murmur with excitement; fishmongers, butchers, tailors, housewives, beggars and friars, their bowls forgotten, waited to see their Queen come by. She, and not Madame Cathérine, reigned in their hearts. Mary Stuart was Queen of France long before her marriage.

I understand the bridges were wedged with horses and riders and folk, but saw none of it. The crowds pressed so close that it was impossible to move. One could see, on its height, the open pavilion erected before the gates of Nôtre Dame, with all the stone gargoyles grimacing above. 'They say it was designed, all of it, by M. le Comte, the Master of Works,' murmured a woman close to me, as though she knew everyone concerned, as such women will. I smiled at her, then turned back to the carved vine leaves and trellises which resembled a cathedral cloister, and the blue Cyprus silk with its fleurs-de-lys, and the brave royal arms of Scotland.

By ten o'clock the guests were assembled, and necks were craned to watch them come, but they would be remembered less well than the bridal party. The Swiss Guards marched in before the Duc de Guise, and I reflected that I had hardly known this eldest half-brother, for he had been away from Joinville on his military service very early, and I had seen nothing of his later marriage with Anne d'Este, said to be the most graceful dancer in Europe, except for the galliard, in which La Reinette herself had no peer. The Archbishop of Paris, in his vestments and lace, and the Cardinal de Bourbon, who was to perform the marriage, were waiting by now; and suddenly Le Balafré made a gesture which showed that he was human, and considered the ordinary people. He swept with his arm to make my lords and gentlemen fall back, and the pavilion was in full view again for all of us, as they had blocked the way with their ruffs and short cloaks.

The young Queen's Scots musicians, whom she loved well, came then, in red and yellow livery, playing and singing, then a hundred gentlemen belonging to the King of France; then the princes of the blood, richly dressed, but that was nothing new. Eighteen bishops and abbots in their mitres followed, with the Cardinal of Lorraine meantime escorting the Pope's representative, the Legate; they were deep in talk, and I wondered if, being used to grand occasions, they were taking the opportunity to discuss the renewal of the Council of Trent, which had lapsed for the time. I would never know that, and my half-brother did not see me, a woman in a plain hood, among the crowd. I felt for the black locket he had given me, and it was still there. I assured myself of its presence frequently, and never forgot it, or my reason for wearing it. If only Madame could have been present that day!

The bridegroom came then, with his two little brothers. None of them were notable, although of course the Dauphin's dress was rich. After the marriage they say François shot up like an onion plant, but he was still no match for his tall bride. Although they cheered his pale face, with the lines already from nose to mouth which should not have been there at his age, they were waiting for the bride. All France was waiting for her; from the Channel ports to the southern mountains, everyone would be thinking of La Reinette that day.

The Cardinal of Lorraine had turned back to escort her. On her other side was the King of France. She wore a white dress and grey-blue cloak, with pearl embroidery, and so rich a jewelled crown that it could not have been from the Scottish regalia; in any case they had refused to send that. The cheers multiplied till one was deafened, and the trumpets and fifes could no longer be heard, and La Reinette was much moved; I saw the jewel on her breast, the Great Harry, which had belonged to Margaret Tudor, tremble, and the bride smiled. The four Maries supported her train, which was of enormous length. She bowed to us, and passed on. I have never seen anyone so beautiful.

Madame Cathérine caused no excitement, led in by the Prince

de Condé, and after her the Queen of Navarre, in appearance a trifle disapproving of all the richness; she was after all a Huguenot. Madame Marguérite, the King's sister, Duchesse Antoinette and the rest were received by the Archbishop, and tapers glowed from within on their silver chandeliers. The ceremony proceeded at once. The King drew a ring from his little finger, and gave it to the Cardinal of Bourbon, who married the boy and girl. The Scots lords came forward to salute their new King, and as they did so largesse of gold and silver was flung in handfuls among the crowd, who jostled forward in such disorder that several were hurt, their caps and cloaks pulled off and lost; in the end it was shouted for further largesse to be stopped for this reason, while heralds' trumpets brayed.

The party had gone into the church for Mass by then, and I saw no more, nor did anyone, till they came out again, then the King made the bride and groom walk round the covered way once more, that all might see them, as some still had not despite everything. After that they went in for their banquet, and I saw no more; but that was the wedding, as I afterwards related it to Madame the Regent.

The two Scots lords, spiritual and temporal, who had been rescued by a fishing boat from shipwreck on arrival in France were destined never again to reach Scotland alive. I was able to witness their demise myself, because shortly before making my own arrangements for return I had encountered Lord Seton and his daughter walking in the Paris market, and he pressed me to travel with them by way of Dieppe. Mary Seton was of course not going with her father; she would remain in attendance on the Queen. She had grown into a quiet, pretty, well-mannered young girl with one of the new small round velvet hats, the colour of a ruby, perched forwards on her dark hair above a high narrow ruff. Everybody followed the fashions of La Reinette, and I asked Mary Seton how the newly-weds fared; she assured me they were very happy. I believe that they were, but in any case one can say no other about a bride and groom. It was never certain whether or not the marriage was consummated, as M. le Dauphin was both delicate and young. As regarded the recognition of him as King of Scots, I remarked to Lord Seton that my lords had all made obeisance to him, in public, in the pavilion outside Nôtre Dame. The fowler's good weatherbeaten face looked doubtful.

'It will have to be debated in Council,' he said cautiously, and I foresaw more trouble for Madame and longed to get back to her. I mentioned this, and it was then that Lord Seton offered me his protection on the way to Dieppe and a place in the ship with them afterwards. The Lord James and the rest would travel with us. I was not overjoyed at prospect of journeying with James V's eldest bastard, but it was better than travelling alone.

I paid my bill at my lodgings and said goodbye to Justine, who wept: we had become acquainted, in fact friends. I gave her two crowns of the sun for her dowry, which greatly contented her, and said farewell.

The journey to Dieppe was uneventful. I cannot recall that the Lord James said a single word, to me or to anyone else. He rode in gloomy silence, while Lord Rothes, long since recovered from his shipwreck, chatted to me as we rode through the windy Norman weather. He was a much-married old rascal with an eye for a pretty woman; in fact, as he confided to me, he anticipated taking a fifth wife on his return, the sprightly widowed Lady Balcaskie. Alas, she never saw him again.

The wind had worsened by the time we reached the coast, and although we boarded the ship at once it put out in heavy seas. I stood on deck with my hair blowing, my cloak clutched about me, and doubted if we would make land. Presently the vessel veered about, and amid general cursing we returned to Dieppe.

We made our way, soaked and hungry, to an inn; Lord Cassilis, who liked everything to go his own way, even the weather, grumbled audibly. We sat down to supper and they served us a dish of mussels. I am prone to a looseness of the bowels after eating these, so asked for some other dish to be brought to me. I was glad that I had done so, for by next morning several of my lords, including the Lord James, were taken ill. The wind was still contrary, and our ship had perforce to wait; in fact the sick men could not have gone on board. The poor old Bishop of Orkney, who had eaten his mussels with relish on the previous night, was so overcome I went up to him at last and tried to comfort him where he lay, as it chanced, on a box containing his vestments and sacred vessels for Mass, lest they be stolen. John Knox afterwards wrote that the Bishop was a miser who would not be parted from his hoard of gold. In fact the old man had been most generous to the poor and had added great improvements to his cathedral at Kirkwall. He died, in great agony. So did poor Lord Rothes, and much later Lord Fleming and the Earl of Cassilis, the latter having at last torn himself with reluctance from the company in Paris of the young Queen's Latin tutor, Master George Buchanan. The Lord James unfortunately did not die, although he complained ever afterwards of a troublesome sourness of the stomach. It may partly have accounted for his subsequent conduct, but he was self-seeking from the beginning. He had asked La Reinette for permission to marry the heiress of Buchan although he was a churchman, but she had refused. Thereafter he had a grudge against her, and against Madame.

That was a long poisoning. Two of my lords lingered for weeks, and one did not die till Christmas. The Scots blamed the French for the poisoning, due to their own slowness in acknowledging the young Dauphin as their King; but as no Frenchman could have foreseen that we would return to eat at the inn at all, I put it down to accident.

Parliament agreed, in the end, to allow the title to King François as ruler of Scotland, but the Lord James, who was elected to carry this news back to France, would not return there. I hardly noted what he did, so concerned was I by the change in the appearance of Madame herself. She had not been in the best of health when I left, and by now was much worse; the hazards of her Regency, the constant suspense concerning France and England, and the insolence of her lords, as well as disease, had greatly aged her. Not only were both legs swollen so that she could hardly ride, their flesh like butter when one pressed in a finger, but her body likewise had swelled, as if in pregnancy, though she hid the disfigurement meantime under her robes. She knew as well as I that it was dropsy, and that nothing could be done, although she joked about it and wrote to her mother in France that she was her own surgeon and physician. I did what I might, rubbing the swollen flesh to ease it and persuading Madame to rest when she could, but there were constant demands on her. Nevertheless it was a relief that the marriage was accomplished; she saw her daughter as safe, the Queen of France, and France governing Scotland whether it would or no, England being prevented thereby from further attacks on us. That had been Madame's intent from the beginning, and who could blame her after all she and others had undergone? Yet it did not suit the Scots; that nation are hard to suit. Now that it appeared that the French were to be their masters, they again wanted the English, though they would never admit it; but they took English money.

The old Earl of Angus, all of whose young sons had died in infancy, was newly dead, of an attack of erysipelas at Tantallon. Of his daughter Lady Margaret we heard nothing; after Queen Mary Tudor's death she lived with her husband Lennox in Yorkshire. As for Sir George Douglas, he was thankfully dead long ago, on one of Châtelherault's justice ayres, while the latter was still Governor Arran. It looked as if the power of the Red Douglas was broken; but the heir of it all was young Darnley, as yet no doubt at his Latin exercises, though later he visited France.

The affair of St Giles's day occurred while I was still abroad, and I can only relate it from hearsay; but it disturbed Madame greatly. There had, on the accession of Mary Tudor to the English throne five years previously, been a fleeing to Geneva from England of many who were of the reformed turn of mind, notably John Knox, who had formerly been high in favour with the Queen's brother Edward VI and had refused a bishopric. Knox had lately, as the Cardinal of Lorraine had informed me, made a short visit to Scotland. During it, they say he climbed Arthur's Seat, imagined himself to be Christ tempted by the devil, and replied in clear tones on being offered all the kingdoms of the world. 'Thou shalt serve the Lord thy God, and Him only shalt thou serve'. We all of us knew that, but did not confuse ourselves with God on the mountain, as the man's subsequent conduct shows that he himself did. At any rate, he helped inflame the fire that was already running high in the Protestant belly, though Knox himself proclaimed that there was an unquenchable fire in Madame's. He always hated her and said and wrote things of her that would not be forgiven from man to man, let alone man to woman.

The feast of St Giles is on the first of September, and each year on that day, often swept by the early clean winds of autumn, a procession would wind down the Canongate carrying the saint's great image and the reliquary which contained his arm-bone. St Giles was not only a favourite of Madame – it will be recalled that she named one of my sons after him – but, also, the patron of Edinburgh; the cathedral with its great brooch spire always guttered inside with candles to him and to Our Lady, and it is sad to think of their being put out now, and everything dark. The procession wound, with its priests robed and censers swinging, monks, trumpets and drums following, the saint's image held high on men's shoulders, and all the folk watching and chanting prayers, about the town and to Holyrood. This happened year after year, and was much honoured among us. It is a mistake to say, as the reformers do, that we worship images; it is God we worship, and the image does but remind us of His saints and the virtues for which they were known in their day, that they may not be forgotten. St Giles had cured the plague often, with prayer; he was said to have shrived Charlemagne; he had led a holy life as a hermit, with his rescued hind for whose sake he had taken a wound with an arrow; and certainly he had never done any harm. On that day in 1558 the reformers inflamed a mob, who attacked the great image, carried it to the Nor' Loch which broods down below the Castle, and threw it in with a splash, yelling insults. Then they fished it out, carried it with more cursing to a bonfire, and burned it. It is perhaps true that the flames were as unwilling to rise as they had been at the slow burning of Patrick Hamilton the reformer, long ago; there was a high wind that day too, and the image was wet.

When the news was brought to Madame, she ordered a smaller image, which was in the Greyfriars, to be borrowed, and put it in the larger one's place to be carried in a shrine. Then she herself headed the procession, and in her presence the crowd dared do naught. It wound on calmly; and as all was quiet now, and Madame was tired, she went with her women into a house in the Canongate where they had already asked her to dine, but as soon as she had gone from among the people trouble broke forth again; they attacked the smaller image as they had done the larger, with ribald shouting about the young and the old St Giles, father being as bad as son, son as father. Madame was forced to watch the tumult from the upper house windows; it had gone beyond her control. This was the second open flouting of her authority; the first had been the turning back of the French at Eyemouth, and already there was murmuring everywhere against French help, the French marriage, and French masters for Scotland. It was all of it tied up with the uneasy war between France and Spain, the position of England, the lack of hope for the barren Queen there, and, maybe, certain arrogance of French officers about our countryside. They were no worse than the English had been; but everyone had forgotten the English invasions, the Rough Wooing of the little Queen, when towns and abbeys and harvests had gone up in flames and been left in charred ruin. Nor did they know that it was English money that already paid for the disturbances, by way of Scots lords. That was the end of the two images of St Giles, at any rate; as for his procession, there would be none in the following year, and the year after that, Madame was dead.

Part VII

Queen Mary Tudor died in November 1558, abandoned by her
Spanish husband, made foolish by false pregnancies, broken-
hearted after the recapture of Calais by our brother, alone,
having alienated her subjects who at first had called her, after
their earlier ordeals, Merciful Mary. Now, with Knox, Foxe, and
their like rampant with both word and pen, she was Bloody
Mary, and so would be remembered; although the open
burnings at Smithfield were perhaps less cruel than the many
secret torments, the rack, the suspense, the hanging by the
thumbs and crushing of testicles, the Little Ease where a man
could neither lie nor sit, and other such methods employed later
by her half-sister Elizabeth, the latter's minister Cecil and their
employed torturer, Topcliffe.

We had not met the Lady Elizabeth that earlier time in
London; she had been too cautious, and caution has been for a
long time, in fact for all of her life till now, her watchword. She is
a Tudor, and therefore cruelty does not appal her; I once heard
that having at last hunted down an especially brave swift deer at
the Earl of Leicester's great feasting for her at Kenilworth,
Elizabeth caused its ears to be cut off and then set it free. That is
perhaps less important to most than what she did to those men
and women who opposed her; even before her half-sister's
burial, she arrested an old bishop who had dared to preach a
farewell sermon on the virtues of the late Queen. Mary Tudor's
coffin lay neglected under rubble at Westminster and no one as
far as I know, has yet disposed of it. By degrees, Catholics

271

suffered increasingly in England; Elizabeth dared not allow them tolerance, for they believed her mother Anne Boleyn to have been the concubine of Henry VIII and not his wife, and Elizabeth a bastard: our Reinette, through her Tudor grandmother, being accordingly the legitimate Queen of England. All this was bad enough before the Pope excommunicated Elizabeth Tudor, some years ago now; but by then Madame was long dead. Henry VIII made war on us in Scotland with fire and sword; his daughter did so with money.

At the time, we noticed changes in the confidence of the Protestants. Men like Knox, who had refused a bishopric in London in King Edward's day and had in fact helped compile the English Prayer Book to its detriment, reappeared in Scotland, well found with Tudor specie. The reformers called themselves, after the desecration at Perth, Lords of the Congregation. There was always money to pay them, whereas Madame had to sell her plate. Once she had admired the fine furnishings and tapestries in Scottish palaces when she came there as a bride, and had planned gardens; but there was no time for such things now, nor any hearing of music, nor patronage of artists such as had painted her portrait three years since. She herself was no better; both legs were still swollen, and her eyesight was beginning to blur; I would see her bend close over the documents she must sign and sign, to the King of France, to her brother the Cardinal, to Argyll, to Huntly, to Châtelherault again at last. It came to that; once more in desperation, she must pretend to rely on the twitching uncertain fool of an ex-Governor, who could command the Scots because he was one of themselves, and supposedly a man. It did not matter how often he changed sides, or his son Arran. That young man, flattered like many others before and after him by the prospect dangled before him of marriage with Elizabeth Tudor, resigned his command of the Scots Archers of the Guard of France and hastened to the Virgin Queen at Greenwich, where he saw her in a summer bower. Despite the fact that he had abjured Rome, fled to Geneva saying his life was in danger from the French, and other attributes – he was still a handsome young man although his manner was already wild – the cautious lady rejected him, not openly, for that was not her way; Arran returned to Scotland full of zeal for the Protestant cause, and later, despite all Madame's determination and charm, persuaded his father to join the former alliance and forsake Her Grace. Châtelherault was, naturally, not alone in that.

The Beggars' Summons was pinned to the doors of all Scottish friaries by the Protestants on the first day of January, 1559. It commanded the inmates to render up their property to the poor and infirm and to be out by Whitsun. When Madame heard, all she said was 'That is not till the end of May. We have a little time. It remains to be seen what is happening in France.'

She was informed, of course, about events, more so than I; within weeks a peace was signed between France and Spain, and young Madame Elisabeth, King Henri's dark-haired daughter, La Reinette's close friend in childhood, was sent to marry King Philip as his third wife. This relieved Madame in that King Henri would no longer ask her to make further incursions into England, as for the moment all was peace. Those who have described Madame as intent on making war at any time malign her. For a little while we had card games, mostly quadrille, to amuse ourselves, even some music. My twins were meantime learning to ride their ponies in the park at Stirling. I heard news of them now and again; and although our main residence had, by reason of events, to be in the capital, Madame rode west to Stirling again in early summer, partly on my account, partly on her own; and I rode with her.

'He took the bread and brake it;
The blessing then he spake it.
And what His word doth make it,
That I believe, and take it.*

'That commits her to nothing. It has served her all through the Protestant reign of Edward VI and the Catholic one of her sister Mary. Now she has recognised the English Prayer Book, in which Knox had a hand regarding the doctrine of the Eucharist, and has proclaimed herself head of the Church in England, as her father did before her. Yet she is near her people's hearts already, in a way I never will be here in Scotland.'

Madame tore up the scrap of paper with Elizabeth Tudor's quatrain; she had it by heart, no doubt. I noticed tears in her eyes, as these days she often wept; and as usual tried to comfort her. 'It does not matter what Knox says,' I told her. 'God can make wheat from earth; why not flesh from bread? He can make grapes from soil; why not blood from wine? Our Lord said that if one did not eat of His flesh, and drink of His blood, one would not gain the kingdom; yet these people deny it, as the followers did who left Him then.'

'You are a comfort to me, Claudine. Our education at the Poor Clares, and with my mother, was perhaps not wasted. Do you remember when you said St Clare ought not to have cut her hair off, and should have married St Francis?' Despite everything, the worn face laughed. I recalled Madame Philippa's behaviour to me on that occasion, and remained prudently silent. Her Grace went on 'These Scots; they think of me still as a foreigner. When I came to this land to marry its King, long ago, they made a broth and called it Lorraine soup, but I have never tasted it. It is as though I have never reached their hearts, though God knows I have tried hard enough all these years. I hope my daughter fares better, if she ever comes here; but perhaps it will not happen when she is Queen of France.'

She turned away, and I reflected on the news of the day, which said that Master John Knox was again in Scotland, this time for as long as he chose; and that Madame had summoned him and the rebel preachers to meet her here at Stirling for trial, but I myself did not think they would come. It was no longer, I knew, as it had been in the days of Cardinal Beaton, when the Church could safely order and the folk here obey. Madame herself was not safe, as our brother the Cardinal of Lorraine had predicted; even while I had been in France, a party of lords had burst into her presence and had clapped basnets on their heads, in defiance. Madame had cozened them with fair words, as was her way: what other was there? She could use no force, except for France; and France, here, was increasingly the enemy.

The rebel preachers did not obey the order to come. Instead, the Beggars' Summons still flapped on the doors of the friaries, its ink long faded in the wind and rain. Before Whitsun, Madame sent Erskine of Dun to tell the preachers they were outlawed, put to the horn in absence. It would have had effect in the time of the King her husband. Now, it had none: except to inflame rebellion itself under the cloak of religion. Madame knew very well that that was at its heart; without it, she would no doubt have left the Protestants to their protesting. She had several times said that men might after all worship God as they would. But it was not to be so for us; neither for Madame nor for myself.

* * *

I heard John Knox preach in Perth, before the destruction there. This was no accident; I had been sent there by Madame, riding with two servants as a private gentlewoman. It would be less obvious than sending delegates or Frenchmen to listen, and I could bring back my opinion of the preacher and his powers, which I did, having slipped in among the rest. I had not set eyes on Knox since that time in St Andrews shortly after Cardinal Beaton was murdered, and before they had apprehended the man and sent him to the galleys. Now, after that experience, he was somewhat physically changed and aged, as might have been expected. He was still short in stature, with broad shoulders, perhaps grown even broader with the exercise of rowing. His hair and beard had been a wispy black; now the beard was long, full, and iron-grey, and he wore a round cap and long gown. Beneath the cap, above the beard, his eyes looked out, blue-grey and compelling, and his mouth still resembled a plum. I could understand the power he had over men even before he spoke, and women too; there was a doting lady of middle years in the congregation whom I understood from whispered talk to be his mother-in-law, a Newcastle woman who evidently followed him everywhere in doting fashion. Knox had eventually married her young daughter, who bore him two sons in proper course; one was called Nathaniel and the other Eleazar. I did not glimpse the wife that day. Knox began to preach, and his sermon was lengthy, perhaps lasting a full two hours. During that time, he thumped the pulpit till I thought it would fly to pieces; the points he was hammering home concerned Christ's evangel, as put forth by himself. There was little enough about Christ's grace. I came out afterwards with the subdued congregation, chilled to the bone though it was summer, and rode home with my opinions to Madame. She was diverted to hear them, but we were both well aware of the man's danger, even before then; a few weeks later, there came the time when, after one of such sermons, a stone was thrown by a boy at a statue in St John's Church in Perth, and then the whole assembly rose and set about wrecking everything in the building, windows, images, vessels, altarcloths, tombs; the destruction was worse than an English invasion would have been. Afterwards they ran through the streets of Perth, their numbers growing, looting and destroying everywhere; finally the Charterhouse itself was hammered to fragments, even the monuments of its founder

James I and his Queen Joan, and that of old Margaret Tudor.
There was nothing left in the end but stone-dust, smashed glass,
bones, and a ruined shell. Her Grace broke her heart when she
heard, almost as she had done that time the English destroyed
the chapel at Holyrood where her husband and sons lay. Such
were the tidings; soon it would be the same all over Scotland. I
may add one thing more about John Knox before I finish; years
later, in his fifties, after his first wife was dead, he married a
young girl of sixteen, a daughter of the minor Scots nobility. His
mother-in-law from the earlier marriage still lived with them.
The situation may perhaps be imagined, but by then I was
elsewhere.

'My lord, I marvel at you, you being second person of Scotland
and none between you and the authority but my daughter, who
has no succession as yet, and I but a woman, that knows not the
nature nor falsity of men and baronage of Scotland; and I
believe they stand in no awe of me because I am but a woman,
and therefore I marvel at you that you will not help to come at
the men that so abuse the common weal and policy of the
country, in casting down of abbeys and religious places, and
destroying the liberty of Holy Kirk.'

Châtelherault, who everybody had said would not appear,
shuffled his feet. Madame had been certain he would obey her
summons; so had I. Any show of firmness confirmed this
vacillating man, for the time, until somebody else got hold of
him. For that reason Madame cozened him, as she had been
used to do, once he was safe in her presence. She flattered the
Duke to the top of his bent; she implied that she could not do
without him, as indeed for the moment she could not; and at last
said that she intended to ride out against the rebels in person,
and could by no means do so without his support and presence.
By her fair ways and subtle words, as they put it afterwards, she
brought the ex-Governor to her way of thinking, at least for the
time.

They rode out of Stirling side by side a few days later, at the
head of such men as could be mustered. It was by no means the
army it should have been, nor in any likelihood a match for that
of our enemies. Nobody but Madame, in her state of health,
would have ridden out at all. I went in attendance on her,
leaving my sons in their tutor's care, because she needed a

woman to minister to her; she should have had a physician as well. I saw her proud worn profile lifted to the sky, and Châtelherault's twitching face borne close in some talk or other; we rode north-east, with the hills closing in, and already there were sounds of squabbling from the men behind, some French, some Scots.

There is a long village in Perthshire named Auchterarder, like other villages with pigs in the streets, middens and straw, and scared folk bobbing and making then swiftly for their bothans. Half Scotland did not know what the war was about; the Evangel had not yet reached the remoter parts of it, and in some places never would.

'We must wait for the guns,' said Madame. She lay down on a bed in one of the thatched houses, and I rubbed her legs. Outside, there were grunts and sounds of heaving as oxen were harnessed and taken off along the way, to drag the guns after us. Unfortunately this was a slow business, and meantime there was a rally of Protestants and a rumour of the Earl of Glencairn, Madame's determined enemy, riding in with reinforcements from the west.

Glencairn and his father had been for the English marriage from the beginning. Also, he was unfriends with Châtelherault and the latter with him, owing to the divorce of his first wife, the ex-Governor's sister. He had entertained John Knox at his house in Finlayston, where he and others had received the reformers' communion of plain bread; and Glencairn had a history of loyalty to Lennox. Although he had been with us on the visit to France in the young Queen's childhood, I had never dealt with him or liked him greatly. He was a close-eyed, thin-faced personage, but at least knew which side he was on. Accordingly, we marched on Perth, when our guns had caught up with us, having few illusions: which was as well. By then, Glencairn had raised some thousands of soldiers. Our small force had no hope, and Madame knew it.

She sent for the Lord James, who came cold-eyed. It was hard to remember, as evidently he did not, that Madame had reared him as her own son and had always been gracious to him. There was talk and discussion back and forth, while on the North Inch of Perth, where long ago the Clan Chattan had defeated the Clan Kay, three thousand Protestant troops waited on the green summer grass, while flies buzzed over their ordure and that of the horses. There was no battle. Madame was concerned about the fate of the people in the town. Finally she ensured that none were to be punished for their support of either side, or for damage caused in the late riots; on the other hand, my lords demanded that no Frenchman enter Perth. They were not to come within three miles of it, nor was Her Grace to leave a French garrison behind her when she left. Otherwise, she might, by their kindness, ride in.

The Lords of the Congregation, grim-faced, rode out, and the Regent entered the town, prepared to endure what she saw. It was worse by far than she had expected; everything that could have been called a church lay in ruins. There was a silence like the silence of death, and no cheers for her. She sent for the Provost, and I saw the bright colour flare again in her cheeks; she had endured much, and she was a Guise.

'I will dismiss that man,' she swore, and when he entered our presence left him in no doubt of it. It would have been less easy to dislodge the former holder of the office, Lord Ruthven, Keeper of the Privy Seal as he had been and married to a rich heiress with much land; but he was dead. Madame appointed her own successor, Edmund Hay, who later became Rector of the new Scots College at our old retreat of Pont-à-Mousson; saw order restored as far as it could be done, and rode then out of Perth, leaving it garrisoned with Scots in French pay; later they said that this meant she had broken the agreement. That lost her the Lord James, in as far as he was worth keeping; the late King's eldest bastard changed sides openly from that day, and was thereafter numbered among the Lords of the Congregation, which allegiance suited his sour looks.

There was a fiery comet seen in the sky at night about then, blazing its orange trail in presage, they said, of disaster to Scotland. We needed no comet. In addition to the man-boy Arran, bandied from one to another of the insurgent lords as their future King and promising to make his swerving father once again desert the Queen Regent's cause, there was news out of France. King Henri had been jousting with De Lorges of old days with us, and had received the splinter from a lance above the eye. Like the poisoned lords, he was long in dying: in fact for a time it was thought the injury was slight. All was not by any means well with ourselves; already, the reformers had ruined St

Andrews and Crail, and while Madame rested at Falkland they moved nearer to her, to Cupar. I feared they meant to encircle and capture her in her palace, but she shrugged that off. 'They will make for Stirling in the end; it means more to them, and I will come when I can. You must go there, Claudine, to your boys; they should not be left alone. My person is of no value to anyone. Do not stay with me, I beg.'

I was unwilling to go without her, for she was no longer in any state to ride, and I hoped would not try meantime to do so. I think she herself knew that she had no more strength, for this time she sent the shifty Duke by himself, with our faithful D'Oysel to steady him, and to command the army. It was D'Oysel who in the end climbed the Hill of Tarvit and surveyed the immense sea of Protestant forces spread out below on the moor. Resistance was as useless as it had been at the North Inch of Perth. They came, as I later heard, to a fresh arrangement, and allowed Her Grace to ride free through Fife, but without supporting French forces or any Scots who were in French pay. How could she escape with her life? But she did so; by some means, having tried Stirling and failed, she got herself to Edinburgh again; and heard that my Lords of the Congregation were by then in Perth to eject her chosen Provost, Edmund Hay. Having done so, they marched to Scone and looted and burned the palace there, and the abbey where Kings of Scotland had been crowned since ancient times. There was nowhere else left for them to come, after that, but the west.

I had gone out to an apothecary's to get ointment for Damien's sore eyes; both boys had had measles. I had done my duty and sat by them, tying their hands by the end in linen bags to prevent their scratching. Otherwise they were company for each other, mostly silent; they were never talkative children. Perhaps I myself did not talk to them enough. I left them, and went thankfully into the town; the streets were quiet. The apothecary haggled over the unguent and its price, and coming out of his shop with it at last I heard in the near distance a sudden dull murmuring, as of a nearing swarm of bees. Presently I saw dust rise, and men approaching on horseback and on foot. They were a rabble, but under direction; in a trice they had blocked the way to the Castle, and I could not go home. I saw at once who was in command; two men, both well mounted; the Lord James and his kinsman and familiar, Argyll.

They came on relentlessly. I should have known, and perhaps did, that their target would be the Church of the Black Friars; after all I had seen what happened in other towns. I saw them stream towards it; they had mallets and other instruments in their hands, and as they drew near began swinging these at the stonework, breaking off fretted carving. Soon there was a jumble at the doors to get in, some to destroy, some to watch. I was borne along with them whether I would or not, for by now the street was packed with folk; and found myself at length inside, but with no peace there any more. Even as I watched, the statue of Our Lady of Pity toppled, and the carved face of Richard of England on his supposed tomb, with the painted beard, whether it was he or not, was smashed to fragments. I closed my eyes and leant against a pillar, hearing the senseless destruction and the shouting; when I looked again, a rabble of monks and nuns were being forced out into the streets, many of them bleeding with blows from fists and mallets, terrified as they were, with no protection. The dust of the ruined stonework rose still, making the air thick as it had been at Pinkie Cleugh. I became aware of a thin figure running, robed like the rest, away from the crowds towards the tabernacle. I thought of what lay in there, and so no doubt did the destroyers, and we raced to it, but I was first, and myself encountered the running man. It was Melville, his lean face contorted in fear, his hands clutching some matter against his robe. He saw me, and lurched forward; and thrust the Host in its containing vessel close at me, gasping 'Take it, and make it safe if ye may,' and then they were upon and over him, scarcely having looked at what he was, let alone what he had held. By that time I had concealed the vessel in my cloak, later thrusting it in my loosened bodice along with that other I kept always for Madame. Who was I, that I should twice bear away next my heart the Body of Christ?

Afterwards, when their fury was slaked and they had gone away, I went back to Melville, or what was left of him. He was dead, crushed flat. His nose was broken, pressed down hard against the stone, his spread hands and trampled body covered with dust and blood. He would perhaps know that he of all men, he, the renegade, had saved the Host, and that I, never in truth his wife, had concealed it, God knows how; maybe they did not suspect me, being a woman. There was nothing I could do for

Melville; God would receive his soul, I thought, for what he had lately done, and would forget what had gone before.

I limped back to the Castle later when all was quiet, for they had not taken it, being too greatly busied with devastating the summer gardens and cutting down the fruit trees with their apples already set. By now they were getting drunk in the streets, and several women, among them nuns, were fugitives; the Castle guards knew me and let us in. I took the sacred vessel straight to Madame's chaplain, who received it gratefully. 'It will be used at Mass,' he said quietly. 'You will be present?'

'I will be present, to pray for my husband's soul,' I told him. After all Melville, in his way, had been my husband. I found that in the agitation of events I had lost Damien's ointment for his eyes, but they got better without it. Both boys recovered from the measles. I heard afterwards that Madame had left Edinburgh, which was no longer safe, and had fled with a few followers to Dunbar. Whether she had resolved to await rescue by a French ship from that sea-rock I did not know, but resolved in any case to join her there.

'King Henri II is dead. My daughter is Queen of France.'

I had ridden through ruined Edinburgh, out of which Madame had lately been driven; the dismal pervading rain doused the smoke from its ruins and had soaked my servants and myself to the skin, like that unforgotten time at Fontainebleau. Yet Madame stood before me not like a fugitive, regal as ever, tall, smiling, assured that her policy of union with France had borne fruit, leaning now on a gilt staff covered with painted fleurs-de-lys. She saw me glance at it.

'Claudine, take off your cloak,' she said. 'This was sent to me on the same ship that brought back Master John Knox to Scotland. That is amusing, but it is sad about King Henri. He was my friend, and I cannot think but that my lords here will rejoice at his death, accordingly. It is true that my brothers will be in power now in France, while King François II is young. How wet you are! Did you find food on the way? Have your servants eaten? It is growing difficult, with no harvests, and ships seized which are bringing supplies; but we will contrive, I am certain. I am glad to see you, my dear. How are the boys? You wrote that they had been ill; I received the letter. Would you have left them? But I am glad you did.' She smiled again, and embraced me.

I told her my news, and that the boys were well cared for; took off my wet cloak as bidden, and freed the damp hair from the nape of my neck, spreading it out to dry. I had ridden in with two servitors and they were, I assured her, being attended to. I myself was not hungry. Presently I persuaded Madame to a chair, hearing the North Sea roar below in the constant rain that battered the walls. If I had ever thought that she intended escape to France, I was convinced otherwise now that I had had renewed sight of her; sick as she was, her eyesight blurred, her body swollen, she was confident. I myself was not. I had seen on the staff, a gift from her daughter and son-in-law, a thing that in itself would cause trouble: beside the royal arms of Scotland were impaled the arms of England and Ireland, as well as those of France. If the Cardinal of Lorraine had advised Mary Stuart to press her claim in such a way to the English throne, he had advised her badly. There would be trouble now from the south as well as from my lords. I knew it, and foresaw it if Madame herself did not; for a second time, I was wiser than she.

Madame had already issued her own proclamation to Edinburgh, in ruins as it lay, with its robbed and mutilated churches, its burned missals, its stolen chalices. 'They are not concerned with God,' she told me, 'but with the subversion of my authority and the usurpation of the crown. They greet the son of Châtelherault like the Son of God, but my informants tell me that although young Arran appears comely, his brain is crazed.' She had issued a command to the Lords of the Congregation to be out of the capital within six hours, and with them all strangers; but of course they ignored that. The way to deal with such persons was in fact to wait till they dispersed to their homes in due course, as they would do when the excitement was over. Meantime, by the end of July, the rebels had seized the coining irons kept at ruined Holyrood mint, and a load of bullion as well.

Madame was furious. She roused herself to an energy I had not seen in her for months. She summoned Châtelherault, Huntly – both of them wavering, both of them weak – to a Council meeting and faced them. 'We will march on Edinburgh,' she told them. My lords backed and shuffled, and Madame added, in face of their uncertain countenances, 'We must drive these persons from our capital. Lord Erskine is loyal, and he keeps the castle in the name of my daughter, Mary, Queen of Scotland and France.'

They protested that their forces were too small, that the plan would never succeed; but by force of will Her Grace persuaded them. 'I cannot ride with you,' she said, indicating her swollen body. As before, she sent Châtelherault alongside D'Oysel, whom she rightly trusted. They rode off and we saw them go, the rest following.

The Protestants had been drifting back to their homes, as foreseen, but got word of our coming in time, and drew up their forces again just outside Edinburgh. The French – I discount the ex-Governor, as by now did everyone else – marched instead into Leith, and took possession of it. This town had been greatly favoured by Her Grace, who had long since given it franchises of its own and had begun to build herself a house there, to be completed in the year she died. It had her name, harebells and thistles and the royal arms carved above the door. Later we would be glad of its shelter.

The rival sides entered into talks at last on Leith Links, by the end of July. My Lords of the Congregation promised to leave Edinburgh next day, to deliver up the coining irons, any coins they had made therefrom, and to leave desolate Holyrood in order that Her Grace might enter it. They promised to obey Mary, Queen of Scots and of France, and her husband. They promised that they would molest neither churches nor churchmen; in truth there were few left. In return, Madame's commissioners promised that the people of Edinburgh should be free to choose whichever form of worship they desired. A surprising number still desired the Mass.

Châtelherault and Huntly rode in first and duly received the coining irons. Thereafter Madame and I, with our train, rode out of Dunbar, leaving the North Sea to its constant murmuring, and returned to the gouged-out shell of the capital. We both stared expressionlessly at the harm that had been wrought there; by now, we were hard as iron in such ways. There were no Protestants in sight, and a few stragglers by the wayside even raised cheers. Madame rode on, her swollen bulk disguised by her summer cloak. I knew that she was in agony and would be glad, when we reached Holyrood, to subside in whatever chair might remain. 'We must wait for reinforcements,' she murmured to me on the ride. 'At all costs, we must wait.'

*

Before we had left Dunbar Madame had sent for me. She was seated at the table where she wrote letters, almost daily, to France. She sealed one with the green familiar seal, and handed it to me.

'You are to keep that by you in case of my death,' she said. 'Do not be alarmed, Claudine; we all die. I have known for some time that it would come soon. Do not grieve for me.'

'Madame –' I could not restrain my tears. Faltering, I told her of the locket the Cardinal of Lorraine had given to me, and asked if I should part with it to her at that moment.

'No,' she said. 'It is safer with you than with myself. When I am dying, bring it to me. You will be with me, I am convinced.' To my astonishment, I perceived a twinkle in the glazed, swollen eyes. 'Those twins,' Madame said. 'They were not Melville's, I believe. They are the sons of the steward at Vouvray, is it not so? You did not deceive me; few ever do. My intelligence is excellently served, and so was that of King Henri, God rest his soul.'

I hung my head. 'Do not be troubled about it,' Madame said. 'I have endured perfidy from the bastards of my late husband; you at least have been faithful. The letter I gave you is to my sister Antoinette, Abbess of Farmoutiers, to admit you there. When I am dead you may perhaps not choose to return to Vouvray. Use it if you will.'

I told her then what had happened to Melville, and she made the sign of the cross. Like myself, she was certain that God had pardoned him. 'I do not know what happened,' I said. 'When I parted from him he was a reformer, and next time he was in a procession of friars, and did not want to see me.'

'His end shows that he had come back to God,' Madame said. 'Do not trouble about it any more, Claudine, but pray for him. I pray for the King my husband also. I think that you will find Farmoutiers, if you decide to go there, less severe than Rheims, the abbacy of my other sister Renée, where I myself choose to be buried. The Protestants would not afford me quiet slumber in Scotland, I fear.'

We parted for the time, and I put the green-sealed letter among my effects, and kept it always by me. Thereafter, as I have said, we returned to Holyrood.

The Lord James and I faced one another across a table. In the background was the Earl of Argyll, whose presence I had hoped to be able to do without; the Campbell had been the first of his quality, as they put it, to desert the old religion, and was grimly fanatical in his support of the new. Anything I had been instructed by Madame to say would afterwards be discounted by the Earl and subtly discredited; but I could only do my best. That sick, but by no means yet defeated woman who could not ride for herself nowadays without pain had sent me, her sister and ally, to do what I could with this man, her husband's bastard, whom she had brought up from a child. Looking into James Stewart's chilly eyes, I forgot my sojourn in the clean and pleasant town of Glasgow, with its cathedral of St Mungo still unspoilt on a rise and the grey stone houses clustering round. One of them was that of the Archbishop, where I and my servants had had refreshment. On the whole, the churchman supported Madame.

'What may I do for you?' had enquired the Lord James courteously. He had then duly ushered me to a chair. He was a tall man, but the fact that he was seated also discounted his height, which would not in any case have troubled me. He wore rich dress, dark in colour, and a narrow ruff enhancing his short black beard. I knew that despite his weak position in illegitimacy, which was the same as my own, he still had hopes of being considered as a candidate for the crown of Scotland and, in this way, a rival to young Arran, on whom most of my lords had fixed their hopes and who was now with his father. For this reason, Madame thought that we might win the Lord James back. Already I knew better; but spoke as I had been bidden.

'My lord, you and others have signed a bond agreeing that none among you shall go to see or speak to the Queen Regent without the consent of the rest. Any private message from her is to be made public. Is not that an admission that her charm can itself change you from enemies to friends? Would it not be better that we are all so in any case? Madame has no wish to force your beliefs; she has never done so, or attempted it.' God knew, I thought, their friendship would be wavering enough if gained: and at least the two men at present were determined enemies. I was aware of the absent influence of Knox, who had gone lately to Holy Island to treat with the English. Being a relatively honest man, he had told everyone of it, which angered my lords both north and south of the Border and, no doubt, Elizabeth herself.

The Lord James spoke. 'Mary of Guise is an enemy to Christ's evangel. To have sent a woman to try to cozen me, as she now does, is evidence of her subtlety.' His mouth set in the narrow line of a much older man. In the shadows, Argyll nodded. I was roused to anger, which is never diplomatic.

'I am employing no womanly wiles on you, my lord. You are a churchman, or were so till lately.' I did not remind him that he had tried, as Prior of St Andrews, whose revenues he had long enjoyed, to obtain, when with the young Queen in France, her consent to his marriage nevertheless with the infant heiress of Buchan, and La Reinette had refused it; the Lord James had kept the Buchan child's rents, and later saw her married to his brother. 'Madame is an enemy to none, and all she asks, when you hold your preachings, is that you do not inflame the congregations thereby against their lawful princes and government. Can you blame her for requesting that? You have already compelled her to endure more than almost any other mortal woman; you and your men have done untold damage throughout Scotland, and now you are in league with the enemy in the south as well. Oh, you are surprised that we already know; we know some things, my lord, even that, the very day after Queen Elizabeth had sent Arran north with promises, she showed Madame's portrait to M. de Noailles in the gallery at Hampton Court, and discoursed on the Regent's goodness and virtue. She says that her signet is very well known, and that you have nothing to show. She is careful. Is she to be a friend or an enemy? Perhaps at least nobody knows that; but as you can, be loyal to your own country and its ruler. Madame herself has shown you much kindness.'

'We have professed loyalty to Queen Mary and to her husband,' he said coldly. Argyll moved a little, but said nothing; he was cautious to say no more throughout the meeting. 'Then why do you promote sedition and tumult?' I asked angrily. 'That is not loyalty. For whom do you fight, except yourselves and your own interests?'

'We have sought English help for God's greater glory,' said the Lord James unctuously. 'Mary of Guise has restored the abomination of the Mass at Holyrood, and would do so in St Giles's were she let.'

'Alternately with your own services, so that it would please all the people whichever way they choose to believe. That is her suggestion. Is that unfair? Is any force being used?' But there was silence.

I had a sense of complete helplessness. I said 'Then you will do nothing to see that civil policy here is respected, that peace is maintained, and that Madame is treated with honour as an anointed Queen and your Regent?'

'She will be deposed of her regency by the sound of trumpets and a proclamation in Edinburgh.'

I rose; my anger could contain itself no longer. 'She will ignore such impertinence, I assure you,' I said. 'She had hoped that by speaking with you, I, not by my own persuasion but by her reason and gentleness, might bring a change of heart in you; but men such as you have no heart. You complain of the French presence in Scotland, but what brought it here except your disobedience? I myself curse you; you are a hypocrite, such as Christ loathed. Whatever happens you will not prosper, and at the end, when you face God, you will at last know right from wrong.' I turned, and upset the chair in my haste to get out; he did not escort me, and I regained my servants and our small body of horse, and rode off, still enraged. I may say that the Lord James, later Earl of Moray, after many changes of coat, was murdered in the street during his own regency by a young man whose wife had been raped to death by Moray's soldiery. Moray himself was eulogised as the Good Regent by his Protestant party and buried, after a sermon by John Knox, in St Giles's, by which time I was thankfully in France, having watched poor Mary Stuart's trials from a distance. For now, I returned to her mother with the admission of my own failure, which perhaps we had both expected. But Madame's courage was so undaunted she would attempt anything in the cause of peace, which by now was impossible.

The Lord James, with Argyll forever by him, visited young Arran and rode with the lad to Stirling, to present him to the lords. Whatever ambitions the eldest bastard of James V had for himself in such ways were kept in abeyance for the time, but he must have summed up Arran and kept his own hopes. As for Arran's father, Châtelherault was induced to waver in his allegiance yet again, but that had been expected. Madame had a remedy for that at last, which has been condemned in her as unscrupulous. 'We must fortify Leith. If I do so they will say I have broken the agreement, but if I do not, how am I to build shelter for our poor French soldiers in time before the lords march again, with that

man and his son at their head, on Edinburgh?' Madame was too
angry to mention the name of Châteherault then, but later she
wrote to the King of France asking that, as a warrant for his
good behaviour, the rents pertaining to his dukedom there be
sequestered and his bastard son David Hamilton, and his servant
James of that name, held in custody.

Leith was fortified, and those who favoured Madame there
had their patience tried because of much hurried erection of
buildings to house the expected men. Also there was ill-feeling
when a thousand French soldiers at last landed, and the rumour
was put about, as some had brought their wives, that the Regent
intended to found a French colony there. Madame was aware of
all this, and that her popularity was not what it had been; but she
contented herself with victualling the place, though sadly short
of money, and with taking pleasure in the hanging, at last, of the
beautifully carved wood door on the house she had had built for
herself in Water Lane, where we would live for the time. It had
her own portrayed head in the centre, our father and King
James one on each side, and two nymphs, the right-hand one of
whom she said was myself, at the upper corners. Below were the
flowers, and the heads of Francis and Mary; the stonework
above was as I have already said, with Madame's name, Maria de
Lorraine, and the year 1560.

Meantime Elizabeth had sent her subtle statesman Randolph
north with the young Earl of Arran. He was reported as saying
that he had heard the Regent was very sick, but that some still
maintained the devil could not kill her. She was indeed sick, but
ordered our gear to be moved in from Holyrood, as clearly as if
she had been well; and in answer to certain insolence of my lords,
sent Lion Herald with a reply suitable to his mouth. She castigated
Châtelherault in no mean terms for his falsity, then stated that she
had as much right, in the Queen's name, to fortify Leith as he had
to do the same to his palace at Hamilton. 'Provide for the worst,
and make yourself strong in all costs,' replied that nobleman
dejectedly. 'For the sake of public tranquillity, I shall do what-
soever is not contrary to my duty to God and the Queen,' said
Madame. 'As for the destruction of law and liberty, it never
entered into mine heart. From whom should I conquer this
kingdom, seeing my daughter does as lawful heiress possess it?' It
was a timely reminder to the pretensions both of Arran and the
Lord James, if they would heed it.

Knox and a preacher named Willock were by now with my lords in Edinburgh, and this no doubt strengthened their resolution; we heard on the wind the trumpets Lord James had promised, though not the voice proclaiming the end of Madame's regency in the name of her daughter. They then sent a message back again by Lion Herald, requiring Madame to withdraw her person and French soldiers from Leith in twenty-four hours. This being disregarded by us, defiance was given, and preparations made for an assault.

The plaster in the new Leith house was still damp, reminding me of the smell at Freuchie. Otherwise, there was little resemblance to that peaceful place. Our food ran short, despite Madame's careful victualling; and the French, who like to eat well, began to murmur, and some tried to run away. Madame hanged five of them. There was one skirmish beyond the walls, wherein a man named Kirkcaldy of Grange slew a Frenchman and drew first blood, which is considered fortunate.

We had our own good fortune, however; the scaling-ladders they had made, in the cathedral aisle at Edinburgh of all places, were too short to approach Leith walls. St Giles perhaps favoured us. We heard the fighting, and I stayed by Madame, who was in no state to venture out; I did not tell her that it was generally assumed she would retire for safety to the island of Inchkeith, which she had once taken back and renamed l'Ile Dieu. She would retire nowhere; although she was not seen, she was at the heart of the siege, and directed it as our father would have done.

There was aid. It came from an unexpected quarter; a gallant young man, tough as leather, who was the son of the Fair Earl of Bothwell, Madame's hangdog suitor, dead four years since. James Hepburn, Earl of Bothwell and Great Admiral of Scotland, resembled his father not at all, either in fair looks or false behaviour; he was forthright, honest, brave, a proper man I could have fancied myself, but he was too young for me. He was said in any case to be handfasted to the widow of Buccleuch by then, but we heard no more of that. Bothwell captured £4000 in English money, sent north by Elizabeth for the rebels' use, and brought it to Madame. I can remember how her glazed eyes lit with laughter; it was almost the last joy she had. James Hepburn knelt and took her hands in both his hard ones, and swore to be her man, and so he was, till her death; and after that he served her daughter well, whatever they say. I was glad of his presence; and glad of the absence, which commenced about that same time, of Madame's smooth-faced secretary, Maitland of Lethington, who was afterwards discovered to have been sending her secrets, even those expressed in code, to England. Maitland had lately deserted to my Lords of the Congregation, and nobody missed him.

Meantime one Haliburton, a convinced Protestant and provost of Dirleton, had raised a battery on the Hawk Hill above Leith. He had enough guns to have finished us with their noise alone; all those of my lords, all those of the city of Edinburgh, except the Castle, where Lord Erskine would not part with any for the purpose. We waited for the thunder; and then Madame sent for me in some excitement.

'There is a man named Clerk in Edinburgh who is for us,' she said quietly. 'He says that all men, lords and commons, are gone to one of their long preachings this morning and that they will be at it many hours. Fetch the small guard; we do not need many men, only those we trust.' And she struggled from her chair, raising her swollen bulk for the first time in days; it was as if health suddenly returned to her with hope.

The men assembled. They made a quiet sortie from Leith, climbing the hill where the guns bristled silently, and took them, slaying Haliburton himself and such men as remained on guard. Then, not content, they invaded Edinburgh, reached the Canongate itself, and the foot of Leith Wynd; slew all in their way, and returned laden with matters much needed by us; sides of bacon, pots and pans, all they could lay hands on in the time; afterwards Knox wrote that the Regent had sat on the wall and bandied pleasantries with the soldiers as they came in. Madame was very far from sitting on a wall, but the return heartened her; we had lost no men at all. We heard a brief discharge of cannon from the Castle, for Lord Erskine was neutral, and desired to show it; I remembered that he had also promised Madame that if in the last extremity, or in danger of her life, he would give her shelter, with her women only. It was a comfort to know.

It seemed as if our luck had turned. On Hallowe'en, at Restalrig, the Lord James and Arran were put to flight like two of their own bogles, and twenty-five of their men slain, which agitated my lords more than if it had been several hundred.

There was consternation among them; the Lord of Hosts had deserted them; at midnight on the fifth of November, they retreated from the capital, taking their wives and children with them, and apart from relieving themselves, at Linlithgow, did not stop till they straggled on to Stirling. I had by now sent Giles and Damien with their nurse back to the Abbey Craig, and it was to be hoped that two small boys would be safe enough among the trees and rocks, away from the distracted, ruined town.

Madame entered Edinburgh in triumph next day. As before, she covered her body with her cloak. We did not go to Holyrood, but to a little house she owned near the Castle Hill, in Blythe's Close; it would, if needed, be nearer Lord Erskine's protection than much-invaded Holyrood, by now almost roofless and without furnishings. Over the door of our house was the motto *Laus et Honor Deo*. It seemed a good omen.

Mary, our young Queen of Scots, our Reinette, had wisdom; they had said at the Court of France that even as a child, she could talk as a person of fifty years old. Nevertheless she had a trustfulness that was later to betray her, for others are of necessity neither good nor wise. In thinking of relieving her sick mother by sending our youngest brother, René Marquis d'Elboeuf, to govern Scotland, she no doubt acted for the best; but she did not yet know her own countrymen. The Scots would have resented fiercely the presence of a French Governor and a Guise; at least Madame, though a Frenchwoman, had been married to their King and had borne him sons. The Scot is a stiff-necked animal. Although they had already entered into bonds with the English, as was shortly to be proved, I doubt if this would have happened without English gifts of money. The Scots lords knew well enough that they themselves were not Englishmen. That animal is very different.

Meantime, Madame took up the reins of government again from our house *Laus et Honor Deo*. She ordered repairs to the ruined buildings of the capital and she had St Giles's Cathedral reconsecrated. Oddly, among her adherents was Châtelherault's brother, the Archbishop of St Andrews, who of late had clung to her skirts. He was not to be relied upon, naturally, but he was present; also, good Lord Seton, whose wife remained in France. There were few others Madame could in fact trust, except myself. As for Châtelherault, she had for some time thought of a way of dealing with him; it was probable that he and the lords would again attempt Edinburgh, and she desired at all costs to discredit him among them before that happened. About Christmas, she revealed her intention to me; and asked if Marion Ogilvy could be sent for.

I was amazed. Those who knew her always said that the Regent forgot nothing; but to have remembered, through all of the strife, that Cardinal Beaton's former mistress had a talent for forgery argued immense recollection, at least. I wrote to Melgund, and its lady rode duly into town. Marion had changed little over the years, except that her black hair had by now turned white in two broad bands at the temples; it gave further strength to her strong face, rendered in some way more so by the loss of her teeth. She had employed her time very often in litigation over land and debt, and was known in the courts, conducting her own cases with the agility of a lawyer. Nothing made her afraid.

We had a copy of Châtelherault's seal. It was a simple matter to compose a grovelling letter to the King of France, regretting all past unfaithfulness and asking for protection. The stopping of his French rents at Madame's request might be supposed to have brought on this change, which was neither the first, the second or the third. 'They open my letters by custom in England,' said Madame, 'and no doubt they will also open this. Do your best,' to Marion, and she, her tongue passing to and fro between her lips, interlimned the message to François II and also carefully traced Châtelherault's own signature, which we had in abundance, from an original. A *carte blanche* was enclosed with the letter so that the King of France might make what terms he would. When it all came out, it would at least cause confusion among my lords; that was intended. We all three sat and drank wine together afterwards, conscious of a task well done. Treachery had been met with treachery; it was the first time Madame had tried it. I watched a little colour return to her pale cheeks with the wine, and was glad.

Young René de Guise, Marquis d'Elboeuf – he was only twenty-three, eleven years younger than Madame and the last surviving son to be born of Duchesse Antoinette, as two since then had died – set out at last with a fleet of ships, which were repeatedly scattered by adverse gales and driven back on the

Norman coast. Eighteen ships of the squadron were lost in one
night. Only a thousand foot-soldiers in the end came, without M.
d'Elboeuf himself. By then Madame had been very ill; her life
was in fact despaired of. It was also very difficult for us to obtain
money. She herself had pawned all her jewels by then, except
for a small gold cross. At last she parted with this to Hume of
Blackadder, who gave her a thousand crowns for it. La Reinette
later retrieved it, on her return to Scotland following Madame's
death. It was not until after all this that Madame debased the
coinage. That was in desperation, and the only thing left to do.
It did not make her popular, and the price of everything rose.

At that time a mighty fleet was seen to enter the Firth of
Forth, and, beleaguered as we were we thought M. d'Elboeuf
had come; he was, in fact, prostrate in France with sea-sickness.
Our guns fired a friendly salute, and a fierce cannonade replied,
killing many at sea. The fleet was not French but English, sent by
Elizabeth Tudor, who only days before had conveyed all
gracious messages to the Scots Regent and had assured M. de la
Marque, presented to her by the French Ambassador to demand
a safe-conduct north, that she believed Madame to be quite well
at present. Perhaps this accounted for her callous and shameful
behaviour in the matter of the fleet.

Madame had rallied until then, for there was good news of
a further defeat of the Lord James and Châtelherault by
Frenchmen at Stirling on Christmas Eve. In addition to our own
meddling letter to the King of France, an old ambition had been
pandered to and Lennox, who still hoped in England for the
recognition of his supposed title to the throne, had been
encouraged, at least, to believe that he was not forgotten. He
and his Lady Margaret, though devoted, were unfortunate;
most of their children had died except Lord Darnley and a
much younger brother, and they were kept as always in great
poverty in Yorkshire; Lennox must often have regretted his lost
days as an officer in the Archers of the Guard of France.

But the English fleet in the Firth, with its supplies of arms,
provender, and ammunition for the Lords of the Congregation,
as well as eight large vessels of war and a quota of three
thousand troops, made bad sight and worse hearing. My lords,
in exchange, promised four Scots strongholds to be handed over
to Elizabeth's lieutenant-general the Duke of Norfolk; Dunbar,
Dumbarton, Inchkeith, and the Border town of Dumfries.

Promises are not however performance, and Madame's men still occupied the fortresses and towns. However Norfolk marched north across the Border. The days of the Rough Wooing might have come again; burning, slaying, rape, and ruin, and all this in the dead of winter. It interests me to reflect now that it was that same Norfolk who later lost his head by order of Elizabeth, as a suitor and plotter for La Reinette in her English prisons.

The English have a smooth way of denying the obvious. Admiral Winter assured Madame that he had not come with any orders to make war; he had decided of his own volition to help my lords, as it were in passing. 'As if,' Madame remarked drily, 'a simple subject and officer had the authority or power to make war without the very express command of his Queen, and as if one could make war at the expense of a Prince without his knowing anything of it!'

She turned to me after the emissary had gone back. 'The Queen of England's actions truly contradict her words,' she said. 'She has eight vessels in the Firth which make war openly and attack the subjects of this realm.' Soon there were more than eight; the sails gathered like gnats in twilight, while the English swore still that they had entered the Roads of Leith by reason of bad weather. Madame pointed out that the wind had been against them, also that they had captured two Scots ships sailing across to Fife with munitions for the French soldiers quartered there.

It was war. 'I have known the inconveniences of it far too long,' said Madame, 'and primarily for the honour of God I desire to avoid it.' But she garrisoned Inchkeith, fortified Leith once again, and was up with the dawn each day, despite her increasing sickness. My lords made ready to attack Leith a second time, so that all our former gains were as nothing; and the French were driven by them out of Fife. Madame summoned all able-bodied men between sixteen and sixty to be ready at an hour's notice to fight, and between Edinburgh and the Border country all households were to put away their food where it would not be found, and break their brewing vessels. This order was not obeyed, and it may be that the French forces were themselves to blame; we had heard of one officer being drowned in a tub by a poor woman whose children's food he had eaten, and who called in her neighbours to help finish him. That

Madame's name was spoken of alongside the French made her unpopular; more and more the ordinary folk turned away, and followed my lords, whose tongue they understood, and concerning whose religion they were increasingly persuaded.

That was a hard winter; at Christmas there was small chcer. In the bitter wind of February, the Lord James slipped away south by sea with company of his choosing, met the Duke of Norfolk at Berwick, and signed a bond. When they brought the news to Madame she lay back in her chair with the tears pouring down her face like rain; she had taken to weeping much lately, and the cruel men in the south said it would ease the fluid in her, and that her bleating, as Norfolk called it, had its own purpose. They could not credit her with honesty in any matter; perhaps thcy did not even believe that she would soon die. The news itself was enough to kill her. Queen Elizabeth was now to accept the realm of Scotland; Châtelherault, by Act of Parliament, was to be declared heir to it, and its nobility subjcct to England's Queen, who was to send into Scotland with all speed 'a convenient aid of men of war,' both by sea and by land, till all the French were utterly expelled. In return, the Scots Protestants promised military aid to England should that country be invaded by the French. They added, as a rider at the end, that they were still obedient to Mary, Queen of Scots and to her husband: the manner of this obedience was left in doubt.

'Nothing that has happened in Scotland has given me more torment. I am a woman. I have perhaps fought as a man. But not even a man can fight an enemy on two fronts.' I led her away; she was fit for no more, and I made her lie down and unlaced the dreadfully swollen body; Madame closed her eyes, but the tears still trickled down her face.

March came and ended, and with the spring the army of invasion entered Scotland. The commander was Lord Grey de Wilton, a man known for his especial cruelty. Six thousand foot soldiers, with two thousand more promised, came; seven hundred great horse, over a thousand lighter horses, and twenty-four batteries of guns. They encamped at Halidon, then Haddington, then Musselburgh, then Restalrig itself, within sight of Edinburgh.

Madame had waited until then, to hearten such troops as she still had; but by now there was danger for her person. I do not remember if she herself made the decision or if we, who loved her, made it for her; at any event we guided her steps, for she could hardly walk, up the slope to the Castle, where Lord Erskine had promised her entry in final extremity of distress or danger. Now, the time had come. The strong old portcullis, the same Margaret Tudor had caused to be wound down in the dead King's childhood, was raised; under it we walked, all of us, supporting Mary of Lorraine, Queen Regent of Scotland, who would never again leave Edinburgh Castle alive. Lord Erskine was waiting, and bowed over her hand; he was a staunch man, although the brother of that same Margaret who had ensnared James V and given birth to the Lord James, now absent with the English enemy. Erskine himself was neither enemy nor friend; he had kept himself altogether aloof from the war; but the sight of Madame now moved him to pity. There was a soft bed, he told her, inside, and a fire; and she was glad of them, and so were we.

She had nine weeks to live, but her spirit was not broken. By some means she established communication again with M. d'Oysel and the rest in Leith, where Lord Seton had joined them. Of all her lords he was the most faithful. As for Lord Erskine, he still maintained evident neutrality, with the stern rectitude his dark-browed family appeared to possess. I dare say he was an honest man. At any rate, he so far succumbed to Madame as to agree to permit nobody to enter the Castle precincts, and to speak with those outside only on her express orders. This was some advance for a fugitive invalid who had come to him in tears, surrounded only by her women.

As for the Protestant lords, they held a conference with their English allies at Musselburgh the day after we had entered the Castle. Guns and munitions were awaited by sea from Berwick; when they came, Lord Grey would attack. What he would attack, and whom, we waited to discover; in the meantime, two messengers, Sir James Crofts and Sir George Howard, both in shirts of mail, were sent.

There was a high wind blowing. Lord Erskine forbade the two Englishmen entry to the castle, as he had already forbidden the French. There was nothing for it but for the sick Regent to stand, buffeted by the wind and supported by her staff, on the parapet of the front block-house, while the two English stood below outside the gates. It was impossible to hear their shouted words for the wind, or to come to much agreement; but John Knox later asserted that the Regent had at that time enchanted Sir James Crofts, who had hitherto been her bitter enemy and was thereafter her friend. Perhaps the sight of her courage convinced him.

On Easter Monday the French commander, M. de Martigues, forced the besiegers' trenches and spiked three cannon, slaying many. Her Grace was gravely ill by then, but rallied when she heard of it. Her lips twitched in the old way as she recalled the words of Crofts, who had blandly assured her that the English army had not come on any enterprise against the Queen or her subjects. 'It is a strange thing,' Madame said, 'to see the army of one Prince enter in so hostile a manner so far into the land of another, if it had no desire for any enterprise there.' But the milk-faced English continued with their protestations, led in such ways by their Queen. At first Elizabeth had refused to order an attack on Edinburgh Castle, because a fellow-Queen was inside its walls; but being later persuaded that the Dowager was worth five hundred Frenchmen, changed her tune.

The English were in fact beginning to desert, complaining of the cold even in early summer. They were short of food: so were we. Their horses were unfed, and altogether they were in worse fettle than when they had first set out. If Madame's scorched earth orders had been obeyed, they would have gone home the sooner.

More parleys were demanded with Madame, and this time, to save further encounters in a high wind, a tent was erected on the outworks. She waited inside it and I stood behind her. How many times, in how many places, had this happened by now! I could remember holding the baby Queen's weight in my arms in such a place; and also looking out, as I did now through the tent's flap, at the darkening town, its remaining houses lurching down the Canongate from their incredible hill, with smoke belching from the chimneys. Beyond was the blue Forth, and Leith. I could see it and Madame could not. Nobody yet perceived, except ourselves, that she was by now, almost blind.

The men came in, took out a paper, and read its terms aloud to Madame; behind us, the servants moved about lighting torches. There was nothing new in the expressed demands; all French soldiers to be sent home immediately, which Madame said was beyond reason and could not be discussed. The second demand was that Protestant grievances should be laid before the Queen of Scots and her husband.

'The King and Queen will not take orders from any other Prince in the world, much less from their own subjects,' Madame replied evenly. 'I myself have always conducted the affairs of the realm according to the country's laws and with the advice of the estates.'

'If you find the demands unreasonable, then confer with your advisers,' said Sir George Howard, a relative of Norfolk; that family have always been noted for their rough manners, in particular to the misfortunate. Sir James Crofts broke in.

'Madam,' he said courteously, looking at her worn face, 'you have composed so many great differences, I beseech you to bring to the settlement of this one all the means in your power for a true appeasement. Everything lies in your hands.'

It was a curious statement when on the day previous, English cavalry had defiled beneath the Castle walls. Madame retired at last exhausted, and at the second discussion was not present. M. d'Oysel represented her, and Lord James, having returned, the Protestants. It was again stated clearly that French soldiers were only in the country at all because of the constant disobedience of the Scots. If civil order were restored, they would be withdrawn. But my lords bargained on. Everyone was waiting now for yet another French arrival, the badly frightened Bishop of Valence, who had seen Queen Elizabeth in London lately and was not in any case a young man; his duty was to say that the King of France would pardon all offences if order were restored in Scotland, but it was difficult to convey such intelligence to the devious red-headed lady in the south who had helped foment trouble on the excuse that she, not the King of France at all, had the right of rule in Scotland. Châtelherault terrified the old Bishop further by declining to give him a safe-conduct through the fearful Border country, where anyone unarmed might well be set upon by reivers in broad daylight and stripped bare. Norfolk prodded the Bishop north nevertheless; in the end it was Madame herself who obtained a conditional safe-conduct for the elderly churchman, Lord Grey escorting him.

By now the English were firing on Leith and fighting outside its walls. A large fleet of English ships still lay in the Roads. Norfolk resented the activity of Madame, but the Bishop, who finally met with her in the last week of April, was alarmed by her looks. 'She is in want especially of health and of everything else except greatness of spirit and good understanding,' he said, 'for she is quite undaunted by these troubles, as if she had all the forces in the world.' Madame was, as always, drawing her strength from God; she still prayed in the chapel daily, and had masses said in thanksgiving for all French victories.

She talked with the old Bishop at length; I was not present, but she told me she had asked again for news of our young brother d'Elboeuf. 'If only he would come!' she said, with tears in her eyes. I myself knew that he would not come now. There was too much danger, not enough hope.

The poor old Bishop was later led to the Duke of Châteherault's tent, where he found the English commanders, and fared less well with them than he had done with Madame. They showed him little respect, cried out in his presence, and forced him at last into a lodging in Edinburgh with a guard of forty men. He dared not speak to his own servitors in his own tongue; if he did so, some Scots intruder would come up, thrust his face between and ask what they had been saying together, and whether the Scots were not as good as the English after all: this is a famous saying of the former. In the evening, smooth-faced Lethington, Madame's former secretary, arrived with the grim Lord James, and they demanded to see the Bishop's commission. The old man quavered that he had given it to Madame. This did not find favour.

Arguments went back and forth for a week, achieving no purpose. The same matters were hammered out over and over again, the same arguments furiously set forth. Nothing the Bishop did or said was right, and in the end he went home, having achieved no more than his journey: in fact many present had not understood a word of one another's language from the beginning. The Bishop came, before leaving, to the Castle and sadly kissed Madame's hand. He knew that he would never see her again, and she that her eyes would never more see France. We watched him go without feeling. He might as well never have come; and there was no further aid, in promise or in fact, from anyone for the Queen Regent of Scotland.

I squeezed lemon juice cautiously on to the empty quill. The lemon had been difficult to obtain, and it was in any case hard to be sure what one had put down in invisible ink; at the top of the paper was a message in ordinary phrasing, asking M. d'Oysel to obtain ointment in Leith for Madame's infected leg. The words below in lemon juice were very different.

I wrote at the dictation of the grey-faced woman in the chair, which Madame found eased her now more than lying in bed, where the distended flesh weighed too greatly upon her heart. It was impossible to lace her any more, and she wore a loose black gown, keeping her swollen feet carefully hidden by its folds. Nevertheless she gave cool orders to the sound of the constant gunfire from distant Leith, the exploding of cannon, the knowledge, somehow gained, that the English were digging under the walls to mine the town, and the French were countermining. There was a fiercely won victory for our side, and the fleur-de-lys banner was raised on the walls: English corpses had been laid out along them and left there in the summer heat. John Knox wrote afterwards that at sight of these Madame, on the walls of Edinburgh Castle, had hopped with mirth and said she never saw so fair a tapestry. I did not have to look at her now to know the truth or otherwise of that. I myself could just perceive what was happening, and report it; Madame herself, with her dim glazed eyes, could see nothing any more but light and dark.

There had been no overtures for some time from the Protestants. We had heard that two of the remaining lords on our side, Morton and Borthwick, had lately decamped to join the Congregation. No doubt they were deserting the sinking ship; the marvel was that pig-faced Morton had remained with us as long. As for Lord Borthwick, his mind was no doubt uncertain; he had always said in public that he would believe as his fathers had believed. Perhaps he was a weak man, married to the strong-minded wife who long ago had kidnapped the Fair Earl pending her husband's release. I did not know. I awaited news of the lemon-juice letter, and when it came it was bad. Lord Grey had suspected the paper, which to a casual glance revealed only a few written lines at the top; and as he rightly said, fresher ointment could be got in Edinburgh than in Leith. He held the letter to the fire, when the invisible writing appeared; honourably enough, he burnt it. 'Tell Her Majesty I will keep her counsel, and say to her such wares will not sell till a new market,' he observed, and when Madame heard of it she turned her head aside, and wept. They still mocked at her tears.

*

Two of our men, Findlater and John Spens, were sent at last to
my lords to ask again for a conference. The latter demanded
destruction of the fortifications at Leith and all Frenchmen to be
sent away before they would agree. 'I am amazed to see that you
men are in her service still,' Lord Grey said to our two. 'She is
oppressing the liberty of your country and has brought French
men of war in to conquer it.'

John Spens was a small man, but he stood up to that. 'Her
Grace has been made Regent by the estates of the realm,' he
answered, 'and all good Scots are bound to obey her.' The
glinting eyes of those present watched him narrowly from above
their ruffs; they did not trouble to wear armour any more. Up
spoke Châtelherault, full of his own injured dignity, determined
to be considered for once. 'She has been deposed,' he said, 'and
is no longer Regent,' and puffed out his satin-clad chest. John
Spens retorted that Madame had been elected at a rather fuller
meeting of parliament than that which had deposed her.

'Ye lie,' barked the Duke, unable to think of a better argument.
Lord Grey, who had no doubt had much occasion for thought
since coming to Scotland, spoke then like a fair-minded man.
Spens and the Laird of Findlater, he said, were loyal and faithful
servants and had spoken as such. With this they returned to us,
and the Duke busied himself with confirming the already signed
Articles of Berwick handing Scotland over to Elizabeth.

Madame kept John Spens by her. The Laird of Findlater she
sent back again, granting my lords' requests on condition that
they gave some surety for their allegiance to Queen Mary and
the King her husband. She asked to see Huntly who had long
deserted to the Protestants, and Glencairn, who had never been
anything else; but, presumably because of her enchantment, it
was a different assembly who came; Lord James, Lord Ruthven,
the young Master of Maxwell, and Madame's former secretary,
Maitland of Lethington. Evidently the latter was unable to blush.
There were the usual harsh words, the accustomed demands.
They complained of taxes.

'Your Scots have spent the money,' said Madame.

'You have tried to change the laws of Scotland. Frenchmen
are appointed to Scots offices.'

'I have not. The French officers were appointed by consent of
Parliament, and also –' she glanced sideways at the Lord James,
remembering the revenues from his French abbeys – 'Scots

enjoy the reciprocal right of being allowed to hold offices in France, is it not so?'

Lord James looked down his nose, and mentioned René d'Elboeuf: he had been about to be appointed viceroy, he said, and would have brought men and money.

'Not so,' replied the Regent. 'I myself would have paid another visit to France to see my daughter; can you wonder at that? Later, I would have returned, having called upon the Queen of England on my way, as I did King Edward.' I cast down my eyes, remembering that long-ago encounter and of how the dead boy would have remained our friend had he lived. Elizabeth herself, no doubt, hoped for the return of Calais.

Madame continued to temporise, her swollen hands resting on the arms of her chair; her wedding-ring had long since grown too tight for her finger. 'I must consult the authorities commissioned by the King of France,' she told them. 'I pray you, give me time to communicate with M. d'Oysel, M. de la Broose, and the Bishop of Amiens.' The latter was with them in Leith since the departure of old Valence. My lords refused, ungraciously. 'I desire peace,' said Madame, and wept. She asked again, and particularly, to see D'Oysel; as before, they refused. A letter of her own, written in cipher, had meantime been translated into English and was handed to her openly. She closed her eyes, and did not try to read it. There had been enough treachery.

Her last act was to summon Parliament for the fifth of July, but we knew she would never see it. The Duke of Norfolk was still proclaiming that nobody was deceived by her bloody sword in a scabbard of peace; but death is peaceful. By the beginning of June, she had ceased to take food, though she walked slowly about still, leaning on her staff. Shortly I took the news to her, wondering how to break it, that four hundred more English soldiers had arrived; the smaller number might mean that Elizabeth was growing weary of paying out money for the conquest of Scotland and for my lords' pensions. Madame stared at me, as if from behind glass; I realised that she did not now follow my words. She was elsewhere; perhaps nearer those she loved than anyone knew. I took her a drink of water mixed with some wine, and she sipped at it. The sounds of firing were still coming from the siege of Leith and that day, they brought down St Anthony's tower, altering the skyline. She could not see it; she did not know. I began to be afraid that she would slip away from me without the Sacrament I carried; at the first opportunity, when we were alone, I whispered to her, and she understood.

'Soon, darling,' she said quietly. 'Not yet.'

Lord Erskine was aware of her condition; and he was a merciful man. He sent his brother Arthur of Blackgrange, who had always befriended the Queen, to persuade my lords to let the Bishop of Amiens come to her, as she was near death. My lords conferred about it; finally they agreed to allow this favour to a dying woman. Lord Grey and the other English agreed also. Only one voice prevented the Bishop's coming. It was that of Châtelherault, the pusillanimous former Governor, the man whose twitching face had sat on many councils, but whose mind had never held to a decision till now. Whether or not he had learned of Madame's deception over the letter to France, and took this revenge for it, I do not know; I only know that he left Madame without succour in the hour of her going, and that I, a former whore, a woman of many sins, who however loved her, was the one who finally put the Body of God in her dying mouth. I hope that the Duke, who died at his palace of Hamilton within a dozen years of Madame, died alone and forgotten. I have heard that this was so.

Madame waited for the Bishop, and when I told her gently that they would not let him come, she gave a little sigh. Then she let us lead her to her chamber, and sent for all my lords. I believe there was suspicion in their camp as to why she had sent for them; even now, there might be some subtlety of the foreign widow to inveigle them into the Castle against their wills, and there make an end of them. But when they came, there were only her ladies, including myself, about her bed. She lay there, seemly in a linen coif, her hair hidden; it had turned grey long ago. Châtelherault entered first, his tears already falling; his emotions were always near the surface. He knelt, and took her hand, which she extended. The Lord James was behind him, and there was no submission in his greeting; in his own estimation, he was already King of Scotland. The Earl Marischal followed, with others of my lords. Next day would be her wedding-day; it was twenty-two years since she had come from France to marry their King.

'I am cold,' I heard her say. Outside, the June sun was shining.

She said that she was thirsty, and I took a kerchief and wet her lips. She tried to speak; she urged my lords to cleave to France, not to the English 'who aid you not for any other respect than for their own turn and commodity.' She assured them that the welfare of Scotland had always been as dear to her as that of France, as she had the honour to be its Regent. She then said a thing that showed her true humility, for all that they had spoken of her as haughty in their despatches. 'If I have ever done anything displeasing to you, it was rather from lack of wisdom and judgment than for want of good will.'

Her breaths were rasping, but she urged them on to obedience to the Queen. She begged them to come to a peaceful conclusion with D'Oysel and to send the English home. 'I fear greatly lest if the French depart, the English will still remain and subdue the land to their obedience.'

She was weeping by now, and so were they. She took each lord by the hand and asked for his forgiveness if she had offended any during her time in Scotland. It was the nearest she could come to a confession, as they would not allow her a priest. They mumbled some kind of reconciliation and left her chamber, much moved despite themselves.

Lord James and the Earl Marischal remained in the castle, as Madame had asked of them. Last of all, she sent for Châtelherault's son, young Arran. He came in wildly, and the dying woman on her pillows gazed with blind eyes at the youth who would never be King. Presently my lords, who had denied her consolation in her own faith, demanded that she see the preacher Willock, a fellow of Knox. Madame agreed, but not as if it mattered. Later, she made her will, with her mind a little clearer. Nothing was forgotten by her, any more than it had ever been; not a servant's wages, not a debt, not the expense of her funeral. In France, Duchesse Antoinette and our brother the Duc de Guise were to be her executors; in Scotland, the Earl Marischal and Argyll's kinsman, John Campbell. After her death, the Earl refused the task.

All that being done, Madame at last sent for me. She could hardly speak, but I heard her whisper, when we were alone in the room, 'Give it me now.' I took out the flat pyx from my bosom, where I had kept it for this moment, and removed the precious wafer, slipping it on to her tongue. It did not matter that the creature Willock came and thereafter preached over her, and heard her answer, and named what he miscalled the abomination of the Mass; as to that, Madame remained silent.

Next day we watched, and her silence was not broken. The sun rose in the sky and then declined, and evening came: when it was midnight, the two shadows who were the Lord James and Argyll entered her chamber. They stood within the shadow of the curtains, watching her go. I had her hand in mine and she clenched it, and I am certain she knew I was there, I, Claudine, who loved her; I do not think that in all of my life I have ever loved anyone as I loved Madame Marie.

Then she was dead, and there was a great wailing among us. She had passed from life to death in silence. Where her mind had been at the end I do not know; perhaps it was with her daughter; more likely it was with God. Whatever they say about souls in purgatory, I do not think Madame would spend long there; she had already had her purgatory on earth.

But she was dead, and I was desolate. I knew that my life was finished; that whatever remained to me now, it would not matter. I went out of the death-chamber and left them to their tasks, which were not my concern; except that when they had done with her body and I saw her face again for the last time, it was peaceful.

They had embalmed the body, finding among other things the heart worn out, at her age of forty-four. At some time one of the doctors asked me if she had ever had a fever in childhood, and I recalled the one she had had at Pont-à-Mousson, in the cold damp convent of the Poor Clares. He nodded sagely, as doctors do; I do not know what it meant.

The unspeakable Knox has written unspeakably about the rest, but they lapped her in lead. The coffin was placed in the tiny chapel near the outer wall, where St Margaret of Scotland used to pray. Nails were brought to secure the door, but we, her ladies and I, took it in turns to guard the closed coffin night and day. Walls can be climbed and doors broken open, and there might have been insult from her relentless enemies for the body of the woman who, had they let her, would have ruled Scotland all these years wisely and in peace. I myself knelt on the cold stone many hours beside where she lay, and gazed at the black pall with its white taffeta cross along all the length, covering the lead. It was not a plain cross, or even the saltire cross of St

Andrew of Scotland. It was the Cross of Jerusalem, the great double Cross of Lorraine. She was a Guise and I had made them remember it, if they did not do so otherwise.

As to that, her last hope of all did not vanish, mercifully, till she herself knew nothing. She never learned that six months after her own death the boy François II died unexpectedly, leaving our Queen a widow, and Madame Cathérine again in power. The young King died of an infected ear, lying on a palliasse with no one but his girl wife to watch by him, for all their furnishings had been taken away in the expectation of a visit to Chenonceaux. Thereafter the trouble of governing Scotland, which Madame had borne for her royal daughter's sake, came home to roost. What irony that they were never to be together in that land!

It can hardly be believed that Madame herself was not permitted a funeral, not even a requiem for the repose of her soul; the reformers do not believe in them. Nor would they, and this would have been, one imagines, a relief to them, allow her body to be sent home to France, for Christian burial. It lay there from June, when Madame had died, till March of the following year. By then, when awareness had itself died down among the people, it was made possible to remove the coffin secretly by night to Leith, the port Madame had once made prosperous, and thence to a French ship. I went with it, and certain of her ladies, and Mr Craufurd her almoner, the parson of Eaglesham in Renfrewshire.

The voyage had none of those storms that had raised themselves constantly while Madame lived. We remained kneeling on deck, black-clad, by the coffin, praying together in the light March wind. A fair wind blew for France, I thought; but it was too late for her, who had intended to travel back this way once again, to see her daughter, and on return visit Elizabeth of England. In earlier days they might have cozened one another cheerfully and become friends, but not now.

Certain persons waited at Fécamp in Normandy, near where we landed, making a slow journey to the abbey itself from the coast. Mary, Queen of Scots, was now Dowager of France at eighteen. Dowager met Dowager there, with the arches of the great abbey rearing above. It had been built in the days of Duke Richard the Fearless and was a fitting place for Madame's body to rest before travelling on to Rheims, where she had asked to be buried.

The young Queen of Scots was pale and drawn, had wept, and

now knelt by the coffin for a long time. I thought what joy mother and daughter would have brought to one another in their lives, and how it had hardly been permitted them. The Queen rose at last, her long white veil sweeping, and returned to her place, maintaining her dignity as she had done that time when, as a child of eight, they had made her read out a pompous speech of welcome to her mother at Rouen. I studied her; her features, partly disguised by the mourning barbe, were those of her father, her height certainly that of her mother; but her hands were her own. I kissed them afterwards, white as they were, most graceful and beautiful. She herself had beauty of a timeless quality; she might have been any age, and when she grew old, I thought, if they let her live as long, she would be the same as now. Her charm and sympathy were genuine. She sent for me later and asked that, as I had known her mother well, I should stay with her now; but I declined. 'Madame, you are young, with all your life before you,' I told her. 'Whatever happens you will not need me. I have my memories, and those are of the past. You have the future. One grows old in time,' and she smiled a little, though still grave with grief.

'I may have to return to Scotland,' she said. 'It is difficult here. I am no longer Queen of France, and there is no one left to govern my country except —' and she shrugged a little and I knew we were both thinking of the Lord James, who wanted power although she still loved him, and of Master John Knox. Her Grace must no doubt go soon; this meeting was, one might say, a crossroads, and one went one way, the other the other. Madame's coffin left Fécamp to the tolling of the deep bell, and the tread of horse, and behind that the flat tramp, tramp, of the tall blond peasants of Normandy who had come, and who followed as far as they might, for the fame of Marie de Guise-Lorraine was known far beyond Scotland. The Normans are not like other French. They are descended from a Norse pirate known as Rolf the Ganger because he was too big for any horse. The English have a great deal of their blood, and their persistence; as to cruelty, I cannot say.

We reached Rheims, and there was the new young King Charles IX whose head was as big as a turnip in contrast to his frail body, rather like the little Master of Angus long ago, and the full Court. Madame Cathérine was here, having endured her widowhood as she had endured her marriage, by now however with the consolation of power. Madame Diane was absent, having retired long since with her customary prudence to her château of Anet on the death of Henri II. Everyone wore mourning, the royalty white, the rest black. Madame was finally interred in the Benedictine church of St Pierre of Rheims where the youngest sister of all, Madame Renée de Guise, was Abbess. I understand that a magnificent monument in bronze was erected later, but monuments do not last. As soon as there is a disturbance or a revolution, they will destroy it, and no doubt also disturb Madame's bones. The Huguenots at present are attacking everything of the kind with picks and hammers, where they can.

As for myself, I had had leisure to think a great deal during the long months of kneeling by Madame in St Margaret's cold stone chapel in Edinburgh Castle. It seemed to me that the only home I had was at Vouvray, and that I should send for my sons. Iain Ruadh would make a life for himself in the army of France, and might now and again visit me; the twins ought in any case to be shown to their father. It could then be decided what was to be done. I had by now written briefly to Andelot, to say I was on the way; no doubt the imbecile Comte could be consulted formally. I could not see any other prospect that I would welcome, and I was, when all was said, Douarière. No reply had come, but that was understandable. As soon as the funeral trumpets and the bells were' stilled, I waited for a litter in which to set out. However, one arrived which I remembered seeing at Vouvray on my last visit and having eventually borrowed to return to Madame. It was used, no doubt, frequently still to take the imbecile Comte for his airings, but had been sent for me, and was presumably Andelot's answer: there was no other. I got in, with my gear and without a maid, but with four attendants lent me by the Queen, who would escort me to Vouvray, whence I would see that they were returned.

I will not state what thoughts occupied me on the journey; I lay sad, sick at heart, but not in truth reflective. The miles swayed on, and when the green country at last grew bright with summer, once we had passed Troyes, I began to feel my heart at rest. Perhaps Duchesse Antoinette had meant well by my first marriage. She had been present for both funerals, old now, widowed, the mother of twelve, but indomitable. We had not spoken other than to exchange formal greetings, but the hooded grey eyes had looked into mine. 'Go with God, Claudine,' they seemed to say. She had after all loved her husband, my father. I resolved to lead an upright life and to remember everything she had tried to teach me when I was young. The journey proceeded, and in time we reached Vouvray, that is to say within a mile or two.

There was a horseman standing like a statue, blocking the forked way that leads in one direction to the château, in the other to the village. It was Andelot, and I assumed that either some catastrophe had occurred, or that my steward was present to afford me a proper welcome. In either case he was blocking the way. The attendants drew rein, their well trained mounts at once standing motionless. My steward got off his horse, removed his hat, and came over to my open litter. As it was summer I had the curtains drawn back in any case; nobody, in sunshine, desires to travel in a velvet darkness unless there is something wrong with them, and although I was still grieving I had recovered outwardly and was enjoying the view.

Andelot bowed, and I saw that he had aged a little; that was to be expected, but also his brown eyes had lost their habitual assurance and seemed concerned. I asked him what he wanted, not reflecting on the last time we had parted; that was finished with. He twisted his round hat in his hands, like a schoolboy.

'Madame la Comtesse, I should perhaps have informed you earlier that I am married,' he said in some embarrassment, the first I had ever seen in him. 'I have been married these two years to a young wife, of whom I am fond.' He paused, but I said nothing; that was natural. He continued 'Vivienne has already had one miscarriage, and now there is a second hopeful situation; I would not have her disturbed if that is possible.'

'My friend, I would by no means disturb her,' I put in. 'You should certainly have informed me of your marriage as your employer, but I bear no rancour. Why are you here, apart from the information you have just conveyed? I have come on a long journey and so have the Queen's servants, and we should like to proceed.'

'Madame.' He twisted the hat again. 'If I may be frank, it is not proper that you should live at Vouvray in the present circumstances of the Comte's residence there: even in his condition, there would be talk. Also, he might not agree formally to such an arrangement; he needs persuasion in such matters. It is my own suggestion, if you will forgive me, madame, that you marry him if it is considered suitable. The rest I leave to your judgment. The Comte sees few people, but I have contrived to persuade him to grant you a meeting.'

I opened my eyes fairly wide at his impertinence, but on reflection, once I was again in the moving litter, acknowledged that Andelot had probably done his best in the circumstances. It would certainly do no harm to inspect the afflicted Comte and see for myself whether or not I could endure the thought of a formal marriage to him. If I could not, there would be some other feasible arrangement; on that I was determined. In any case I had seen worse sights in my time than an imbecile. I dismissed Andelot and bade him ride ahead of the escort. In a short time, and without further incident, we reached the château. As before, ducks were quacking in the stream, shaking their feathers in the spring sunshine. It seemed that whatever happened, I must always return to Vouvray.

I emerged, shook out my skirts, demanded refreshment for myself and for the men, also for the horses, ready for their return on the morrow. I myself partook of a light collation before going up to visit the Comte, considering that it would give me strength after my journey. I was not aware of any sensation except mild curiosity, and a certainty that I could in some way make matters conform to my plan.

One thing had disturbed me. As I came out of the litter, a creature whose like I had never before seen slipped out of the sunlight into the shadows cast by the high pitched roofs, moving swiftly like a shadow himself. He was brown, thin, and naked except for a white turban and loincloth, and I had the curious certainty that he was neither male nor female, but something else, which is impossible. I asked Andelot, who gave a little bow, his dark eyes fixed on me with, perhaps, a hint of lingering regret.

'That is Satki, the poor Comte's constant attendant,' he said. 'He is Indian.' He did not comment further and I went in to eat as I have stated. I was more than ever convinced that Vouvray must become my home, despite its two strange inmates. Where else could I go? It could not be Joinville, Pont-à-Mousson or even Châteaudun, and my home had certainly not been in Scotland, except for the bothan. As for Madame's letter to the Abbess at Farmoutiers, I would keep it meantime.

The great hall was as unchanged as on my last visit, and this time I took more notice of its state; the furnishings were well brushed, and everything appeared to be in order. The place was in fact kept as neat as on board ship, and I knew I could have no complaints about Andelot in that respect; I had been right to keep him on in my employment.

Satki reappeared to escort me to the Comte. I was aware of a faint scent, like musk or verbena, emanating from him; it was not unpleasant. He moved before me, but with deference, upstairs, and at last we came to the door of a room.

'M. le Comte. Madame la Comtesse.'

The Indian had moved silently away. I was left with the sight of the room, which I once knew, in shadow now except for the firelight from the hearth, and two candles. On an invalid couch – my mind fled back to Madame Madeleine long ago at Blois, since when I had not seen one – there sat, propped up, a lean old man with white hair, longer than was the fashion. The eyelids drooped over his eyes in a manner which veiled his expression. I advanced, and saw that he was watching me with interest; he had, it appeared, some wits. As I drew nearer, I noted again that he was spare of build; not too tall if he could stand, and clad in dark clothes. I assumed that perhaps he was unable to speak, and held out my hand. He spoke.

'Be seated, madame. I regret that I cannot rise to greet you, but I have an affliction of the bones. Sit there, where the candlelight falls upon your face. I can then observe you clearly.'

The French was correct, a trifle cold, yet amused in a worldly fashion. I seated myself as I was bid, and sat bewildered; certainly this man was no imbecile. I had time also to reflect that whereas I had come upon this visit to satisfy myself that I could endure marriage to him, he was possibly doing the same for me. He might even reject me. The eyes, now that I had grown used to the half-dark, surveyed me not unkindly beneath their lids, with knowledge in them.

'M. le Comte, I –' I began, a trifle confused, and he smiled. 'Do not talk yet,' he said. 'I want to look at you. I seldom look at anyone but Satki, whose graceful movements do not disturb my thoughts. His name is the female version of the three incarnations of the Hindu god. I rescued him from extreme poverty in Howrah. He will bring you wine presently.' As if by a spell, Satki reappeared with two flagons and a beaker, which he placed nearby; then he vanished again. The Comte raised his hands and poured the wine, holding out my flagon towards me. The hands were long, white, and beautiful, reminding me of those of Madame Marie.

We drank. 'It is, you will agree, an excellent Bordeaux,' he said. 'So you know wine?'

I replied that I had drunk it as others do, but had never thought of telling one from the other and in fact knew very little on the subject. 'Then that is one thing I could teach you,' he replied. 'There is much enjoyment in the careful choice, and tasting, of wine. One must not, needless to say, drink it to excess.'

'I have never –' I began, but the Comte motioned me to silence. 'No, that is one thing I am sure you have not done,' he admitted. The eyes opened a little wider, revealing amusement in their depths, and I had the feeling that this man in some manner knew everything I was, had been, and had been forced to become. I sat silent, my eyes fixed on my flagon and the dark living depths of the wine. Presently he spoke again.

'I will speak of myself first, although it is perhaps not good manners to do so. You will have heard that I lack wits and that accordingly I meet no company. The first is not true: the second, by the age and disillusionment I have reached, is so. There are very few persons whose presence I can by now endure for more than half an hour, and one of them, for some extraordinary reason, is Andelot. It may be the fact of his Vouvray blood. He is moreover an excellent steward. If you had shown signs of dismissing him, I should have been obliged to forbid it. Fortunately the situation did not arise. I see very little of him, except when he renders me the accounts each month. Otherwise he does not trouble me, and I must make it a condition that during my lifetime he does not trouble you either.'

I said nothing. There was nothing to say. The Comte smiled a little, keeping his lips closed.

'I see that you are not a fool, madame. Most women would have babbled denial at such a moment. I assure you that Andelot has said nothing of you to me personally. However, when you were last at Vouvray – I know who comes, as visitors are rare by my own wish – I heard a thing I have not heard these many years, coming from the great bedchamber; a woman's cry of ecstasy, on more than one occasion. It could not, in that place, have come from anyone but yourself. From that moment I admit to some curiosity regarding you, but at the time it was hardly suitable for us to meet.'

By this time I was blushing deeply, which I seldom do. I saw him laugh, and perceived a thing which intrigued me; most old persons, and he was old, let their mouths wither for greater comfort. The Comte had not done so. He had a set of false teeth the like of which I had never before seen, evidently carved out of a double piece of ivory, upper and lower, with great delicacy so that they almost resembled nature. I assume that he got them in India, but I never enquired; one does not ask concerning such things. It argued a fastidious taste, and I found myself increasingly attracted to this Comte and to the widened horizons he could evidently offer me. He went on to speak further on the subject he had lately raised, which evidently did not embarrass him.

'I may say that I myself could satisfy you in such ways still, though perhaps with less abandon than our steward. There are many kinds of pleasure, which is why I gave up the world itself some years since. Its distractions disturbed my thoughts, which themselves entertain me. I know philosophy, the Hindu religion to a certain extent, though it repays increased meditation; the myths, Christianity in its various forms, and mathematics including the study of the stars. The latter two can fascinate indefinitely, even in a close prison with a single window. There is also music, but here it is unlikely to be made. However I can remember what I have heard, a little.'

I felt that I had to put in a word. 'You have travelled much?' I asked, and he smiled the closed smile again, his pose remaining languid but at ease.

'I think that I have visited every country in the world where civilised conditions obtain. There are, of course, others where they do not. One of them is Scotland, where I understand you have spent much time. I even know something of your prowess there.' He bowed a little, as if to imply that not all of the latter had been infamous. 'Presently, as I have already talked a great deal, I will allow you to do so in your turn. Tell me anything you please. I shall be, I may say, more than interested; your person delights me, and your presence I do not yet find tedious. That at least is a beginning. Now speak on.'

I was by now afraid of failing to please him, but decided to tell the truth; had I not done so, he would certainly have known at once. I sat with my hands clasped in my lap and told him everything that had ever happened to me, while the remaining light outside faded and the ducks quacked beyond; my beginnings, how I was the daughter of Claud Duc de Guise by a lady who was not discreet, and my upbringing by Duchesse Antoinette after her fashion. 'She is still alive,' I said. 'They used to say the devil would never kill her daughter; but Madame herself died at forty-four.'

'Your Madame was a great and courageous woman; but continue about yourself.' I did so, and recalled Pont-à-Mousson where I had run away from the nuns, and he laughed again and agreed with me that it was a pity about St Clare cutting off her hair. I told him of my first marriage thereafter to the earlier Comte, his impotence, and the rape by Andelot on the night of his death. I looked him in the eye as I said it, and he did not flinch when I mentioned Andelot's name.

'He is no doubt bitter to be so near the title, and unable to obtain it,' said the Comte de Vouvray. 'Urged on by his mother, and with your own undoubted attractions in youth, which have not diminished, one can understand it. Provided there is no recurrence, which is unlikely, there is no need to consider it further. Continue, madame; you interest me more than anyone has done for years.'

The rest followed, and I left nothing out; the second rape by James V, the birth of Iain Ruadh, my marriage to Alasdair Dorch, and the death of Mhairi. The tears came into my eyes as I remembered Alasdair's long anger with me, and my search, and how I had found him dead at last. The Comte said gently 'He is at peace. No doubt one day you will be reunited. The dead, I believe, are by now at the centre of a wheel, which is eternity. The spokes are the time we understand, and we travel towards the hub, which is out of time and beyond space. It is easier to contemplate that than the thought of time stretching backwards in an infinite line, because then there can be no beginning.'

'There is not much more to tell,' I said. I mentioned Melville and how I had left him; I had sketched briefly over the time when I had become a whore. 'That must have been instructive,' said the Comte calmly. 'Provided you have not caught the pox, to which I would object even at my age, there is no harm done.

The Valois are degenerates because of it. I will not, however, expect you to bear me more children in course of our pleasures. The sons you have given Andelot will do very well, and will correct the inheritance. I have always felt it a trifle unjust that I, the son of a younger branch, should fall heir to Vouvray.'

I let him pour me more wine, flattered that, at my age of almost forty-five, he should think me capable of bearing more children in the event; but some women have done so. I was relieved in any case that it would not be necessary. We drank together, I finished my wine, and the Comte then dismissed me kindly and said that if I agreed, he would make arrangements for our wedding as soon as possible. 'Kindly let the world continue to think, at that rate, that I am the imbecile you expected to find,' he said. 'It is infinitely more restful than having neighbours call.'

We were married, and lived together in supreme happiness for eleven years, at the end of which the good Comte died in my arms, having attained a great age. I mourned him sincerely, not only for what he had done for my body but for the improvement to my mind. Old men, even with an affliction of the bones, are not always impotent; and the Comte in his youth had become an adept in the arts of love. Also, he had introduced me to certain of his philosophies, and I will never again lack material for thought; perhaps, in a way, I never did. I buried him, with deep regret at last, in the De Vouvray vault at Troyes, and one day hope to join him there. The creature Satki disappeared then: I do not know what became of him. On the whole, I have passed a virtuous widowhood, or at least did so until Andelot's wife died some years ago of a blockage, having never produced living children. Now that our spouses are both dead there is no doubt that I have occasionally accepted a trifle of consolation from my steward, together with his continued services in other ways. The Comte would be the first to understand the necessity.

Meantime, my sons, brought over in course from Scotland, have been reared to look after the estate, also an adjoining one I purchased on the bankruptcy of the owners, an ancient local family. Their daughter was married to Damien, and Giles is betrothed to a lesser heiress who will no doubt bring him sons in time: as the Comte used to say, if anything happens to one there is always the other, and I feel that I have done my duty by the elder branch of the house of Vouvray.

For myself, I have not changed except to grow fat over the years with contentment: as the Comte used courteously to put it, the more flesh the more delight. Nevertheless Andelot, who by now resembles my first husband, might well become a permanent temptation, and it is time I practised certain mortifications for the saving of my soul. I have at last, accordingly, sent Madame's letter by courier to her sister Antoinette de Guise, Abbess of Farmoutiers, to ask if I may be received by her as a postulant. I understand that conditions at that convent are not too severe, which is why Madame thought of it for me rather than Rheims. It seems odd that I should have to begin, and end, in charge of an Antoinette de Guise. The old Duchesse is, naturally, by now long dead. I can pray, in my convent, for the Comte's soul; for that of my dear Alasdair Dorch Gregarach; and also, and always, for Madame Marie, who hardly knew that youngest sister of hers before it was time to sail to Scotland as the King's bride, long ago.

Mary, Queen of Scots, as the world knows, has had many and cruel experiences over the years, but not more so than her mother. I have admired her courage, which she should possess, having inherited it. She has spent many years now in Elizabeth's grip, and it is possible that an even more terrible fate awaits her: they have after all tried to kill her ever since she was a child. She will die bravely, if so. We all die; I pray for her and also for myself. I am no longer young, and I have a feeling that it will happen soon. Tomorrow, or as soon as an answer comes from Farmoutiers, I leave Vouvray for the last time. Andelot and my sons will no doubt kiss my hands and weep, the way Madame Philippa de Gueldres' children wept long ago when she entered the Poor Clares and nevertheless lived there to be eighty-five; but I shall not. I conclude this in haste, therefore, having written it at leisure. The world goes on, and some of the happenings in France, at the time I write, are terrible; history will no doubt tell of it, but old women are no longer a part of history. I hope to join those I have loved in heaven shortly, if after all my sins God permits me to enter there; and heaven, after all, will be quite different.

Written in the hand of Madame la Comtesse,
at Vouvray, Ash Wednesday, 1587.